Flower from Castile

Trilogy

BOOK THREE: A SAFE HAVEN

Lilian Gafni

FLOWER FROM CASTILE TRILOGY - BOOK THREE: A Safe Haven by Lilian Gafni

First printing
Published by Lifeline Publishing Books
Book and cover design by Ellie Searl, Publishista®

Cover painting: *Sunset. A Lone Sailboat*, 1853
Artist: Ivan Aivazovsky (1817–1900)
Oil on canvass

ISBN-13: 978-0-970273536
ISBN-10: 0970273533
LCCN: 2014938705

Printed in the United States of America
10 9 8 7 6 5 4 3 2 1

LIFELINE PUBLISHING BOOKS
La Quinta, CA

Also by Lilian Gafni

FLOWER FROM CASTILE: BOOK ONE
THE ALHAMBRA DECREE

FLOWER FROM CASTILE: BOOK TWO
THE NEW WORLD

HELLO EXILE

LIVING A BLISSFUL MARRIAGE: 24 STEPS TO HAPPINESS

Praise for

FLOWER FROM CASTILE: BOOK ONE
THE ALHAMBRA DECREE

"A MASTER STORYTELLER, GAFNI WILL reveal to you a world that will open your eyes and show you a piece of important history while keeping you riveted, wondering what will happen next. A must-read!" ~ C. S. Lakin, author of *Someone to Blame* and *Intended for Harm*

"GAFNI'S UNDERSTANDING OF THE TIME period seems paramount, and her plot is solid. Isabella's movement between different cultures allows readers to explore what it was like to be a Catholic, Jew, or Moor during one of history's darkest periods." ~ Kirkus Reviews

"*THE ALHAMBRA DECREE* IS AN accessible novel that inspires interest in, and relays the complexities of, a fascinating period in history." ~ ForeWord Clarion Reviews

"GAFNI USES HISTORICAL FICTION TO retrace the steps of displaced Jews during the Inquisition. She writes with passion—her experiences a springboard." ~ *The Desert Sun/My Desert*

"THIS BOOK IS A MONUMENT to the Marranos that suffered and lost their lives." ~ Manuel Luciano da Sílva and Silvia Jorge da Sílva, authors of *Christopher Columbus was Portuguese!*

"Both my husband (who has very different literary tastes than me) and I loved this book and enjoy discussing it. Gafni is a superb author!" ~ Ann White, Rabbi and Chaplain, Radio Host, Transformational Author and Speaker, author of *Living with Spirit Energy: Bring Balance and Harmony into your Life and World*, and *The Sacred Art of Dog Walking*

Praise for

FLOWER FROM CASTILE: BOOK TWO
THE NEW WORLD

"History has never been so exciting. The author marries historical events and fictional characters to create a page-turner. I awaited the release of this book with high expectations after reading the first of this trilogy, *The Alhambra Decree*, and I was not disappointed. I am looking forward to the final book; I'm sure I won't be able to put it down." ~ Patty MacFarlane, founder of Immigrant Ships Transcribers Guild

"Although it would be best to read the first book in the trilogy, *The New World* stands alone beautifully. This second book follows the characters as they try to find safe havens. Gafni has done a tremendous amount of great research, which shows so keenly in her novels through the detail and care she takes to convey the era and locals. I'm excitedly waiting for the final book that will resolve all the riveting story lines!" ~ C. S. Lakin, author of *Someone to Blame* and *Intended for Harm*

"The sequel does a fine job of balancing the plot . . . and themes that permeate in the sequel. It continues with the same themes: risk-taking, faith, and endurance. Not only is it just great story telling, it leaves one to ponder the validity of history and humanity. That is equally as important, to me, as good drama. Like its predecessor, *The New World* is tightly enticing, and it flows with the rapid movement of true adventure without depleting the weight of history." ~ K. P. Kollenborn, author of *Eyes behind Belligerence*

Dedication

The giants in history are the unsung people who endured and searched for a better land for themselves and their families. May all persecuted masses of this world find the peace and freedom they seek.
To those seekers I dedicate this book.

Acknowledgments

I want to thank Susanne Lakin for her amazing skills as a copyeditor and her patience in polishing the manuscript to where it now shines; to copyeditor Katie Vorreiter, for looking over the entire book and pointing out improvements that highlighted the story; Ellie Searl, Publishista®, who formatted and designed a great interior and cover; and my family: my husband, Joel, and my children, for their input and suggestions while I burned the midnight oil for hours, months, and more than a year to reproduce a small corner of the world where injustice, cruelty, and disregard for human life occurred.

My deepest thanks to Wikipedia and the many faceless people who help input free data and information online that we authors use daily. The support we get from this source is invaluable.

Many thanks as well for the words to the song in Chapter 35 from *The Bride Unfastens Her Braids. The Groom Faints – Ladino Love Songs* by Etty Ben Zaken/Eitan Steinberg

Last but not least, my sincere thanks to these publishers for the use of Taíno words found in their publications: William F. Keegan and Lisabeth A. Carlson's book, *Talking Taíno: Caribbean Natural History from a Native Perspective*, © 2008 The University of Alabama Press, and to Magoria Books for *The Carib Language*, by Henk Courtz.

A list of characters is found at the end of the book

1493

1

Return to Sea

ISABELLA STOOD ON THE STARBOARD side of the *Liberação*'s quarterdeck, her untied black tresses flowing free, breathing salt air into her lungs. The ship left port in clement weather, and they'd had a warm sun and good currents since leaving Lisbon's docks at dawn. The continuous rumble of shouts and yells from the sailors as they loaded the vessel with final goods, deployed the sails, and unraveled the rigging had made her head burst from the loud sounds. Now the sea's pleasant silence enveloped her, leaving only the sound of water swooshing against the ship's bow. In the midst of this euphoric sensation that came with being part of the sea, she felt the sharp memory of her son left behind. *Salvadore will be well taken care of by Ana*, she reassured herself, to lessen the pangs of missing him.

She tilted her head back, looking up to the sky, her hands stretched on the railing as she savored her newfound freedom. She was now rich beyond her wildest dreams. A chest filled with gold and silver maravedís remained in Ana's safekeeping. She was the owner and captain of a trade ship, and possessed an estate filled with workers. She owed it all to Isaac Abravanel, who had heaped these riches upon her and Miguel. But she lacked one thing that tipped the balance negatively: there was an empty spot in her heart created by Miguel's absence. She would fill this void by achieving her mission to find him.

"*Senho*—" Lourenço da Sintra, her second in command, startled her.—

He'll never get used to me, she thought as she let out a sigh. "What is it, Lourenço?"

"I mean, Captain. So far we have come sixty leagues and are making good progress."

Pleased by the swiftness and the vessel's momentum, she said, "Very well, Lourenço. Tell the cook to serve the crew's meal."

She followed Lourenço with her eyes on his way to the cook's corner and caught sight of Avram monitoring the crew on deck. Avram, her first in command, worked with the sailors as if he were part of the crew, pulling and heaving the rigging, preparing and dragging the port and stern anchors with the sailors' help, and showing a naked torso glistening with sweat in the noon sun. She quickly struck away from the scene, trying to control a strange beating in her heart. She pushed away wayward thoughts in her mind from taking hold and returned to her cabin.

The cabin was a comfortable room, holding her bed, a table, and two chairs. Furled maps and instruments were heaped on the tabletop. She sat down and unfurled one map, hovering over the chart to determine the distance left to complete the voyage. If the sea kept cooperating with a swift wind, as it had since departure, the *Liberação* was bound to be in sight of the African coast within two days.

How strange. Last year she had been captured and sold as a slave in Tangier. Now she was the mother of a young child and commander of a caravel, shuttling goods from Portugal to the African markets. Fate had deemed to reward and punish her at the same time. She blamed herself for causing the death of her mother by her hasty decision. Her Catholic upbringing and a deep sense of guilt still plagued her, Isabella felt that Miguel's death or disappearance was punishment from heaven. She fought against the sudden emotion and held back tears.

She leaned against the backrest of the chair, rearranging the seat cushion, and let her thoughts wander. Her whole mission was centered on searching for Miguel. Yes, she knew quite well—according to everyone from Ana to Avram—how foolish it was attempting this voyage, let alone believing Miguel lived. How long had it been since he disappeared into the waters? Was it more than six months, a year, or perhaps an eternity? She still longed for him, his touch, and his gentle words and vowed to look for him— even if it took her a lifetime!

A sudden ruckus startled her back to the present. Anguished voices rose from the deck, then the sound of steps racing toward the cabin. The door swung open, and Avram stood on the threshold, his face red, his breath gasping.

"Isabella, quickly slip on your black garb!" he cried and rushed out.

She jumped out of her seat and with quick breaths went to open the wooden cover to a chest to reveal her dresses lying one on top of another. She searched along the bottom and pulled out a long black cotton robe and an abayajilbab coat to top it with. She slipped them on and covered her head, leaving only a narrow opening exposing her eyes, and stepped out from the cabin onto the upper deck.

In the distance, she saw the dreaded black pirate flag sailing toward the *Liberação* with great speed, helped by a fast wind. By now Avram had hoisted the black flag on the topmast, signaling to the pirate ship easy access to their ship. When he made a sign for Isabella to not be seen, she hunkered down on the quarterdeck's wooden plank floor, sitting cross-legged.

As the waves tossed their caravel, the pirate ship closed in, their sailors holding knives in their teeth and hanging by the rafters, where Isabella could see the pirates' menacing features. A tall man dressed in a rich overcoat stood with legs apart on deck, his hands holding the railings. From her seated position on the quarterdeck, Isabella looked down on the imposing man, his head covered by a white turban, spooled around a red cone jutting from the middle of the hat. His clothes showed distinction with the silk brocade overcoat over a white gown.

The man crossed from his ship to the *Liberação* on a wooden plank thrown across the two caravels. Isabella observed that the pirate ship was unnamed—perhaps to better disguise themselves from their prey.

That isn't how a pirate is supposed to look. In Isabella's previous experience, pirates were the image of tattered clothing, musty smells, and foul wine stains, but this pirate exuded wealth and power. Isabella grimaced. All his wealth came from ships blackmailed into paying for "protection," a mercenary arrangement made by Matigoro in an attempt to rein in the pirates.

Close to twenty pirates followed their leader and ran onto the *Liberação*'s decks, staking their positions throughout by waving their cutlasses and threatening with menacing gestures to kill anyone who made the first move. Isabella watched her sailors' contorted faces and overt displeasure at being overtaken by pirates. These were profiteering men who wouldn't hesitate to slit her crew's throats. Her crew used great restraint to keep from spitting at the pirates' feet.

"As-salamu alaykum." Avram bowed to the young pirate chief climbing on deck, his chin covered by a red goatee and tufts of red hair escaping the white turban at his temples.

"Ahlan wa sahlan!" replied the pirate.

Avram signed for the man and his aide to follow him to the cabin on the quarterdeck. As the pirate climbed the three steps past where Isabella sat on wooden beams, he fixedly eyed her with his coal-black eyes. She turned her head away from his penetrating stare.

As soon as Avram closed the door to the cabin, she got up and rushed to Lourenço.

"Quickly, tell the cook to prepare food for the effendi."

Lourenço rushed to carry out her order, and Isabella ran to the cabin and barged in.

"What's the meaning of this?" The effendi turned to Avram, his hand clasping his sword pommel.

"Please, Effendi Aruj, don't pay attention to her. She's mute and dumb and can't hear or understand our dealings."

Isabella cringed under her veil, and went to sit in a corner.

Aruj settled down and gave a chortled laugh. "By Allah, I'd whip her if she were my wife."

"As I was saying, Effendi . . ." Isabella noticed Avram taking on a serious tone, to distract Aruj's attention away from her. "We made a bargain of two thousand dirhams per ship, per voyage, plus your share of wine."

Aruj waved his hand back and forth in front of his face. "When we met the first time with your intermediary, Matigoro, we spoke of four thousand dirhams and one fourth of your cargo."

Avram shook his head at the exorbitant sum. "With all due respect, Effendi Aruj, we only spoke of that reward sum if you found the man we are looking for, not for the protection you will give us."

Aruj stroked his red beard, his eyes holding a distant look. Isabella, seated on the floor near Avram, was bursting to say something—anything—to shake him out of his greed. She bit her upper lip. Just then the cook, Juan, came in with refreshments of water-filled goblets and a pot of Ana's jam. Isabella got up and went to dish out a spoonful of jam, then dropped it into the water, mixed it, then offered it to Aruj.

Aruj smelled the liquid, then drank it. Pleased with the taste, he licked his lips. "Do you have more of this jam?" he asked.

Avram broke into a big smile. "We have ten of these pots for you, Effendi."

"All right then, let us conclude this meeting with the two thousand dirhams and the wine. And don't forget the sweet jam."

Avram took out a money purse and handed it to Aruj. His aide quickly grabbed it and looked inside. He nodded to Aruj.

When Aruj and his pirates left the *Liberação*, their ship retreating in the distance, both Isabella and Avram let out sighs of relief.

"We planted the seeds. Now let us see if they sprout," Avram said.

"Yes," Isabella replied. "Let's see if the word spreads about Miguel."

2

Seville

JOÃO TREVES NOTICED A DEEP stillness as he stood on the threshold of Don Arturo Obrigon's estate. The hour was still early—he had just heard the bell on the Giralda tower announcing matins. The household was probably asleep. With apprehension, he grabbed the cord attached to a bell and gave it a pull. The sound reverberated through the cobblestone alley where he stood, and he feared the neighbors would come out at him in anger. After a few seconds he gave the bell a second pull, while his mule brayed with the sound.

João spoke softly into the animal's long ears, "Hush, hush, we don't want to wake the entire neighborhood."

A sound came from within the building, and a servant stood by the opened door. *"¿Qué quieres, señor?"*

"I must speak with your master, Don Obrigon. It's urgent!" João stressed.

The servant disappeared inside the house then returned shortly. "My master agreed to see you. Leave your mule in the front yard."

João abided by the request, tying the mule to the post in the yard, then followed the old servant into the house.

"Wait here." The servant indicated a reception room, then left him.

João first paced the comfortable room, then sat down on a divan and looked around him. A strange feeling overpowered him, and a lump grew in his throat, as he stood in the same home that had cradled his Isabella. He envisioned his niece barging into the room unannounced, or leaving in a swirl of expensive dresses and robes, as he re-created her protected childhood in his mind. He rejoiced that he had made the right choice when he brought her here as an infant. From her appearance at his friend Maria's farm last year, he noted that she had grown into a most beautiful young lady. He had liked her fiery voice as she demanded to be freed by her captors. She had shown character of spirit, just like his dearly departed sister, Sarita, had done in the past.

"Señor, señor . . ."

The voice startled him out of his reverie. He looked up to see an aging gentleman in front of him whom he did not recognize.

"Forgive me, Don Obrigon, I was dreaming."

"And forgive me too. For I don't know your name."

João took a few moments to answer him, his throat tight. "Don Obrigon, my name is João Treves." Obrigon's face turned an ashen shade. The old man shuffled slowly to a chair by the hearth and sat down as he invited João to take the chair opposite his.

João sat with discomfort on the red velvet chair.

"I remember you well," said Obrigon. "My memories of you include gratitude when you brought us the baby."

João was about to acknowledge Obrigon's comment, but the old man stopped him with his hand.

"I also remember my anger at you for what you'd done to my family and to your niece!" Obrigon's voice rose.

"Please let me explain—" João was interrupted again by a now-furious Obrigon.

"I'm surprised you show your face here in my home. I can have you arrested for having kidnapped my daughter!"

"Please, please, Don Obrigon, I came here with pure intentions. It's for Isabella's sake that I come to you." Seeing that he'd captured Obrigon's attention, he continued. "I bring important information to her. It's about her birth father."

Obrigon looked at him without expression, the words not having an effect on him.

"Please let me talk to her and give her the information."

"What information?" Obrigon asked. "I thought her real father was dead, like your sister. That's why I consented to adopt her. One look at her and my wife would've killed to keep the baby. We fell in love with Isabella at first sight."

João remained silent at Obrigon's tenacious memories. Then he said, "Yes, her mother, my sister Sarita, did die right after childbirth. I didn't lie to you or your wife, but her real father is still alive."

A somber expression appeared on Obrigon's face. "What you don't know is that my wife died because of the grief of having lost her baby. She lost all will to live." Tears appeared on Obrigon's face. He wiped them with his hand. "I too lost Isabella."

João lifted his eyebrows. "What do you mean? Isn't she with you? In your home?" Now it was João's turn to feel anguish. If Isabella was dead, he may as well die too.

Obrigon looked at him silently at first, then a flood of words spilled from his lips. "Isabella came back to me, but she fled again." The old man proceeded to tell João about Isabella's return to Seville with the Beneluz family, her wedding to Miguel, Miguel's mother's death by the Inquisition, then Isabella's flight on the ship that left August the third of last year. "So you see, I've lost her twice. I don't know where she is now." His voice died.

João was stunned. His determination to kidnap her had changed his niece's fate. All he'd wanted was to hide her in Granada and protect her from any reprisals from the Inquisition. He only wanted to follow his sister's dying wish: for Isabella to marry within the Jewish faith. He bowed his head with the burdensome weight of guilt.

Obrigon continued. "So you see, your callous act has banished my child from Spain. Isabella should have been left who she was. A good Catholic who would have married Juan de Santilla."

João could hardly contain his anger. "But you swore to me that she would marry within the Jewish faith. Remember?"

"In the end she did as you predicted," Obrigon said with irony. "Although Miguel was a Catholic, he was born of a Jewish mother. You too are a Converso. You became Catholic," Obrigon reminded him. He added as an afterthought, "I love Miguel as my son, because Isabella loves him."

João didn't reply. "Where could she be now?" he asked, his voice distant.

"You could look for the ship she sailed on. I was there that day when she left."

"You were? Why was she sailing? I don't understand."

Obrigon recounted the events of that day, when the overzealous Inspector Guerida, hungry for promotion and a stooge for the Inquisition, dragged him to the port in Seville to apprehend Miguel and his brother José aboard the refugee' ship . "I didn't see her that day . . ." Obrigon fell silent. "But I knew, somehow, that she was safe."

João said, "I will track the ship to see where it headed. I'll find her!" He clenched his right hand into a fist. He got up to take his leave, when Obrigon stopped him.

"Who is that father of hers?"

João looked at him silently. He finally uttered, "I can't divulge his name right now, but he's an adventurous and illustrious man." João bowed to Obrigon and said, "I will never forget my debt to you and your dear wife for making a safe home for Isabella."

Obrigon nodded silently. He then said with great sadness, "When you find Isabella, tell her how much I love and miss her."

"I will." João turned to leave, when Obrigon stopped him again.

"I'd almost forgotten. When you see Miguel, make sure to tell him that Guerida arrested his brother. I later found out he'd been sent to La Rábida monastery to become a priest."

João was shaken by the news. "Poor José. Lost his mother and torn from his brother, Miguel, too." He then took leave of Obrigon.

3

At the Court in Barcelona

AMONG THE REVELERS IN HIS honor, Columbus was surrounded by many nobles and dignitaries feasting him and his new discoveries. Wine poured from casks right in the hall, filling delicately engraved silver goblets, drunk from one after another. Columbus only wetted his lips, preferring to stay lucid. A crackling fire burned in the vast marble hearth in the Saló del Tinell. The music of the lute played in the background by the court musicians accompanied the conversations at the long table in the sonorous hall. Paintings and draperies covered the walls in a festive and joyful atmosphere. All had come to celebrate him: the adopted son of a wool weaver.

Around him many men welcomed his return. The stories of his discoveries traveled throughout España and beyond by courier and caravels sailing every day to Venice, France, and the Germanic lands. *I wonder if my adoptive family in Genoa has heard about my discovery of the Indies?* "Admiral Colón?" A melodious voice reached his ears. He turned his head to face Queen Isabella's inquisitive eyes.

"Pardon me, my queen, for my lack of attention." He bowed his head to Isabella.

"You must continue your wonderful tale of reaching San Salvador." Her eyes held admiration for him. She turned to the animated King Ferdinand, who was talking to the aged Don Fernando Núñez Coronel, and put a finger to her lips.

King Ferdinand acknowledged the queen's interruption and encouraged Columbus with a nod. "Please continue, Admiral."

Columbus continued. "As I was saying, Your Highnesses, after we saw the flickering light in the distance, we stayed awake the entire night before landing. My men were silent, yet tense with anticipation and excitement . . ." Columbus recounted the tale of San Salvador island appearing at dawn. "It was an apparition sent by the Savior, a tether to life."

Queen Isabella nodded, pleased by Columbus's fervor. She crossed herself, then everyone in the great hall did the same.

Columbus thought, *All Barcelona is at my feet, holding their breath, entranced by my words.*

"Admiral Colón, we must baptize the Indians you brought back on Trinity Sunday. It is to take place right after the festival."

"Certainly, Your Highness." Columbus approved.

One of the nobles spoke directly to him. "Tell us, Señor Cristóbal—we have in our great country of España many cosmographers and mariners who would have found the New World whether or not you had discovered it. Wouldn't you say so?"

Columbus didn't reply for a few minutes. He looked around the table and spotted an egg basket. He took one of the hard-boiled eggs, and raising it asked the assembly, "Gentlemen and nobles, would anyone care to try to stand this egg on its head? Without using sand or salt to prop it up?" he added. "As I was without help in discovering the Indies."

Many in the hall attempted to stand the egg on one end. King Ferdinand tried and failed but laughed at the effort. Others tried and failed as well. When the egg came back to Columbus, he hit it on the table, crushing one end, and stood it there for all to see. The assembly turned confused eyes toward Columbus, followed by a glint of comprehension.

"So you see, gentlemen? It's always easy after the deed is carried out to claim another could have done it too."

Bursting laughter filled the hall, reaching the carved wooden ceiling.

When the laughter stopped, Queen Isabella said, "Let us drink a toast to the admiral!"

4

The Search Begins

ISABELLA AND AVRAM HAD ARRIVED at the port in Tangier. The usual hustle and bustle of passengers disembarking, the loading and unloading of cargo onto and off ships proceeded as it had for millennia. They found an open carriage ride to Matigoro's house and arrived within a half hour. Isabella could hardly contain her excitement at seeing him again.

The door opened up, and at first glance Matigoro displayed his open joy at seeing Isabella.

"What did you have?" Matigoro asked with both his hands in a prayer gesture, close to his mouth.

"A boy. His name is Salvadore," Isabella said with pride.

Matigoro embraced her with effusion and joy. *"Mazal tov! ¡Gran alegría para la nueva madre!"* He escorted her to a divan, exaggerating his show of attention.

As she sat, Isabella was overtaken by a sudden rush of emotions, wavering between her own delight at the precious life in her keeping, and anger mixed with guilt for having abandoned Salvadore when he needed her most. This voyage had not, so far, panned out the way she had anticipated. The pirate ship had come and gone, the protection money paid and promises made to find Miguel. What more could she want? She'd known the search might take months, if not years. But now she felt stumped.

"I feel disappointed. So far nothing's turned out."

"Isabella," Matigoro said. "There's no need to despair. You've made contact with the pirates. Now it's their turn to come up with some leads. If they want the reward, that is."

"What's to stop them, when they can attack the ship, kill us, and take their booty?"

"Sure, they could do all of that. But don't forget the reward money is good bait. They will come back for more." He stopped, then added, "There's also a silent agreement among pirates to beware of anyone double-crossing them."

"I don't understand," Isabella said.

Avram, who hadn't said a word until now, nodded. "Matigoro is right. We need to create competition among the pirate ships and make them be wary of each other."

Isabella shuffled on the low divan. She straightened her posture and asked, wide-eyed, "What do you mean Avram?"

Matigoro raised his hand to stop Avram from replying. "It means, what we do is promise the same thing to other pirates. This way they compete against each other for the prize money." Matigoro said.

Isabella's face felt hot. She restrained herself from shouting at Matigoro, then said, "You mean we have to do that all over again? Give each and every one money and goods too!"

"We can lower the protection money and the reward, but tell them they're getting more than another pirate."

Isabella kept quiet, trying to make sense of it all. She turned to Matigoro. "But you'd be double-crossing them!"

"Yes. But they won't know that." Matigoro had a smirking smile on his lips.

Isabella sat still for a moment, trying to digest the information. It was a dangerous game to play in the company of ruffians and cutthroats. A game she preferred not to play. But then, she had a mission. If she wanted to find Miguel, dead or—she pushed the thought away. She had to play among these pirates and beat them at their own game.

"All right. But I will control the payments and reward, and how much wine they will receive."

Matigoro nodded. "You're the boss now, Bella."

Isabella was surprised but pleased by the endearing nickname. She smiled at him and turned to Avram. "Let's see if any slaves are to be found in today's market."

5

The Pope Rules

POPE ALEXANDER VI, RODRIGO LANZOL Borja, opened the discussions with all the parties present in the consistory of the Sacred College of Cardinals. He faced the two rows of seated cardinals in their scarlet red gowns with white fur and silk biretta hats. The main representative to Spain, the rotund Cardinal Carafa—trusted camerlengo and new vice-chancellor in addition to serving as chamberlain—sat across from his enemy, Cardinal Ascanio Sforza, also a suburbicarian bishop. Borja knew to keep his most vehement dissenters close to him. He was fully aware of their hatred toward him—a Catalan Pope who had acceded to the papacy and won over the Italian prelates. Ironic in their seating choices, the two rows faced off against their mirror images of mutual loathing. Della Rovere faced Virginio Orsini, bound together in a long suit over land and towns, as well as Fabrizio Collona, who hated both of them.

Pope Alexander knew he had made the right choice with Cardinal Carafa, whose allegiance sided with King Ferdinand of the House of Aragon and King of Sicily. Carafa had been a competent man in the service of the church; however, his most distinguished career was as an outstanding military leader. Pope Alexander felt reassured to have retained him as chamberlain. Now Carafa was Bishopric of Salamanca, Spain. *A good and able man*, thought Pope Alexander.

With Cardinal Sforza, however, he had to tread carefully, because of the man's allegiance to Portugal.

"Your Eminence," Cardinal Carafa said. "We have been petitioned by both the kingdoms of Spain and Portugal to put to rest the claims to the New World."

Pope Alexander took a deep sigh, clasped both his hands together, and nodded in agreement. "We must be extremely careful not to antagonize John II of Portugal," he said. "He's liable to start a war again, over what seems to him preferential treatment by the church toward Spain and Aragon." He stopped to take a breath. "Yes, yes, I'm aware of it. The Treaty of Alcáçovas has lasted so far. No wars have been openly fought between Spain and Portugal since they signed the treaty in September 4, 1479." He stopped again with another sigh.

Carafa held a questioning gaze. He said to the Pope, "I don't understand, Your Eminence. The Alcáçovas Treaty of 1479 specified exactly where the boundaries lay between the two countries."

"This treaty, ending the War of Castilian Succession, has been threatened since the discoveries of the Indies by Columbus. We must initiate another treaty to keep Portugal and Spain from warring against each other. These boundaries must now be extended," said Pope Alexander.

"Extended how?" Carafa unfolded a chart showing the lands and continents disputed by Spain and Portugal, and held it at arm's length for the Pope to see.

Pope Alexander moved forward and traced an imaginary arc with his dry and scaly hand at a distance from the chart. He moved his index finger from the North Pole to the South Pole. "We will push the boundary lines west, from north to south poles, starting along a meridian of three hundred leagues west of the Cape Verde islands off the west coast of Africa."

The consistory remained silent, unable to comprehend their religious leader's intent. Pope Alexander knew their confusion was due to their ignorance or fear of speaking out in front of their enemies.

"What I mean is," Pope Alexander stressed, "Spain and Portugal will inherit all lands in the Western Hemisphere. The line will divide all lands east, which will belong to Portugal, from the lands west, belonging to Spain."

"But, Your Eminence," said Cardinal Sforza, who had listened silently until now, "this will shortchange Portugal. We know now that the lands discovered by the explorer Christopher Columbus are vast, and greater than Portugal's holdings on the African coast. We could start a dangerous precedent that could lead to more wars."

Pope Alexander replied, "If this treaty is signed by those kingdoms, there will be no wars because it will be in their interests. Any land that belongs to Portugal or Spain can be taxed between the two countries. If Portugal trades in Spanish lands, then Portugal pays a share of access to Spain. The same goes for Spain trading in Portuguese lands."

Cardinal Sforza's face displayed surprise mixed with controlled indignation. "But, with due respect, Your Eminence, I still believe that this new line will anger the Portuguese crown. They won't abide it. That goes without saying for the other European kingdoms."

"I'm aware of that. I don't think the Kingdoms of Naples, France, or England will object, since they haven't traveled that far west. First, we have to get the crowns of Castile, Aragon, and Portugal to agree to the new treaty by offering future benefits in trade for their kingdoms." He turned to Carafa. "You will find the Spanish sovereigns in Barcelona at this time. Have them sign first, then report to me."

Carafa, who stood silent and reflective, said, "We will also issue an *Inter caetera* papal bull—the Alexandrine Bull to honor your papacy's reign, Your Eminence."

Pope Alexander nodded to Carafa with gratitude in his eyes. He turned to his scribe seated next to him and dictated the details of the new bull.

"This new bull named 'The Treaty of Tordesillas' will give Castile exclusive trading rights for all the newly discovered lands and oceans west of the meridian at one hundred leagues from the Azores and Cape Verde Islands. To the King of Portugal, John II, all territories . . ."

When he finished dictating to the scribe, he turned to Carafa. "You have my full support, Camerlengo, to carry this new treaty and have the monarchs sign it with haste in this blessed year." Pope Alexander made the sign of the cross, followed by Cardinal Carafa and then Cardinal Sforza, who didn't seem too pleased by the decision.

6

The Gold Mines at La Mina

ALI STRAIGHTENED HIS BACK, LAID the pick at his side, took a sip of water from his sheep water skin, hooked it back on his belt, then wiped his brow with his dirty sleeve. He couldn't shake off the dank smell rising from his body—a smell he still hadn't gotten used to by now, since there was little water to be had, and washing was restricted to once a month.

The scene in front of him, seen through a yellow curtain of dust, could only be called nightmarish. Hundreds of men labored at breaking a ten-foot-tall rock wall under a hot orange sun. A gritty brownish dust hung in the air, invading nostrils and lungs, and dusty faces strained under the backbreaking labor in sweltering heat.

Today's heat had penetrated his skin, and the more he drank, the more he perspired. He looked down at his tattered clothes and grimaced. His shirt with ballooning sleeves, white at one time, was now gray and stained. His trousers fared no better, with a large tear at the calf. He had mended the tear with a thin rope he'd found lying on the sand to hold the pieces together. He glanced at the miners chipping at the rock wall in front of them, the dust propelled in the air with each blow, the dryness in the furnace they stood in, and wished he'd wake up from this perpetual nightmare.

"Hey! Get back to work!" The guard's voice, carrying down the hill, startled him. From the deep pit in which he stood, the miner squinted up at the guard above him on a small hill with a waning sun behind him, and returned to his task.

"*Ya habibi,* Ali," The miner working next to him said. Then in poor Portuguese he added, "This guard dangerous . . ." A coughing fit interrupted him. When it stopped, he wheezed, then said, "He bad guard. He beat you."

"*Shoukran*, Sekou," said Ali. "Speak for yourself. You forgot the lashes you got a few weeks ago?"

The aged Sekou looked at the lacerated scars on his arms and grimaced. "I quiet." He wheezed again.

Both prisoners continued aiming their blows at the wall in front of them, while other prisoners piled the smashed pieces of granite into rubber baskets. A large mound in the distance was their destination.

Ali wiped his dripping brow again and took the last sip of water from his water skin.

"You no more water," Sekou mumbled, his sparse yellow teeth showing in a wrinkled, graying, bearded face. Then, seeing the guard's attention directed away from them, he boldly said, "You no told me what a white man doing in garbage hole!"

Ali checked on the guard, and not seeing him around said, "I was captured and sold as a slave. Just like you."

"I African. I captured in Mozambique. You white man's world."

After another glance at the guard, Ali said with somberness, "Better not talk about it!" Ali turned his back to Sekou and continued working with his pickax, concentrating the blows on a quartz vein in the granite. He scraped a rust-stained mound with the sharp side of the pickax's head. If it yielded gold flakes, he'd be rewarded with additional food tonight. Otherwise he'd receive the same tasteless gruel with hard bread.

A bell rang in the distance, and all the workers laid their pickaxes down with deep sighs. It had been a long day in the baking heat, and everyone wanted to crawl to the huts to stretch out their aching bodies. Ali, too, felt drained, both in body and mind, and couldn't wait to wash the festering sores on the soles of his feet caused by torn sandals.

Sekou's curiosity and questions had startled him. He couldn't give him any information that he hadn't asked of himself over and over: who was he, and where did he come from? The only traces that came to his memory were shreds of images and words. He could only remember awakening on a ship, then being dragged to a market to be sold as a common beast. He also recalled being asked, *"Sho ismak? Sho ismak?"* then being beaten several times on his back, shoulders, and head. In a nightmarish recollection, a man kept yelling at him over and over: "What is your name? You dog! What is your name?"

When the blows kept coming at him repeatedly, he yelled, "Ali! Ali! Ali! I'm called Ali!" He'd heard a boy being called by that name and latched on to it. He couldn't remember any other name.

He'd been at odds and angry with himself for not remembering, until, exhausted from searching his mind, he pushed the questions haunting him deep down. Now all he needed was to rest his weary body.

7

The Docks in Seville

OÃO MADE HIS WAY THROUGH the docks filled with sounds of hammering, the loud voices of dock supervisors and workers calling to each other, and the noise of saws grinding through wooden boards. The length and breadth of the drydock was a scene of activity and fevered pitch. As many as seventeen vessels, lined up like soldiers before an assault, were secured in each berth alongside the quay, crawling with sailors applying pitch to sideboards, and unfurling and checking sails before long voyages.

This flurry of activity was in preparation for the next big voyage led by Columbus to the New World in the Indies. João had but a few months to find Isabella before he too sailed on one of the ships. He had blackmailed Columbus on the previous voyage into helping his cause by smuggling Conversos and Jews to the Indies. His mission now was to gather them before the admiral sailed back. He felt an overwhelming burden on his shoulders: a mission to which he had devoted his entire life. His old shipmates Hernán Çavallos and Alfonso Sabatin had as good as deserted him since their return to Seville. It was all up to him now.

He smacked his forehead with a sigh of desperation. *How am I to find her in such short time?* He would start by asking questions. Not far from the noisy docks, he spotted a small tavern to begin his search. He opened a creaky door, descended a few steps, and entered the dark confines of the tavern lit by candles and no windows. A few customers drank beer and wine in booths, and he sat down at an empty table.

The proprietor came to him with a rag to wipe the table. "What can I get you?"

"Beer," João said.

The tavern owner came back with his drink. "That'll be one blanca."

João paid him, then asked, "Were you here when the exodus of Jews happened last year?"

The owner squinted, his eyes questioning. "Why do you ask? You don't want to remember that time, do you?"

"I do remember," João said boldly. "Not only was I here, I also sailed with the *Santa Maria*."

The owner's face relaxed instantly, and his eyes widened. "You must tell me about it! The town hasn't stopped talking since then. How was it? How did you cross the dark seas? Weren't you—?"

João stopped him short. "First, I need information."

The owner retreated, narrowing his eyebrows. "What sort of information?"

"I need to know who the captains of those ships were on the third of August of last year."

The owner placed his hands on his hips and bellowed with roaring laughter. When he stopped, he wiped his teary eyes and, still laughing, said, "I'm not that important to have known those captains." He stopped, then said, "But they used to drink here at the tavern."

"All right," João said. "Then you must remember some of them, don't you?"

The man reflected a moment, rubbing his chin. "There was Alonso Pérez Roldán with his caravel the *San Juan*, and Fernando Núñez on the newly Christened *La Gallega* . . . there're too many!"

"All right," João said with a frustrated sigh. "Where can I get information on all the ships?"

"You'd best go to the maritime office at the end of the docks." With that, the owner left João's table for new patrons coming into the tavern.

João sighed with relief. The owner had forgotten to hear all about his exploits in the New World. He quickly slipped out the tavern and looked for the official building. He located a structure standing in the distance. It was a small, run-down one-story building with a tower in the center.

He entered and found himself in a crowded governmental office with many desks holding piles of papers in disarray.

He asked a clerk rushing by. "Please, Señor? Where can I find information on departing ships?"

The clerk pointed at an office in the back of the room, then left João in a hurry.

João approached the office, where another clerk sat at a desk laden with piles of folders in front of floor-to-ceiling bookcases holding hundreds more records.

"¿Señor? I'm looking for the manifests of ships that left last year."

"What month was it?" the clerk asked.

"August of last year. The third, that is."

The clerk walked him to a wall cabinet filled with volumes held tightly on shelves. "You must pay a fee to view these records. One silver maravedí, please."

João paid him, shook his head at the task before him, then plunged into the first dusty volume.

After two hours, during which he hadn't made a dent in the hundreds of pages before him, he realized he'd been wasting precious time—he had searched for the wrong names. Don Obrigon told him that Isabella and Miguel had accompanied the Beneluz family on the spur of the moment. It stood to reason that they wouldn't be listed. Only the Beneluz name would've been written down. João initiated a new search for that name and found it on a page at the end of the tenth volume. His heart jumped with joy. To his delight, the Beneluz family's names were scripted on the page: Isaac Beneluz accompanied by his spouse Rivka and their four children. As he had suspected, Isabella's name wasn't listed—nor Miguel's. The ship's name was *El Mouro*, and it had sailed to Tangier.

João left the maritime office in distress and in a quandary. He had little time left to search for Isabella and Miguel, let alone sail to Morocco. The best solution was to look for the captain of that ship. During another search, he was told of a house in Seville that housed Juan de Luna, the captain of *El Mouro*. He found the captain's house at the end of an alley.

Juan de Luna greeted him at the door and graciously asked him to enter. "What can I help you with?" de Luna asked, standing in the hallway.

"I'm looking for a family of passengers who sailed on your ship on August third of last year."

De Luna first stroked his small goatee then said, "I have a passenger list in my storage room. Let me get it." He disappeared then returned with a large volume. "What were their names?"

"Beneluz. A family of six, accompanied by their nephew and niece."

De Luna searched for the name and pointed to a line in the records. "I see their names. They had four sons. I don't see anyone else besides their name."

"Their nephew and niece were traveling with them," João insisted. "The young woman happened to be my niece too."

De Luna asked. "Can you describe them?"

"My niece is a beautiful young woman with striking green eyes, and her husband a young—" João stopped when the captain threw him a strange look.

"Did she have your eyes?" de Luna blurted.

"Yes!" João cried. "They were sailing to Tangier!"

The captain's face turned ashen all of a sudden.

João's heart sank. "What is it?"

"I don't know how to tell you this." De Luna paused. "We were accosted by a pirate ship . . ." His voice trailed again. "Many young people were taken by the pirates. I'm afraid your niece and her husband were among them."

João took the blow hard. His legs went weak, and he sat on the nearest chair in the hallway. "That can't be. It can't be!"

De Luna nodded with sadness. "I'm sorry."

"I can't believe it! I don't believe it!" João repeated over and over, as if the repetition of those words could wipe away the ugly truth.

"If it's any consolation to you, there's a man in Tangier who buys back slaves sold in the market there."

João lifted his head with hope. "How can I get in touch with him? I'm pressed for time."

"You can hitch a caravel leaving tomorrow at dawn and be in Tangier in a few days, given good weather. He goes by the name of Ansar."

"Thank you, Captain. You've been a lifesaver." João bowed his head to the captain and took his leave.

At the whisper of dawn the following morning, João, who had slept on the docks among bundles and crates, boarded a caravel bounded for Tangier.

8

The Return Home

FOR A NUMBER OF DAYS after returning from Tangier, Isabella sat silently at meals. Ana, who knew her to be communicative about her latest journeys, looked at her curiously but didn't say a word. Finally she decided to query her. "Did you find any link or any trail in your search?"

Isabella continued her silence.

Ana turned to Avram. "What about you, Avram? What does Matigoro say?"

Avram first looked to Isabella, reluctant to say anything to Ana. "Matigoro said it would take months if not . . . Well, a lot of time. We did, though, strike a bargain with the head pirate, Aruj. We dangled a reward in front of him, and you should've seen his eyes light up." A rare smile appeared on Avram's lips, at which Isabella replied in a harsh tone.

"They're brigands, thieves, and cutthroats!"

Both Ana and Avram exploded in laughter. When they stopped, Ana said, "But you knew that trading with them would be no walk in the garden."

"What's more," Isabella said, "Matigoro put us in danger by suggesting double-crossing other pirates and letting them believe they will get a larger reward."

Ana wrinkled her brow. "That could be dangerous and worrisome." She turned to Avram. "Is the *Liberação* equipped to fight any pirates who discover they've been double-crossed?"

Isabella replied, "We carry five bronze cannons, an arsenal of metal balls, and plenty of swords and lances to face them all. I've got my crew trained for any pirate ship that might confront us."

Ana gasped. "I didn't know how much knowledge you'd gained these past few months. I feel more at ease now. We—"

Raquela entered the room with Salvadore asleep in her arms, quickly changing their mood.

"I just fed him and he's fast asleep," Raquela said.

Isabella went to take her sleeping infant son from Raquela's arms. "My little Salvadore," she said softly. Salvadore smiled in his sleep. She rocked him in her arms and walked slowly out of the room, oblivious to everyone, and straight to the gardens still in spring bloom.

She sat on a wooden bench and held his little hand and his well-formed fingers. She kissed his fingers one by one and sang to him in a low, almost hushed voice.

Mi hermoso niño,
las cosas que tú verás
y las cosas que va a hacer
le sorprenderán al mundo

9

Plans for the Second Voyage

HAMMERING, SAWING, AND POUNDING—DEAFENING sounds burst from Cadiz's docks, with hundreds of dockworkers outfitting the many caravels. An astonished Juan de la Cosa stood with his mouth open, witnessing history in the making. He scanned the harbor, and beyond the caravels standing with naked masts devoid of sails, every ship was being prepared to embark on a long voyage to the Indies. He counted, as best he could, and came up with seventeen ships total. Indeed, the queen had been most magnanimous to provide and furnish an entire fleet of vessels at the admiral's disposal.

De la Cosa rubbed his hands with joyful anticipation. This second voyage to the Indies would seal the Christian faith upon the islands and their inhabitants. The admiral had always been keen on bringing the Catholic faith to the New World. Now his dream would take forth the true faith. De la Cosa felt proud to have been chosen at Columbus's request to supervise, hire, inspect, and set in motion the greatest expedition by sea the world had ever seen.

"Señor, are you searching for something?" A voice behind his back startled him. He turned to face Vicente Yáñez Pinzón, youngest brother of the deceased Martín Pinzón.

The two men embraced, and de la Cosa pulled away to gauge his former fleet shipmate from the first voyage.

"I'm so sorry, Vicente, for the death of your brother. His loss to navigation will be missed. He was a great man."

Vicente's eyes became teary. "I miss him too. It goes without saying that his son, my nephew Arias Pérez, hasn't yet recovered from losing his father."

Vicente fell silent. He then said after a long pause, "He vowed to take revenge."

De la Cosa was puzzled. "Why? What kind of revenge?"

"He claimed that his father should have gotten the reward money for finding land first."

"But you know that isn't true! The *Santa Maria* was first to sight land. I was there to witness it."

"Look, de la Cosa. I have much respect for the admiral, but I was on the *Niña*, so I don't know how accurate the claims of the admiral are."

"Tell me," de la Cosa said, not wanting to take sides. He felt split between his duty to the admiral and his friendship with Vicente when they were thrown together on the *Niña*. Without rescue from the *Niña*, after the *Santa Maria* ran aground, they would never have made it home. "What exactly does your nephew intend to do?"

Vicente was silent for a few moments. Then he said, "He'll appeal to the queen and bring a lawsuit against the admiral."

De la Cosa was stunned. Arias Pérez, Martin Pinzón's son, had the gall to stand up to Columbus and the Spanish crown? It didn't bode well for this second voyage. If Columbus was to be detained, the whole expedition would be too.

"Forgive me, Vicente, but I'm on my way to Seville's port to recruit sailors for the next voyage."

"I've already been contacted by Juan Niño, owner and master of the ship *Niña*, to pilot the ship," said Vicente. "I've declined. Out of respect for my dead brother." With that, Vicente nodded, turned, and walked away from de la Cosa, who remained pensive. *Will Martin Pinzón's family put the threat into action to delay Columbus's grand voyage?* It would remain to be seen.

10

Revelations

ALI SAT IN THE SHADE of a hut constructed of bamboo sticks and covered by palm fronds. The rest of the slaves also sat, too tired to stir. Their day began before sunrise and continued until darkness set in. By then the famished slave workers fell upon the gruel offered them and drank the lukewarm water brought by the slave masters. When their meager portions were wolfed down, they'd form a queue to go behind the sand dunes to relieve themselves, always within one guard's presence while another watched the other men.

When Ali's turn came, he had lingered to watch the horizon fade in front of him, and the guard dealt a blow to his head.

"Bastard! Be done already!"

Ali warded off the wooden club's blows. "All right! All right! I'm done!" Dragged by the guard, he ran as fast as he could toward his hut with his ankles chained. He collapsed in front of the hut. He massaged the sore spot on his head while the guard chained him to the other prisoners.

"O que aconteceu?" Sekou, sitting outside the hut, slid closer on the sandy ground after watching the guard leave.

"I took too long to urinate."

Sekou burst out laughing, then quickly extinguished it, afraid to attract the guards' attention. "You lucky, my friend. I big trouble do that."

Ali looked at his only friend in the deepening darkness and wondered what he meant. Sekou was older than him by twenty years, making him at least forty. Although, perhaps, this life of slavery had taken a toll on his health and aged him beyond his years.

"Tell me, Sekou, how long have you been a slave?"

Sekou said with some hesitation, "Long time, my friend. I boy fifteen when Arabs come to my village, kill my family, then put chains." His voice broke as he rattled the chain around his ankle. "I want escape, but guards here day and night."

"Perhaps you didn't plan your escape right."

"No escape. If catch you, they beat and you dead!" Sekou's voice rose in anger. "I see this happen. Guard beat poor Mohammed and he dead now. We scared running away."

Ali was silenced by that argument. Was it better to die from a beating or from a short life of exhausting work? Either way, their oppressors made sure to end a man's usefulness.

"Where you come from to here?" Sekou questioned him again.

"I don't remember. All I know is the slave market and being carted off to this godforsaken mine."

"You white man not smart. Why your name Arabic? You don't have white name."

Ali felt pressed to end the conversation. "All right, Sekou. Don't needle me, or I'll report you to the guards."

That threat silenced Sekou. He then said, "I your friend, your one friend."

Ali felt guilt pangs for alienating Sekou. "I'm sorry, Sekou. You are my only friend. If we ever get an opportunity to escape, you're the one I'd run away with."

Sekou laughed with relief. "I remember this."

Ali extended his hand to Sekou, who took it. They shook hands on a silent pact.

11

A Clue

In Isabella's cabin, the pirates sat crossed-legged on the floor and in close proximity while Avram led the discussion. To his right sat Aruj, the chief pirate, his head turbaned in immaculate white with the red cone jutting from its center, his gold robe covered by a long damask coat. His aide—dressed similarly but with less richness—fingered a necklace of green beads.

Isabella sat on the floor, behind the men in her black garment, her face partly hidden. She held the edges of the hood between her teeth to keep it from sliding off her hair.

"As I was saying, Effendi, for the last months, we haven't gotten one clue. I wonder if we made a mistake about you," said Avram.

This direct insult brought Aruj's hand to graze the silver pommel on his sword. His nose flared and his face reddened by the insult.

Isabella trembled inside at the thought that Avram had pushed him too far. She shifted her position back on the floor of the cabin.

"I can pierce your heart now for this affront to my honor! You'll retract your words!" Aruj eyes glared at Avram.

Without flinching, Avram said to Aruj, "My dear guest. You're welcome on my ship, and if I slighted you in the least, curse me and my words."

Aruj lifted his hand off his sword and said, "All right. Let me tell you what we've learned so far. We found the pirate ship responsible for your brother's disappearance. The ship's name is *Al-Aziz*, after our beloved prophet."

At that moment, Isabella breathed a sigh of relief by this news and by the fact that Aruj believed that Avram was looking for his "lost brother" and she was a grieving widow. She sighed again. This time it was a sigh of grief. The last time she had seen Miguel was last year when he had sailed to Tangier's market to retrieve Jewish slaves.

Avram's voice pulled her out of her thoughts when he asked Aruj, "What's the size and build of the *Al-Aziz*?"

"It's a seventy-ton caravel, carrying cannons and many slaves. They sailed to Africa, where slaves are traded at a higher price."

Avram nodded. "We're grateful to you and to your God Allah for this information."

"Allah is merciful." Aruj nodded back, seeming to be pleased with Avram for acknowledging him as a pious man. No longer a pirate in the eyes of Allah.

Avram took a purse filled with coins from his trouser pocket and laid it in front of Aruj.

Aruj made a sign for his aide to grab the purse.

"Let us now drink to this welcome news," Avram said.

Refreshments of fruity drinks were served, and a contented Aruj turned to Avram.

"My sympathy goes to you. We will find your brother, dead or alive."

Isabella grimaced under the veil, and pain stabbed at her heart. She took a long breath, staring silently as Aruj and his aide got up and followed Avram from the cabin. She remained alone in a conflicted state of mind. *So they found the ship.* She ran the words in her mind. Could Miguel have found a lifeline to another ship?

12

A Chance Encounter

JOÃO DRAGGED HIS MEAGER BELONGINGS in a canvas bag. One pair of trousers, one shirt, and several bandanas for his neck and head. All around him, the voices in Tangier's port and bazaar came to his ears with strange words. He had been as far as the dark Atlantic sea to the Indies, but other than that, Spain and Portugal were his frontiers. Now he faced a foreign land with a tongue unknown to him. The only brush he'd had with Arabic tribes were the converted Moors—the *Moriscos*—who served their Christian masters on Spanish and Portuguese soil. How would he communicate with the inhabitants here?

"Hal beemkani mosa'adatuk?"

He turned to see a beggar man wrapped in a tattered cloak with questions in his eyes. João must have looked lost to this man.

"I help you with one dirham—only one dirham," the beggar man said, switching to Spanish.

João dug in his pocket and brought up a copper sueldo. "That's all I have," he said, raising his shoulders, his hands face up.

The beggar bit on the coin and, satisfied with the metallic taste, broke into a smile. "What you need for?"

"When will the slave market open?"

"You lucky. This afternoon you see slaves. Not much money."

"Show me the way," João told the beggar.

He followed the man through several cobblestone alleys until they came to an open market. The beggar disappeared to continue his lucrative begging back at the port.

João dropped his canvas sack and waited near a large fountain where camels drank water from the trough. He approached and took a sip from the spigot. The water tasted heavenly and refreshing. His thirst quenched, he looked at the market buzzing around him with activity—from vendors selling their wares and food being cooked on open spits to children running through the tables laden with pottery, satchels, leather purses, and intricately etched saddles. The smell of leather mixed with the aroma of grilled meat, while flies buzzed on the food and camel dung lay in piles in the market's alleyways.

Soon a commotion began. Bystanders moved away, leaving an empty circle around the large fountain. The sounds of feet clasped in metal chains came to João's ears. From one of the alleys, a pitiful display of men and woman trekked into the plaza. Their soiled shirts and trousers hung in rags, their hair was matted and blood caked, their feet were barely protected by torn sandals filthy with dust, and their arms displayed fresh lash marks.

The activity grew pitched as João watched the unfortunate young men and women be sold to the highest bidders. Money changed hands, and the slaves' voices rose in anguish.

"I've got more fresh merchandise coming. Do not leave yet!" the rotund slave merchant yelled at bystanders about to leave the plaza.

Just then another column of slaves came through, dragging their sandals, some tripping over the ground's uneven stones.

"Who'll give me ten dirhams?" the merchant shouted.

"You want too much!" a bystander heckled.

"Look at them. They're skinny and sick with starvation. I'll give you two!" another bystander shouted, cloaked in a long white linen robe, his head covered by a wide burnous hood.

"Two! Are you crazy! They're young. They'll fill in with the proper master. I'll lower the price for you. Yes—you, hoarding your dirhams." He pointed at the last heckler. "Seven dirhams."

"Still too much." The man turned his back and started to leave.

"Wait! Wait. I'll go five. No lower than that."

The bystander in the white robe faced the merchant, "All right, but I'll take the whole lot of twenty for three dirhams each."

The merchant stood astonished and indignant by the offer and by the dare to bid him down. He stroked his graying beard, and after some hesitation he nodded. A large purse changed hands, and the new master cracked his whip in the air.

João watched, amused by the scene and the cunning skill of the negotiator who left the slave merchant unable to refuse.

"Follow me!" The new master's voice rose in the plaza.

The column of twenty men and women slaves turned with submission and followed their new master.

João stood back with curiosity, his pulse rising, eyes blinking. That voice had a familiar ring. One he'd heard before. *But where?*

He rushed to catch up to the slave column that had disappeared from sight and reached the last row of slaves turning an alleyway corner. Running past the slow-moving slaves, he caught up with the master heading toward a group of camels near the outskirts of town.

"Wait, wait!" João yelled at the man. He tapped him on the shoulder, and the hood fell off the master's head. When he turned around, João stood astounded! Here was Benvenide Matigoro—one of the Conversos at Téresa's home! The meeting where it all began. Téresa had taken a risk that evening when all the Conversos and Jews met to discuss leaving España for a new haven. In a way he blamed himself for her death and for Miguel and his brother José losing their mother to the Inquistion.

"Don't you recognize me? I'm João."

Matigoro let out a raucous laugh and embraced him. João embraced him back, then held him at arm's length.

"I can't believe it! It's you! We wondered about you and Téresa," João said.

"I left ahead of the refugees last July. But I'll tell you all about it soon. Follow me."

Matigoro walked to the waiting camels, braying their impatience to leave, and turned to his newly purchased group and spoke to the wretched lot.

"We have a short walk. Then you'll be fed." He turned to João. "Climb on board." He pointed to one of the camels that had kneeled for him to mount.

The slaves moved again, reluctantly and passively following the mounted camels, and within a half hour they arrived at Matigoro's camp near the shore. At the sight of food waiting to be served from a hot cauldron, the slaves fell upon the men dishing out hot rice.

"Come with me inside," Matigoro said to João.

They entered a small whitewashed dwelling composed of several rooms, where two servants served them rice and lamb, flat bread, and a nutty paste that João recognized as ground garbanzo beans. The taste brought back memories of accompanying Téresa's husband, Nahum Costa, on his travels to Berber lands.

During the meal and after indulging in fruits and sweets, Matigoro related to him all the events that had taken place during the past year. He told him of Téresa's arrest back in Seville and her death, Maria's arrest by the inquisitors and consequent disappearance, his own escape to Tangier with Abravanel's help, and his role in retrieving Jews and other slaves up to the present moment.

"You have served our people well after their exile from Spain," said João, still reeling from the news that Téresa had died to help his niece. "Can you tell me where Isabella is?"

Matigoro looked at him intently. His face had taken on a pained expression that tugged at João's heart. But at his question, Matigoro's eyes widened, and a reassuring smile crossed his lips.

"Your niece is alive and well." Matigoro lifted his hand to calm João's alarm. "She has a young son called Salvadore."

Amazement at the news and surprise to have found Isabella filled João.

Matigoro then related all the events that took place, and how Abravanel, an angel in disguise, had come again to their aid.

"So you see, *HaShem* saved them from the evil following them to the ends of the earth. God was there to help them in their hour of need. Although, I'm afraid that Miguel is lost to us."

"But how? They were together, weren't they?" João almost yelled in agony over what his niece must have suffered.

"Miguel was killed as he sailed to Tangier, helping us shuttle slaves. That's where the pirates struck."

João sat stricken by the news. Isabella was so young, and yet so soon a widow. Fate had been cruel, but his niece had survived. He sighed. "Where is she now?"

"She has taken over Miguel's operation, with Avram's help." Again he filled him in on Avram's miraculous find and his help with their mission. He then added, "I don't want to give you false hope, but Isabella believes, deeply in her heart, that Miguel may still be alive. Avram had told her that he was thrown overboard after a blow on the head. He'd seen Miguel disappear into the waters." Matigoro stopped again and shook his head. "I'm worried that she's taken on a dangerous alliance with the pirates."

"But it's madness. She could be killed too. Pirates bent on booty roam from the Tyrrhenian Sea to the Alboran Sea and beyond!"

Matigoro nodded with hopelessness. "Nothing could change her mind. She's fixed on the idea that Miguel is still alive. She's now the captain of the ship, and Avram is there to protect her."

João felt a crashing weight on him. "Please tell me where to find her." This time his tone commanded Matigoro. *Will I find her in time before sailing back to the New World?*

13

Life at Court

COLUMBUS SAT WITH COURTIERS IN the palace at Barcelona, relishing his every moment of luxury and attention. Already his detractors were fewer in number, and the number of his followers grew daily. His loyal friend, Luis de Santangel, came to visit several times to confer on his next voyage. Juan de la Cosa had returned from Seville and stood by his side, carrying out plans for the voyage, and monies were pouring in from the Crown's treasury for expenses to the Indies. Fray Perez, his trusted friend who had made the grueling trip from Palos, sat across from him. Two other officials were there to discuss the voyage, including the young noble Marquis Juan Ponce de León, a protégé of Queen Isabella's.

"My dear Colón, have you set a date for the return voyage?" Ponce de León's voice disturbed Columbus's deep thoughts.

Columbus turned to Ponce and nodded slightly at him. "My apologies, Ponce de León, I was rehearsing in my mind the steps to the voyage."

Ponce de León laughed a deep belly laugh at Columbus, without malice in his eyes. "That's why we're here—to help you plan it. Why don't you tell us instead about your romance with the beautiful Leonor de Bobadilla, eh?"

Columbus felt reddening as heat rose to his face. He struggled for words to reply to Ponce de León, when de la Cosa came to his rescue.

"Marquis, I hear the queen has authorized you to join us on the voyage?"

De León appeared surprised, as if caught stealing a trinket. He gagged, coughed, then cleared his voice. "This news had been well guarded until now. The queen herself was to let you know at tonight's banquet. How did you learn of it?"

Columbus intervened to save de la Cosa. "We would be honored, Ponce de León, if you were to represent your famous Basque father and your illustrious line from the kings of Vasconia by accompanying us on this dangerous journey."

De León looked pleased with Columbus's praise, and he bowed his head. "My old man, I thrive on danger. The queen has been most gracious to give me this appointment for further exploration."

Columbus didn't know what to make of this upstart, barely twenty years of age, calling him old. He might be older, yet wiser and more experienced, he thought with glee. He decided to forgo the slight insult and smiled at the youth.

"We'll certainly feel safer having your impetuous and vigorous youth to guard us against danger."

Ponce de León looked as though he vacillated between replying angrily to Columbus and accepting his praise again. "Don't forget my relative, Rodrigo Ponce de León, Marquis de Cadiz, who fought bravely against the Moors."

"How can we forget?" Columbus said, then got up to end the session between the planners of the voyage and the supporters waiting to question him. "Gentlemen, we've discussed all there is to discuss of our grand voyage. I will leave you now, my dear friends, for an important task is waiting for me."

"And what is that important task, Admiral?" de León asked, with a cocky smile upon his lips and a wink of his right eye.

The assembly laughed raucously in unison.

Columbus replied abruptly, "I'm to give thanks to the Virgin of Guadalupe, as I vowed on the return voyage. She saved us from peril on the first voyage." He turned his back on the men and with de la Cosa walking beside him heard sighs of disappointment follow.

The assembly watched him leave the hall. With his back turned, Columbus imagined their facial expressions of having been shortchanged on the primary purpose of the meeting—hearing gossip about the beautiful Leonor de Bobadilla.

14

Plans for Escape

ALI SAT BY THE DOOR of the stifling hut to breathe in the night air. He leaned against the tightly knitted palm-frond wall, which prevented air from penetrating the hut. The temperature hadn't cooled much from the blazing heat of the July day, but any breeze coming from the sea refreshed his sweaty body. Sekou, too, sat chained near him. Both men lingered in the moonless night that felt overbearing. Only stars shone above, lighting shadowy outlines in the slave camp. From time to time, a lone vulturine fish eagle, looking for crabs or mollusks near the lagoon off the sea, chimed in with a guttural squawk.

"You thinking . . ." Sekou's voice trailed as he saw Ali turn his head sideways to check whether a guard was near. He continued. ". . . escape." His voice died down to a whisper.

"Yes," Ali replied. "All the time."

"I want to go to Mali and my people." A sigh escaped Sekou's lips.

"It's good you remember where your people are. I can't remember my beginnings." Ali remained quiet afterward.

"But," Sekou said, "why you no remember?"

Ali then decided to tell Sekou his affliction: his memory loss with no shred of images or words coming to mind. "I don't remember because I don't remember."

"Why you no remember?" Sekou repeated.

"All I remember is a ship and being beaten daily. And now I'm here at La Mina's mines."

Sekou stayed silent at his last remark. He then said, "Scars on back, arms, is from beatings?"

"The scars, yes, but the gash on my arm was there when I woke up on ship. From before I could remember."

"That's why your name Ali? You take from air?" Sekou waved his hand in the air.

Ali smiled in the darkness. "Not exactly from the air. I heard a father calling his boy."

"So, Ali, one who no remember his name. How we escape? You no go far in the night. Guards, animals, heat kill us."

Ali moved close to Sekou and spoke in a low voice: "Did you see that when the guards get their food, they leave a few men watching the campground. That's when we can run to the dunes on the edge and hide from their sight."

Sekou gave a short chuckle. "And what you do with chains and dogs?" He pointed to his ankles.

Ali whispered in Sekou's ears, "I found a metal file hidden between two rocks."

"Você encontrou o que?"

Ali laughed softly. "I slipped it under my trousers when the guards weren't looking. I tell you, I had trouble all day with the file grazing my thighs. Sitting was also a pain."

Sekou laughed silently.

"The night is getting deeper. Better get some sleep," Ali said.

15

Commerce

ISABELLA HELD SALVADORE ON HER lap at the dining table, trying to feed him a purée from solid foods. The boy swallowed some of the gruel, but spit out the rest as his small tongue stuck in and out of his mouth.

"I think it's too early to give him solid foods. Raquela can still nurse him." Ana gave Isabella a sideways glance.

Isabella kept feeding Salvadore. "No. I think he's ready for it."

Ana waved her hand in the air. "Well, you're his mother, and there's no changing your mind."

Avram, who usually kept quiet through meals, turned to Ana. "Isabella knows her mind. After all, look at what she's accomplished in one year."

Ana nodded. "I grant her that. Our granaries and orchards produce so much that wine and jam fill the storage shelves. We're having a tremendous year. You are now a very rich woman."

Isabella didn't reply to Ana's praise, but she raised her head from Salvadore's feeding and smiled at her.

"It was a stroke of genius to buy the land next door," said Avram. "Now we can continue to diversify our crops. We can start a new vineyard too."

"Perhaps now you can stay at home and leave sailing to Avram," said Ana, looking down and picking at her food while hiding the sheepish look on her face.

Isabella wiped Salvadore's mouth, laid him in the basket near her, and looked fixedly at Ana. "Nothing will stop me from sailing. You know why, and that's final." She rose with a quick movement. "I will be sailing next week to Morocco."

Both Avram and Ana looked surprised.

"I thought we were going to stay home till next month," Avram said, his eyebrows raised in question.

Ana looked down, resigned. "How long do you intend to look for him?" She didn't dare pronounce Miguel's name. "It's been over a year, and you've exhausted every possible means, even trading with criminals—pirates—and rewarding them."

Avram remained quiet, knowing too well not to interfere. He couldn't say or do anything that would dissuade Isabella from continuing her search for Miguel.

Isabella shrugged, then smiled at Ana and said in a calm voice, "They've left us alone, haven't they? This is the price we pay for peaceful sailing."

She turned to Avram and said, "Contact Lourenço da Sintra to prepare the *Liberação*."

16

Searching

THE SIGHT OF LAND ON the horizon made João's heart beat faster with anticipation. One year had passed since he glimpsed his niece Isabella at Maria's farm, if only for a brief moment. He longed to see his sister Sarita's features in her face. Above all, he must see that no other harm came to her or her son. At that thought, he marveled at having a grandnephew to love and cherish. And as the caravel approached Portugal's shores, he prepared himself to meet his new and only family.

The docks in Lisbon were the same as he had left them many years ago for Spain, except for a few new governmental buildings scattered around the port and ships trading as before. He recalled his sailing years before he was caught in the web of inquisitional vengeance that was unleashed on the Conversos of Spain. He wiped his brow to chase the bad memories away, and with a lighter step went down to the sheltered harbor near the Tagus River estuary. He rented a horse, and within an hour he reached Sintra and stopped at a tavern to get his bearings.

"What can I get you?" the elderly, tavern owner asked.

"Ale."

The owner poured the gold liquid from the barrel behind him and served it to João with a head of white foam.

"You look familiar to me," the owner said.

João stayed silent at first, then said, "I had a sister who lived here many years ago."

The owner's face lit up. "You mean Sarita! God works his blessed ways! I saw her daughter here, under my roof, a number of months ago." He took a curious look at João and added, "That's what hit me first—you all have the same eyes."

João laughed freely. "I'm glad our family resemblance is shining through. As a matter of fact, I'm looking for my niece, Isabella. Do you how far the farm is?"

"It's up yonder past the Castelo dos Mouros on the hill, then thirty minutes by horse."

"Muito obrigado, senhor." João left the tavern, mounted his horse, and followed the directions on the dusty road. He passed the Moorish castle with its rectangular towers and entered a dense wood, where thick vegetation was watered by sea mist. Birds sat in rows on vines connecting trees, watching him and his horse penetrate this green sanctuary.

When he emerged from the forest, his eyes caught sight of a large property, elevated and sprawled beyond a line of trees. He could hear the surf rolling from his vantage point, and the two-story house overlooked the sea. A sudden urge to turn his horse around grasped him. *What if Isabella shuts me out? What if she hurls vindictive blows? What if*— Enough! He shut out the guilt-ridden thoughts at once.

João dismounted, and leading his horse behind him, he slowly advanced to the front gate of the property and opened it, alerting two women sitting and working on the front porch. One woman nudged the other to see to the stranger walking toward the house.

A young woman approached him at midpoint and asked, *"O que você quer, senhor?"*

"I'm Isabella's uncle."

The young woman left him to report to the other woman.

João's heart jumped to discover it was Ana running out of breath toward him.

"João! Is it you? I can't believe it!"

He embraced Ana. The last time he'd seen her was at Teresa's home. She hadn't changed since that time. "I can't believe that it's you either! When Matigoro told me you were all together near Sintra, I thanked the Lord many times!"

"Come. Come inside," said Ana, leading him toward the front porch. He tied his horse to a post and followed her inside with the young woman holding a dish of peeled carrots.

The interior of the house was bright, spacious, quiet, and peaceful. They had found a haven in heaven. *But for how long?* he asked himself with a nudging worry.

"Where is Isabella?" he asked.

Ana took him to the kitchen without answering. Under the supervision of another woman, two children played in the vast room while a babe rocked in a crib. He approached the child and was struck; there before him was Columbus's grandchild. The red hair and blue eyes revealed the glaring patrilineal thread. He grabbed the boy's soft hand, and Salvadore grasped João's index finger. He smiled at the boy, and Salvadore smiled back with cooing sounds.

"Isabella isn't here," Ana finally answered.

João let go of Salvadore's hand. "Where is she?"

"She sailed with Avram, just yesterday, for Tangier."

João could barely conceal his deep disappointment. "And I've just returned from seeing Matigoro." He took several steps back and sat down by the large table.

"She'll return in a few weeks."

"I'll be gone by then. I must rejoin the ships leaving from Cadiz in September."

Ana reflected on his words, then said, "In the meantime, let's celebrate your visit. Raquela, bring us the wine by the pantry." She turned to João and said, "Raquela, her two children, and Juanita have been with us for almost a year."

Juanita raised her head with a smile.

João peered at the two children now playing on the floor with a ball made of sheepskin, the oldest girl directing the young boy's hands.

Ana then proceeded to tell him where Raquela and her two children lived before. "So, you see? There are many Jewish families still wandering in poverty since the edict. A pox on the monarch's house!" Ana spit on the floor, which brought a smile to João's lips.

"This is also why I'm here, Ana. To save them from danger and harm." He told her of his plans to smuggle refugees from the Inquisition to a new world free of fear and death.

"But how can you succeed? Danger is always at our door. Granted, we found here in Portugal a haven from evil men in Spain."

"But how long will it last?"

A shadow passed over Ana's face.

"This is what I plan to do in the next months." João revealed his scheme to find a new land and shuttle Jews and Conversos to the New World.

"I'm aware of the quest you put before us. Will that bring us the peace we yearn for?"

"Yes. In my heart I believe so, and with HaShem's wisdom it will be done."

"If you're looking to help Jews and Conversos escape danger, you might want to go to the Castelo dos Mouros. They all found shelter in the ruins."

"Then that's where I'll start my search," said João.

"What shall I tell Isabella when she returns?" Ana asked him.

"Tell her that next time I'll bring news she'll want to hear." He quickly put his finger to his lips to quiet Ana's curiosity. "I must speak with her first."

"All right, João, I'll tell her to be patient until then. *Mientras tanto, ve con la protección de Dios.*"

They drank a cup of wine, and João embraced her and left on his horse to return to port and embark for Cadiz.

17

Pilgrimage to Guadalupe

EAR ADMIRAL, YOU HAVE MY leave from Barcelona to begin the second voyage to the New World. It is clear what your mission is: secure the conversion of infidels and find the gold. We gave strict orders to Archbishop de Fonseca to assist you with all negotiations regarding ships and provisions. We have also contracted several servants from the royal household to accompany you on the voyage and send five baptized Indians to be returned to their land.

Signed, I Queen Isabella de Trastamara   Queen of Castile and León

Columbus, swaying to and fro on his horse, read and reread the queen's letter with difficulty, then kissed it with reverence. Queen Isabella had been munificent to him personally and a great patron in his quest. It remained for him to prove to her his services to Spain and the church.

They were now traversing the immense Ebro plain and heading to Saragossa. Behind him were the officials traveling as his servants on their horses, also supplied by the Crown, and a bevy of other officials to accompany him. Riding down in the valley, along the many castles on the Sierra de Guadarrama peaks, they ascended the higher plains of New Castile. When they reached the lands of the Duke of Medina Celi, one of Columbus's most avid patrons, they entered Madrid. Its citizens lined the streets, welcoming the column of men and horses with shouts of joy, clapping their hands, playing instruments, and throwing rose petals from opened windows. Columbus raised his face to the cheering public welcoming him to their city. He saw many young lads, their eyes open in amazement at seeing the man of legends, which reminded him of his own childhood when he'd go to port every day in Genoa to see the caravels and carracks leave on their long voyages. *Perhaps one of these youths will grow up in my footsteps.*

Archbishop de Fonseca, riding by his side, turned to him and said, "You are much admired and loved, Admiral."

Columbus lowered his head in humility. "I'm only a messenger for God. In his wisdom I dwell to bring glory to his house."

The archbishop nodded with admiration, and though Columbus knew that they'd been at odds with each other, he didn't let it show. "We will sleep in the town of Trujillo tonight and by morning will reach the Sierras. Tomorrow we'll arrive at the monastery," said de Fonseca.

"Though I'm weary, I can't wait to see the Virgin's statue at the monastery of Santa María de Guadalupe," said Columbus.

Upon reaching the inn at Trujillo, Columbus wearily left his horse in the capable hands of his trusted Indian, then followed the archbishop into a reception hall, then to a series of sleeping rooms. "Good night, my dear archbishop." He left de Fonseca to manage the rest of the lodgings' arrangement.

He found his bed comfortable and plunged into a recuperative sleep.

The first sun ray awoke Columbus with a jolt. He slowly walked to the windows to find the expanse of the ocean but instead found hedges and trees blocking his view. His primary mission to get to the monastery came back to his mind.

Within an hour, the party of officials, Indians, de Fonseca, and Columbus were back on the road heading north. By now there were many pilgrims on the ascending road, all heading for the monastery of Santa María de Guadalupe. The defiles in the Sierra Mountains were narrow and dangerous, and Columbus kept his unsettled horse from rearing or buckling by whispering calming words into his ear.

"You do control your horse beautifully," remarked de Fonseca. His horse had stopped several times, refusing to go any further.

Columbus said, "Use your rowel spurs sparingly on your horse. Their flanks are tender from too much pressure." He then caressed his horse's neck, at which the animal nickered quietly.

"I'll remember that," said de Fonseca.

By now the party had reached the mountaintop and the Jeronymite monastery of Guadalupe. The base of the crenellated walls was filled with beggars preying on tired pilgrims to part with their coins.

Columbus dismounted and gave alms to some of the poor, then entered the sacristy sheathed in gold icons of the Virgin. The statue's golden cope blinded him, along with the chasubles, candleholders, and dalmatics made of fine silk and embroidered with the lily flower. Above his head were great vaulted and finely decorated golden arches.

Columbus recalled the legend of the Virgin's statue being buried near the Guadalupe River to protect it during the conquest of Seville by the Moors. A poor shepherd boy, minding his sheep, had been summoned by the Virgin's apparition to build a great cathedral on the spot where her statue was found and excavated.

This gold display was a great message from the Virgin for him to discover gold in the New World and bring it back to all the cathedrals in España. This mission drove him. Then the conquest of Jerusalem would become his most ambitious dream to achieve. He crossed himself and knelt to pray and give his thanks to the Virgin, who protected sailors and rulers.

Deep in sacred thoughts, his mind wandered to Córdoba. His next detour was to pay a visit to his son, Fernando, and his mother, Columbus's mistress Beatriz Enriquez. His other son, Diego, from his deceased wife Filipa Moniz Perestrello, had also been left in Beatriz's care. He couldn't wait to see both his children.

Just then another face superimposed itself in his thoughts. It was the vision of a beautiful young woman with dark hair and emerald eyes. That was how he envisioned Isabella's features would appear, resembling her mother's. Sarita had first captured his heart and soul when he was a young man living in Portugal. Their love created a bond between them, and he promised to return and marry her. But life had other plans for him; it was the sea that won in the end.

18

Escape

ALI DIRECTED HIS GAZE TOWARD the guard standing on the hill above him and Sekou in the pit. The guard shuffled back and forth sluggishly, his long-barreled *espingarda* firearm hanging from his shoulder, a knife at his belt, and a stare fixed on the prisoners.

Ali stood near Sekou at the end of a long row of prisoners shackled with chains on one ankle. He glanced at Sekou and shook his head twice. He wasn't ready. Both men went on chipping at the rock wall in the dust and heat of a long day winding down. In another hour, the sun would descend below the horizon, and forms would begin to disappear in the night.

"Hassan! Hassan!! Ta'ala ma'ee!"

The guard looked down the other side of the hill, where voices called to him, then, taking a last look at the prisoners working below, he disappeared from view.

"Quickly!" Ali whispered.

Sekou replied by lifting his pickax and swinging it with force toward Ali. The ax fell on the chain leading to the metal band encircling Ali's ankle.

"Again!" Ali's voice rose, and he looked around him if anyone had heard. The other prisoners were still working at the rock wall, their attention on finding a gold vein.

Sekou brought the pickax down a few more times and the chain broke, releasing Ali from the next slave in the row on his right.

Ali breathed a sigh of relief. "Your turn now."

The blows kept coming down until Sekou, chained on his left, was also freed.

"Quickly! Let's run in the opposite direction!"

Two prisoners had taken notice of Ali and Sekou's broken chains, glancing at them with surprise and shock, but neither sounded the alarm. A silent pact existed between prisoners—should anyone escape, the guards would not be called.

Ali, flanked by Sekou, climbed the hill above and ran toward the dunes in the distance. Sekou began to fall behind, and Ali turned to see him limping. He ran back to help his friend.

"What wrong?" Ali asked.

"My leg," Sekou replied, out of breath.

"Here! Lean on me!" Ali grabbed him under the arms and pulled the limping Sekou toward the dunes. As they reached the first dune, a call sounded, then a shot was fired into the air. The barking of dogs followed.

"They discovered us!" Ali said out of breath.

Sekou yelled, "You go! Go!"

"Are you mad? They'll beat you until you're dead!"

Sekou shook his head. "I wait for them. Go!" he urged Ali.

Ali took a long look at him, turned his back on his friend, and ran further inland. If he could bridge the distance between the lagoon and the fort on the hill without being seen, he might have a chance. The problem would be the metal band around his ankle.

The dogs' yelping and barking came closer. Ali ran the last distance in the soft sand to the lagoon and jumped into the water, where he hid among bamboo reeds in the shallows. He snapped a hollow branch and placed it in his mouth, then plunged into deeper waters. The dogs were upon the bank, circling, barking, and being egged on by the guards.

Ali sat still on the sandy bottom below the water, using the reed to breathe, but the air couldn't reach his mouth and lungs through the thin tube. He held his breath. He could see the guards' boots stepping through the murky water around him as they disturbed the sandy bottom of the lagoon. He used the murkiness to swim down to deeper water, his lungs ready to explode.

After thirty seconds that felt eternal, the waters stilled. Ali surfaced, gasping for air. He waited a few more minutes until silence prevailed with no signs of guards in the distance. He lay exhausted for a few moments on the sand, and noticing the descending darkness, he moved stealthily through the dunes toward St. George's Castle on the lagoon's shore. As he fled, he looked behind him to see if torch lights appeared on the horizon.

He breathed a sigh of relief. It seemed the guards were long gone, as were the sniffing dogs. As luck would have it, the dogs didn't pick his scent in the water. He now looked for a hiding place to spend a long night.

19

Second Voyage Underway

COLUMBUS STOOD ON DECK ON the *Mariagalante*, supervising the loading of barrels, crates, horses, pigs, cattle, and building materials for settlements in the Indies. Further down the docks, caravels bobbed with their naked masts, awaiting provisions to be carried on board. If all went according to plan, the seventeen ships with more than one thousand men would furnish the many towns he planned to build in the New World.

From his vantage point, Columbus felt he was master of the seas. His greatest plan, though, was to establish trading posts all along the coasts of Juana and Española and convert the Indians. With all the honors, rewards, and further promises by the monarchs, his future was assured.

"Admiral! Admiral!"

Columbus recognized Juan de la Cosa's familiar voice. He looked at his faithful second-in-command and waved to de la Cosa as he maneuvered around the horses being loaded up a plank. When Columbus reached him, de la Cosa hugged him with joy.

Columbus returned his friend's hugs by enveloping him in his large embrace. "How was your voyage to your relatives in Santoña?"

"It renewed my strength and faith to see them all."

"Now that it is done, we'll need you here to get the voyage underway."

"Very well, Admiral. I'm at your disposal," de la Cosa said with a large smile. "By the way, Admiral. Before leaving for Santoña, I ran into Vicente Pinzón . . ." De la Cosa seemed reluctant to speak further.

"What is it, de la Cosa? Speak."

"He said a lawsuit against you would be presented to court."

Columbus stood shocked at first, then puzzled. "Why would Pinzón want to do that?"

"It isn't Vicente Pinzón, Admiral. It's Martin Alonso Pinzón's son, Arias Pinzón, who's claiming the reward for finding land in the Indies."

"But Martin Pinzón received his monies for the voyage, through the Crown, who paid those sums out of their coffers."

"It isn't his dues that the lad is seeking; its revenge. Revenge for his father being denied the honor for the discovery."

"But they all know that I sighted the first light from the sterncastle! I showed it to Pedro Gutierrez, the steward of the king's dais. He confirmed it."

"You know, Admiral, that no one is disputing your word of honor, but the Pinzón family is trouble."

"Well then, let them arrest me!" Columbus was furious. He'd had to fight detractors and enemies at his throat for the last twenty years. Now the fame and honor he fought so hard to earn was being coveted and threatened to be stripped from him. He wouldn't allow that—the queen would see to it. After all, he was bringing an entire new world to her and to Christendom.

20

In Hiding

ALI HID ALL NIGHT NEAR the lagoon, yet close to Elmina's Castle. Sitting on high ground during the night and dozing on and off, he observed two large vessels waiting offshore. He then heard moaning and crying as slaves were dragged through a door in the wall of the castle and shuttled in canoes to the waiting ships.

In a flash of memory he saw himself being collared by the neck and one ankle with chains, then marched outdoors from the same slave's cavern, where he had awaited his outcome. He didn't have to walk far. His destination ended beyond the lagoon in the mining camp.

Ali's attention returned to the torchlights illuminating the harbor, where slaves were being hauled aboard two ships. Pitiful, muffled screams, filled the night as children were snatched from their mothers who were then whipped harshly to move them toward the ship's plank. Ali heard the sobs of those on board in a crescendo of voices, ascending and descending like a desperate wave. He felt their pain and distress. But how had *he* gotten to La Mina and to this dungeon?

These thoughts disturbed him, but he was brought back by sharp wails. He looked yonder at the docked ship and saw a guard hitting a slave on the head with the pommel of his sword. The man touched his head in pain and raised his hands to block the next blow coming down on his head. Ali felt a sudden rush of emotion and images: a pirate beating him on the head, then throwing him into the sea!

Snatches of memories burst in front of his eyes as he recalled the blow to his head and warm blood dripping onto his eyelids. He relived again the choked feeling of drowning and sinking down in dark waters, then he gasped and came back to the present. By what miracle had he been pulled out of the sea?

He remembered the iron file he kept strapped by a rope to his thigh. He reached into his trousers and pulled out the rusty file, then began to grind away at the metal band around his ankle. After a full hour, when the dawn began to whisper on the horizon, he despaired that the band was sturdier than he had imagined. Again he tackled the filing and ground through half of the cuff. Another hour and he'd saw it off completely.

A weak sun already showed on the horizon over the dunes, the castle and the lagoon becoming distinct to the eye. Flocks of birds flew above him, oblivious to his struggle, but he continued until a final effort cut through the loop, and it fell by the wayside. He stopped with relief—his arms, shoulders, and hand cramped and sore. He buried the metal band under the sand near a rock and stood up free. Now he must move on before the guards resumed searching the area.

His first thought was to approach one of the vessels and stow away without being noticed. On second thought, he feared he might be caught again, and the cycle would renew into slaving for the gold masters. His only other recourse was to flee the coast, hiding by day and traveling by night. But first, he needed to find water and some food.

21

final Details

COLUMBUS FINALIZED THE LAST DETAILS for the grand voyage under the watchful eyes of the archbishop of Seville, Juan Rodriguez de Fonseca. It was due to de Fonseca, the royal chaplain, and his excellent skills as planner and developer, that the fleet of seventeen ships was assembled. *The queen made a wise choice in selecting him*, thought Columbus with satisfaction. All he had to do now was chart the voyage and give the order to sail. He still relied on the maps used on his first voyage and the coordinates he concealed in his secret journal. He let out a chuckle, remembering when King João of Portugal had asked to see his coordinates to the New World. But he had outwitted the king and evaded his request. Time was growing short before the voyage, and Columbus knew that they were nearing launch.

"Admiral, you have over twelve hundred men to supervise and seventeen ships to monitor for smooth sailing. Are you quite ready?" Archbishop de Fonseca asked as he adjusted the black cloak caught between his corpulent body and his horse's saddle.

"I'm as ready as I'll ever be, Venerable Sir."

"The heathens of the New World must be converted as soon as we reach land. It's most imperative that we start at once."

Columbus nodded in approval. "It shall be done."

"As I was saying, Admiral. The men have been picked, the stores are bulging with supplies, and the chandlery is stocked with—" The archbishop pushed back his red cap, then unfurled a document. He read, "—additional tools, cordage, tar, pitch, and linseed oil. We also have plenty of arms, crossbows, espingardas, and fireballs for the cannons. Likewise the farming implements and seeds to be planted immediately."

"These preparations will exceed São Jorge da Mina's colony on the Gold Coast, which I saw in 1482," said Columbus. "I can't stress enough that we need our Spanish and local foods to feed the men. They won't survive on an Indian diet alone. We must have plenty of flour, biscuits, oil, molasses, vinegar, wine, and salted meat."

"My dear admiral, what I provided should be plenty. We can't have the men imbibe their way there. We need them to be sober," said the archbishop.

"I've already made my requests to the queen. I know she'll abide by my demands."

The archbishop scrutinized him for a moment, seeming surprised by Columbus overstepping his advice, but he remained silent. Columbus, too, felt the archbishop was challenging his leadership. He had to tread a fine line not to challenge the archbishop's authority—or the queen's, for that matter. Above all, no scandal should mar Columbus's name or family.

"Dear archbishop, I will see to it personally that no man is drunk during the voyage, and certainly not when we land. We need all hands to build a new world for God."

The archbishop sat tall on his horse and smiled at Columbus's religious fervor.

"Now, Archbishop, I must add the final touch to our voyage."

The archbishop raised his eyebrows and turned his eyes to Columbus.

"Go ahead, de la Cosa!" Columbus shouted at his second-in-command.

A large flag hoisted above the mainmast unfurled before their eyes. It was a coat of arms emblazoned in blue on a gold field. The arms featured a gold castle and purple lion in the upper two fields, and islands and five anchors in the lower field. The colors of gold, purple, and green on the flag flew gaily in the breeze.

The archbishop turned up the palm of his hand and looked at Columbus with surprise. "What is the meaning of this?" His voice held an impatient tone.

Columbus quickly rushed to explain. "Her Majesty has authorized me to use these arms on the flag, issued on May twentieth of this blessed year. This is my own coat of arms," Columbus said with pride as he unfurled a cylindrical parchment.

"Why wasn't I told?" The archbishop toned down his voice. "In that case," he conceded, "we'll bless your coat of arms for safe and productive passage to the New World."

"Admiral, Admiral?" A voice called.

Columbus lifted his eyes to see his young brother Diego Columbus standing in front of him.

Shocked for a moment, he then opened his arms to greet him. "Diego? Is it you? I can't believe my eyes!" He embraced him, tapped his shoulders, then hugged him again.

"Yes, it's me." Diego said laughing as he returned the warm embrace.

"When did you arrive? Why didn't you send me word?"

"I didn't want to miss your voyage. So here I am."

"Admiral?" The archbishop interrupted the joyous reunion between the two brothers. "I will take your leave now."

"Of course." Columbus nodded. "Archbishop, this is my brother Diego who will shortly enter the priesthood."

The archbishop smiled at Diego as he examined him with his hands clasped over his stomach.

"It's my pleasure to meet you, Venerable Sir." Diego said with reverence.

"The pleasure is mine, Diego. I think you'll make a fine priest," said the archbishop as he walked away.

Diego blushed under the praise.

"Come, little brother," Columbus said. "We have much to discuss."

22

Ghosts in the Night

JOÃO STOOD ON THE *CAPITANA'S* deck, directing sturdy, seasoned sailors and haulers willing to do the job. He first retained permission to hire additional help from Juan Manrrique, his foreman. He also hired five youths of fourteen and fifteen years of age, for whom he felt personally responsible, but who could be useful on the ships.

"Are you sure those youngsters are able to do the job?" asked Manrrique.

"Absolutely!" João stressed. "They're young and healthy—and what's more, they'll take anything you pay them. I can tell you they're starving."

Manrrique took another look at the five adolescents, their tattered clothes and hooded hats that made them look like monks instead of dockworkers. He nodded. "All right, but make sure they don't dawdle!"

"I'm on top of it, señor."

"All right. Put them to work." Manrrique turned his back to attend to other chores.

João had now been promoted to supervisor, working under Manrrique, leaving him responsible over the newly hired. That promotion had come at a price. Columbus had yielded again under the threat of extortion so that João would keep the admiral's real identity hidden from the Crown. Disgrace and ruin would follow if anyone discovered that the great mariner and explorer to the Indies was none other but a Converso. The first voyage had already been accomplished under a lie. No monarch or court would have allowed a Converso the leeway, let alone the responsibility, of being trusted with commissioned ships. João felt a perverse sense of power over Columbus. But he was on a mission: to save his brethren from misery and death.

He turned to the newly hired. "Quickly! Lift those crates and bales stacked on deck and start loading them into the hold!" he told the five youngsters.

The five youngsters went to work at their task, and João lent them a hand in lifting, sliding, and making sure the cargo was securely lowered into the dark abyss. Several hours later, as the supplies filled the vast hold, he waited for the young recruits to come down one by one into the hold. The hired youngsters collapsed with fatigue.

"All right, you can stop now," João said. The vision in his mind of family members hugging and saying their good-byes to the youths, perhaps never to see them again, suddenly overwhelmed him. He quickly took hold of his emotions

"Follow me," said João.

Making sure no one was looking he led them to the recesses of the crowded hold, where darkness fell, and said, "You'll hide and remain in the hold. I'll bring you food and water. You must be silent until we sail tomorrow. Is that understood?"

One of the youngsters said, "But where can we relieve ourselves?"

"You'll find a chamber pot near these crates," João said. "Once the ship reaches high seas, you will resurface and use the 'head' by the bowsprit near the figurehead like anyone on this ship."

"Won't we be arrested on the spot? And who knows, they might throw us overboard!"

A frightened murmur came up.

"No. You won't be arrested or tossed in the sea," João said. "I'll make sure of it. Now do as I say, and I will return shortly. The sun is setting, and we sail at dawn."

João left the five frightened youngsters and headed for the upper deck. Upon surfacing, he noticed Columbus talking to Juan de la Cosa, and quickly hid behind the mainmast, busying himself with the cordage.

"João!" It was the admiral's voice. He turned to face him.

"Yes, Admiral?"

"I want to talk to you after your work is finished."

"I'll wait for you, Admiral." João tried to keep his voice level, unworried.

When João met Columbus at nighttime, he found himself cornered in the admiral's cabin. Columbus closed the cabin door and turned to João with anger. "I saw you leaving the hold. What's the meaning of that?"

João stepped back. "I was just making sure the cargo is secure. That's all." João's heart was pounding.

Columbus's face looked taut under the dimmed lamplight. "As you brought up the subject on the first voyage, I know that I haven't given you permission to bring unauthorized sailors on board. If anyone is stowed away on this ship, I'll hold you personally responsible!"

"Aye, Admiral."

23

New Horizons

ISABELLA SQUINTED AS SHE SURVEYED the sea for pirate ships. So far they had been left alone. They'd given tithes and merchandise to Aruj, the feared pirate captain. Other ships, too, received a smaller amount of coins to satisfy them. The word spread among all the pirates—that Aruj was paid the same amount—brought grunts of satisfaction as they pocketed their coins and left the *Liberação* with jars of jam and bottles of wine. *I wonder if they'll eat and drink, or sell them on the black market?*

"Avram?" Isabella called.

Avram lifted his head from coiling the rigging and looked in her direction.

"I want to see you in my cabin," she said.

A smile appeared on Avram's lips, but she paid no heed to it. Avram was used to her giving him orders and never complained. He was an efficient and dutiful first mate.

She turned her back and entered her cabin. The small room immediately brought up images from the past. Reminders were all around her. It was still Miguel's cabin, with the bed he'd slept in, some of his clothes folded in the small chest in a corner, and his hat hanging on a nail by the door. At first she had refused to get rid of any of his belongings. But then she gave most of it to the poor in Sintra, keeping a few things back. These remnants of Miguel's presence kept him alive in her thoughts. *I haven't given up on him yet*, she reiterated silently.

A knock on the cabin door brought her back to the present. "Come in."

"You asked for me?" Avram's questioning eyes peered at her.

In them she saw a hint of something else. Something she may have put there herself: a glint of hope. A feeling of discomfort pervaded her thoughts. She must correct that impression and not let it take hold.

"I asked you here because I want to make corrections to our voyage."

Avram's eyes turned somber. She was now certain of having disappointed him.

"We already went over those measurements and set coordinates for the voyage before we left," he protested.

"Yes, we did. Now I want to change that." She walked to the table holding charts, instruments, and her journal. She unfurled the chart and pointed to a spot on the western African coast. "This where I want to sail. Along this southern coast."

He came close and looked down at the chart, then raised his head with bewilderment. "Why would you want to do that? That would put the *Liberação* out of a safe sphere. You will endanger your crew and our lives."

Isabella didn't reply. Avram had hit a chord she had tried to block out. The safety of her crew was uppermost in her mind. Could she in good conscience compromise that safety?

"I'm well aware of this possibility. However, we do have means to repel any ship trying to board her. We have cannons, firepower—"

"I know all that. But can we defend against bigger caravels and bigger cannons?"

Isabella didn't answer, deep in thought.

"And why would you want to go there? Eh? Is it Miguel?" Avram brushed the chart away and left the cabin.

Isabella sat down, shocked by Avram's bursting temper. She had lost hope that pirates would find leads, yet needed Avram's help to find Miguel. A nagging voice in her head whispered to turn back. A voice pounded at her conscience. *No!* She wasn't going to listen to it!

She studied the map patiently, looking for possible routes. By sailing along Morocco's western coast, then further down to the western Sahara and in line with the meridian for the Canaria Islands, she'd glean more information on slaves loaded there on boats for the market.

She stepped out of the cabin and called Lourenço da Sintra, her second-in-command.

"Change our coordinates from Tangier west to the furthest point south of Morocco."

Lourenço was speechless. He then spoke in a low voice, "Is Master Avram aware of these changes?"

All her patience and willingness to cooperate with Avram changed in that instant. "I'm the captain, and you'll do as I command!"

Lourenço's face blanched. He nodded silently and left without a word.

"That will teach these men that I'm the commander!" She spoke out loud, then burst into laughter as she realized the power she possessed.

24

Eve of a Grand Voyage

IN CADIZ, THE NIGHT DESCENDED fast on the docks brimming with voyagers, longshoremen, dock loaders, horses, and cattle eager to be taken care of, and on the sea of sails from seventeen ships flapping and swaying in the gentle breeze. The final remaining crates were lifted and moved by many hands, maneuvering the heavy cargo with pulleys and large nets into the almost-full hold. The cargo was lashed with ropes and secured to dunnage boards with stevedore knots in order to protect the parcels from bilge on the hold floor.

Columbus stood on the *Mariagalante*, also nicknamed the *Capitana*, his two-hundred-ton flagship, with its owner and master Antonio de Torres. The other ships before him included the trusty old *Niña*, a veteran among ships, and both the *Colina* and *Gallega*, which were equivalent in tonnage to the *Capitana*. The remaining fourteen ships were smaller and fit to enter narrow inlets and rivers. All vessels were square-rigged on all masts.

He had entrusted his brother Diego to Francisco Niño, pilot of the *Niña*, to induct him into the ship's operations and to be useful on this grand voyage. He suddenly wished that his other brother, Bartholomew, was here with them on this voyage.

"That is a wonderful sight, isn't it, Admiral?" De Torres turned to Columbus with eyes wide, his left hand pressed against his heart. He lifted his lamp with his other hand to better see the flotilla of ships becoming indistinct as night fell.

Columbus felt giddy, and his heart pounded fast. "Yes, Antonio. This is a blessing from the Lord. To watch all those caravels being prepared for Christendom and glory brings me to tears." He rubbed a dry eye, but felt, nevertheless, the emotion inside him as he tapped his foot on the wooden deck.

"Do you think, Admiral, we'll be ready by tomorrow at dawn?"

"Yes, Antonio. We'll be ready," Columbus said with satisfaction. "Now, why don't you show me the hold?"

"Follow me, Admiral." Antonio directed Columbus to the hold, unlocked the bolt and removed the chains, then slid the heavy cover to let the admiral peer inside. He lifted his lamp for Columbus to see the vast dark hold.

At first Columbus saw dark masses of crates, but couldn't see the bottom. "How high are those crates stacked?"

"As you can see, Admiral. All the way up to the underbelly of the main deck."

Amazed, Columbus said, "Let's take a closer look."

He descended the rope ladder with Antonio following him and reached the vast hold packed tight with cargo. Narrow aisles separated the crates, bales, water casks, equipment, and farm implements for the long voyage. Columbus raised his head to the light falling from the hold opening and tried to see through the dark space below. A solid crate wall piled to the ceiling affirmed the astonishing volume of costly cargo. He proceeded to study the narrow aisles.

"Anything amiss, Admiral?"

Columbus said, "All right, Juan. Bring up the written inventory to my cabin for me to study it."

"Aye, aye, Admiral."

When Columbus emerged from the hold, he took a deep breath. He also fought a nagging and undefined thought. Hopefully, the musty air he smelled down in the hold would not affect provisions. On deck, navigation tools, rigging, horses, and farm animals filled all remaining space. Not one single space remained empty. He wondered where the crew would sleep, when his eyes caught sight of the gifted Indian hammocks hanging one above the other near the row of boats moored on deck. Good! He rubbed his hands together.

"Get a good night's rest," he told Juan before heading for his cabin.

In the dark hold, with the doors now bolted and shut tight, scurrying movements took place among the cargo. The five stowaways gathered silently, then one of them spoke. "That must be the famous admiral."

"Yes, Elías. It must be Christopher Columbus," said another.

"João promised that we'll be released as soon as the ship hits the high seas."

"Don't count your eggs yet, Enrique. We may be trapped in here for a long time," Elías said.

"But we'll die without food or water. This will become a tomb for us," lamented another youth.

"You must have faith, Moisés," Elías urged him.

The other two youths remained silent and detached from the rest, when one of them spoke. "My young brother Emanuel is my responsibility. If we're stuck in here more than a day, I'll give myself away. I couldn't see him die from hunger."

"We will be rescued, Isaac. I promise you," Elías reassured him. "Besides, we have all the food and water we need right here in the hold." He made a sweeping movement of his hand in the darkness. The reassuring comment failed to cheer them. They all remained silent.

"Let us sleep now until tomorrow," said Elías.

25

New Seas

THE CREW SCRUBBED THE *LIBERAÇÃO'S* decks while Isabella looked on from the upper railings. They had accepted her as a woman captain, but were more comfortable receiving orders through Avram. *I must teach them to follow my direct orders.*

She called to Lourenço. "I want a drill today on the cannons and fireballs to be discharged."

"But, Captain . . ." Lourenço hesitated. "We had this drill the first day we left."

"I know that, Lourenço. I was on ship, remember?"

"It's all in working order."

Isabella tapped her foot twice on the quarterdeck, which raised a fine dust that shouldn't have been there. Then she realized how childish the gesture was, trying to reinforce her authority.

"Thank you, Lourenço, for following my command. I want this drill done again. We can never be too sure or become complacent. And have the decks scrubbed again." She left Lourenço, who was about to protest, and descended to the lined cannon carriages on the lower deck and drew back the canvas covers. She looked through the five cannons, checking to see whether animals had built nests. Then, finding them clear, went to check the cannon balls piled up in pyramid fashion.

Lourenço stood to the side as she made her cursory check. "Is everything in order?"

Isabella looked up from one pile of cannon balls and said, "There are fewer fireballs next to this cannon. You want to make sure we have enough on hand."

"Yes, Captain," Lourenço said, and called one of the men to find and restock the missing fireballs from the hold.

A loud cannon bursting in the distance startled Isabella, who ran starboard to see a ship headed their way. A large pirate flag flew from the highest mast. Apparently it wasn't one of the "protection" pirate ships.

She shouted at the man in the crow's nest. "Pedro! You were supposed to be looking out for those ships!" She looked around for Avram and found him emerging from the tiller hole.

"What's going on?" he called out.

"This man was asleep when he should've been checking for pirates!" She paced back and forth, then turned to Avram. "I'm going to my cabin to get ready. Raise the flag!" She headed for her cabin.

Just then the other ship fired another lombard, hitting their mainmast and chipping it in two places. Isabella lost her balance and hit the deck, unharmed by the blow. She stood up on her feet and turned back to the main deck to supervise the *Liberação*'s men ready to fire a volley of cannon balls.

"Fire!" Avram ordered.

Isabella and the men around her covered their ears as the five cannons fired simultaneously, deafening their ears and tearing their eyes with the lingering black smoke.

"Fire!" a second order rang out.

A second volley of metal balls hurled through the air, hitting their targets. The pirates' mainmast took the brunt, then collapsed partly on deck, part of it hanging over the gunwale. From the *Liberação*, Isabella saw wounded or dead men hang from rafters and ratlines aboard the crippled ship.

"Isabella! Take cover! Go to your cabin!" Avram shouted.

"I'm not leaving my men!" she shouted back.

He took a brief look at her and turned to the artillerymen. "Fire again!"

Another volley catapulted from the cannons. This time it took down the pirates' foremast. The men on the *Liberação* cheered and hugged each other in their first taste of victory. Avram turned to Isabella and hugged her too.

She blushed. "You can't hug the captain."

Avram stumbled on his words. "But you're like . . . one of the men. A . . . woman captain."

The men around them exploded with laughter. "Captain, we're glad you're a woman! Hurray for our woman captain. Hurrah! Hurrah! Hurrah!"

Pleased, Isabella turned to the men cheering her and shouted, "There'll be extra rations and extra wine for you tonight!"

Again the men raised a loud ruckus, happy with their captain.

Isabella turned to Avram. "Now I will go to my cabin. See that the mainmast is repaired immediately and the cannon balls replenished!"

"Aye, aye, Captain," Avram replied with a grin.

She reached her cabin, and before entering watched the disabled pirate ship make its retreat with one mast left.

26

Slow Progress

FOR TWO DAYS ALI TREKKED through hot sand dunes while heading north of La Mina. He passed several small towns, but stayed away out of fear. Near the last town, he stole a water skin hanging on an unattended camel and filled it with water from the nearby well. He skirted several tent encampments, then came to a garrison of Portuguese guards blocking the way. Hiding behind a sand dune, he observed the guards monitoring the traffic of caravans to and from their posts. Many camels were overloaded with sacks containing goods. *Gold, most likely*, Ali deduced. But why were these shipments made by land rather than by sea? Perhaps they were booty stolen from the main post in La Mina?

He'd been able to move surreptitiously at night under a black sky, gathering leftover bread near smoldering campfires. The nights were cold, and he longed to warm his tired bones. Yet he couldn't succumb to the mesmerizing warmth beckoning from the embers.

One night, days later, he came close to being caught when a camel began braying and woke his owner. Ali flattened against the dunes hoping the dark night would swallow him. A tall Berber sat up on his blanket on the ground to check the noise, stared into the darkness, then lay back down. Luckily, the camel also settled down.

That was close! Ali breathed a sigh of relief. He waited for the man to fall asleep again before approaching the camp. With caution he neared the sleeping, snoring men and searched for provisions. A few uneaten pieces of flat bread remained on a blanket. A plate of dates and small pieces of meat, still attached to the bone, made for a good catch. Ali stuffed his trousers pockets with the food, grabbed a filled water skin, and moved with caution past the encampment, making his way north.

A cold breeze rose from the sea, and Ali rubbed his arms for warmth. His hand brushed the scar on his right arm. *Where did I get that scar? Where was I?* Again, no answers or images came to mind. His brain had shut tight around any memory he tried to find. He knew for certain, though, that he wasn't an African slave. His skin was lighter and his features different from those slaves. One of the most puzzling thoughts that kept running through his head was his knowledge of many languages: Moorish Arabic, Spanish, and Portuguese. *Why or where did I learn them all?*

Tired from his swirling thoughts, Ali trekked through the dunes, placing a greater distance between himself and his pursuers.

27

Back to the New World

THE FLEET OF SEVENTEEN SHIPS manned by twelve hundred men had left Cadiz two days prior with the blessings of Grand Cardinal Pedro Gonzalez de Mendoza. All the city's inhabitants had turned out at the port, traveling by horse, donkey cart, and foot to see the fleet set sail on a clear, sunny day. Columbus stood on the *Mariagalante* to see his two sons, Fernando and Diego, wave their good-byes from the docks. He sensed his sons' pride in his success and popularity among the throngs cheering him. Sadness crept into his heart over leaving his boys behind, but they would be well cared for by Beatriz. Queen Isabella had personally promised him that they would be welcomed at court as page boys to Prince Juan.

During the two days that followed, the elements were merciful and the sea obedient to their wishes. The winds blew into their sails, breezed across the surface of the sea, and caressed Columbus's temples, while the hand of God propelled the ships toward the promised land. Columbus's heart trembled with joy at the thought of seeing the garrison left at La Navidad again and the new islands he would discover. He was keen to explore the coasts further south. He believed that a greater land mass lay below the large islands of Juana and Española.

First he longed to see Doña Leonor de Bobadilla. Her beauty and intelligence had dazzled him on his first voyage to La Gomera. She was a lady of great renown, having fought many of her enemies and those of her late husband, Peraza, among the natives of La Gomera. Pleasant memories of his first voyage last year flooded his senses. Now he yearned for her—to hold and make love to her. If she would ever accept his hand in marriage, he would recapture the nobility he had enjoyed when his late wife Felipa was alive.

"Admiral?" De La Cosa's voice interrupted his pleasant wandering thoughts.

"What is it, Juan?"

"I don't know how to say it . . ."

"Come on. I'm listening." Columbus encouraged him.

"I'm not sure, but there are more men on the *Mariagalante* than we counted originally."

"What do you mean?"

"When we left"—De la Cosa's worried eyebrows knitted—"When we sailed, we counted seventy men total. Now I'm seeing five additional sailors."

Columbus felt baffled, and a sigh escaped him. "I took the count myself," he said distractedly. "Show me these men."

De la Cosa directed him to a group of young adolescents scrubbing the deck.

Columbus observed the five boys thirteen to fifteen years of age, wearing knit caps down to their eyebrows with their heads bent toward the deck planks.

"Who are you?" asked Columbus.

One of them raised his head and squinted at the sun blinding him. He put his hand above his eyes. "We were hired in Cadiz to help load the ship."

"But who hired you?" asked Columbus.

They all remained silent, heads down, scrubbing the deck in slow motion.

"If you don't answer, you'll be put in irons in the hold!" Columbus said.

De la Cosa came close and whispered in Columbus's ear. "Admiral, they must be lashed. If the sailors found out, they'd grow bold and not fear you."

Columbus hesitated, and then said to the boys, "First you'll be whipped, then thrown in irons."

"No, please wait!" the youngest boy cried. "I'll tell you who hired us, but only to you." His face turned ashen.

"No! No, Moisés!" the oldest one cried. "Don't do it!"

The youth who was about to confess fell silent.

Columbus stood stunned. The name Moisés was a Jewish name. Who other than João could've carried out this deed? Columbus had been forewarned on the first voyage, but he'd dismissed the threat. Now it came back to haunt him. If anyone on the ship discovered stowaways had escaped to the New World, he'd be the first one to be disciplined. The law was stringent, and these young boys should be shackled and sent back to Spain to be dealt with by the Inquisition.

"De la Cosa, return to the tiller to check on coordinates. Find João and send him to me."

De la Cosa hesitated, no doubt curious as to how the admiral would deliver the blow, but he obeyed. "Aye, aye, Admiral."

As soon as de la Cosa left, Columbus looked over the five youths, still scrubbing the decks. His breath came shallow and fast. He took a deep breath of the wind swirling around him, but still panted for air. He suddenly felt the burden of responsibility and punishment weighing heavily upon his conscience. No matter—he had to carry out justice.

"Admiral Columbus? You wanted to see me?"

Columbus turned around and looked at João's face staring at him. "Follow me to my cabin!" His voice came out harsh, almost barking.

João took one look at Columbus, then at the young men—eyes fixed on the plank floor—and his face became somber. Nevertheless, he followed the admiral to his cabin on the quarterdeck.

"Close the door!"

João obeyed and turned to face the admiral.

"Did you stow these young boys on my ship?" Columbus was now yelling at him.

"I can explain, Admiral."

"I give you two minutes!"

"Well, it is that—"

"Explain yourself!"

"You agreed on the last voyage that Conversos and Jews could travel on your ship."

"I never said that!" Columbus protested. "I said I would think about it. Not that I would physically bring them on board." He began to pace the cabin. "You put me in an untenable position. How will I explain this to de la Cosa, or to de Fonseca, who watches my every move?"

João stood silent during the outburst. He then said to Columbus, "I thought you'd want to help brothers in need. I, too, consider myself one of your brothers—both by blood and kin."

Columbus looked at him as if João had gone mad. "We're not brothers! Nor have we the same blood! I never married Sarita. And why should I believe your story about Isabella?"

João looked pained. "You promised Sarita you'd come back to her. Isabella is your daughter whether you believe it or not. As for our blood, it courses through Isabella's veins as well as mine and yours." His voice lowered. "It's the same blood that runs in other Conversos, Marranos, or Jews. You can never get away from that."

Stunned by João's impudent words, Columbus remained speechless.

"I'll leave you now," João said. "Please don't harm the youngsters."

"Go back to your chores!"

João turned his back and left the cabin.

For a long time Columbus sat in his cabin, torn between putting his threat in motion and his reluctance to apply it. De la Cosa had warned him—use his authority or lose it. He stepped on the quarterdeck and hailed de la Cosa.

"What is it?" de la Cosa said, out of breath.

"Tomorrow we'll have a flogging of the five stowaways. Prepare the crew for it."

De la Cosa observed him for an instant and said, "Admiral, I know it was a hard decision. This way no one will question your authority."

Columbus nodded, and after de la Cosa left he bent down as if a heavy load was pressing on his back. *All I wanted was to discover new islands and a new passage to the Indies. Fame is a heavy burden.* Perhaps he ought to postpone the flogging for another day?

28

flight

*A*LI LABORED UNDER A BLISTERING sun in a land covered with hot dunes spreading to the horizon. He had left the cooling ocean coast as more and more ships appeared in the sea. At all costs, he wanted to avoid being found by slave merchants and resold again to the highest bidder. The only way to evade human traffickers was to return inland to the desert dunes.

His progress was slow, with a blazing sun and little water left in his leather gourd. He'd have to wait till sundown to return to shore and look for more water. How? He had no clue. It was just as well that he had no more visions of how he'd gotten here in the first place. The earliest memory was the suffocating drowning, then surfacing the waters and lying in seawater on a ship deck. The next nightmarish encounter came back to haunt him—a boot kicking him repeatedly and a voice yelling in Arabic, "Speak! *Maa ismuk*? Speak!"

When the rib pain became unbearable and he couldn't take it anymore, he had yelled at his attacker, "*Tawa-qaf! Tawa-qaf!* I don't know anything!"

The Berber pirate stopped in his tracks. "You speak my tongue? Don't think it will get you anywhere!" He resumed kicking him.

Ali had moved his chained body away from the dreaded boot, but he was just as surprised as the pirate. Where had he learned to speak Arabic? He looked at his hands, then his arms folded against his chest holding his bruised ribs. Though his skin took on a dark shade of golden brown under the blazing African sun, it was still whiter than the Berber's.

"Please stop! I can't remember."

The pirate stopped. "Ha-ha! I haven't heard that one yet. You lie beautifully." He was about to swing his leg with the dreaded boot, but Ali grabbed the man's leg.

"Let go of me!" the pirate yelled. "Let go!"

"What's going on here?" A voice boomed above Ali as he lay on the deck's planks. He squinted through the sun's blinding rays under his cupped hand and could make out the figure of a young Barbary chief pirate. He was better garbed than the rest of pirates going about on ship. Dressed in a long white tunic covering red silk baggy trousers, he had a red beard and a turbaned hat covered his head.

"I'm disciplining this dog!" said the pirate.

"What's he done?" the chief asked.

"He won't tell me who he is, Aruj. Maybe another kick or lash will loosen his tongue."

The chief looked at Ali with curiosity and waved his hand at the pirate. "No. Wait! He'll bring us many dirhams at the market. Don't damage him! Bring him some food." With that the chief had walked away to supervise his men on deck.

Ali laughed at the recollection. He was then treated more fairly, until sold for a high price to a merchant and he found himself in La Mina. It was another boot and more lashes that made him adopt the name Ali. But who was he really? This question came back to haunt and torture him with recurring thoughts that made no sense. The beautiful vision of a smiling young woman kept coming back. *Who is she?* And why the smile? Again his mind wouldn't yield.

Shrugging his shoulders, his attention came back to the present as he detected a dark column trudging along the horizon. A camel caravan slowly approached him. Panic set in. Where could he run? He'd be spotted quickly against the bare dunes! He plastered his body against the sand and with slithering movements retreated to the higher dune behind him, then lay there waiting.

He heard a sudden bark, and in seconds several dogs were upon him. He fought against the large incisors and canine teeth tearing at his shirt and gashing his arms. Blood ran from his forehead, obscuring his eyes, when a strong voice called the dogs back.

"Qef!" The large dogs pulled back, but kept on growling and barking repeatedly.

Two guards came to Ali, lifting him off the ground. He looked in the direction of the voice to see a short, white-garbed Berber man wearing boots with a whip in his hand and a smile on his face!

Ali swayed, trying to find his footing in the sand, when the man who stopped the dogs said, "Take care of his wounds! I don't want rotten goods!" Then he turned his back on Ali.

So much for daydreaming, Ali scolded himself. He should have been looking out for danger. *Now I'm finished*! He'd be returned to La Mina and the mines after auction in the slave market. They might as well kill him now and end his misery.

He bolted and began to run, but the guards ran after him with the dogs in tow. In no time they were upon him, and this time he was chained hand and foot. He lowered his head in despair, when a vision presented itself in his mind: the beautiful face of the young woman smiling at him. It then faded, and he followed the caravan on foot in the hot sand.

29

Return to La Gomera

COLUMBUS STOOD ON THE MAIN deck, anticipating docking at La Gomera. The fleet of sixteen caravels followed the *Mariagalante*, bobbing around her like young ducklings swimming after their mother. The sight of colorful flags on ships' masts, men assembled on their decks, and captains shouting orders faded from his eyes. One thought only resided in his head—his heart burned with desire for Doña Leonor de Bobadilla y Peraza. His eyes searched the island for the Torre del Conde, the tower that pinpointed Doña Leonor's house in the town of San Sebastian, and his heart skipped a beat. After the many months at sea since the discovery of the Indies islands, he couldn't control his happiness at seeing her again. As his men rowed closer to the black sand beach, he could hear and see the white-crested waves crashing onshore as if Doña Leonor's arms drew and beckoned him on.

"Halt!" Juan de la Cosa shouted to the rowing men. With a thud, the boat dug into the sand, and they all alighted.

Columbus searched the beach and saw a welcoming party galloping in approach to receive him.

"Admiral, we welcome you on behalf of Governor Doña de Bobadilla," said Alfonso de Lugo, the governor of the neighboring island of La Palma. He presented an empty mount to Columbus, who climbed into the saddle of a fine Arabian horse. The rest of the party had other horses that followed the lead.

"Gracias, Don de Lugo. It's a pleasure to see you again." Columbus nodded to the envoy as he rode his horse at a slow trot.

Don de Lugo replied, "The pleasure is all ours, Admiral."

Before long they reached Doña Leonor's San Sebastian house. Columbus dismounted, turned around, and looked with unconcealed delight at the sight before him. The magnificent island revealed the protected harbor crowded with his seventeen ships' masts and colorful flags swaying under a light breeze. The Canarias Islands, spread in all directions, dotted the vast expanse of the blue ocean, and white cloud formations floated in the sky. And the woman he desired most anticipated his arrival. He gave a silent thanks to the Lord and held in check the pleased sigh budding inside him at what awaited him. At that moment he wished with all his soul and the fibers in his body to remain here with Doña Leonor for the rest of his life, but other duties awaited him.

Columbus turned to de la Cosa and Archbishop de Fonseca. "Let's give our compliments to the governor."

She waited for them in the great hall, greeting them in a flurry of blue brocade and silk robes with precious jewels dotting her hair.

"Welcome to my humble home, *hidalgos*."

Archbishop de Fonseca was first to kiss her hand, dazzled by her beauty. "*Dios* has blessed us to be in one of the most beautiful islands of the Canarias and in your presence."

"Your praise of La Gomera is well deserved, but not for my own sake. I'm a humble servant of the Lord and his design upon us," Doña Leonor said with a modest smile.

De Fonseca clearly approved of her comment. He nodded graciously and kissed her hand a second time.

Next came Juan de la Cosa, following the same ritual. "The Madonna has shed blessings upon you and your house."

"Master de la Cosa, we're delighted by your presence—a great cartographer, I hear."

De la Cosa blushed. "You give me undeserved praise. I'm just a tinker of the world's image."

Columbus stood aside. *When will she acknowledge me?* He felt a secret bond between him and this beautiful woman, and waited patiently for his turn.

Doña Leonor then turned to the dashing young Juan Ponce de León. "I hear Queen Isabella has favored you to accompany the admiral?"

Ponce de León bowed to her. "I'm also a humble servant of the realm, Doña Leonor." He bowed and kissed her hand.

"My dear admiral," she finally said to Columbus. "It's a pleasure to see you again." She gave him her hand, and he kissed it with a reverence due a queen's royal hand. After all, she was his queen, for him to adore for the rest of his life.

Doña Leonor then directed them to a table laden with food and wine. As they ate and spoke, Columbus tried to capture her eyes and attention, but she heeded only the archbishop, Ponce de León, and de la Cosa's words. Again he waited patiently while suffering painful angst, hoping she would lay eyes on him.

"Let's drink to your second voyage, Admiral. With luck and many blessings from the Lord."

"Admiral? Admiral!" A voice startled him out of his trance. He looked dumfounded at the company cheering him.

Columbus quickly raised his glass. "My apologies, everyone, for not hearing you. May the Virgin bless this voyage! We will conquer the New World again!"

"Hear ye, hear ye!" all voices called.

"My dear distinguished guests. The hour is late, and the voyage begins early. We must all get a good night's rest," said Doña Leonor with a seductive smile to all her revelers.

None of the guests appeared offended by the send-off. The men received the summons to disperse with smiles and bows. They left the hall, still conversing with each other as they disappeared down the corridor.

Columbus had remained behind, determined to talk to Doña Leonor. He waited for the servants to empty the cluttered table, all the time avoiding looking at her. When they found themselves alone, she got up to close the doors to the hall. She came back to him and looked in his eyes. Columbus gave her a mutual gaze, but found something missing in her eyes.

"My dear admiral, I sense that you want to talk to me?"

Columbus rose from his chair and went down on one knee. He took hold of her hands, brought them to his lips, and held them there for a moment. He then cleared his throat and said, "Dear Leonor, I suffered a thousand deaths away from you. I worship and love you above all else. Will you do me the honor of being my wife?"

Doña Leonor looked at him passively. Gone was the passion and love she returned a year ago. Had he been mistaken of her feelings? He squashed the thought and waited for her response.

"My dear admiral. I admire you in return, and it is a great honor you just bestowed upon me. In different times I would have been greatly happy to return the love you hold for me, but I have been a widow for—"

"I know that you still hold great regard and feelings for your deceased husband, Don Peraza. His memory be blessed for eternity. But you're still young, and you—"

This time she interrupted his passionate protest. "I have been and will remain Don Peraza's widow. I made a vow to keep his memory alive by not marrying again."

Columbus was dumfounded; he had never heard of such a vow. He couldn't believe her words, or her denial of what had passed between them. He lowered his head and felt his heart shrinking. Then he lifted his heavy body off the cold stone floor.

He nodded to her. "I will take leave . . . of your hospitality." He left the hall with a slouched gait.

30

The Search

THE *LIBERAÇÃO* PLOWED THE DARK Atlantic waters, sailing close to shore, while Isabella searched the sand dunes on the coast. She could see a sparse tree line at the horizon and few settlements. She thought of men working in dusty pits, straining and sweating in the heat, living on a meager pittance. Any slaves working for their masters would have to be chained to the grind and under the supervision of guards and dogs. Perhaps if Miguel had survived the unforgiving depths of the ocean, he was slaving in one of those pits now.

She sighed with impatience at their slow progress. The last suggestion she'd heard was by a merchant, suggesting they search slave markets from Tangier to the southern tip of Ghana. It was unlike her to become impatient with a task or project. She may have acted with impulsiveness in the past, but now she had methodically studied the best way to go about finding Miguel. Matigoro had been instructed to look out for Jewish slaves for sale in all markets in Morocco, and to search ships unloading these poor wretched souls along the coast.

"Captain? We're approaching La Mina."

Isabella turned from her portside coastal watch to see Lourenço waiting on her orders.

"Give order to the men to begin furling the sails and unload one of the boats."

"Aye, aye, Captain."

Isabella smiled after Lourenço left. She had earned the crew's respect and admiration in the last pirate attack, and taking orders from a woman captain had become routine among the men. Her orders were followed without delay or hesitation; she had won their trust. The only crew member not responding as the others was Avram, her first officer. Since their last disagreement, he hadn't spoken to her, carrying out her orders silently.

She turned her attention to the approaching jutting peninsula, with the port of La Mina and its surroundings. The only vegetation seen from her ship was a few palm trees hugging the hill leading up to St. George's castle.

"Boat ready, Captain!" Lourenço shouted in her direction.

Avram was already waiting in the boat, and he sat silent at the stern. Isabella struggled with her long skirts as she tackled the rope ladder. When she finally stepped over the gunwale, she signaled to the first boatman to begin rowing.

The shore came fast into view, and they landed with a thud on the soft sand. Isabella, without any help, sidestepped over the bow and jumped onto shore.

"Make sure to fasten the boat securely, and leave one man behind to watch it," Isabella ordered Lourenço. She hailed Avram, walking behind the men.

When he came close, she spoke in a low voice. "As first in command, you must walk alongside me."

Avram nodded but didn't reply.

She continued in a hushed voice. "I don't know what I've done to merit your silence, but whatever I said to you doesn't justify your behavior."

Avram stayed mute. He then uttered, "You have nothing to apologize for. It is I who beg your pardon for my ill manners."

Isabella flashed a smile with a relieved sigh. "All right, Avram, let's make peace and go on with our search."

Avram nodded in agreement.

The ten men accompanying her were armed with swords and crossbows, and Isabella carried a long knife in the deep pocket in her skirt folds. In no time they arrived at the high square brown walls of the fort, and she entered the military premises with Avram and Lourenço in tow, leaving the rest of her men outside.

A Portuguese soldier in charge in the first chamber stood at their sight. *"A que devo o prazer da sua companhia?"* he asked as he noticed Isabella, sizing her up with his eyes.

"I'm Senhora Isabella Obrigon, captain of my ship, the *Liberação*."

The officer's eyes now flashed with admiration. "The pleasure is all mine, senhora. I'm captain of the fort. What is your pleasure?"

"I'm looking for a runaway slave. Perhaps you may have seen him?"

"We have few runaways. They're usually lashed severely, and too afraid to repeat it. Some die from their wounds."

A shadow passed in front of Isabella's eyes as she restrained a mournful sigh from escaping her lips.

"Can you describe him?" the captain asked.

"Tall. Black hair and blue eyes."

"This doesn't sound like the black slaves we keep here. Most are from southern Africa and Saharan countries."

"I would like to visit your open mines and the prison hold with slaves." Isabella took from her pocket a small purse and slapped it on the table in front of him.

The captain bowed, then quickly pocketed the purse. "Please follow me."

He led them to the open mines, where slaves had already begun their day cracking the granite wall with their pickaxes, their bodies white with dust plastered to their sweat. The sound of metal on stones dominated the pit, and the dusty soil hung in the air, prompting Isabella to cover her nose.

"This is no place for a *mulher*," the captain protested. "You will be more comfortable inside the fort, no?"

"I'll be fine," Isabella replied.

Row upon row of slaves, chained all in a line by one ankle, had enough slack to maneuver without tripping over one another. The party continued viewing the spectacle, while Isabella walked the rows of workers resting their pickaxes briefly between blows. In a cadence, one man hit the volcanic rock while another lowered his pickax. Then, like a well-rehearsed dance, the next one swung his tool at the hard, unyielding granite. They all looked malnourished and skinny with ribs protruding through their thin chests. When Isabella finished the last row, she turned to the captain.

"May we now see the ones in prison?"

"Please, senhora." He led his visitors onward.

The captain checked the guards posted at intervals, then led the party to a section in the fort's hold. The dank air smelled wet and musty, and moisture dripped from the walls. Dark forms lay on the ground with chains around their necks and ankles. Repeated coughing came from several men, and again Isabella brought her handkerchief to her nose. They stopped in front of sickly men wallowing on the ground.

"As you can see, senhora, we only keep black slaves in here. You'd be hard pressed to find a white man in this hellhole." He quickly covered his mouth, and with eyes wide said, "Forgive me, senhora, for my twisted tongue."

Isabella nodded but said nothing. As she passed an older black man with white hair, she felt a pull on her skirts. She looked down and saw bleary, red-veined eyes fixed on hers. She stopped for a moment and turned to the captain.

"This man is old. He shouldn't be here."

The captain covered his mouth again, this time to control laughter from bursting. "My dear senhora, this man is a runaway. He tried to escape about a month ago with another slave." A sigh escaped the captain's lips. "The other one fled, but he's good as dead now. No one gets out alive from this evil Saharan furnace."

Isabella cringed at the dreadful words. "Never mind," she said with a choked voice. She then caught Avram nodding his head and agreeing with the captain, but remaining silent.

"How much do you want for this slave?"

The captain looked at her with surprise. "Why would you want an older slave when I can sell you a young, strong one?"

"I want this one. He reminds me of another slave I had while growing up."

"All right, senhora. Since he's outlived his years and strength, you can have him for one silver piece."

Isabella slipped her hand in her pocket and brought out the silver coin. The coin passed hands quickly, and the captain nodded at one of his guards to remove the chains from the older man.

When they stepped out, the captain bowed to Isabella and said, "I'm sorry we couldn't find your slave, senhora."

"Thank you, Captain." Isabella turned to Lourenço. "Take us back to the ship."

Upon boarding, Isabella turned to Avram—silent during the three hours they spent at La Mina. "Please see that this slave is washed and fed." She then retired to her cabin.

31

Westward Bound

COLUMBUS STOOD ON THE *MARIAGALANTE'S* DECK, peering at the horizon for the fleet following his ship. The caravels glided along like happy little ducklings following their mother. His enthusiasm for reaching land had been dampened by Doña Leonor's rejection. She had broken his heart, but more so injured his pride. As an admiral he had earned the right to elevate himself to nobility. After his wife died, he had lost that coveted status and reverted to the common rank of navigator or Genoan foreigner. With Doña Leonor, he had hoped to recover that title, and now had to content himself with the titular name "Admiral of the Ocean Seas." He still loved her, however, for she inspired in him the passion he had lost years ago.

The vision of a beautiful woman with emerald eyes and jet-black hair appeared suddenly before his mind's eye. Of all the women he had known, including his mistress, Beatriz de Arana, and mother of his son Fernando, Sarita had captured his love forever. The name Isabella came to his lips, channeling his thoughts to the daughter he had never seen nor cherished until now. Since João divulged her existence to him on the previous voyage to the Indies, she had become now part of his life.

"Admiral, we have bridged the first four hundred leagues," de la Cosa said, startling Columbus out of his deep thoughts.

"That's good news, de la Cosa. Another two weeks and we'll be back to La Isla Española, where I long to see the men in La Navidad. "

"As do I, Admiral. Who knows? By now they might have gleaned much gold from the Taínos."

"I should hope so. They were left to cultivate the land and the natives. I hope they used their time wisely."

"Admiral? It's time to administer punishment to the stowaway lads," de la Cosa reminded him.

Columbus hesitated. He then spoke reluctantly, "Is it that time already?"

"We've been remiss in that task," de la Cosa said. "Any longer and the crew will doubt your command."

Columbus sighed. "Go and fetch them." Then he hailed him back. "Assemble all the men on deck."

When all his men were called on deck, they stood with curiosity in their eyes, unsure of what to expect. Likewise, sailing behind the *Mariagalante,* Juan Niño, owner of the caravel *Niña*, hailed Columbus, anxious as to why the men were assembled on deck. The *Niña* and *Pinta* caravels and the other ships were too distant to see the commotion on board the *Mariagalante.*

Columbus disregarded Niño's call and turned to his men. He pointed at the five boys assembled on deck, and spoke to his sailors. "These five youngsters came on board illegally and without papers! This is what happens to men who don't obey the law." His voice quivered.

Columbus caught João looking straight at him with a contorted face and angry eyes bulging from their sockets. He averted João's gaze and quashed the self-loathing guilt bearing upon him and returned to supervise the punishment.

Within minutes, the five youngsters were lined up and the first youth tied to the mainmast. His billowy shirt was torn off his back, and Columbus nodded to the flogger to proceed. At the first leather whiplash, the youth closed his mouth tight to the violent pain. Then the next lash unleashed a painful cry. By the third and fourth whip he moaned after each blow.

"That's enough!" Columbus shouted after the tenth lash. "Bring the next one." His voice failed him, his stomach heaving from revulsion at this violent act.

The other four youths each received the same flogging. Afterward they lay on deck, bleeding from their wounds.

"Have the physician attend to them!" Columbus ordered. He shouted at his men. "You can all go back to work!"

One by one his men walked slowly back to their chores, shaking their heads.

"I had to do it. I had to," Columbus mumbled to himself. He made for his cabin, when a voice hailed him.

"Admiral?"

He turned to face João's anger. "What is it you want?"

"Why, Admiral? Why? These are young boys who have never harmed you."

Columbus cast a furtive glance about him and said to João, "You don't question your commander. I'm your superior."

"I know that. But why did you demand these savage beatings?"

"I've explained myself. There's nothing more to say."

"You could have let it pass. You've become a harsh man."

"Again, this is nothing that concerns you!" He turned away from João and walked away angry, not sure whether the anger was at himself or João's questioning his authority.

32

Revelations

ISABELLA TENDED TO THE OLD man, bringing him food and drink to satiation. The frail man held gratitude in his eyes and once grabbed her hand and kissed it. She had placed him below deck near the cannons, protected from the scorching sun and the sea that periodically drenched the decks. She knew not why she was helping the poor wretched soul or what prompted her to purchase him in the first place. Perhaps she missed her father Don Obrigon and the ancestral home back in Seville. What was her adoptive father doing right now, and most importantly, was he well? He was probably occupied with Miguel's young brother José. Tears came to her eyes, and a drop spilled over onto her cheek. She stared at her empty hands.

"*Mut'asif*, why you so sad?" The old man spoke haltingly in Arabic. A cough rattled the old slave's thin body. When he stopped he finished with, "My daughter?"

She raised her head, surprised that he detected her sadness. "I was thinking of my father," she replied in Arabic.

Surprise reflected in his eyes that she spoke in Hassaniyya Arabic—his tongue.

"What do they call you?" she asked him.

"Sekou."

"All right, Sekou. You rest here."

"Lourenço?" she called her second in command.

"Yes, Captain?"

She took him aside. "Make sure this man is watched over. He's feverish and may not last the week. Also, send for the physician."

"Right away, Captain."

Isabella smiled. Now Lourenço called her "captain" every time he addressed her. *He's making up for each time his tongue had been tied*, she mused.

She added, "Oh, and call Avram to my cabin."

"Aye, Captain."

Heading to her cabin, Isabella felt saddened that this old man might die alone in this big and unjust world. Her thoughts went back to her small family: her son, Salvadore; Ana who had become a mother to her; and Avram, who, though stubborn, remained what little family she had and a close friend. Her adoptive father, Arturo; her adoptive and now deceased mother, Estrella; Miguel; José; Sarita, the long deceased mother who had given birth to her; and her former nanny, Hannah, all swirled in her mind with images of her past. All were snatched away from her life. The longing to be with her father in Seville was becoming oppressive and overwhelming.

She went straight to her cabin and the table laden with maps and documents and retrieved the map of Africa's coast. "Let see . . ." she mumbled. "What other slave posts are there to explore?" She turned to face Avram, who had come in without her noticing.

"You need me?" Avram said.

"Yes. I want the ship to stop at two other posts as we head north."

"Why?" he asked without hesitation.

"There might have been someone who saw him." She didn't pronounce Miguel's name, not eager to repeat the angry scene she'd had with Avram. He remained quiet. She might need to convince him.

"What makes you so sure that you'll find him?" he asked. "We've been traveling up and down this Gold Coast, where slaves are sold and bartered, and no sign of him has come up."

She let out a long sigh. "We've been over this many times, Avram. You've opposed me from the start, and I want to know why."

He moved close, grabbed her by the waist, and kissed her savagely on the lips. She fought to free herself from his grasp and turned her anger on him. "You know that my heart is with Miguel. You knew this from the start. I could never love you!" Her words were heartless and cruel, but they were out of her mouth nonetheless. She felt the guilt weigh on her immediately, as if she had stabbed him with a knife.

He stood stricken for a moment. "Yes, you're in love with a dead man, when I could give you all the love you need." His voice came out passionate but sounded harsh, almost sarcastic.

She took the blow hard. If Avram believed Miguel dead, as did Ana as well, and everyone who knew Miguel, then what hope was left to find him?

She composed herself and said in a cold voice, "You will stop at the next two outposts. That is all."

He looked at her frozen. Lowering his head, he turned his back on her, and left the cabin without a word.

33

Mists of Memory

*A*LI TOILED AGAIN UNDER THE hot sun, while shackled as before with a rusty chain around his ankle. This mine was further inland, at the confines of the Sahara's edge in Algeria bordering Morocco. He had been handed down from the previous slaveholder and sold to the present one, Effendi Yusuf Zaim. His master exhibited pride in all the slaves he owned, and there were more than a thousand. He had a cocky smile on his lips as he moved along the rows of slave workers mining minerals, looking for gold.

Gold! Ali spit on the ground. The source of all that was evil! His life would be spent extracting the precious mineral for other men to get rich. Fury engulfed him. He swung his pickax against the wall in front of him with fast successive blows. After a few moments, he stopped, out of breath and drenched with sweat.

"Hey, Ali. Leave some for us!" At those words, the slaves stopped directing their blows on a large vein in the rock that appeared to hold promise and burst into laughter.

"Yeah sure. We'll be rich with our labor." Another man's sarcastic remark brought a new wave of laughter.

"Get back to work!" All heads turned to the sound of the guard's angry voice.

Ali hailed the guard. "We're finding a lead; see for yourself."

The guard approached and examined the rock wall. He came closer and passed his hand over the gold grain shimmering through the granite. "I don't see that there's much here. But you shouldn't be laughing on the job," the guard barked as he looked at the workers. Meanwhile the slaves kept on throwing blows at the wall, hoping for a breakthrough vein.

"We were overjoyed for the effendi and his good luck," Ali said coyly, hoping the guard—who was too dumb to know gold from pyrite that glimmered with the same intensity but without its precious value—would not detect the irony in his remark. He scratched his temple with a dusty hand as he felt his stomach flutter. He was dumbfounded. How did he know about pyrite, fool's gold?

"You worry about your own luck." the guard barked at him. "It'll run out soon if you don't go back to work!"

Ali turned to his work without a word.

When the guard left their group to supervise other slave workers, low renewed laughter was heard from the workers.

Ali spoke quietly to the coworker on his right in the long chain of slaves. "The bastards use us to gain wealth and kill us with hard work."

"You said it," his coworker murmured with a sigh.

"When will it all end?" Ali exhaled his own sigh with despair.

"When we're aged and then dead from hard toil and malnutrition."

This remark threw Ali into a deeper mood, one that tore at him. *I have no memories, and I will die in this desert!* His chest heaved again.

"He's the one!"

The voice came from behind Ali's back. He turned to see the guard charging his station with a finger pointed at him. Effendi Yusuf Zaim walked a few steps behind the guard.

"Now you've done it," his coworker let it slip.

Ali waited for the blows to hit him when Effendi Zaim walked straight to him.

"What do you know about the minerals?"

Ali felt mute for a moment. Then he said, "Your Excellency, I know very little."

"How do you know?"

"I'm not sure, but I know that gold will be found in a vein surrounded by quartz veins and clay. You can spot it usually in clay deposits surrounding the vein. This outcrop isn't the best for this sedimentary cliff." The words came pouring out of him. He bent and picked up a rock fragment lying on the ground to show the master. The effendi meanwhile followed Ali's explanation with curious eyes.

Ali turned the sample over. "This host rock has a reddish and orange hue, which isn't bad, but a deeper green color is much better to find higher quality gold. It means a better and richer crop." He felt again stunned by the information coming out of his brain and mouth without being able to control it. *How do I know this?*

This time, a smile appeared on the effendi's face. "I want to hear more of your knowledge, boy," he said and turned to the guard. "Release him!"

The guard stared at the effendi, but obeyed as he reached around his belt and pulled a key that released Ali from his shackles. The band on his ankle was lifted, and Ali bent to rub his chafed skin.

"Come, boy!" the effendi ordered him.

Ali followed, and couldn't help asking himself why he was called *boy*. He certainly wasn't a boy. The reflection that had stared back at him in La Mina's lagoon told him otherwise. He saw himself as a grown man, but not as old as Sekou. Where was Sekou now? Had he been lashed by a vicious guard or thrown in irons? Was he dead? Ali's conscience weighed heavily upon him. If it weren't for his urging Sekou to escape, his friend wouldn't have been exposed to cruelty and beatings.

"So what exactly do you know, boy?" The effendi's voice interrupted his thoughts as they walked to his tent.

Ali paced himself as he delayed answering the effendi, then said, "In all honesty, Effendi, I don't know much more than what I already told you." For a moment, he regretted his words. Would they take him back to the pit and lash him?

"But how do you have this knowledge? Who taught you?"

Again, he had to answer before the nearest guard would come down with a whip. "My father taught me, Effendi."

"Your father was a wise man. Come to my tent."

He followed him to his tent and upon entering saw it was the headquarters for the mining operation. A table held paperwork and charts. A plate of dates and a jug lay side by side. Ali's eyes were fixed on the dates, and the jug reminded him how thirsty he was.

The effendi noticed the look. "You must be hungry. Eat!" He pushed the plate toward Ali, then poured water from the jug into a goblet near it.

Ali fell upon the dates, gobbling a dozen in seconds, spitting the pits clean on the sandy floor, then quenched his thirst with the clear water.

The effendi broke out laughing. "Ha-ha, we keep you hungry so you don't escape into the killing desert."

Ali kept his mouth in check from responding to the taunt to escape.

"I'm going to keep you in my tent to study the charts. Find me outcroppings like the one you described."

"But, Effendi, you have to survey the land," Ali protested. "You have to see it on the ground."

"But you can look for descriptions on the map and choose the right deposits, *lah?*"

Ali nodded. He had no choice but to agree.

"And don't think again about escaping. The jackals and hot sands will kill you in no time," the effendi said.

Ali nodded again. At least he would have more food and less work.

34

Crossing the Atlantic Again

THE SEVENTEEN-SHIP ARMADA HAD been plowing west, riding the waves as their sails blew in clement wind. Fish flashed on the water's surface surrounding the caravels, and a few black–and–white terns flew low by the bow to catch this abundant food. Columbus communicated daily with Juan de la Cosa sailing on the *Pinta*, to coordinate their progress in leagues. The other ships regularly passed their measurements forward to Columbus as they followed behind his flagship, the two-hundred-ton *Mariagalante*. Columbus preferred the *Mariagalante* and *La Gallega*. They were both carracks, nao ships with deep, wide hulls that carried large cargo.

The ships communicated via a pulley system and wooden bucket to send notes and coordinates. The main ships under his command, the *Colina*, *Niña*, *San Juan*, and *La Cardera*, were all sturdy caravels, and the remainder were smaller ships that could sail close to shore with shallow drought, requiring just 3.2 meters to the sea bottom. Columbus remembered all too well not being able to land on several islands on the first voyage because he had no such ships in his fleet.

As Admiral of the Ocean Sea, he commanded the fleet. He also had power over Spanish ships traveling to and from the Indies. This command began when westward-bound ships crossed the meridian between the Azores to Cape Verde. He held the highest command in this ocean jurisdiction, while Don Alfonso Enriquez governed from land to the Azores. What gladdened Columbus's heart with pride was his emblazoned coat of arms, flying its gold castle on the green field from the highest mast of his flagship.

The air had turned sweet and the temperature mild, but most of all, the compass needles had moved one point from northeast to northwest as they crossed the first one hundred leagues west. It was as if a curtain had separated the Old World from the New World in mid-ocean. Likewise a carpet of weeds appeared out of nowhere on the ocean's surface. The sea turned a deeper green, leaving behind the dark shade of European waters. God extended his blessings upon the fleet to enjoy a paradise of sea, fish, and sky as if no seasons existed—just the constant pleasure of good weather.

"Admiral, we crossed the seven-hundred-league point this morning," said Pedro de Terreros, his personal steward, who also shared duties such as cooking for the crew of seventy men.

Columbus sighed with pleasure, and a rare smile crossed his lips. "We should be on the lookout for land very soon. Meanwhile, monitor the men in the crow's nest. Make sure they don't fall asleep on their watches."

"Aye, aye, Admiral."

Pedro left to carry out his orders, and Columbus caught João's eyes fixed on him. *What could he want from me now?* Turning abruptly, he climbed to his cabin.

Inside the cabin he looked for his most prized possession: Zarco's map. The man had bequeathed Columbus all his maps and documents. He pored over the charts, making small crosses in various parts to indicate newly found islands. If he navigated south to chart new islands before going to La Navidad, he would have more feathers in his cap and more territory to claim for the Crown.

He pushed the map aside and reclined on the chair, letting his mind wander. He had reached the pinnacle of success with his discoveries. A sense of well-being at his conquests flooded him.

Immediately, he was struck with a negative thought that he couldn't shake—the idea that he was considered a foreigner by many Spaniards who had opposed him in the past. He had proved them wrong, but nonetheless still suffered from having few loyal friends, even among his officers. No matter. He would keep on conquering and achieving the height of fame for himself and his family name.

A knock at the cabin door startled him from his thoughts. "Come in!"

The door opened to reveal none other than João. Anger rose to Columbus's face. "I didn't summon you," he snapped.

"I know, Admiral." João's voice fell silent.

"Then what is it you want?" Columbus's annoyance was surely visible; he felt a vein throb in his neck.

"Admiral, you know that as a mariner for many years now I'd acquired much skill in sailing and directing ships on many voyages on the Mediterranean."

"I have no knowledge of your skills. Come to the point."

"I would like very much to help with those chores."

"And what chores are you referring to?" Columbus refrained from sneering.

"Why, the coordinates involved in reaching the Indies, of course. I accompanied you on the first voyage, remember?"

"Yes. I'm painfully aware of that. What do you want?" Columbus got up from his chair and stood towering over João.

"To help you check coordinates on the compass in the binnacle box, and jot them down in the journals." João looked fixedly at him.

"I already have de la Cosa doing that and Antonio de Torres with Ruiz. I don't need anyone else."

"But, Admiral. If you allow me to relieve the men every few hours, they can get a well-deserved rest."

No doubt João's argument was convincing, but Columbus hesitated. After all, João was originally of Portuguese stock, as was his sister Sarita, even though those were different times then. Now Portuguese meddling and attempts at dominion over the seas was a threat to his claim on newly discovered islands. The Portuguese monarchy had tried before to guess the coordinates for the Indies, and perhaps João might be their spy. These coordinates had to remain secret.

"I can't let you take on this task," Columbus said.

"But, Admiral. I can help. Unless you don't trust me."

Columbus remained silent.

João continued, as if he'd read Columbus's mind. "I can keep the coordinates secret from prying eyes, and my lips will be sealed."

Again Columbus stayed silent. Then he said, "I need to think about it. Return to your chores now."

João took a long penetrating look at Columbus, then turned on his heel and left the cabin.

Left alone, Columbus mulled João's request. *Would he use it as another blackmail attempt?* He sighed. In the end, he knew he would have to relent to João's request.

Over the following days, João was inducted at the coordinate watch on deck. His duty was to write with an inked quill the cardinal directions as the ship plowed ahead. Columbus also put him in charge of communicating those directions to the other ships and receiving their coordinates. At the compass in the binnacle box on deck, lit by a lantern at night, the leagues were added to the journal provided by Columbus, who demanded to see it at each watch. De la Cosa, helped by his assistant Ruiz, kept a record in the second binnacle box by the tiller. Each day the two journals had to be reconciled down to the last league, to ensure the flagship and the rest of the fleet were on course.

Tonight, after the admiral retired at the second watch, João replaced him and kept a close eye on the compass, jotting down coordinates and leagues in the journal. Tucked between the pages, he also kept duplicate notes of his own on blank parchment he had stolen from Columbus's cabin. He copied coordinates from previous watches as well. When done, he folded the duplicate records and slipped them in the long pocket of his trousers.

"Fourth place, fourth place, we sailors finished the fourth watch; wake up, wake up, wake up all," the gromet announced.

Startled by the announcement, João had done an additional watch without realizing that the time had gone by without waking Ruiz to replace him.

Ruiz was already running toward him in a disheveled state, while trying to tuck his long camisole into his trousers. "Why didn't you wake me at the third watch?" he roared.

"Take it easy, Ruiz," said João. "I didn't have the heart to call you."

"If the admiral finds out, he'll throw me in the hold!"

"The admiral isn't going to find out." He winked at Ruiz. Seeing that his mate was reassured, he went to lie down and fell asleep immediately.

35

Return to Sintra

ISABELLA SNATCHED SALVADORE FROM RAQUELA'S arms and covered him with kisses and hugs. She looked over her son, marveling at the growth he'd had during the three months she'd been away. His face had rounded into the plumpness of childhood, and his hair exploded with red hues. His blue eyes smiled at her, recognizing her features. She was grateful he hadn't forgotten his first mother. Raquela had done a fine job nursing him, but now his real mother would be alongside to guide him.

"He's almost ready to walk," said Ana with a smile. "And we often took him outdoors to look at the sea."

"Did you repeat my name to him so he didn't forget me?" Isabella asked coyly.

Ana raised her hands in protest while nodding. "Of course we did."

"We certainly have," Raquela added. "I also sang to him." She repeated the melody Isabella had sung to Mica, Avram's little brother, on the exiled ship.

Bre, Salvadore, bre ojos tienes tú
Manzana de comer!
Por mi vida el Dio me los dio.

Isabella looked up at Raquela gratefully. *These women make up my small, cherished family.* "Yes, God gave me a child with eyes like apples to eat."

The three women broke out in laughter as Avram appeared at the door.

"I made Sekou comfortable in one of the huts." His voice carried neither inflection nor emotion.

"Thank you, Avram," Isabella replied with a smile, not knowing how to cheer him. He still hadn't forgiven her for rejecting his love.

"I need to speak to you two," Ana said with grave eyes.

Isabella turned her head to Ana. "What about?"

"Please, Raquela, take the child outdoors for some sun," said Ana. When the door closed behind Raquela and Salvadore, Ana turned to Isabella and Avram. "While you were gone, we had a visitor."

Isabella raised her eyebrows, and Avram stirred with curiosity.

The mysterious look on Ana's face worried Isabella, but then a smile reassured her that no threat would come to them.

"Your uncle João found us and was deeply disappointed not to find you here."

Isabella was stunned. She'd been looking for her uncle, alongside the search for Miguel, and now he had come and gone. "When was he here? What did he say? And was he followed?" She stopped, out of breath. The questions had popped out one after another.

"You see, Isabella?" Avram said with reproach in his voice. "If we had stuck close to home with our search with Miguel, we might've found out more clues."

Isabella turned to Avram, surprised. "I don't think that's fair."

"All right you two. Stop fighting." Ana called them to attention. "Let me first tell you all about it." She told them of the meeting with João. "So you see. It has nothing to do with your search for Miguel. He went to see your father in Seville and communicated news about José. Poor Joselito. Already lost to our faith. A priest they'll make out of him. Of that I'm sure."

Isabella fell into stunned disbelief. On one hand she felt joy that her father was safe and well, but the news of José's fate was grim, hopeless. After a long silence she said, "I'm heartbroken for the poor boy. I know that my father must have done his best to prevent his snatching by Guerida. I should have thought of the consequences when Miguel and I left for Seville's port that day to find my uncle. It's all my fault." She paced back and forth and fought tears.

"That's nonsense." Ana's voice rose volumes. "It's no one's fault. It's Guerida's hatred and diligence in helping those Inquisition devils!"

"What can we do to help José?" Isabella asked.

"There's nothing more we can do. In the meantime, I have heard many rumors in town about bringing the Inquisition to Portuguese soil," said Ana.

Both Isabella and Avram were shocked by this news.

Avram protested, "They wouldn't dare! King João II promised to protect Jews. He was overjoyed that Spain let its Jews go. He knew their usefulness with trade and money."

"No matter our skills, we'll always be hounded." Ana flailed her arms in the air. Her face became red with indignation. "Why couldn't we have a land of our own?" Her voice broke in lament.

"We did at one time." Avram said. "When the Romans destroyed the second temple and drove us from the last land our ancestors had." Avram's voice was charged with emotion. "I remember my father, *Zichrono le Braha*, may his soul be remembered, who spoke the same words."

"Yes. His memory be blessed," Ana said.

Isabella was heartbroken by the ominous threat that Ana had related to them. "Let's not fall prey to this rumor mongering." She tried to reassure them. "And let's not forget that we've been productive in Portugal. We've enriched ourselves and the country too."

"So we have," Ana said.

The sudden image of a large bird swooping down and snatching Salvadore came to Isabella's mind. She felt the strong urge to run out of the house, find her son, and hug him close to her heart. "When will they stop hounding us?" Reluctantly, she let out the words pass her lips.

Neither Ana nor Avram answered her question.

"Your uncle João also mentioned that he had important information," Ana said.

Isabella looked at her. "What do you mean?" She felt a flutter and put her hand to her chest. "Is it Miguel?"

"I'm sorry to disappoint you; it's not. He didn't share the information with me, but he'll tell you when he sees you next."

Isabella could hardly conceal her disappointment, but felt intrigued by Ana's words. "When is he coming back?"

"Unfortunately, he left on another voyage for this new land they found in the Indies. That's all I know."

Isabella didn't answer and left the room silently. She went looking for Salvadore to grab and hold her son's small body in her arms.

36

New Islands

COLUMBUS STOOD ON THE QUARTERDECK, peering into the semidarkness for land. It was four o'clock in the morning, and a waning moon showed a slice of the round disk. He felt a slight chill in the air signaling winter coming to paradise, though he recognized by now that a cold season didn't truly exist in the Indies.

His thoughts pondered the three-week voyage during which the sea had taken on shades of sapphire to ultramarine blue and had treated his men to visual delights accompanied by varieties of flying fish. He also enjoyed each night at Compline, the last prayers of the day, and when by the light of lanterns the *"Salve Regina"* was sung with the sixteen ships surrounding the *Mariagalante* as the Franciscan priest, Fray Bernal Buil, conducted the service. Columbus hoped that his brother Diego was doing his best to participate in the services on board the *Niña*.

With the help of trade winds, they had sailed for twenty-one days and were now close to the magic number of eight hundred leagues, where they anticipated seeing the nearest land. The other ships had reckoned seven hundred and eighty leagues as reported by their captains. The difference was due, perhaps, to the gromets' faulty counting or failure to turn the sandglass each half hour. The pace of the *Mariagalante* had slowed the smaller and faster ships, creating impatience among the sailors who had to shorten their sails to let the flagship catch up to theirs.

Columbus had altered the coordinates from the previous voyage's reckoning to a south-southwest or west by south and one-half south from the Canarias, sailing in a straight line, hoping to touch land south of the eastern tip of Española.

"Land! Land! I get the reward!" A voice pierced the air. It was the voice of his new man in the crow's nest.

Columbus peered through the darkness lifting in the distance and could distinguish a mountainous cone surging above the mist covering a tree line. His heart began to beat fast, and his head grew light with excitement at being back in the New World.

"We've arrived! We've arrived! Blessed be the Virgin!" The sailors standing on deck let out a roaring shout echoed by all the other ships. For the men, land signaled freedom from repetitive and exhausting hard work— from manning the water pumps in the holds to checking and rechecking rigs, sails and masts. It signaled as well an end to their great impatience to arrive on terra firma. They hugged each other, jumped, and did a traditional *Jota Aragonesa* Spanish dance.

Columbus grasped with tingling hands the railing on deck, his excitement as great as his men's, as if he were seeing land for the first time.

"Shorten the sails!" He gave orders to the ships as they glided by an island on the port side then another to the starboard, and yet more emerging as dawn broke. The first island had majestic mountains, and the next was thickly wooded and flat. When the light increased, they counted a total of six large islands. All around them tall mountains rose to great heights with waterfalls spilling from peaks. His men were astonished to see waterfalls seeming to fall from the skies.

"We'll land at the first island with a good harbor!" Columbus shouted with a bubbly voice from his perch on the quarterdeck.

The search began for a suitable harbor, but they sailed two leagues along the coast without finding one. They had, though, spotted the island's vibrant green trees close to the water. The men delighted in the contrast to Spain, where no green vegetation was to be found at that time of year.

"The *Mariagalante* will head off to the next island. The rest of the fleet will wait behind," Columbus ordered.

The flagship approached the larger island, which sat at a distance of four to five leagues from the first, and the men's hopeful eyes searched for a safe harbor. When they spotted hut dwellings and a number of Indians on shore in the distance, Columbus told his first-in-command, "Let's go back to the fleet now." By noon they had rejoined the ships, and to be prudent had remained on their ships in a safe harbor found at the first island.

As an astonishing number of sailors—in the hundreds—landed on the beach from the fleet the next morning, Columbus noted there were no signs of inhabitants on the island. Carrying the royal banner to take possession in the name of Their Majesties, he walked ahead of his party. Then, finding a good spot on a low hill, he planted the Spanish banner in the soil.

"We'll call it Dominica for the first Sunday following All Saints' Day!"

His brother Diego followed his lead by kissing his rosary and falling to his knees on the soil of the New World.

All the men fell to their knees and crossed themselves while Columbus gave a short prayer of thanks. Thick wooded trees bearing fruit and flowers encircled them as witnesses to a new people having reached heaven. A strong smell from laurel-like trees brought clove scents to their noses. Some of the men, without asking, tasted a berry-like fruit on some trees. The immediate reaction was a burning sensation on their tongues. They screamed in agony and ran down to the water to cool their mouths. When they came back, they panted with pain, tongues hanging from their mouths while they fanned their faces.

Columbus and his men searched the island, and upon finding dwellings realized the inhabitants must have fled. The houses were clean and contained large quantities of spun cotton ready for weaving. In one hut they found several colorful parrots with blue, red, and green feathers, chirping and squawking on their perches. Columbus appropriated two parrots, which looked different from the parrots offered to him on the first voyage. In one hut, separated a distance from all the others, they came upon wooden statues. Columbus believed they might be gods or reproductions of their ancestors, each statue having a name carved at the base.

The party came upon an iron pan in one of the huts, and marveled at the inhabitant's skills. Columbus immediately set them straight: "These men have no iron or skills to fashion this pan. It must have been brought by the Caribs who plundered other islands, then brought it here."

Columbus found bones of a human arm and leg. He recalled the Caribbee islands, where the inhabitants ate human flesh. He creased his brows under weighty thoughts. The men he had left at La Navidad were safely housed behind large, tall fences built from the remnants of the *Santa Maria* wreck. The Virgin protected them.

He crossed himself. The hour was late, and Columbus gave the order to return to the ships.

37

New Clues

*J*SABELLA BEGAN HER MORNING BY touring the property, checking on the vineyards and workers already grafting and toiling by the vines, and looking in on the huts on the outskirts. The workers had very few possessions in their dwellings. In one hut, a few articles of clothing, such as a change of clothes, hung on nails, and two tin plates and a goblet lay on a bench near a wooden bed with a straw mattress and woolen blankets. Isabella paid her workers well, but their wages went to their families residing in various cities in Portugal or overseas. The young workers who had found a home away from a life of slavery kept their wages safely hidden on their bodies.

The mornings were getting cold for mid-November, but the skies were clear and no rain had yet fallen. Isabella wrapped her long coat closer to her body and went to look for Sekou's hut. She found him lying in his bed, uncovered and shivering. She rushed to him and heaped on the woolen blankets, pulling them close to his chin, but he still shivered. She laid her hand on his forehead and found it hot.

"You're running a fever, Sekou! Why wasn't I told?" she said to him with a hint of reproach.

He replied in Portuguese, "No worry, pretty boss."

"I am worried. Come, come with me!" she ordered him.

He stared at her. "Where boss take me?"

"I'm taking you to my house. Here, lean on me."

He stared again, apparently not used to attention from others, and shuffled out of the hut as she supported him. They crossed the grounds at a slow pace and arrived at the front entrance to the house, both straining with effort.

"Ana! Raquela!" Isabella called, out of breath.

Ana came tearing out the door with Raquela following in her footsteps. At the sight of Isabella holding on to Sekou, Ana's eyes popped. "What are you doing?" she yelled with outrage.

"He's sick with fever. Put him in the room at the back behind the kitchen. This way we can monitor him closely."

"You don't know what he's sick with. We have young children in the house!"

"We'll keep the children away, and I'll tend to him," Isabella said with a smile. She knew that by now Ana didn't argue with her, knowing full well it was useless.

"All right, Isabella." Ana led them to the back room, where a single bed stood in a corner with bedding. She lit a fire in the cold hearth with dry alder logs stacked in a woven basket nearby. The logs first gave off white smoke, then glowed red, giving their warmth to the room.

Sekou watched the fuss created over him with unbelieving eyes. When Isabella arranged his pillows, he grabbed her hand and kissed it. *"Obrigado, Patroa. Obrigado,"* he said in halting Portuguese mixed with his melodic native African twang.

"Ana? Bring him some of your hot soup right away."

Ana stared at her, then headed for the kitchen.

Sekou dozed off, and Isabella turned to leave, when she overheard mumblings coming from his mouth. She approached his bed and bent down to listen. He spoke in his light sleep, repeating words. She came closer to his mouth and heard faint words: *Branco Ali, branco Ali, correr, correr*! What could it mean? White Ali run? She tilted her head to the side and shrugged, but her curiosity was aroused. She tiptoed to the door, then went out and quietly closed it.

When she reached the kitchen, she stopped Ana from bringing the soup. "Give him time to sleep, then feed him."

"All right, Isabella. But you know this isn't sound, especially since we don't know what's making him ill."

"Yes, you're right, Ana. I just couldn't abandon him alone in the hut. I wonder why Avram didn't say a word."

Ana gave her a blank glance. "Perhaps Avram is angry with you?"

Isabella shook her head and tapped her right foot twice on the floor. "What do you mean, angry? I haven't done anything to merit his anger."

Ana gave her a strange look and shook her head silently.

"What is it?" Isabella asked with impatience. She guessed why Ana gave her a muted message, but let it pass. Now was no time to argue or worry about why Avram's anger prevented helping a sick man. Nevertheless, it was cruel on his part to punish the old man because she had rejected him. She'd have to watch Avram's behavior from now on.

38

Exploration

COLUMBUS AWOKE FROM A DEEP sleep feeling feverish and weighed with the sense of unfinished tasks. They had explored the various islands throughout the previous days and found more lush vegetation, spectacular tall mountains, large plains, and an abundance of flora and fauna. The vibrant green trees grew close to shore, all decorated with multicolored flowers—the names for which he knew not. He had instructed Archbishop de Fonseca to record and name all plants and fruit he collected.

He got out of bed and went to wash from a terrine filled with water. He rubbed his gums with his index finger, splashed water on his soapy face and neck, and promised himself to wash his body in the clear waters of inland running rivers. The water cooled his warm forehead, and feeling a slight resurgence of vitality, he walked to his cabin door and opened it to call Pedro de Acevedo, his cabin boy. The lad had now grown to the age of fourteen and showed all the impetuousness and health of youth.

"You called, Admiral?" Pedro said, gingerly entering the cabin.

"Bring my breakfast and call Archbishop de Fonseca. I want to talk to him."

Pedro left to attend to this task, and Columbus pondered his mission of exploration. He was anxious to arrive at Española and see the men he left at La Navidad. He hoped that by now they had accumulated the gold they'd been told to mine with the Taínos' help. The chief, Guacanagari, had offered his friendship to the Spanish on the previous voyage and treated them as princes of España. The men on the flotilla, too, were anxious to unload their cargo and begin the construction of towns in the New World.

Just then de Fonseca came into his cabin. "What can I do for you, Admiral?"

"We should depart soon. I'm concerned for the men in La Navidad and want to leave immediately for Española."

De Fonseca hesitated replying, then he said, "We can't leave just yet."

"And why is that?"

"Because a party led by inspector Diego Marquez went inland yesterday and hasn't returned."

Dumbfounded, Columbus restrained his anger. "Who issued the order for him to explore inland?"

"No one, Admiral." De Fonseca fell silent, anticipating that Columbus would mete out punishment.

"All right, de Fonseca. I'll deal with them when they return."

De Fonseca left him alone in his cabin to mull the nagging thought coursing through his mind. *This delay to La Navidad is driving me mad!*

All that day, the small fever didn't let go, and Columbus lay lethargically on his comfortable bunk. The cabin was spacious, as opposed to the one he endured on the previous voyage. This bed accommodated his large frame, and he took pleasure in resting. He called Pedro again to his cabin.

He sat up and said, "Call the Indian on board to come see me."

"Right away, Admiral."

When Pedro returned immediately with the baptized Taíno Indian, Columbus said to him, "Sick. I'm sick." He touched his forehead, then lay down on the bunk.

The Indian came close and laid his hand on Columbus's forehead and nodded. *"Aji, ciba cohoba cinchona."* He waved his hand in the air while blowing as if to put out a fire. He then left the cabin as fast as he had appeared.

"Where did that blasted Indian go now?" Columbus asked. He closed his eyes, and when he opened them up, the Indian stood in front of him with a black basalt *molcajete* mortar and a hand-held grinding *tejolote* pestle. He put dry bark into the mortar bowl and began to grind it to a powder. While he worked, the Indian raised his head and smiled at Columbus frequently. Pedro, who watched the whole procedure, waited as anxiously as Columbus to see the outcome. When he finished grinding the leaves, the Indian mixed them with water and brought it to his patient in a tin cup.

Columbus took one look and hesitated.

The Indian nodded and said, *"Pyjai. Pyjai"* Columbus assumed he meant to drink, but the Indian looked up to the ceiling of the cabin, and he understood that he conjured God for his help and blessings.

Pleased, Columbus smiled. "You're following in the words of God."

The Indian returned the smile and waited until Columbus drank the last drop. Immediately, he began to feel its effect. Drowsiness took hold of him. He lay down and in no time was asleep.

When he awoke, it was evening and he felt refreshed. His hand went to his forehead, and it felt cool to the touch. The powder had worked miracles on the fever—that and God's blessing.

Just then a sudden commotion came to his ears. He got up and felt dizzy for a moment or two, then walked out on the quarterdeck. Outside, sunset had begun to fall. He noticed some of the captains from the other ships in canoes alongside the ship holding a young Indian boy about the same age as Pedro. The boy tried to resist the hands gripping his shoulders, but he was dragged on board, accompanied by women captives who came on board on their own accord.

"What have you brought us?" Columbus said to the three captains.

"This boy told us the Caribs possess much gold. We brought him on board for you to witness."

"Come here, boy." Columbus encouraged him. When he came near, Columbus patted his cheeks and smiled at him.

The boy seemed to take to him immediately. He came close and wrapped his arms around Columbus's waist.

"All right. See that this boy is fed. Tomorrow we'll send an expedition to find where the gold is."

One of his captains asked, "Shouldn't we wait for inspector Diego Marquez to return? By the looks of it, the party will have to spend the night in the dark forest with the Indian women." The men around him laughed and made obscene gestures with their hands.

Columbus replied with anger, "This is no laughing matter. Tomorrow we'll send a party to look for them and the gold."

39

Hope

THE DAYS MERGED INTO EVENINGS, then nights, and each new day began in succession. By now Ali perceived his life as a repetitive blurred cycle with no past or future. His life had improved with better food, no beatings, and his ankle free of the cursed metal band, though guards accompanied by vicious dogs watched his every move. He began each day charting bed deposits for the effendi, then inking them with a cross. The map in front of him showed only mountains, so he had to divine what kind of soils and bedrock they held. He knew that only solidified lava flows contained precious minerals and that some sandy deposits might hold the key to their find. But from what source did he know those facts? Again his thoughts were in turmoil. Apparently he must have known these bits of information in his past. Was his memory coming back? His eyes returned to tracing the sheepskin chart—not for bed deposits but for an escape route.

"Well, Ali? Are you finding a new source?" Effendi Yusuf Zaim's voice coming into the tent startled him.

He turned to face Yusuf. "I'm still looking, Effendi. I'll have something for you soon."

"I need new outcrops," Yusuf said, pointing at him. "Remember, you're getting free food without producing anything."

Ali bowed without words, and Yusuf left the tent.

Where was he to find new gold for this master? Perhaps it was high time for him to escape his captors. He was in full health, thanks to his master's feeding and greediness for the gold metal. He looked at his hands, and Sekou's words *White Ali* ran through his mind. He searched the table, then the tent, for a weapon or crossbar, but none were seen. To add to the difficulty, the camp was situated away from the shore, where temperatures would have eased his escape. But he had access to food and water to provision his trek through the desert. For now he would keep his eyes open for the opportunity to flee.

40

Preparing for La Navidad

AFTER A FEW DAYS' REST and more of the Indian's potion, Columbus felt well enough to step ashore. He hoped that all his captains were ready for the voyage to La Navidad. He longed to see the men left there to prospect and barter for gold and to begin the establishment of new towns for the Crown. Pedro, who tended to him through his fever, said, "Admiral, the lost men haven't returned."

Columbus rose from his bed and said, "Call Antonio de Torres immediately, and the captains from the other ships, to the *Mariagalante*."

Within the hour, ten of his captains were assembled on deck. Columbus, waiting on the main deck, said, "I want a report on the lost captain and his six men."

Antonio de Torres spoke with drooped shoulders. "We searched for them in the forest with forty men and trumpets, but no one responded." With a grave expression, he continued. "I fear the worst with the Caribs searching all islands."

Columbus didn't reply. De Torres had echoed his suspicions and worst fears. Father Fray Buil standing near him crossed himself; Columbus did so as well.

"Yes, Admiral," confirmed Cristóbal Pérez Niño, master of the caravel *Cardera.* "We also went to the south side of the island. We didn't encounter the lost men."

"If it's any consolation, Admiral, during our search for the men we found numerous exotic birds, aromatic plants, and many rivers," said de Torres with a smile.

Columbus remained momentarily pensive. "I can't understand those men. They were able to navigate from Spain, but cannot find their way back to this harbor" He shook his head with puzzlement. "We'll remain on this island until the men's return. In the meantime, let's go ashore to look for the inhabitants."

They canoed ashore and saw several women, but no men. The women were naked except for a cloth they wore over their genitals in the same manner as those they had encountered on Guanahani. Twenty-five of them were young girls. They all wore bands of woven cotton around their knees and ankles. When the landing party approached, the women came boldly forward. *"Taíno! Taíno!"* they repeated in unison while tapping their chests with the palms of their hands.

Columbus turned to his Indian and said, "Tell them we don't like the Caribs. They're savages."

"Carib lu lucairi pinagua," the Indian translated. "They said, 'We women Taínos. No Caribs. We Caribs' prisoner. Caribs sail to islands.'" The Indian said some words to the women, and they broke out in smiles.

One woman took Columbus's hand and led him away from the beach. They all walked into the thick forest of interlacing trees to a clearing where huts were built in a circle. At least fifty of those huts displayed dry white bones and skulls hanging from their roof's edges. *These must be Caribbee islands, and they must be honoring their dead relatives,* Columbus thought. *"Bohio, bohio,"* the woman said to him, pointing at the huts.

"I think they mean houses, Admiral," said Cristóbal Pérez Niño.

Upon entering, Columbus was surprised to find the huts were clean with looms and cotton piled up near them. Some of the cotton had been woven into sheets, which he found comparable to Spanish sheets.

When he emerged from one of the huts, Columbus saw a few young boys under the age of eighteen. They huddled on the edge of the clearing, hiding behind trees. The native women signaled for them to come out. They approached with caution and stood shaking with fear, close to the women. The youths also wore cloths over their genitals like the women. The Indian translator came close to Columbus and said in his ear, "No men." Columbus looked at his translator and couldn't understand what he meant.

"You mean they're not yet grown?"

The Indian shook his head, then waved one hand vertically on its side, back and forth, near his pubic area to signify cutting.

Columbus stood shocked, and then shook his head. Rather than asking to see the boys' genitals, he said, "You're joking!"

The Indian understood right away. He shook his head. "No joking," he repeated.

Columbus said, "Ask the women."

After some words with the women, the Indian came back to Columbus. "Women say Caribs cut manhood."

"I think he means mutilated, Admiral," said de Torres standing near him as he crossed himself.

Columbus replied with anger in his voice. "I know what he means." He was aghast! These Caribs were not only savages but also murderers and wanton men.

"We will stay on the ships for the night," Columbus said. "Gather the men, and let's go back to the boats."

João, who stood aside during the whole scene, felt sick with concern. His five young charges had been left back on the ship in safety. What if they fell into Caribs' hands? He would have to keep his eyes on them the whole time—to make sure that the young men never went ashore. *Hmph*! *Easier said than done.*

41

The Search Continues

STANDING IN HER BEDROOM, ISABELLA felt she had exhausted all avenues to find Miguel. She had sailed the western coast of Africa on the *Liberação* down to Ghana, and wanted to go further south, until Lourenço da Sintra, her second-in-command, stopped her.

"Captain." Lourenço's tone had been firm. "I can't in good conscience sail this ship into dangerous waters nor endanger the crew. We've been lucky so far that no more pirates have attacked us."

Isabella had fallen silent at that argument. Lourenço had no knowledge of her complicity and the bargain she had made with the head pirates. And they abided by that bargain, as long as they got their share of booty and gold coins. Lourenço had been puzzled why the pirates didn't loot the cargo, but he hadn't questioned her. The greater reward hadn't been claimed. Miguel's whereabouts remained elusive. And the *Liberação* had sailed home.

Concern tugged at her heart. She glanced into the convex silver mirror on her chest of drawers and saw a reflection of poor skin coloring and dark circles under her eyes. She had been driving herself now for more than a year, and her body felt the effects of constant anxiety in pursuit of a mission. Both Ana and Avram had discouraged her from further searches. The constant effort to find Miguel had become an exhausting and intangible dream. She bent her head in the agony of surrendering that dream and winced with despair.

She left her room and went to check on Sekou, lingering in his bed. This morning, his fever had subsided, and his forehead felt cooler to the touch.

"Good morning, Sekou." She smiled at him, and he returned a pitiful smile.

He nodded. "Master Isabella. A bright morning."

"Don't call me Master. Isabella is enough."

"Isabella. Isabella," he repeated, rolling it around on his tongue and marveling at the sound.

"All right, Sekou. Tell me, where do you come from? And when were you caught as a slave?"

Sekou lowered his head and closed his eyes. He then opened them and looked up at Isabella. "I young boy. Arabs come in my village. My brothers also slaves before." He shook his head with the recollection. "My father, mother, old with pain." He stopped, overcome by emotion. He wiped unseen tears from his eyes.

"It's all right if you don't want to tell me," Isabella said.

"No, no," he protested. "I talk. I honor memory. Berber, slave master, sell me from Mali."

"You must miss your family very much."

"Yes." Sekou nodded. "Their faces come in dreams. Me better catch. Not White Ali."

"You were mumbling that name in your fever."

A smile appeared on Sekou's face. "He my friend. We free when dogs and slave guards take me."

Intrigued, Isabella thought to question him further. "I'm looking for a white man of about twenty years of age. But his name was Miguel."

Sekou searched his memory. "No. Not know name."

"You're saying this young man called himself Ali? So he was African like you?"

"No. He white." Sekou reclined on his pillow and began to cough.

Isabella thought she had fatigued him enough. "You rest now. Soon, we'll have someone carry you outdoors in the sun."

He closed his eyes and she left the room, shutting the door quietly. On the way to the kitchen, Sekou's words ran through her mind. White slavery abounded in Africa; unfortunates were caught by rough traders to be used as cheap manpower and servants to aid their masters. But then, why was this white man called Ali? She came into the kitchen disturbed with heavy thoughts.

"How is Sekou?" asked Ana.

"He's better."

"Good." Ana breathed a sigh of relief.

Isabella smiled at her. "Don't worry, Ana. He won't die in this house if I can help it."

"We've done everything to help him. The physician said on his last visit that Sekou's health is like that of a man of sixty, not forty-five as he claims to be."

"If he said he's forty-five, then he must be that. Don't forget he struggled many years working without respite. It's a wonder he made it so far."

"Don't forget about your health, *mi niña*."

Isabella smiled at being called her girl. "I'm fine. Don't worry about me. It's you who needs care—with all the work you do in this house."

Ana threw back her head and laughed with her hands on her hips. "I'm not afraid of hard work. It keeps me alive."

Isabella smiled again at Ana's good humor. "I'll be outside checking on the workers."

She left Ana to her kitchen and stepped outdoors, when a discomforting thought occurred to her. White Ali? Who *was* this White Ali? She turned back and made a dash for Sekou's room. She grabbed him by the shoulder and shook him out of his sleep.

"Hmm?" He opened his eyes and stared at her, questioning her action.

"This 'White Ali'—how did he look? Tell me? What did he say, and what language did he speak? Tell me!" She was yelling at him and shook him harder.

"What's going on?" Ana came running into the room, alerted by the yelling. "Why are you shaking the poor man?"

Isabella whirled on Ana, her eyes bespeaking torment. She turned back to Sekou and in a calm voice asked him, "Please tell me about Ali."

Sekou leaned back on the pillow and answered, "He slave worker, like me. He young."

Isabella leaned toward Sekou, her voice trembling. "How young?"

"Twenty years. He speak Portuguese with big scar on arm."

Isabella leaned away from Sekou. "Tell me more."

Ana, who stood silent, puzzled by Isabella's unusual behavior, came closer to the bed. "Why are you asking him all these questions?"

Isabella raised a hand to silence her. "Tell me, Sekou."

"He white like Portuguese. He black hair. Blue eyes."

Ana took a step back with surprise.

"But why was he called Ali?" Isabella muttered. "I don't understand."

"I say that. He not speaks much. He not remember."

"Where did he come from?" Isabella kept at him.

"He not know this. He smart. He break leg chains." Sekou closed his eyes for a moment.

Isabella thought that he looked weary. "Thank you, Sekou. I'll let your rest now." She stood up from the bed and left Sekou, with Ana on her trail. She felt shaken and disturbed by this development. She wanted to believe that this Ali and Miguel might be the same man. Yet she feared being disappointed again.

"What are you going to do?" asked Ana.

Her voice came out resolutely. "I'm going to search for a man called Ali."

42

The Return

A FEW MORE DAYS PASSED on Dominica since the small party of men accompanied by Inspector Diego Marquez had been lost. Columbus had waited long enough, yet he still feared departing for La Navidad's fort. Knowing that Dominica was in close proximity to the Caribs, he trembled for his men's safety. He knew the Caribs would soon return from their pillaging of neighboring islands. Time was growing short and his patience thin. He yearned to return to Española and see the men.

Just when he thought he would have to abandon his lost men, that night a fire was spotted on a mountain at a distance from where the ships were anchored. His men shouted with joy.

"We found them, Admiral!" All hands pointed west at the island.

"We don't know who built the fire, but we'll send a boat to wait for them near shore. I can't afford to send another party to get lost too," said Columbus. "We'll sail by dawn tomorrow if they're not here," he told de Torres.

"But what about the men, Admiral? How can we abandon them to the Caribs?"

"I'm sure they'll be safe with their firearms. We'll return shortly to get them."

That night the ships laid to in the lee of the island. At the following dawn, a Sunday, they all waited anxiously for the lost party, when Columbus decided to leave. He gave the order to lift the anchors. No sooner had he uttered the words than a rousing noise came to his ears. His men ran to the port deck railings, and thunderous shouting rose from the other men on sixteen ships. "Hurrah, hurrah! The men are back!"

Columbus ran down from the quarterdeck to the main deck to see the lost party emerging from the green canopy of the wooded forest. "Lower the boats!" he shouted.

The lost men came on deck, haggard and emaciated. Ten Indian boys and two Indian women accompanied them.

Columbus confronted Diego Marquez. "You know your way on the vast ocean, but get lost on a small island?" he said furiously, trying to control his anger.

Marquez protested. "Admiral, we became disoriented. The canopy was so thick we couldn't see the sun or stars."

"Yes, Admiral. It's true," another sailor confirmed. "A few men climbed the trees and couldn't see through the tops that were so thick."

"All right, men. We've lost eight days waiting for you. Rejoin your ships and lift anchors! Before we leave though, go back to shore and destroy all the canoes you find. This will cripple the Caribs from waging war on friendly Arawak Indians to the west."

By noon the fleet sailed by another island twelve leagues from the island they left behind. The island seemed deserted with no huts or natives on shore.

Columbus asked his Indian translator, Dieguillo, to question one of the woman brought on board. "Ask the Indian women what that island is."

Dieguillo said, "The women said the island is empty. The Caribs took all the people away."

"In that case, let's sail on," Columbus ordered. "But we will name that island Santa María de Montserrat."

By evening, another large island came into view under bright moonlight. Their ships laid a lombard shot from shore. "Drop anchors here!" Columbus ordered.

"But, Admiral, we could find a safer harbor for the ships," said de Torres.

"Yes, but we could also run into shoals. Stay leeward." He knew de Torres was right, but he also feared repetition of a similar fate the *Santa Maria* carrack suffered, when she ran aground the year before. *Better to be safe*.

43

Glint of Hope

ALI PORED OVER SHEEPSKIN CHARTS, searching for more opportunities to prospect gold. By now time had no meaning, and all that transpired was morning, noon, and night. The following day everything happened again with precise regularity, including his meal of chickpea paste with flat bread and dates that was brought to him with water for drinking. The heat in the tent rose early, then humidity took over. Sweat dripped down his forehead throughout the day, and he had to remove the shirt off his back to squeeze out moisture. He stood on hot sand covered by a cotton rug that barely cooled his sandaled feet. He wondered which was better—working in the hot sun or in a humid tent. All he had to look forward to now was for winter to cool the land.

A guard entered the tent and said, "Effendi Zaim wants to see you in the pit."

He raised his eyebrows but walked slowly, looking back at the guard's hands holding an espingarda firearm. It was the first time Ali had seen this type of arm with a serpentine lever attached to the gun's body. The guard pushed him forward with the metal gun, and he complied. When they arrived at the pit, he was led to exposed iron deposits cut in the hillside soil.

"Come, come, Ali," Zaim called out to him. "See if this is what you're talking about."

Ali approached and scraped a small portion in the wall that crumbled down to the ground. The red tint gave a hint of the ore that accompanied gold deposits. Judging from the layers, it definitely was a dry bed where a river ran many centuries ago.

"I think this deposit may hold promise," said Ali.

"And . . . ?" Zaim awaited further explanation.

"And we follow this deposit throughout the hills for some kilometers, then look for gold mineralization in folding bed layers."

"What kinds of layers?"

"Bent layers of very old rocks."

Zaim looked at him perplexed.

Ali tried to explain, "Look. I will follow these layers going north. Give me two guards to watch me, and I'll find them."

Zaim thought for a long time on the request made by Ali, scratching his head. "You'll leave tomorrow. But if you find nothing, you're back on the line."

Breaking rocks in the line of slaves was not what Ali wanted, but finding gold deposits might be difficult. Therefore, his only hope was to run away. He planned to take the guards as far as possible from the mining camp. Once there, he'd look for the first chance to slip away.

44

More Islands

AT DAWN, THE FLEET SAILED past several small islands, and Columbus christened them Todos los Santos. The *Mariagalante* approached a larger island, which his Indian translator called Kerkeria. Columbus named it Santa Maria de Guadalupe. He had now fulfilled the monks' request from the monastery named after the Virgin.

More islands appeared before their ships. On one, a high volcano peak disappeared into the clouds, while many waterfalls fell on its wooded flanks. All around them nature had excelled in beautifying sea, land, and sky. Columbus had never seen more beauty than in this chain of islands before him. A cerulean-blue sea spread to white shores with abundant emerald forests and vegetation, watered by clouds above. Large formations of birds flew by their masts, some stopping and pausing on the riggings, then squawking between them.

Up till now, not one trace of gold had been spotted, and Columbus felt great anxiety over its lack. None of the islanders wore jewelry or headdresses made of the precious metal, and all the promises by the Indians had come to naught.

His men though, far from any worries, enjoyed the beauty of each island they landed on. The trees covered the hills all the way up to the highest volcano peak. Parrots of bright colors were as numerous as the small birds flying through the trees. He recalled seeing how Indians of other islands used the multicolored feathers to adorn their heads in reds, yellows, greens, and blacks as in a peacock tail.

Columbus made contact with the cacique, who invited them to dine with him. Their food offered a new taste to the palate, and Columbus asked Dieguillo what they called the bread and the other foods.

"Casabi, chicha, yucca, mahiz." The cacique chief pointed to each food on the table.

When they tasted a juicy yellow fruit that was sweet yet tangy, their palates met heaven. The chief showed them the outer shell of the fruit, which had a repeated diagonal diamond pattern. He said, to their delight, *"Yayagua, anana."*

"This fruit reminds me of a large *piña* cone," said Columbus. "Take many samples to plant them in Spain," Columbus told de Torres.

When Columbus asked about the wooden lattice placed over a fire to smoke turtle meat, the chief replied, *"Barbacoa."*

The following day, his men discovered a large piece of timber that had come from a ship. Columbus thought that perhaps it had come from the *Santa Maria*'s wreck. Then, on second thought, he realized it may have come from a Portuguese ship and floated on equatorial currents from Africa.

"As much as I yearn to go home to La Navidad, we will stay on this island a few more days," he told Alonzo de Ojeda.

"Admiral, the men you left at La Navidad are probably pining for your arrival. I strongly suggest we get there soon."

Columbus nodded in agreement, but gold was foremost on his mind. He had promised the monarchs gold and silver to enrich Spain. Now he had to deliver on that promise.

Another thought also perturbed him to the point of distraction. He admitted to himself that he feared João's threats to reveal his real identity as a Converso, although the discovery of a grown daughter and grandson made him smile. He imagined seeing himself sitting with his grandson on his lap.

Somehow, since the five youths had been flogged, João had avoided confrontation between them. That suited him fine. He had enough on his mind without having to worry about stowaways, interlopers, and a blackmailer. Discipline had been administered and his authority restored, thanks to Juan de la Cosa. And as it so happened, João had turned out to be a fine measurement-taker on the crossing. Columbus recognized talent and obedience, and for that he appreciated João's help.

"Admiral." De Torres's voice reached him over sound of the crashing surf.

Columbus turned. "What is it, de Torres?"

"The captains from the other ships are finding discrepancies in the number of men on their ships."

"What do you mean?"

"They found more stowaways working among the men on all ships. They haven't disciplined them yet. But I strongly suggest floggings."

Shocked, Columbus became deeply disturbed by the news. How these men evaded being discovered was beyond him. He replied, "We'll leave the matter at the captains' discretion. We have too many fish to fry right now.

"All right, Admiral."

45

The Search Goes On

IN ORDER TO MOVE FREELY among men, Isabella shed her cumbersome long skirts for trousers and a vest over a long-sleeved shirt, and hid her long black tresses inside a wide cap. She also wrapped her breasts tightly with strips of cotton to hide her female identity, appearing like a graceful young man. Everyone on the *Liberação*—from Lourenço da Sintra, her second-in-command; to Joham Alvaro, the pilot; and Hanrrique the cook— turned a blind eye to this metamorphosis and didn't dare ask questions of their captain.

Isabella had rebounded from the last bout of despair. She now searched the western coast of Africa with renewed vigor and a fixation on finding Miguel. She had also neglected calling on Matigoro in Tangier, and Avram was still cross with her. He had stopped speaking to her and several times disregarded her commands. Their relationship as commander and subordinate had hit a low point and became untenable. One day she confronted him with anger.

"How much longer are you going to ignore and disobey me?" Isabella tried to tone down her voice, but it came out shrill and close to exploding.

At first Avram tried to disregard her verbal lashing by keeping silent. He continued wrapping the rigging into a coil as if she wasn't there.

Isabella waited while tapping her right foot. Avram raised his focus from the pile of ropes and addressed her calmly. "I don't know what I've done to merit your anger and hostility. Haven't I followed your orders all along? And haven't I done all your bidding on this wasteful voyage to find a phantom?"

She was about to explode at him, but then exerted great restraint and calmed down. "Look, Avram, it's no use being at odds over Miguel's whereabouts. You either come with me or stay home. You can help Ana supervise the men."

"It's all right by me. I'll stay on the estate on your next voyage. Meanwhile, we haven't purchased any more Jewish slaves. Think of these poor creatures without a home." Avram tried to stir her pity with a frown of disapproval.

"You're right, Avram. The next voyage will be dedicated to transporting these poor men and women to Portugal. I, too, long to see Matigoro."

The tentative peace between them fell into a quiet lull, and they both returned to their duties. By now they had visited many mining camps, but many more awaited their exploration. The *Liberação* sailed in choppy waters under a gray cloud-covered sky. The winter season had now advanced, and Isabella feared running into storms or gales that could damage the ship or even destroy one of her masts. It was late morning when they approached the coast of Senegal. The ship glided into the peninsula's large bay at the port at Dakar, and they dropped anchor.

A port inspector came on board and asked, "What do you have to declare?"

"We're only searching for slaves," Isabella replied.

Following a brisk search of the hold, and seeing that no dangerous cargo was hidden, such as arms, the inspector gave them permission to disembark.

Avram came near her and whispered, "What do you intend to do?"

"These men come in contact with shipments and cargo," she said, preparing to disembark. She cloaked herself in a white cotton garment and hooked a sword to her waist. "That includes human cargo."

Avram didn't utter another word, leaving her to handle the operation.

Isabella and Avram rowed their boat to the docks, where porters heckled them as they disembarked, but she sent them away. She then spotted a beggar standing aside and hailed him.

"I can help," he said eagerly as he came near.

"I want to see a slave merchant," she told him. She gave him a coin, and he ran to find the merchant.

A short while later, a portly Berber man came to them, huffing with great effort, tripping over his long burnous cloak and wiping his forehead dripping with sweat. He rubbed his hands with a smile and asked, "How many slaves do you seek, Captain?" He then unabashedly examined Isabella's face with curiosity.

She tried to deepen her voice. "I'm looking for strong men who can work on my ship. Preferably white slaves."

The slave merchant laughed with raucousness. "We have mainly African slaves, but only a few white ones."

"I'd like to see for myself," Isabella said.

He bowed. "Please follow me, Captain."

A short walk followed for Isabella, with Avram walking alongside. The Berber led the way to the nearest mining camp. Isabella felt the heat of the morning rising, along with a humidity that felt overbearing. She wiped her wet face with her large sleeve while trying to look manly by taking large steps in her boots. They climbed a small hill, dislodging the sandy mixed earth beneath their feet. When they stood at the top, overlooking the deep pit in the ground, they gazed upon hundreds of men extracting and separating precious minerals from their source. Dust hung in the air, and pickax noise filled the cavernous pit, rising from the ground to their ears. The fine dust covered the men's bodies—they appeared ghostly and no longer human.

"As you can see, Captain, all the men down here are Africans. The white slaves we have are used mainly as servants or attending to the masters."

"Could I see them?" Isabella asked.

"They're not for sale. The effendi will not sell them to you."

"Who is this effendi, and where can I meet him?"

By now, the Berber looked annoyed at so many questions. "The effendi is busy at another camp and cannot be disturbed." He then turned and left them stranded.

Avram, who had stood by during the whole conversation, said, "You won't break through their resistance. Let's go back to the ship."

Isabella thought for a moment, then said, "No. I'm in town to do business." With that she left Avram speechless with disbelief in his eyes. She quickened her pace.

46

La Navidad

COLUMBUS STOOD ON THE PROW of the *Mariagalante*, admiring the islands they sailed by. Each island was more beautiful and stunning than the last. He named them one by one. The first they passed was called Santa María de Monserrate after the monastery back home in Catalonia. The next was Santa María la Antigua. An island north of Antigua Columbus named Barbuda. One particular island that was squat and bulging like a pregnant woman he named Santa María La Redonda. Another small island appeared as the round belly of a man lying in water.

One man coiling the ropes called to him. "Admiral? How about we nickname the island La Isla Gorda? Like the healthy fat lady I left at home, heh!" Roaring laughter from the men on board followed the comment. A few sailors broke out in a dance, gamboling to the delight of others. A rare smile appeared on Columbus's lips, and he nodded to the men. On other ships surrounding and following the flagship, sailors assembled, leaning on railings, curious to see the gesticulating and dancing figures.

Further northwest, Columbus saw three islands rising to great heights at a distance from the island arch he pursued. He mentally noted to visit them on the return voyage. He felt a great hurry to arrive at his destination: La Navidad Fort in Española. Other islands he passed were dubbed San Martín, Saint Anastasia, and San Cristóbal. By now his men were delighted by the warm November weather and the beauty of various hues in the water, from cyan to deep cornflower blue as they came close to land, then vivid sea green and teal when sailing away. The mountains, too, complemented and competed with the sea in vibrant shades of their own in jungle green, apple green, and lime green. A clear sky held a comforting sun, and clouds blown by the trade winds gathered and surrounded mountain peaks. By afternoon, showers fell with precise intervals. Columbus promised himself to return and visit each island of the Islas de Barlovento, lying windward.

As night approached, Columbus sent orders to all sixteen vessels to lay to. "Make sure the ships watch against drifting and running into each other."

"Aye, aye, Admiral. But with this weak moon, I doubt the captains will see clearly," said Antonio de Torres

"Let the captains know to be extremely careful about who holds the tiller. They'll pay out of their own pockets if any accidents happen!"

De Torres crossed himself. "Right away, Admiral." He left to carry out the order, and Columbus peered into the deepening darkness. Outlines of masts and spars that formed quadrilateral and square patterns when viewed telescopically began to fade. He feared losing any ship to negligence or faulty assignments at the till. As each ship lit their cressets, he sighed with relief, and the lit vessels remained as beacons to each other in the dark night.

The following morning, on the thirteenth of November, the fleet reestablished their formation from their scattered and drifting positions over the night and sailed behind the *Mariagalante* as subjects following their ruler. The first island that greeted them was shaped like a shoe, and Columbus named it Santa Cruz. The island was windswept, and they sailed along a protected harbor. His men were getting restless and sorely needed a shore leave, but Columbus decided to hold off landing and to lay to one more night.

On the fourteenth, as they prepared the boats to go ashore on the island at the mouth of a small river bay, they sighted a line of trees thick with vegetation lining the shore. Many of the Caribs, indigenous people, had worked the land and it was ready for crops to be planted.

Columbus shouted, "Send an armed boat to shore now!"

A group of Caribs lingered behind trees, apparently hesitant to advance to the beach, and a canoe appeared in the water with four men, a boy, and two women. They floated at a distance of two cannon shots from the *Mariagalante*, and the crew on deck could see amazement on the Indians' faces at the fleet. The natives remained in their boat for nearly an hour. The party of Indians already onshore positioned themselves to block the sailors' access to the beach. From his perch on the quarterdeck, Columbus confirmed these were definitely Caribs by the way they clipped their hair behind their heads, as opposed to the Arawak, who wore their hair long. These Caribs had their faces and heads painted black to appear fearsome. Near them was a group of Arawak prisoners they had captured.

One of the Spanish fleet's shallow vessels approached the canoe, and the Indians floated in place, not knowing whether to flee or keep gazing at the amazing sight of all ships and the Cantabrian barques and barges crowding on the water. Meanwhile, the men on one barge came closer still to the canoe, and the Caribs began to flee.

Columbus's men on the *Mariagalante* and other caravels began to shout, "Catch them!"

Columbus's feelings of animosity toward the cannibalistic and barbarous Caribs drove him to yell above his shouting men. "Don't let them escape!" The barge came nearer still, and Columbus shouted, "Corner them now!"

When the Indians in the canoe saw it was too late to flee, they raised their bows then let fly their arrows, wounding two men on the barge. One sailor received an arrow to his breast and another to his side. The Indian canoe had, meanwhile, capsized in the scuffle, and the four men swam and waded into shallower water, while the two women and the boy clung to the overturned canoe.

The four Carib men still aimed their arrows from the water, but did not hit anything except the *Mariagalante*'s hull. By then Columbus had ordered his boats to land with many of his men carrying lances. At the sight of so many boats coming toward them, the Caribs onshore fled into the thick forest, but one who lingered was slain by a mortal lance blow. Another Carib fought the Spanish men bravely until he was pierced by a sword and dumped into the water. After a few seconds, the injured man all of a sudden revived and tried to swim ashore, but a Spaniard shot him while he waded toward the beach. After several arrow shots, he lay mortally wounded as his blood pooled around him.

Columbus, who had watched the whole scene, trying to avert his eyes at the killings, said, "We'll call the high point of this island Cabo de la Flecha for the arrow that vanquished the fearsome Carib."

When his men came back on board with the captured Caribs, their Arawak captives claimed that the next island, called Cayre, had plenty of gold.

While Columbus had the Arawak Indians questioned, the aristocrat, Michele de Cuneo, boarded ship, dragging behind him a most beautiful Indian woman.

"What have you got there?" Columbus asked him.

"Admiral, I request permission to keep this woman."

Columbus looked at him curiously. "What for?"

"Why, Admiral, to be my servant, and for my pleasure."

Cuneo's offensive and shocking words put Columbus in a quandary. He'd been a mariner all his life and couldn't measure up to military heroes with long histories of sword fights and warring feats. His aristocratic shipmate, Michele de Cuneo, had power back home with the Crown. To antagonize him would place Columbus in jeopardy and bring derision from his men.

"You must treat her with kindness."

"Of course, Admiral." the noble gentleman, Michele de Cuneo replied. He then took her to the admiral's cabin, where, from her screams, Columbus gathered she was being raped.

He stood frozen by the series of events taking place and not being able to go to the woman in distress. He continued to question the Indians and closed his ears to the piercing cries coming from his own cabin.

47

first Clue

AS SOON AS ISABELLA AND Avram reached town, they looked for mules or horses to ride. A vendor selling foods nearby attracted her to his table.

"What is your pleasure, young man?" the vendor asked.

For a moment she startled at the address of "young man," then answered quickly, "I'm looking for mounts to take us to the mines."

"And what would you want with the mines?"

"I'm a buyer for my captain." She turned to point at the *Liberação* with its proud Portuguese flag flying high on the mainmast, when she tripped over Avram behind her. "What are you doing here?" she asked, miffed by his presence.

"I'm helping you to get your rides," he said hastily.

She was about to reply with sarcasm, but instead said, "I don't need any help."

The vendor, listening to both of them, said, "Well, I haven't got all day."

"Where can we get two horses?" she asked.

"It will be two silver coins."

Avram took two coins and rolled them on the table.

The vendor caught the coins before they rolled off his table. "At the end of the bazaar you'll find a stable with horses."

They found the building at the end of the street as the vendor had said. Isabella, followed by Avram, saw a farrier shoeing one of the horses. He raised his head as they entered the stable, then wiped his hands on a leather apron and waited to be addressed.

"We want to purchase two horses," Isabella said with a low voice.

The farrier showed them a couple of young, hardy black Barb horses that were whinnying and hoofing at the ground with stamina to be let out of their pen. Isabella walked around the pen to examine them. They appeared healthy, and she thought they'd be useful on the estate back home.

"How much?" she asked.

"You can have each for seventy silver reais."

Isabella reached for her trouser pocket and pulled out a purse. She paid him the silver coins, and while the horses were being saddled, Avram whispered, "You paid too much."

"Maybe, but now we have our rides to the mining camp."

She turned to the groom. "We need directions to the mine."

He pointed to the only road out of town. "Take that road for an hour ride, and you'll see the mine."

Isabella and Avram mounted and turned the horses inland. An hour later, they arrived at the mining town. They asked right away for the foreman.

Avram took the lead. "We're looking to purchase white slaves."

The foreman examined them for a moment and answered with the now too-often-heard reply: "We only sell black slaves we can't use anymore. The others are needed for mining."

Just then, a man clothed in better clothing than the foreman approached them. "What do you seek?"

"This is Effendi Yusuf Zaim." The foreman bowed as he introduced his master.

Avram inclined his head, acknowledging the introduction. "I'm the captain of a ship, and we're looking for a white runaway slave. We're ready to pay handsomely."

Isabella didn't flinch at Avram's taking over the lead. She stood aside, willing to relinquish her captain's title for the moment.

"If you'd come sooner, I'd have one for you, but—"

Avram interrupted Yusuf. "But what?"

Isabella, too, hung on every word Yusuf uttered.

"But he fled yesterday. The bastard had a good life as my servant and surveyor. We're still looking for him."

"When you find him, would you contact us through Effendi Aruj?" Avram asked.

Yusuf didn't flinch. "I see you purchase your slaves from the same source. I'll send word if the white slave is found."

Isabella burst from her silence. "What was the slave's name?"

"We called him Ali."

48

Heading North

ALI BURNED THE KILOMETERS AS he trudged, sweating along a sandy shore. He had escaped the mining operation camp the previous night, putting a distance between him and his pursuers. Several times he'd heard dogs barking in the distance and he searched for meager vegetation or old desiccated trees to hide in. When the dogs did not materialize, he'd reemerged from his hideout and continued his trek. His feet burned from the hot sand penetrating his sandals, but he felt possessed and driven to head in a northerly direction, as if an invisible tether drew him ahead without respite. He couldn't understand the pull that drove him forward. All he knew was a force kept him moving along.

He stopped several times to dip into the cool water of the Atlantic and refresh his heated body. His water pouch was getting light, and he scanned the horizon for a drinking source. His eyes only met more and more sand dunes and few places with shade. His stomach growled for food. The previous day's meal had left him wanting for more, and he had run out of food. If he could reach a town soon, his struggle would end.

His mind replayed his daring escape, and he smiled as he remembered. The foreman had asked him to remain in the tent while he went behind a dune to relieve himself. Outside the tent, the guard walked around the perimeter with his firearm slung over his shoulder. Ali waited for the guard to do his round. When the guard walked behind the tent, Ali quickly dug the soft sand below a rug. He made a shallow trough, laid down in it and covered himself with the rug. He hoped that with luck, no one would think of looking below the table holding the charts and instruments.

As soon as the foreman's shouts signaled his escape, Ali left his trench and scanned the horizon behind the tent. He could see the guard and the foreman searching in the distance, then disappearing south behind the dune in the mine's direction. He burst into laughter at their stupidity and bolted in the opposite direction, knowing his tracks in the sand would give him away. A dry branch was the answer.

Sweeping the branch back and forth behind him, he ran leaving a zigzagging swath in the sand. All he hoped for now was a slight breeze from the sea to obliterate those marks. Within minutes he breached the tree line and ran east toward the mountains in the distance. This time no branches would aid him—only sand dunes and no vegetation could be seen for kilometers.

Each minute that passed put a larger distance between him and his pursuers. Now, after a number of hours, he had slowed down, exhausted and out of breath. As thoughts crowded his mind, a slight breeze blew, cooling his forehead, and his feet directed him toward shore.

The sun still beating down gave him a glimpse of a town in the distance. A fort and crenellated towers rose from the sand by the shore, and many tents squatted outside the iron gates. Sounds of activity took place near a makeshift bazaar, and he approached the gates. Two guards kept a watch for everyone coming into and leaving town. The Berber tent dwellers were busy around their temporary homes, with women cooking on fires, camels braying to be let off their tethers, and young ragged children laughing and calling as they tagged each other.

"Anta! Ibta!" A voice called to Ali. The guard by the gate signaled for him to move away.

He lowered his head into his torn shirt and felt ashamed at his shaggy look. He knew his appearance was one of a dirty man, no more than a beggar, with his haggard and malnourished body and face drawn with hunger.

As Ali passed a tent, he peered inside, but a man squatting on a rug stood and chased him away. The next tent offered some hope; it was empty. No doubt the owner had left momentarily. A low table held a stack of baked flat breads, dates, and figs on a tin plate. He fell upon the food and stuffed his mouth while hiding several flat breads inside his torn shirt, then fled. A well surrounded by women met him as if a beacon. Without stopping or waiting for his turn, he fell to his knees and drank the cool waters from the wooden bucket.

The women waiting to draw water yelled and showed their fists. *"Saariq! Intadhir duuruk!"* The next moment, the women attacked him from all sides, hitting him with their pots, pans, and bundles.

The guards by the gate left their post and assailed him too. They grabbed his arms and led him inside the fort and threw him onto the ground, the bread inside his shirt falling out in the dust.

"You're a nuisance and a beggar!" one guard called out in Portuguese. Just then a Berber man ran inside yelling, "Someone stole my food!"

"We have him here." One guard tried to appease the robbed man. The Berber stooped and gathered the flat bread, blowing off the dust, and ran back to his tent.

The guard struck Ali with his club. "You're a thief too!" He beat him several times until Ali felt faint with pain. The guard dragged him by the arms, wrenching his shoulder sockets, and threw him in a cell. He locked the door and peeked through the bars in the small window. The guard's face, contorted by a protruding lower lip, disappeared from the window, and Ali heard footsteps down the hall.

Blood dripped down his face from a head wound that made him grimace with pain. He rose slowly from the floor and walked haltingly to the door. "What a mess!" He pressed his forehead against the small window. "Now what awaits me?"

49

Grim Welcome

THE FLEET OF SEVENTEEN SHIPS, including the *Mariagalante*, *Gallega*, and *Colina*, sailed along numerous islands that Columbus dubbed the Eleven Thousand Virgins after the legend of Saint Ursula and her 10,999 companions.

Columbus smiled as he remembered the legend in which Saint Ursula was reputed to have remained a virgin and refused to marry the pagan king of Brittany. She begged her father, Dionotus, to give her three years of sailing with her companions, after which she would marry. A memorable voyage then began for her friends and every young woman who resisted marriage, wanting to remain a virgin. Her father, the king of Cornwall, supplied the eleven ships to transport them.

The further the ships sailed, the more islands appeared, until Columbus stopped counting them and relegated the task to Dr. Chanca.

"I beg of you, Dr. Chanca, take notes for the voyage. I must return to my duties to supervise the fleet and the men's safety."

"It'll be my pleasure, Admiral. Besides a few scrapes here and there, the men are in good health. Must be the pure air they're breathing."

Confident in the physician's promise to keep a log, Columbus turned his attention to his maritime duties. By November 19, the fleet had passed an island called Borikén by the Taíno Indians that he named San Juan Bautista for the venerated Baptist in Genoa.

Columbus sent the order: "We'll stop here to find fresh water."

The reefs encircling Borikén were uniquely luminous with their multicolored corals, seen from the crystal-clear water that formed a buffer from the invading ocean. Tall green mountain peaks dominated the background, with pockets of bushes vibrant with crimson color dotting the slopes. Columbus surmised they were hibiscus bushes.

The sailors marveled at hundreds of small yellowish-brown-and-green frogs with two stripes down their backs, called *coqui* by the Taínos on the island. The tiny frogs stopped their deafening croaking and whistling chant and leapt into the forest as the men's boots trudged the sandy beaches. An abundance of giant silk-cotton trees formed a perimeter at the base of the mountain slopes. Striped-headed tanager birds perched and chattered on many branches among the trees. The magical enchantment of the island was beyond compare. Once they filled their fresh water containers, they boarded the ships.

As they sailed south along the rich green and forested background of the island, Dr. Chanca communicated that the length of the island was thirty leagues long.

"That's sounds accurate, Doctor. Note it in your records." Columbus was pleased with the physician's help and sound input.

"I already have, Admiral."

By November 23, they had entered a bay Columbus called Boqueron, where they spent two days loading food supplies and more fresh water. Columbus sent in the shallow barges while he remained on ship with the rest of the fleet anchored in deeper waters. The party inland found a village of huts encircling an open space in its center. The inhabitants had vanished, just as the Spaniards had come to expect, except for one old Taíno Indian his men captured and brought back with them to the ship.

Columbus questioned the aged Taíno with the help of his Indian translator. After a few brief words, the translator said, "He says the inhabitants fled to the other side of the island when they saw the ships."

"Ask him if there's any gold on the island."

To which the translator said, "There's no gold. The people are poor but happy."

Columbus took a moment to digest the information. Turning to his men, he said, "We'll lay to for the night along the shore. Let's sail for Española at dawn!"

As evening set in, Columbus stood at the railing on the upper deck and marveled at the thousands of stars in the firmament. He felt part of this luminous sky as if he were one of those shiny suspended objects that guided the mariners while he had guided his ships and crew. He felt satisfied with his men's progress and Dr. Chanca's help with the journals. Pleased with himself, he proceeded to turn in for a restful night, when he remembered something odd Dr. Chanca said to him when they returned from Boriquén. The exact words ran again in his head.

"Admiral, I want to commend one of your men," Dr. Chanca had said.

Columbus asked with surprise, "Which man?"

"João, Admiral. I was surprised by how furiously he took down notes throughout the survey on the island. You've made a wise choice in selecting him."

Columbus twisted and turned for a long time before falling asleep.

The following morning they set sail northwest for Española and proceeded with a calm breeze blowing starboard from land. They were sailing by the northern coast of Española, when the sailor wounded back on Santa Cruz died of his wounds.

"We will land ashore and give him a proper burial," Columbus said somberly.

This was the first funeral in the New World, and Columbus stood over the open grave, watching the wrapped corpse descend to its final resting place. Columbus felt proud of his brother Diego officiating alongside Fray Buil.

When it came time for each one attending the burial to throw a handful of soil into the shallow grave, Columbus stirred with a fright that unsettled him. An unnatural horror at coming close to the grave assailed him. He recoiled when he had a sudden image of himself scattering soil along a grave, and an old man wiping his hands. He felt a strange pull to dig into the grave and search the soil. Nausea rose from his stomach, and he took a few steps back. *What could it mean?* He felt deeply frightened and disturbed.

"Let's sail for La Navidad," he ordered Antonio de Torres. "I'm extremely anxious to get there."

"Aye, aye, Admiral." De Torres complied, and the order went to all sixteen ships. The sailors fell busy on decks, unfurling the sails to ready for departure. The riggings were coiled and tied, and one by one the ships, powered by the majestic sails, glided out to sea as white birds in formation with the *Mariagalante* leading. The fleet rounded the coast northward toward Monte Cristi as they sailed north fifty-three nautical leagues.

By sunset, Columbus gave the order that went out to the rest of the fleet. "We will lay to for the night."

On the morning of November 27, the fleet sailed northward into Monte Cristi's harbor. Columbus scanned for a permanent site on which to build a new town. The boats were lowered, and he came ashore with his men.

On the banks of the Rio Yaque River, the Spaniards found two dead men, bound in ropes. A few meters further, two other corpses lay rotting. One dead man had a red beard—clear evidence of European roots.

"¡Oy! Qué calamidad el cielo ha traído sobre ellos!" Columbus's men moaned in shock and pain.

Columbus stood with a sick feeling in the pit of his stomach. Now he knew they had to make haste for La Navidad.

"Make sail for the settlement!" Columbus ordered to weigh in the anchors.

The fleet followed the *Mariagalante* as if a funeral procession, the men somber, their joy extinguished. The mariners worked on board each ship in complete silence, scrubbing the decks, straightening the ropes, examining the sails from the ratlines, and communicating to the young sailors perched on the spars with a nod of the head.

They arrived at Caracol Bay by dusk, the fleet illuminated by the orange rays of the sun sinking on the horizon before night surreptitiously enveloped them in darkness. The lanterns and tallow in the cressets were lit, and Columbus ordered the ships to lay to until morning. A shudder fell over him, recollecting the *Santa Maria*'s wreck the previous year.

"Sound the bottom!" Columbus ordered. The sounding bells were dropped, then retrieved, filled with sand in the shallow cups. The ships were safe to anchor for the night.

"De Torres," Columbus called. "Send flares into the night. The men will see them from the fort and be ready to meet us by morning."

De Torres conveyed the order to his men, and several flares illuminated a sky partially lit by a waxing crescent moon. The smell of sulfur hit their noses.

No return flares or lit fires illuminated the skies. "They probably ran out of tallow or oil," Columbus deduced. "Fire the cannons!"

Cannons booming toward the sandy shore brought no sound or activity back. "We'll wait till morning," Columbus said with a shiver and a heavy heart. His men fell silent, as did all those in the fleet. Silence and anxiety hung heavily in the night air.

"*¡Almirante! Almirante!*" Voices coming from shore brought Columbus and all the men portside. Out of the dark waters, a canoe paddled by Indians came close to the hull.

"What is it?" Columbus asked de Torres.

"They want to see you, Admiral, but they won't come on board until they see you."

Columbus grabbed a torch from the cresset and came close to the railings, showing his face lit by the fire's glow. The Indians' voices rang with laughter, and they climbed on board. Once on deck, they presented Columbus with gold masks.

"*Cacique Taíno Guacanagari caneyes. Lu y guey.*" The Taíno who spoke crossed himself as he'd no doubt seen the Spaniards often do.

De Torres translated, after he conferred with the baptized Indian. "'The cacique Guacanagari is in his square house. Your people are well. Come with the sun.'"

Columbus breathed a sigh of relief. *But why isn't the chief here to greet us? And why do my men not come forward?* It was troubling.

In the morning they lowered the boats, and a throng of men invaded the beach. Columbus stepped onshore, followed by Antonio de Torres, the *Mariagalante's* master; Cristóbal Pérez Niño, master of the *Cardera*; Juan de la Cosa, master of the *Pinta*; and several other captains. The sight that awaited them froze their blood. Many bodies, some in a decomposed state and others partial skeletons exposed to the air, were lying on the beach. Other bodies were found hidden in tall grasses and further up the hill where the fort had stood when Columbus left to return to Spain. Not one brick remained, and ashes and debris filled the ground. Not a single man remained alive.

Stunned, Columbus fell to his knees, crossed himself, and said a prayer for the dead. He rose from the ground and said in a mournful voice, "Dig graves for the dead men, and see that they're all buried with dignity by day's end." He stopped, trying to control a rising anger in his heart.

He then directed de Torres, "I want the area searched. Before I left the men for home, I warned and commanded them to bury their gold. Also, prepare a party to accompany me inland. I want to question the cacique."

The Indians had, in the meantime, moved a distance away from the Christians onshore, staying away from the party. Columbus got hold of the Indian who had brought him the gold masks and started to question him. "What happened here? Speak, or I'll have you speared!" His voice boomed as the anger resurfaced.

Trembling for his life, the Indian had his words translated to "Christian people killed by the Caonabó and Mayreni. Guacanagari is wounded."

"We'll see about that!" Columbus shouted, and accompanied by his captains and men, marched for the cacique's house.

The village was arranged in a circular pattern near the shore. The men searched many of the huts and found many articles that had belonged to his men. One new mantle, still in its unfolded package, lay alongside clothing in baskets. Columbus didn't believe that his men could possibly have bartered them. When they arrived at the cacique's hut, they found Guacanagari lying in his net hammock with his legs all bandaged.

Columbus turned to Dr. Chanca. "Remove his bandages!"

Dr. Chanca stared at Columbus with his mouth open. "Why?'

"Because this chief is a liar!"

The physician nodded and proceeded to unravel the cotton bands about the chief's legs. The skin on his legs was smooth with no lesions or scars.

Guacanagari at once began to talk volubly and didn't stop for an instant. When he finished talking, the Indian translator said to de Torres, "Christians take many wives and young girls for their pleasure. Jealous husbands killed Christians."

Columbus remained deep in shock and grief. These deeds had been done by his men, those under his command. He was the one responsible for their behavior and, ultimately, their deaths. He, the admiral, would have to answer to the Crown for the loss of those men. With great difficulty, he turned aside his grim thoughts.

He said to his men, "We will bury them with Christian honor for their bravery and courage."

A hasty service took place in the evening led by Fray Ramón Pane, the Jeronymite monk, Fray Buil the Benedictine monk, Diego Columbus, and the three Franciscan monks. Holy water was sprinkled on the bodies wrapped in white cotton, and the *De Profundis* Psalm and *Miserere* Psalm were intoned and repeated.

"We're all gathered here," Fray Buil began, "to entrust our brothers and commit their bodies to this earth . . ."

Columbus felt stricken and grieved at the loss of so many men. Among them was Luis de Torres, the interpreter, and Diego de Araña, cousin to Columbus's mistress, Beatriz de Arana. He could never face Beatriz now, the mother of his son Fernando. This was a catastrophe from which he might never recover.

When the service ended, Columbus said to the men, "Tomorrow begins a new era for España. We'll lay the foundations for the first of many towns in the New World."

That night, under the lantern's light, Dr. Chanca wrote in his notebook:

Today we buried the men at Navidad, and the admiral was heartbroken over the tragedy. That so many courageous men had died in the line of duty was disastrous. The admiral wanted to leave this accursed island, but tomorrow we sail southward toward Monte Cristi. By December 7 we will sail from here, before the bad weather sets in from easterly trade winds blowing along the northern coast. This might make sailing upwind a great hardship. We might stay put until the weather improves.

During his nightly watch on deck, João had meanwhile gone over his notes of all islands they had encountered since the voyage began. He had noted their coordinates and particularly underlined the island of Boriquén. He liked that its distance, about twenty-three leagues from Española with her anticipated gold mines, was far enough from greedy and power-hungry Spaniards. As he lay on deck wrapped in his blanket, heavy thoughts burdened his mind. He realized that most of the islands would be colonized by Spain and marred by the boots of men prowling every centimeter of land in their search for gold. His dream to bring his brethren to the New World rested precariously in the balance. *Where could they find a safe haven?*

50

feverish Search

ISABELLA PUSHED FORWARD WITH HER search for Miguel. The last clue that a white slave had been seen and had recently worked for Effendi Zaim was evidence that it had to be Miguel. She went over and over a map to discern just what terrain a runaway slave might cover as he made his way north. Sekou had confirmed that Ali was a white slave, and that he had a scar on his arm—a scar that corresponded to the injury Avram saw Miguel incur during his last moments on the pirate ship. All the evidence was irrefutable and conclusive proof that it was Miguel—the man she still loved.

"Captain?" Lourenço's voice interrupted her silent determination.

She turned her face to him. "What is it?"

"We will be touching upon the coast of Morocco within the hour."

"Thank you, Lourenço. Prepare the crew for docking in the harbor in Tangier. And saddle the two new horses."

Lourenço went about carrying out her orders just as Avram appeared from the tiller box. He walked straight to her position on starboard and faced her. With a serious face he said, "I want to apologize for my behavior. I doubted you when I should've supported your search for Miguel."

Startled by Avram's admission of his insubordination, Isabella didn't know what to make of this. She lowered her head silently—not to show approval but to let him know that she hadn't forgiven him yet.

"We have much to do before we dock. Go and help Lourenço with preparations."

Avram nodded and turned to carry out his duties.

She followed him with her eyes, then felt pity for him. He had lost his entire family, and she had rejected his advances. Now he had to help with the search for a rival who might materialize only to rob him once more of connection and affection. As her thoughts centered on Avram, the coast became larger and closer. Within thirty minutes, they were docking in Tangier.

The noise and hubbub in the port included calls from vendors, the brays of camels, and shouts from slave masters flogging their charges to keep them moving toward the marketplace. As soon as the *Liberação* cleared customs, Isabella disembarked with Avram in tow.

"Let's first go to the bazaar!" Isabella shouted. Now, in her manly attire, she could avoid the staring glares from men and disagreeable looks from women. No one saw her as anyone other than a young man following his shipmate. With the cap that hid her hair adjusted over her eyes, she could avoid fixed glances coming her way.

Isabella and Avram reached the market and waited for the slaves marching from port to arrive. Long rows of slaves were already displayed, and trading took place with vigor and interest. Isabella sat by the sidelines, examining each slave that was bought forward or rejected and delegated to the last row, only to be brought back up front as a last offering.

"Who'll give me top dirhams for those healthy, young slaves?" the slave trafficker yelled for all to hear.

"Ten!" a voice from the spectators shouted.

"Not enough!" shouted back the auctioneer.

"Twelve! And no more!" another buyer insisted as he showed his money purse, ready to buy.

Isabella reached the front row to inspect the slaves closer, but they were all black men from the African coast, or perhaps snatched from as far as the Congo inland or Tanzania on the east coast. No trace of any white slave was among them. She began to despair and turned to Avram for his confirmation.

"Apparently no white man can be traded in the open," she said.

Avram nodded. Isabella noted that he seemed ready to agree with her beliefs and views.

"I suggest we make for Matigoro's house soon," Avram said.

Isabella nodded, trying to hide bitter disappointment. Within the hour they reached Matigoro's home, a short ride from the marketplace on their Arabian horses.

Matigoro came forward as they entered. "Come, come, my children." Then came his utter surprise at Isabella's appearance. "What is this handsome young man doing in my house?" He burst into laughter, and then embraced her and Avram.

"I find I can talk to men and bargain with them easier dressed this way," said Isabella.

"Clever of you, my daughter," Matigoro said affectionately. "Tell me, what news do you bring?"

Isabella filled him in on their last voyage along the African coast, where they had found the slave Sekou, and who had set them on the trail of a white slave, and the fruitless search for Miguel. "We spent weeks searching the slave markets and mining camps with no results." She could barely conceal her frustration.

"No matter." Matigoro tried to give her back some hope. "Recently the market has had fewer slaves. But now, with winter, a resurgence is about to begin." He stopped then raked his hand through his beard, which now grew thick. For a moment he appeared to Isabella as an Arab sitting cross-legged in his home. The only thing missing was a masbaha necklace of amber beads to finger while reciting the ninety names of Allah and God's glorification— as with the Trinity rosary. No doubt he had to assimilate among the Muslims to continue his slave trade. He then said. "What's more, there seems to be no sign of Jewish slaves being traded either. Perhaps we've seen the last of them. And that is good news. You will have to return home empty-handed."

To Isabella, Matigoro's last words were another bitter reminder of disappointment at the fruitless search.

Matigoro said. "What I find curious is why this white slave, or Ali as he is called, is hiding behind an Arabic name, and why he keeps escaping then re-escaping his shackles? I find a curious pattern—perhaps he's heading north to find you."

Isabella sighed with relief, hanging on to any words of hope, to lift her. "That is also my strong wish—that he's getting nearer to me and his son." She fell silent, then she said, "What I don't understand is why a slave isn't returned to his previous master but keeps changing hands."

"Because this way money is traded for his value. Bringing back a slave is not profitable for any slave trader."

Isabella mulled over Matigoro's words and didn't reply to him.

Avram, who usually kept quiet, said, "I suggest we return home and wait for your word, Matigoro."

"As soon as a new trail appears, I'll send word to you."

"Thank you, Matigoro. You've been a true savior," said Isabella.

They hugged, and Isabella and Avram left for the harbor to return home.

1494

51

La Isabela

COLUMBUS WOKE UP ON ISABELA Island to the sounds of banging, sawing, nailing, felling of trees, and—most loudly—the boisterous voices of hundreds of men calling, yelling, and giving orders. A shiver overcame him. The realization of the dream he harbored to conquer and settle the lands he found was unfolding. It was true then. This was the first of the permanent settlements in the New World. It was the New World that would magnify God's glory by converting heathens into good Christians. He gave the order to erect the first fort, christened Esperanza, near the river. He anticipated adding two more settlements later that he would name Magdalena and Santiago.

He jumped off his makeshift straw bed in the small hut loaned by Guacanagari and stepped outside. The sight that greeted him was a balm to his eyes: the entire forest and the clearing in front of him swarmed with workmen, talking and giving one another instructions.

All livestock had been taken off board and housed in pens, construction material had been unloaded, and twelve hundred sailors—men-at-arms with several cannons, lances, and espingardas—began to find their footing on this new land.

Columbus went to find Fray Buil to conduct a service. "Your blessings for this land and the men dwelling in it are sorely needed."

"Dear admiral, as soon as the dwellings are constructed, I will pour holy waters onto them. Right now, some men are still ill from all this sailing."

"I want to put the Indians on mining gold right away."

"But, Admiral, we can win the Indians' help first through trust. They are gentle people, and we must baptize them first."

Columbus acquiesced. Feeling sheepish for his haste, he went to look for Antonio de Torres.

"I want you to organize a party of men. I want to explore El Rio de Oro, the river of gold we found last year. The river is a league distant, south-southwest away from Monte Cristi."

De Torres expressed surprise upon hearing that gold was ready to be mined. "You must have kept this secret from all your men on your last voyage, Admiral."

"No, I didn't. Juan de la Cosa was aware of it. We didn't want to lose time going back to La Navidad. Time was growing short to return home." Columbus felt de Torres's eyes on him.

"I'll have the men ready within the hour, Admiral," said de Torres.

When the two dozen men were ready, including the capable and devoted Christian Alonso de Ojeda and his subordinate Ginéz de Gorbalán, as well as a slew of Indians, Columbus instructed them to head inland toward Cibao and the river of gold.

"Make sure to travel along the Yaque del Norte River, and then go down Yaque del Sur, heading south by its tributary." He reminded them, "You'll find in the river many gold flakes mixed in the bottom sand."

"*Sí*, Admiral, we'll follow your instructions," said Ojeda.

Columbus returned to the *Mariagalante* to wait for the men to return with the gold. Feeling a little feverish, he decided to remain behind in Dr. Chanca's able and caring hands.

52

Shreds of Memories

ALI STOOD MANACLED IN A long line of slaves to be traded. His wrists chafed at the chains, his feet burned through torn sandals at the touch of hot stones in the plaza, and his thirst tormented him. There was one thought that drove him mad: the vision of a beautiful woman calling to him by a white house. *Who was she? Where was she? Was it a dream?* No. It wasn't a dream. Nor were the chains around his hands and ankles dreams either. She must have been real. The thought swirled in his head. Meanwhile, the column of fresh slaves was brought into the marketplace near a fountain that quenched both men and beasts.

"All right, you dogs, good for nothing—you can drink one at a time!" The slave owner and master shouted at the ghostly men. With their hands unchained but ankles manacled, they fell to their knees and scooped murky water from the trough.

When Ali approached the fountain, he saw his dark and distorted image reflected as a bearded man with long matted hair. He drank to his heart's content, though the waters were soiled. When he dunked his whole head into the water, a whip slashed him across the back. He winced with pain.

"You filthy dog! You've dirtied the waters!"

Quickly, Ali returned to his row, where a man chained his wrists again. His burning back couldn't be soothed, and he squirmed under the pain.

"Stand still, or I'll whip you again!" the master threatened him.

Ali looked through the rows of slaves waiting to change masters and viewed the entire marketplace from his vantage point. Somehow it gave him an eerie feeling as if he'd been there before. Across the plaza, two alleys bifurcated into narrow lanes. That gave him a shiver. It was all too bizarre and confusing. He must have been there too, at the opposite end of the marketplace, but neither as a spectator nor a slave. Further down the plaza, he saw a vision of a military man or police. That too brought a sharp memory, then the image disappeared from his mind. *What could it mean*?

Meanwhile, trading went briskly as the slaves were purchased. A Berber man clothed in expensive garb came forward with his helpers, then stood examining the men. Somehow Ali had the strange feeling he'd seen him before, but where? When Ali's turn came, the man bid on him.

"This is a handsome specimen!" shouted the auctioneer. "He's young, strong, and white. He'll work hard and is suited for digging gold!"

No, not that again! Ali lamented inwardly. Apparently, judging by the rush of thoughts and emotions roiling through him, he must have been purchased in this very market, but when? He couldn't tell.

"I'll take him for thirty dirhams!" the Berber man said. A murmuring wave went through the crowd.

"Going once, going twice, he's yours!" the auctioneer shouted at the Berber.

Ali was brought to his new master, who eyed him from top to bottom. "You'll do fine." he said.

A few men waited for Ali's new master outside the marketplace, accompanied by camels. The men mounted the reluctant animals and headed into the desert bordering the ocean. The camels majestically placed their hooves in the sand with dignity and a swaying rhythm that balanced their riders.

Ali walked behind, tied to one of the camels. One step, then another step, then another, in a trancelike dream. Following the riders in front of him made him wish he had remained at the gold mines and not escaped to fall back again into a nightmare with no end. A groan, then a sarcastic smile, cracked his dry lips. He broke up in demonic laughter that rose deep from within his throat, roaring and tilting his head back to the skies.

"Take me now, God. Take me away from this slow death!"

The men riding the camels turned to view the commotion and started to laugh. "This slave doesn't know he has it good. Ha-ha!"

The Berber man rode from the top of the column to see to the noise. He took one look at Ali and said to one of his men, "Let him ride behind you." His servant stared silently at his master.

"You heard me!"

"All right, Effendi Aruj." The man obeyed, stopping his camel and extending a hand to Ali, who took it. Ali was pulled to the top, where he sat uncomfortably behind the rider.

In a sudden flash of recognition, Ali remembered the pirate who had sold him to the mines! He had come full circle, and he reeled under the searing thought of discovery.

"Hold on to me," the rider said, tearing Ali out of his crushing thoughts.

Ali nodded and remained seated for the trip that took an hour to reach the sea. In the distance, he saw a caravel riding the waters and a boat waiting by the shore for the travelers. They all piled into the vessel, leaving the camels on land with their keepers. As they reached the caravel, Ali saw it flew a Portuguese flag. That pricked his curiosity. Neither his new master nor his men resembled a European crew. It was all too intriguing. After he was hoisted aboard, he saw more Berber men awaiting their master, and it all became clear—it was a pirate ship in disguise!

The Berber master came to him and spoke in Portuguese. "Follow me to my cabin."

Ali trailed behind him and entered a small cabin with low furnishings and pillows strewn across a bed of satin and brocade coverings. He wondered why he was being summoned. Perhaps he had been chosen to be the master's servant?

Effendi Aruj closed the door and turned to Ali standing quietly. "What do they call you?" He examined him carefully as he walked around him.

"Ali, master."

"You're a white man, and your name isn't Ali. Are you trying to fool me?"

"No master, not at all. I can't remember my name. I took this name in the meantime."

"Why?" he asked as he paced the cabin. Effendi Aruj stopped his movements about the cabin, and when Ali didn't reply he said, "You'll attend me and will be treated fairly. You can have plentiful food while you serve me." Aruj came close to his face and looked into his eyes. "But if you try to escape, it's hanging for you from the highest mast. You understand?"

Ali nodded. "I'll serve you, master, with obedience." He then kept quiet, not wanting to overdo his docility.

"Go and help the men prepare for departure."

The words *for where?* almost slipped out of Ali's mouth, but he bit his tongue. That would come later when he won the man's confidence.

53

Month by Month

THE GRAPE HARVEST TOOK PLACE as it had the previous year. Jams and cakes were prepared for market, and the estate thrived and hummed with the activity and production of a peaceful life. Salvadore had now grown into an inquisitive two-year-old. His flaming hair and smiling blue eyes endeared him to all. The workers called him Red, and he reacted with uncontrollable giggles and rollicking laughter at this nickname. Isabella had to correct the men each time they called him Red.

"His name is Salvadore. Don't you forget it."

They protested. "But, mistress, we can't help it. He makes us laugh so." They then broke down in laughter themselves.

As the months went by, so did the second year since Miguel's disappearance. When Ana had suggested the first year they say a short service and prayer for the one-year anniversary, Isabella reacted first with anger, then went into a moodiness that lasted for days.

Ana came to her on one occasion as she sat forlorn on the front porch. "My dear Bella." Ana lifted and adjusted her long skirts as she sat next to her. "You've mourned long enough. You must begin to live—at least for Salvadore if not for yourself."

Isabella didn't reply and kept staring at the sea. Then she turned to Ana and said, crying, "I . . . could never forget Miguel. Never!"

"No one is asking you to forget him. You can still cherish his memory, but you have to start thinking about your child. He needs a father figure. I know—" Ana was interrupted by Isabella turning her head away abruptly. "I know that you're not ready yet. And I also know that Avram will never hold the place in your heart that Miguel did, but won't you give him a chance?"

"I appreciate your concern, Ana, and everything you've done for both Salvadore and me, but I'm a widow now and can never remarry."

"But why not? Why must you go on suffering and being unhappy? Life is to be lived, no matter what happens to us. We must try very hard to live despite the miseries."

At Ana's words, Isabella broke down crying uncontrollably, choking while tears ran down her face. Ana grabbed and hugged her as they both sat, one sharing her grief and the other extending the gift of soothing wounds.

After she calmed down, Isabella pulled away, still trying to control her sobs. "Thank you, Ana."

"*Shh, shh*, I'm just doing what any mother would do." Ana tilted her head toward Isabella and smiled.

Isabella tried to smile back but grimaced instead. She wiped her tears and stood calmly. "I'll check on Salvadore now."

"That's good. He'll be happy to see you. You'll find him with Juanita and Raquela."

"I'm going—" Isabella stopped as she noticed a rider entering the premises, approaching slowly on his horse. Isabella's heart skipped a beat.

Both Isabella and Ana stood abruptly and faced the rider, who was dressed in moderate clothing without the fineries of a nobleman. The rider dismounted and, taking off his hat, bowed his head. Isabella bowed her head with deep disappointment.

"What is your business here, señor?" Ana asked in a neutral tone of voice.

"I'm taking a census on how many people live on the property."

Isabella was about to reply, when Ana raised her hand to stop her. "It depends what you mean by 'live on the property.'"

The census-taker said with irritation, "Just as I said. How many people live here all year round?"

"If we include our servants," Ana said, counting mentally, "it would be nine altogether."

"What about fieldworkers? They too live on the property, don't they?"

"Not all year. We contract them at harvest time, and they disband after. Each returning to their families and homes."

"So these huts I see here"—the man turned and counted the shelters in the distance—"they serve as their homes away from home, don't they?"

Isabella saw that Ana was fuming with impatience she was trying to control. "If you say so." She gave up trying to outsmart the inspector.

He said firmly, "I do say so, and your taxes will increase for the part of the year those dwellings are occupied."

Ana put her hands on her hips, but before she could explode, Isabella intervened. "Thank you, señor, for your visit. Now we must go back to our chores."

The man bowed again, mounted his horse, and left them.

"Why, those thieves! Scavengers!" Ana was beside herself, her face and throat reddening. "They want to bleed us dry. All so that the monarchy and nobility can live in riches while we slave to accommodate them."

Now it was Isabella's turn, to calm her down. "Shh, shh, Ana. We have no choice in the matter. Taxes are taxes, and there's not much we can do."

Ana had fallen quiet. She said, "I'm just worried that it might be more than taxes."

"What do you mean?"

"Remember last year when they checked on Don Abravanel under the pretext of assessing taxes?"

"Yes, I remember."

"They were snooping on him and on us. They know by now that Don Abravanel left Portugal for good, but they're still checking on us."

Isabella was mystified. "But for what purpose?"

"For the purpose of counting foreigners and Jews."

"You can't mean that. We've been given asylum in Portugal, and we've contributed plenty to the economy of this country." Isabella felt blood rising to her head.

"I've been hearing rumors in Sintra's market and everywhere that the Spanish princess is about to marry again, into the Portuguese royal family."

"Yes, I remember the rumor. But the princess of Asturias has been promised to Manuel of Portugal for many years since the death of her first husband, Afonso. There's no talk yet of a wedding."

"Yes, but if she accepts him, she will leave her mother's palace in Spain and reside here in Portugal till the wedding."

"I still don't see what it's got to do with us," Isabella murmured.

"If that happens, God help us. They'll get rid of us just like they did in Spain."

"I can't believe it. Why would they do that? We're valuable and peaceful citizens."

"Because the princess, like her mother, is deeply devoted to the church. She'll insist on ridding Portugal of all Jews. Mark my word, Isabella—we'll be pushed out again and again and again."

Isabella mulled Ana's words, not wanting to get swept up in rumors that might not come true. As a Jewish woman though, she would suffer the same fate here as Miguel and his family suffered as Conversos in Spain. The pursuit by the church, surveying and keeping tabs on Conversos for relapse into heresy, wouldn't give them a moment's peace. And what about Salvadore? Would he be subjected to the same prejudices they all experienced before? She went into the house holding Ana's arm.

"We'll be on our guard if anything new comes up. Let's keep our eyes and ears open," she told Ana.

Ana didn't reply. She cupped her cheek and shook her head back and forth.

54

Gold and Sickness

COLUMBUS HAD RECOVERED QUICKLY from his latest bout with fever. He looked forward to the work being performed on the island, purring with satisfaction. Next, he needed Ojeda to return from the Cibao Indians with news of gold. The little gold he had collected so far was a handful, except for the two masks. He had postponed sending word to Spain and to the monarchs. The monarchs had invested heavily in the fleet, and he had nothing yet to show for it. Perhaps he ought to wait until he had substantial gold by the barrel to send the fleet back.

A sudden roar was heard, and Columbus ran outside his hut to see to the commotion.

"Admiral! Admiral! The men are back!"

From his vantage point, he saw the men he had sent out marching toward the settlement. Alonso de Ojeda and Ginés de Gorbalán were at the head of their men with several Indians, their arms raised in victory. From the smiles on Ojeda's and Gorbalán's faces, Columbus knew they had been successful.

"Admiral, see—we brought gold!" Ojeda said. He opened his hand to show Columbus three large nuggets worth at least thirty-six castellanos.

Columbus cracked a smile of pleasure. The good Lord had heard him by coming to his rescue. He crossed himself. "Where did you find the samples?" he asked Ojeda.

"We came upon a great valley by the Rio Yaque near a village and mountains the Indians called Cibao. You should've seen the streams coming down the mountains with gold flakes. I could hold them by the handful!"

Ginés de Gorbalán added, "Yes, Admiral. We saw a native goldsmith in a village district forming the gold into thin strips on a polished stone. Just like we do in Spain!"

"You've done well, my friends!" Columbus slapped Ojeda's back in his happiness. "And you too, Gorbalán. Good work. Let's celebrate tonight. Tomorrow we'll prepare an expedition of workers and Indians to start mining in that district."

Following the good news, Columbus called for all the captains to assemble near his hut. When they arrived, he presented to them his plans for mines to be developed.

"We're going to need at least one hundred men to conduct the operations, while the other men will remain here to finish building."

"But, Admiral, it's vital to speed up construction of forts," said Cristóbal Pérez Niño, master of the *Cardera*. "Who's to say? Indians might attack us any moment, or the man-eating Caribs."

"He's right, Admiral," said Antonio de Torres. "I also agree that we're sleeping onshore with fear. I don't think we can trust the Indians."

Columbus, opposed by his men, stood motionless without direction or thought on how to enforce his authority.

The twenty-three-year-old noble Ponce de León intervened. "I say, Admiral, let's plow forward to Cibao and the gold. I can lead the expedition inland with at least two hundred men."

"Yes, Admiral. We came here for the gold," another captain said, affirming Ponce de León's proposal.

Columbus nodded to all the captains and the gentleman explorer at his side. "I summoned you here for yet another reason. We've had many blessings in finding a Taíno cacique ready to nourish us with his earthly bounty. But it isn't enough. We need more meat supplies to support the colonies until our crops are self-sustaining." Everyone hung on to his words, anticipating the next pronouncement. "I will send twelve ships back for more food supplies, especially to bring hogs and cows for meat. We'll keep the *Mariagalante*, the *Gallega*, and the caravels *Niña*, *San Juan*, and *Cardera*."

The captains of those five ships nodded several times with approval, large smiles upon their lips. Columbus knew their appetites for gold were bigger than their counterparts', the captains of the other twelve ships.

"But, Admiral, we anticipated this voyage for many months. We were promised much gold," said one of the captains assigned to return home, showing a soured expression.

"Yes, Admiral. It was you who promised us all the rewards and precious jewels we'd find."

"You were promised nothing of the sort!" Columbus bellowed, his face flushing. "You were paid handsomely for the voyage and the use of your ships. Your share for the voyage will be given to you upon your return to Spain. Now, let's talk about who'll lead the return voyage." He turned away from the angry faces and looked among the crowd.

Antonio de Torres came forward. "I would like to volunteer to lead the return."

"So would I," another captain said.

"Admiral, Admiral!" Dr. Chanca burst into the hut where the men were assembled. His flared nostrils palpitated with indignation.

"What is it, Doctor?"

"Admiral, the men are getting sick by the dozen, and we're running low on medicaments!"

"Can you coordinate with the cacique and their shaman?" Columbus asked.

Dr. Chanca's mouth fell open. "But, Admiral, they have crude if not strange medicine and customs."

"This crude medicine helped me get well."

Dr. Chanca pressed on. "But the men are tired. They've been exposed to rain and mosquitoes, and lack of proper food and rest. This diet of fish, cassava, and maize with tubers isn't enough! We need pork, beef, and wheat right away!"

"That is why the ships must go back immediately," Columbus said as he turned to the assembly. "Make sure to take gifts for the monarchs; get donations from the Indians. And go with the blessings of the Lord," Columbus told Antonio de Torres as he crossed himself.

"Aye, Admiral," said de Torres. "I will go to prepare the men and ships!"

"You will use the coordinates by following Hispaniola's coast, sailing northward until you catch the easterlies. It should take you at least twenty to twenty-five days to reach Portugal's coast, then two days to Cadiz."

De Torres nodded.

"Make sure to take along enough cinnamon, pepper shells, sandalwood, and at least sixty parrots. You'll take twenty-six Indians from all the islands we visited, along with three captive Caribs."

"Don't worry, Admiral. I'll make sure to follow your orders."

Columbus nodded with a smile. "Now go and call the *contador*, Bernal de Pisa, to my hut." He then dismissed all the captains still standing with disappointed faces. They left one by one without another look at their leader who had brought them to paradise. De Torres left him, and the contador came in. "You called me, Admiral?"

"You'll return to Spain with all the gold we've found so far. What's your estimate in ducats?"

"Up to the last hour, I counted thirty thousand ducats."

Columbus let out a sigh of relief even though the figure didn't yet justify the expense of the voyage. "That's good," he said.

As soon as the contador left, Columbus boarded a boat and returned to his cabin on the *Mariagalante* to write a letter to the sovereigns:

Your most excellent Highnesses: By the grace of God, we have accomplished much during our first week on the island of Española and in the first city, Isabela, named so after your illustrious name, Queen Isabella. The new town's construction has begun with the Lord's help and blessing, the men eager to finish the cities in the New World and begin mining the plentiful gold here. We only request that new provisions be sent immediately back with two caravels. We need beasts of burden to do heavy hauling for constructing forts. We also need beef, pork, salt, wine, vinegar, wheat, molasses, honey, rice, and medicaments for the ill.

I'm sending to Your Highnesses gold nugget gifts from the Indians, accompanied by cinnamon spices, pepper, and sandalwood. The many colorful parrots and the twenty-six Indians from different islands of the region are a token from their cacique Guacanagari in his affection for Your Highnesses.

Sending slaves captured from these Carib cannibals in Cibao can pay the costs incurred for these expenses. Their cruelty to the Taínos can be relieved by baptizing them and forcing them to learn our language. The merchants back in Spain will come at their own cost and licenses to trade slaves.

My only complaint, Your Highnesses, concerns the soldiers who refuse to work and won't allow anyone to use their horses while they lay ill. There are, however, men who are and should be rewarded for their work and their pay increased. I submit that the two hundred volunteers be on the payroll. I want to recommend especially that Dr. Chanca have his pay increased to fifty thousand maravedís per year. A commendation also for Alonso de Ojeda for his services; Gaspar and Beltrán, for being known servants of Your Highnesses; Pedro Fernández Coronel; and a few others—to have their pay increased. Most of all, I ask your most gracious Highnesses to send mining experts from Estremadura near Mérida. We also need one hundred arquebuses and as many cuirasses and crossbows as can be spared. I send many blessings to Your Highnesses for a most healthy year.

Christopher Columbus, Admiral, your most obedient and grateful servant

By dawn the following morning, all twelve ships were ready to sail. Columbus, his brother Diego with Fray Buil and accompanied by other friars and the men in Isabela, saw to their departure. After the blessings, embracing, and handshaking, Antonio de Torres said to Columbus, "Good-bye, Admiral."

With a sad voice, Columbus replied, "Go with the Lord's blessings, my friend."

Absent was the customary fanfare that typically accompanied a send-off. All that remained was a parting sadness and anxiousness at the task ahead for the men in Isabela.

55

A New Master

ALI STOOD AT ATTENTION AS his new master, Aruj, ate his meal. Aruj had so far prevented him from doing menial work on their ship, and left him with the sole task of tending to his needs. Each morning Ali helped Aruj wash, dress, and recite the ritual prayer on the floor, and then he served the effendi breakfast. A couple of times the ship ran into pirates, but no fighting occurred, as if two merchant ships had passed each other. They each exchanged two courteous cannon blasts to be acknowledged. When Ali asked Aruj why the pirates didn't fire more salvos, his master said, "You are not to inquire in these affairs."

Put in his place, Ali nodded and never asked any more questions. He was grateful to have escaped the exhausting mine work, the hot sands, being chased by dogs, and starvation. Now he needed another plan for escape, but in the middle of the Atlantic, the choices were nil. He wondered what the purpose of the voyage was, and he soon discovered it one day as he passed the hold's opened latch. Moaning and crying voices came from within the dark cavity of the ship, indicating that slaves were hidden in the hold. The ship shuttled those slaves from the African market to Europe. What use they were put to then, he couldn't imagine.

By now his body went from gaunt to regaining its youthful fullness, his face rounded, and his skin had turned a dark-golden shade from months of sun exposure. His mind, too, had gained more connections to traces of visual memories. One night he dreamt of an older woman standing near the young woman he had seen before in memory flashes. He wasn't surprised by now at the rush of images and emotions taking hold in him. He sensed that the young woman was somehow related to him, but how he knew this, he couldn't explain.

"Daydreaming again, Ali?" the voice of his superior rang out. "You're a slave, and slaves aren't supposed to loaf around. You hear me?"

"Yes, Master Mustapha." Ali scurried to Aruj's cabin and hurried to gather up the rest of the breakfast dishes lying on the low table. He aired out the cabin and straightened papers on another table that held documents and sheepskin charts. As he lifted a chart, a rolled document lay beneath it. He unrolled one end, and his eyes were drawn to a word on the document: *Miguel*?

What could it mean? He read the few lines that began with "Find the slave Miguel for the sum of four thousand dirhams and one-fourth of your cargo—" His thoughts were interrupted as he heard the door lever releasing the latch. He dropped the map on the document and jumped aside to let Aruj in the cabin.

"What are you doing here?" Aruj asked, his eyes searching his.

"N-nothing but cleaning the breakfast dishes." Ali gulped, gathering the pile of messy dishes. He rushed to the door, but Aruj obstructed him.

"Don't you ever touch my documents! You hear?"

"No. Of course not, master. I can't read."

In Aruj's eyes he saw incredulity, and a fleeting smile crossed his lips. "All right. Off you go."

Ali burst from the cabin to the tiller cubicle, which housed a pail for cooling the sternpost-mounted rudder with seawater. The helmsman inquired with his eyes to have Ali explain his presence.

"I'm to clean the master's dishes." Ignoring the helmsman, he dropped the empty pail by its rope into the sea and drew it back filled. He dumped in the dirty dishes to soak and walked away. Striding on deck, his thoughts went back to the document. In another vision, one which came more frequently now, he heard the voice of the same young woman calling, "Miguel, Miguel."

56

Seasons

THE RAINY SEASON BEGAN FOR the Sintra region, and it brought with it a lull in activity. The winter crept in unannounced, then made its presence known with dropping temperatures, and storms in the night. Yet the forests and woods still teemed with life. The ducks frolicked joyously in water puddles during the rain's interlude. The Sea Lavender from the salt-marches filled the meadows with their variegated colors and competed with their counterpart the orchids. The cork oaks stood above the teeming life on the ground, protecting the wildflowers and birds as their elder with its wide branches.

Isabella stood holding Salvadore's hand in fields lying fallow with wildflowers that also draped the hills and meadows beyond. She looked down at her son, who grabbed a wild orchid with his little hands, trying to smell it. He raised his blue eyes to her for her approval.

"Smell the wild and free flowers, my son. You're as free as they are!" She lifted and swung his little body around hers, to his delight. His laughter filled the valley, his voice rising to the skies, celebrating life and all nature in bloom.

"Come on, Salvadore, let's go back to Nana Ana."

"Ana back."

Isabella smiled at the way he formed and pronounced new words each day as he heard them.

While she led him back to the house, she felt a great burden lifting. Salvadore had a way of cheering her most when gloom overtook her. She saw in his face similar lines that had graced Miguel's face. Except for his reddish hair, Miguel was alive in his son's features. She bent down and hugged him again, desperately trying to find Miguel's essence in his son.

"Isabella! Isabella!"

Isabella looked beyond the fields to see Ana calling her in the distance. She lifted her son, then sped toward the house.

"What is it?" she asked, breathless, and put the boy down.

"We have a visitor," said Ana. A mysterious look gleamed in her eyes.

"Who is it?" Her heart skipped a bit at the thought of Miguel, but she held it in check. No need for disappointment, she told herself.

"Come inside. Ana took Salvadore's hands and let Isabella go ahead.

Isabella rushed to the sitting room and, to her surprise, found Matigoro sitting comfortably by the fire in the hearth.

"Matigoro? What are you doing here? I thought you were in Tangier." The questions flew one after another.

Matigoro got up and went to hug Isabella. "One question at a time, please," he begged.

"I'm surprised and pleased to see you."

Matigoro sat back down, with Isabella following his lead. Just then Ana entered, still holding Salvadore's hand. She turned to Isabella and said, "I have sent for Avram."

"What a lovely son you have." Matigoro smiled at Salvadore, who returned the smile. "I can see his father . . ." He hesitated.

"It's all right, Matigoro. He resembles Miguel in many ways," Isabella said with calm.

Matigoro stroked the boy's hair and smiled at him again. He raised his gaze from the child and said, "I know you're dying to know why I'm here."

"If you don't tell us soon, I'll explode!" said Ana with a scowl.

"This may come as a surprise," Matigoro began, "but the flow of Jewish slaves has died down."

Ana said, "That's good news, isn't it?"

"Well, yes and no," said Matigoro.

Isabella sensed what he was going to say next, but she waited to hear it from him. Nonetheless, a deep sadness tightened her chest

"After waves of black slaves coming up from Africa, and some from the white slave market, only a trickle of white slaves remains. The bulk, mainly from Guinea and Dakar, are somehow channeled to other markets."

"I don't see what you're getting at," Ana said.

"I've made the decision that I have served my purpose in this part of the world. I'm leaving Tangier and will settle in Naples."

"Isn't that where Don Abravanel fled to?" Isabella said.

"Yes. I will help manage his shipping line that his sons oversee. He's been most magnanimous with his fortune and benefaction. I owe him a tremendous debt."

"So do we," Isabella echoed. "But then, what will happen to our operation? We took over the *Liberação's* operations for the sole purpose of freeing and shuttling Jewish slaves to Portugal. We use the ship now only to trade our products into North Africa."

"You should continue your trade until this part of the world is closed."

Ana displayed surprise. "What do you mean?"

Matigoro was silent for a moment. He then said solemnly, "As Jews and Conversos, we have much to fear in this world. Last time it was Spain that expelled its Jews. Before that it was France. Now we fear the same mongering and hate knock at Portugal's door." He stopped to gauge both Isabella's and Ana's faces. He must have read in them the danger she and Ana sensed.

"I, too, feel these peaceful times may be at an end," Ana murmured as if she were sitting alone in the room. "But where can we go?"

"Yes. Where should we go?" Isabella echoed Ana's worries. "We can't go back to Spain. We'll be caught in the same web of fear, pursuit, and reprisals as before."

"I agree with you. Perhaps you may want to join us in Naples with Avram, where you'll be welcome."

Both Isabella and Ana sat pensively without reply to Matigoro's invitation.

"All right, young ladies," Matigoro said, smiling at Isabella and Ana. "Let's forget about doom and gloom for now and enjoy our time together before my departure."

Isabella smiled with relief. "Avram is about to join us for a meal. Let's wait for him."

57

The Search for Gold

THE DAWN BROKE WITH AN eerie spectral light that rose from the horizon. The orange light ascended to the skies, bathing the columns of men ready for a send-off. The temperature had risen a notch, and the men began to scratch their necks where shirt collars or vests rubbed against their skin. But it was the humidity that made for discomfort at such an early hour.

Columbus hurried to outfit himself with the help of Beltrán, one of his two servants on loan from His Majesty King Ferdinand.

"Call Ojeda to my cabin," he told his cabin boy, Pedro de Acevedo.

When Ojeda appeared, he asked him, "Are the men ready?"

"Yes, Admiral. They're waiting for you to give the signal."

"Give me a report of the equipment and the men ready for the expedition."

As Beltrán turned up the cuffs on Columbus's sleeves, Ojeda listed the many items ready to be processed. "The men traveling with you are the finest noblemen in the cavalry, also the best crossbowmen. Plus, those on foot are armed with arquebuses and swords."

"What about implements for mining, as I instructed you?"

"I took care of that too, Admiral. We have twenty men skilled as carpenters, masons, and diggers. I inspected all the tools personally, and they're all in working condition."

"You've done well, Ojeda. Their Highnesses were most gracious and wise when they recommended you."

Ojeda smiled and bowed with pleasure.

"I'm ready now. Call Fray Buil for a Mass to bless this expedition."

"Right away, Admiral."

Ojeda left him, and Columbus made a grand sortie from his cabin. The sight that greeted him warmed his heart. Lined up on shore, the largest expedition he had seen and represented was under his command. The expedition now grown to at least three hundred men were assembled on the beach—their helmets shining in the sun, their horses whinnying and pawing the sand, their swords and lances reflecting the sunlight. Surrounding them were makeshift palates made of wood planks that held construction material, food supplies, and cooking instruments to be drawn by horses.

Columbus went ashore in one of the boats and joined his party on the beach. Fray Buil waited with his brother Diego attending him, was ready to conduct Mass.

"Dear sons of España," Fray Buil began. "You are the first men to march forth in this land for the glory of God and your monarchs and to claim your place in history. I bless you with the grace of the Lord, and may you have a successful, productive march." He sprinkled drops of holy water on the assembly.

All the men assembled mounted their horses.

"March!" Columbus ordered.

The column of men made its way inland, waving banners to the cacophony of trumpets blowing, drums beating, and the cheering of the men remaining behind. Indians standing by the tree line ran into the forest, spooked by the trumpet sounds.

Columbus now felt in earnest his role as the Lord's carrier of his teachings to the heathens and the purveyor of gold for the realm. The column of men headed toward the tall, majestic Cordillera Septentrional Mountains in the west and to Cibao, where the gold awaited them.

For the first kilometers, the men walked at a brisk pace, silent and still reverent over the sacred call they were heeding for their country and families and the legacies they would leave behind. Sometime in the future, by a warm fire crackling in a hearth, they would tell their grandchildren of their search for the elusive El Dorado, a tale that will have been told and retold throughout the years.

After a two-hour march, they arrived at a large river the Indians called Rio Bajabonico, which meandered through a vast plain of undergrowth and dry brush. The green-shaded river, swollen by the rains, flowed swiftly before their eyes. Columbus gave the order to secure ropes across the river to traverse its churning waters. Men, animals, and supplies were moved slowly across to the other bank.

On the other side, they came upon a forest of low trees. The hour was late. Columbus gave the signal to encamp for the night in a dry, elevated clearing away from the river. Above them, jagged peaks of the Cordillera Septentrional Mountains stood against the darkened sky as backdrop for the men below in the valley. Columbus contemplated this background and thought the cliffs appeared as sentinels to protect them. He couldn't help but feel as defenseless as sitting ducks in their position. He sent for Ojeda to come to his tent.

"Send a party at dawn to clear the dense forest ahead of us," Columbus told Ojeda, who had made the first excursion.

"Aye, aye, Admiral. The men will rest tonight and be ready tomorrow."

Columbus reflected for a short moment, his face warmed by the glow of the fires burning throughout the camp. He added on a somber note, "We're vulnerable in this land. I don't want another repeat of La Navidad, especially if Caribs are near our position. Post fifty guards on hourly watches, and leave the fires burning until dawn."

Not far from Columbus's tent, João sat around the brazier sending embers into the air in fiery tongues, with the five young charges he inducted into the New World. The young mariners had matured over the last months since they left Cadiz. Their backs were still etched from the lashes administered on board, and they'd grown to fear a repeat of the shameful exhibition on deck. *Their wounds have healed, but not their pride*, thought João. They had suffered the rite of passage on board. It had been his charge to protect them, and he had failed. As soon as an escape presented itself, he would send them inland with the other one hundred renegades from Sintra he had stowed away on the other ships.

He got up from his spot by the fire and walked to another brazier burning by neighboring tents. Several men sat around it, silent, staring at the fire while a gentle breeze blew through the palm fronds, carrying quickly extinguished sparks into the sweet-smelling air. Though the starry night called for peace and enjoyment in this tropical land, João sensed the men were worried. He'd have to reassure them of his long-range plans.

"¡*Hola*, Léon!" João said to one of the men as he sat on a nearby rock.

The sturdy, stocky man with curly black hair turned his head toward him. He asked quietly, "Tell me, João. How long before your plan goes into action?"

João glanced around and lowered his voice. "We're near our goal. This march is bound to put down roots. I'll see that you stay behind and learn as much as you can from the natives."

"How can we break away? We escaped the flogging after being discovered. The admiral won't give us a second chance if we're caught."

"You'll stay put for now. I'll make sure you and the men stay here."

"Tell me, João—you seem to have some power over the admiral. Any reason for it?"

"Don't concern yourself with other matters. Just follow my instructions." João fell quiet, then said, "The time is near for us to find a new land for all our brothers."

At dawn on March 13, 1494, a trumpet call sounded, leading to rising chatter, calls from cavalcade leaders, loud sounds of mallets dismantling the tent camp, and horses eager to be untethered.

Columbus called Ojeda to his tent, instructing him about the day's march. "Make sure to place crossbow men at the head of the column, the middle, and the rear. I want tight formations."

Ojeda raised quizzical eyes.

He hastened to explain. "God forbid if a group of men fall behind. They'll be Carib targets. I'm sure they'll be watching us."

Ojeda nodded.

"Have the scouts left yet this morning?" Columbus asked.

"Yes, Admiral. I also made sure each scout was armed."

"All right, Ojeda. We're ready to march."

On this glorious morning, when birds sang in trees and colorful parrots skipped on their perches on branches clacking and whistling, the column of men began the march on a path of fine sand. As time went by, the terrain elevated, and the column of men and beasts trudged higher into the mountain. Ojeda's men had already cleared the path on their reconnaissance trip, though only two riders could navigate the narrow Indian trail. In front of and behind the horses followed crossbow men narrowly placed between the parties of men carrying loads of construction and mining equipment. As the sun rose in earnest, the men struggled against the elevation in terrain crisscrossed with small rivulets of water flowing down the mountain and began sweating, their faces and brows glistening in the early morning humidity.

"Whoa, whoa!" Columbus urged his horse to stop climbing, then turned his mount around to gauge the column's slow progress as the trail narrowed to allow only one man to pass at a time. The men at the rear found it hardest to maneuver against the rise in terrain with the weight of tools and equipment.

Columbus dispatched Ojeda and more men to help push the load up the mountain. With the boost in manpower, the supplies gradually made it to the top, while the rest of the men still struggled to climb the mountain.

Ojeda joined Columbus at the head of the column. "Admiral, we're almost to where the hidalgos cleared the pass for us."

"That is a most suited name. We'll call this pass El Puerto de los Hidalgos."

Columbus encouraged the men by his presence, and when they reached the summit through the narrow pass, they found themselves in a glen crossed by a spring. The column of men stood at the jagged top, gazing at the other side of the mountain and out over a large valley. A forest of tall dark-green palms shot over reddish-brown mahogany trees in a luxuriant and fertile black volcanic soil. Columbus felt a knot in his throat, overcome by such beauty.

"We will call this valley Vega Real, after our sovereigns." He then made the sign of the cross.

The men followed him by kneeling and crossing themselves too. And as they descended the narrow mountain trails, they came upon various trees reaching up to twelve meters above their heads. The deep-red-brown bark on the trees appeared smooth, and their leaves were long, with leaflets up to seven centimeters in length. Other branches had no leaves, but from the limbs sprouted the most beautiful bright pink and lilac flowers with a yellow band at the base. Long yellow-brown pods hung directly from large branches, and one of the Indians cut down an orange pod and sliced it open. He tasted it, then offered it to Columbus, who hesitated at first, then partook. The bitter taste in his mouth coursed through his body and delighted his senses with a floral aroma and a mellow richness. It was food for the gods.

"Cacao," the Indian said as he smiled at Columbus.

"I want you to collect as many pods as you can," Columbus told Ojeda, who rushed to convey the admiral's wishes to several men.

As the columns of men descended into the valley, they encountered cotton plants—silky to the touch—as well as ebony trees and more mahogany trees. Leaves gleamed dark green in the sun, with many parrots screeching high-pitched strident cries. Columbus thought he had reached paradise.

They finally arrived at an extensive river, as large as the Guadalquivir in Spain, that Columbus called Rio de las Cañas because of the great amount of canebrakes, or native bamboo, growing thickly along its banks. Further on, the column passed small villages of huts covered by palm leaves. The cacique came out to greet them with food. Then the Indians produced little bundles wrapped in green leaves. When Columbus opened the small package offered him, to his great surprise he discovered gold dust inside.

He quickly called Ojeda. "We've been showered with gold gifts."

"Yes, Admiral. On our reconnaissance trip they also offered it to us, and we turned it in to the contador." He quickly repeated, "Every bit of gold was turned in."

Columbus waved his hand, confident in Ojeda's honesty. He said solemnly, "We'll establish our camp not far from the river, on elevated ground. As soon as the fort is built, we'll call it Santo Tomás."

He bent down to the ground and scooped up a handful of black soil. He stroked the soil grains with his fingers, pouring his emotion into those remnants of a violent volcanic past. He raised his head to Ojeda and said, "This rich earth in this blessed and plentiful land is where we'll begin our collection of gold."

58

Joyous News

AT THE NEWS OF HER brother's death, Henry IV of Castile in 1474, Queen Isabella had accepted her destiny as queen of Castile and León. The duty she had inherited with the monarchy was to oversee not only the kingdom but also the souls of every one of her subjects. She adhered to her Catholic faith as a birthright. As a young child growing up in Arévalo, her first confessor, Fray Fernando de Talavera, had supervised her religious upbringing.

Sitting in her antechamber, Queen Isabella's thoughts drifted. She mused that Talavera had taught her well the virtues of piety and having a moral compass. In his mercy, God the Creator directed his goodness and blessings to all creatures that worshiped Him. Thomas de Torquemada, her second confessor, also channeled her pious beliefs to rule Spain under Catholicism and permit no other religion that would corrupt theirs. She bent to her crucifix and kissed it with reverence.

She concentrated on mending Ferdinand's doublet, a skill she taught all her daughters—discouraging vain and luxurious frivolities, and instilling belief in economy. In her youth, Isabella had seen the waste of resources and funds squandered at court by her brother the king. She had sworn to institute reform and austerity in the kingdom.

With a teacher's eye she surveyed her daughters, each busy with their embroideries. She then set her gaze on her cherished son John, Prince of Asturias and heir to the realm. He appeared sturdy to her eyes—a mother's eyes. At the age of sixteen, he was ready to be promised to any of the best potential brides in Europe.

He gently bent his head over his first oil painting, seemingly engrossed at his task, and applying the brush strokes under the supervision of his able tutor, Señor León de Castañeda. Prince John had her features and strong constitution. He had inherited her probing eyes and complexion but had the bearing of his father, King Ferdinand. Queen Isabella suddenly smiled at the recollection of Ferdinand's proposal to her. His countenance had surprised her in that moment—he had stood erect as he proposed, rather than bending on one knee before her. It was understandable. As the future king of Aragon, he was taught that his subjects should bend knees before him. Isabella had, of course, accepted him.

"Juana!" Isabella startled Princess Juana out of her slouched position. "Sit up straight or you'll become a hunchback!"

Princess Juana nodded to her mother. *"Sí, mi madre y reina."*

Queen Isabella approved with her eyes. That was another habit she insisted on. Each of her children were to call her queen before any member of the family or at court. "Concentrate on your sewing, *mi hija*."

Her court attendant came into the room and bowed. "Your Highness, an emissary from Portugal is here to see you."

"Let him in," Queen Isabella said.

A hidalgo emissary dressed with the Portuguese flair for fashion held his plumed hat under his right arm, bore his sword on his left side, and wore a red silk vest over brown velour breeches. He bowed his head to the queen but without bending from the waist.

"What news do you bring me, señor?" she asked.

The emissary first looked at her daughter Isabella, Princess of Asturias, and smiled at her. He then looked back at the queen. "With your permission, Your Highness, I have here the agreement terms from Prince Manuel I." He handed a scrolled document to the queen's attendant.

A small cry escaped Princess Isabella's lips, the Princess of Asturias. Her mother glanced at her eldest daughter, cloaked in the black widow frock, and the princess lowered her eyes in confusion. However, a corner of her mouth lifted in a partial smile. Her other sisters, princesses Joanna of Castile; Maria of Aragon; and the youngest, Catalina of Aragon; sitting nearby could hardly contain their curiosity as they stopped embroidering and moved restlessly in their seats.

Queen Isabella put down her sewing and, unrolling the document, she read, "I, Manuel I, prince and heir to the throne of Portugal, promise to marry Isabella, Princess of Asturias and Aragon . . ." Queen Isabella stopped to gauge her daughter's controlled happiness at the news.

"Tell Prince Manuel that we're delighted. I will confer with King Ferdinand when he returns from his campaign in Naples and Sicily, and we will reply to the terms of the agreement."

The emissary bowed while walking backward, then turned and left the presence of four happy women and a smiling prince.

"I want to marry too!" cried Princess Catalina.

"You're only nine years old! Prince Arthur of England will wait for you," Princess Joanna teased her.

Catalina, red in the face, was about to spring from her chair to answer her sister, when Queen Isabella put a stop to it. "We should all be happy for your sister Isabella and her betrothed." She turned to Princess Catalina and reassured her. "In a few years you will be engaged, then married, to Prince Arthur."

59

Cibao

THE EFFORTS MADE IN SANTO Tomás bore fruit, with a sizeable amount of gold dust found from panning the Rio de las Cañas. Columbus was called *Guamiquina* by the native Taínos, or the "Great Lord" of the Christians, and was rewarded by their cacique with gold nuggets and food. The nuggets weighed at least twenty-four castellanos, and the combined amount collected by the Contador Ojeda was two thousand castellanos. Columbus knew that his men had found and hidden more gold, but he couldn't prove where they had hidden it. If gold dust or flakes were found in their possession, they would be whipped, or worse—have their ears slit. The Indians, too, were watched and searched for gold and were punished severely if gold went missing.

"Admiral, we gathered all the Indians in Cibao for mining," said Ojeda as he entered Columbus's tent.

"Very well. I'll leave fifty men here under Mosén Pedro Margarite to supervise the mining, and the rest will follow me."

Ojeda raised his eyebrows in surprise. "Where to, Admiral?"

"We'll march back tomorrow to Isabela."

By dawn on Friday, the column of men took horses, a vast number of plants, food, and a few more captured Indians and left Fort Santo Tomás, crossed the river Yaque, and made their way up the Cordillera Central

Mountains. It had poured the night before, and the incline and ascent put their strength to the test. The horses buckled and slid backward on the slippery wet soil, only to land on the valley floor where they had started. The soldiers egged the horses on by whipping, which made the animals freeze and not budge, and many of their supplies came rolling back down to join the rest at the bottom of the mountain.

After a second try, the men and horses succeeded in getting up two-thirds of the mountain. Then torrential rain began to fall again. With a final effort by everyone in the party, their boots squishing in the sliding mud, they reached the top at El Puerto de los Hidalgos, where a week earlier they had gazed upon a green paradise. Tents were quickly erected across the narrow pass for the drenched men to take shelter in while the animals stood in the pouring rain. When the rain let up, they dried their horses as best they could and resumed the march downward toward the Yaque River. The rain had swelled the rapid-moving body of white-crested waters, and Columbus halted the column of men and beasts.

Columbus felt wet to his bones and needed a rest. "We'll break here for a meal."

Shivering, the hidalgo nobles, soldiers, and volunteers shared a cold, tasteless meal of cassava bread and tubers.

Juan Ponce de León stood glaring, spat out the insipid food, and wiped his lips forcefully. "Worse food I ever ate!"

"If you want a share of the gold, you must put up with it," de Fonseca bellowed at Ponce.

Columbus kept quiet during this altercation, preferring to stay aloof and not get involved in the incident. *The bounteous food the Indians provided for us has spoiled them rotten!* His men had adapted to poor weather and slim rations since leaving Isabela. But they had been trekking for many days with swollen rivers and the threat of dangerous Indians lurking in the forest who could attack at a moment's notice. He decided he owed his men some consolation and hope.

He got up and addressed the gathering. "We have a few days' march to base camp at Isabela. I promise every man here extra rations and wine for a week as soon as we get there."

"Salut." The men raised their hands without fanfare. It was more of a subdued acceptance.

Columbus gave the order, "Let's prepare ourselves to cross the Bajabonico River!"

The hidalgos, soldiers, and workers lifted their loads, and each man, whether riding or wading into the torrent, crossed the river tied to the next man by a rope. The first man to reach the opposite bank collapsed on the sandy shore, out of breath. One by one the caravan of men and beasts made it to the other side in safety. Columbus crossed on the shoulders of an Indian, as did Fonseca, Ojeda, and a few other nobles, including the young and energetic adventurer Juan Ponce de León.

An entire week was spent laboriously marching back to camp at Isabela. When they arrived, tired and frazzled, a flurry of trumpet fanfare and arquebuses firing into the air greeted them. The men from the fort ran to the column of exhausted, hungry men slowly marching into camp, embracing them jovially, happy to find them safe.

Diego was happy to see his brother back. Columbus hugged him with joy.

Dr. Chanca came to greet Columbus. "Welcome back, Admiral."

"It's good to be back, Dr. Chanca. What news do you have?"

Dr. Chanca's face turned somber. "I'm afraid I have bad news, Admiral."

Columbus trembled slightly. "What is it?" he asked.

"A good number of the sick you left behind to go inland have died," Dr. Chanca said. "Our rations have diminished. No more wine or biscuits are left—just cassava and tuber plants."

Barraged by the bad news, Columbus asked, "How many men have died?"

"We lost twenty men, Admiral," Dr. Chanca said with gloom. "But we buried them with all honors not far from the fort."

Columbus felt heartbroken. More men had died under his supervision. Now he had to deal with the food shortages. "What about the seeds? Have they germinated?"

"I'm glad to announce that cucumber and melons are ripe and ready to be picked. Sugarcane and wheat will soon be ready for harvest."

"Then we have more than do paupers in the cities of Spain." Columbus directed his gaze at the colony as he studied the more than two hundred wattle huts and pictured the sturdier stone houses they would build around a plaza, a church to be proud of, and a mayoral palace. Later he'd see that a mill and a water canal would be constructed to prepare for thousands of people to inhabit this land.

60

Seasons Passing

ISABELLA SAT LOOKING OVER HER books in the kitchen while Ana was busy preparing supper near the fire in the hearth. For Isabella, the seasons came and went, and with the rains, the harvests, and the trading excursions, she felt her years bearing down on her. Salvadore had now grown lithe and strong. His language was a mixture of Castilian and Portuguese, picked up through Ana's teaching him new words every day. Avram taught him Galician words and songs. Surprised, though pleased that Avram spent time with Salvadore to educate him, Isabella couldn't help wondering why the Galician dialect.

"Where did you learn that old Portuguese language?" Isabella asked him. "Your parents were natives of Córdoba, weren't they?"

"My father . . ." Avram hesitated for a moment. He continued, "He told me that his great-grandparents originated in Galicia. He taught me some Old Galician words."

Isabella nodded, but no expression of gratitude passed her lips. Though the enmity between Avram and her had healed, she stayed on her guard. She knew that any word of praise or interest would rekindle Avram's desire and interest in her. He kept his distance and never again mentioned her rejection or the fact that he had kissed her by force. He had, though, been an affectionate mentor to Salvadore—taking him to the vineyards during harvest, teaching him some rudimentary planting and harvesting lessons, and seeing to his protection as a hen would to her chick. Salvadore soaked in the words, the sights, and the attention. Several times he called Avram *papai,* at which Avram grinned broadly. As long as Isabella made no objection, he delighted in being called padre.

Ana watched the interaction between Salvadore and Avram with a maternal gaze. But when Ana turned her intense gaze to Isabella, Isabella turned away. She didn't want to raise false hopes that Avram and she would ever unite. It was a natural inclination to Ana that a healthy young widow could use a healthy young man to protect her. Deep in her heart, Isabella still pined for Miguel, and she fought a small voice inside her head that said Salvadore needed a father now.

Her search for Miguel had supplanted her previous all-encompassing desire to discover her own real father. He had become part of a myth in her heart and probably never existed. She smiled at the thought. To have had a mother but not a father would be something of an immaculate conception. That could no longer be possible. Her Catholic upbringing had melted away like a winter snow and with it all its superstitions. Instead, she longed to see her adoptive father she had left behind in Seville. *Poor Father, he didn't deserve that fate.* If it hadn't been for her impetuousness back in Seville, which contributed to her kidnapping, her adoptive mother would still be alive.

"Isabella!" Ana's voice startled her out of her thoughts. She looked up to see Juanita carrying a basket of ripe grapes in her hand while holding Salvadore's hand with the other. Raquela followed behind, grasping both of her children's hands. Aron, who was a head taller than Salvadore, and Sarina, having grown into a lovely ten-year-old girl, were good companions to her son.

When he saw her, Salvadore came running to Isabella's arms. She lifted him under his arms and swung him around and around. Salvadore's laughter filled the room. The other children also ran to Isabella. She put Salvadore down in the middle of the tiled floor and, holding Aron and Sarina's hands, danced around him in a circle. After a while, they all collapsed on the floor laughing and out of breath.

Isabella looked up from the floor and noticed Avram standing by the door with a somber look. She asked, laughing, "What is it, Avram? Looks like you've seen the dead!"

Ana had turned her head too, and her expression soured. "What is it?" Her voice trembled.

Avram entered, walking slowly. He sat on a chair and looked at everyone around him. "I've heard news at the market in Sintra."

Ana gave a darting look. "What news?"

"It is done. The wedding between Isabella of Aragon, Princess of Asturias, and Manuel I of Portugal will take place next year."

Juanita had quickly lifted Salvadore off the floor and held him against her.

A silence descended on the room. Neither Isabella nor Raquela immediately grasped the implication of Avram's words. The children kept tugging on Isabella's arms to continue dancing with them. She pulled away and looked into Ana's ashen face.

Raquela asked, "What could it mean? It's a joyous event. Isn't it?"

Ana turned to her. "It is our doom, Raquela. Next they'll ask us to leave Portugal. The only home we've had since we left Spain."

Raquela turned white. "But where can we go? How will I protect my children?"

"No one is going anywhere." Ana's sharp voice rose. "Nothing has been proclaimed publicly yet. Besides, King John the II is still alive and won't allow his subject Jews to be harmed."

Avram looked up and uttered the dreaded words. "It's been published in the plaza in Sintra. They're giving us a year. We are to convert or leave."

At once and in unison, a muffled cry, suppressed so as to not scare the children, escaped the women's lips.

Ana lamented, *"Oy mio Dio, oy, oy, oy."*

Isabella sat on the floor, too dumbstruck to get up. *When will it end?*

61

A Chance for Escape

THE MONTHS HAD PASSED THROUGH Ali's life like the sand grains through the narrow neck of an hourglass. He had served his master Aruj well and was rewarded now and then with additional food and sleep, but it was a life no better than a leashed animal under an owner's command. All eyes followed him throughout day and night, including those of the guards, the pirates, and the cook who checked that his meals were eaten. A tin plate still full would mean that he had escaped.

At one point Ali asked Aruj the question that burned in his mind. "Why am I your prisoner and slave?"

Aruj at first burst into long unbroken laughter. When he calmed down, he said, "You were purchased with good dirhams. You are my property and my slave forever."

"But you see that I'm white and European. Not a slave from Africa or Guinea."

"It doesn't make any difference to me if you're black or white. If you're noble, I'll get more for you from the highest bidder." Aruj fell quiet as if reflecting on the future sale.

Ali's heart skipped a beat. "When do you plan to sell me?"

"Enough questions!" Aruj yelled, his face turning as red as his beard. *For a Berber, he has interesting coloring*, thought Ali.

"Go and get me Mustapha," Aruj said.

Ali nodded and left Aruj's cabin. Outside, the pirates scrubbed the decks with pumice stone, as he'd seen done many times. He'd seen it . . . ? He stopped, mid-descent from the quarterdeck. Where had he seen it beside this ship? And when? Those were troubling questions. If he had seen the operation done on deck, then he had sailed on other ships, but which ships? Waving his hand in the air, he rushed to Mustapha, Aruj's second-in-command.

"The effendi wants to see you," Ali said.

"What have you done now?" Mustapha's face showed contempt.

"I don't understand your hate, Mustapha. I do my work and serve the master faithfully."

Mustapha turned on him with a lash of his whip. He slashed it across Ali's shoulders several times.

"Qef! Qef!" Ali shouted, running across deck and ducking to escape further blows.

Aruj appeared on deck to see to the commotion. "Mustapha, come up!"

Ali saw the look of hate on Mustapha's face as he stalked to Aruj's cabin. The cabin door closed on both men, and Ali wondered why Mustapha had been called. Perhaps Aruj wanted to preserve Ali's value on the slave market, and thus prevent Mustapha from "damaging the merchandise." Despite his lashed shoulders, Ali succeeded in smiling at his misfortunes. He gazed at the span of sea in front of him as he imagined himself free of slave shackles. He'd run directly into the arms of the beautiful woman calling him. *Beware though, she may be a mermaid.* He smiled again.

One way to escape would be to disappear at the next port. Perhaps he could steal some of Aruj's clothes and use them as a disguise. If he were caught, he'd be lashed to the mast.

Another way would be to hide in one of the crates on board that contained stolen and pirated loot. Their ship had stopped several times over the last two years to unload these crates. What was their destination? He didn't know. He had heard, from the other pirates on board, that Aruj had an estate hidden in the dunes south of Tangier. Perhaps that was their final landing place.

Ali would have to listen to every bit of information trickled down about the next port and plan his escape. He would keep his eyes and ears open.

62

Explorations

COLUMBUS STOOD OUTSIDE THE PARTIALLY built fort, gazing out to sea. He had learned by now that Española was an island and not the mainland Cipangu. Every Taíno on this land had confirmed that they were on one of many islands. Perhaps now was time to explore further to find the mainland without delay.

He called his timid brother, Diego Columbus; gregarious Fray Buil; nobleman Don Alonso Sánchez de Carvajal; Pedro Fernandez Coronel; Juan de Luxan; and a few other men to his hut.

"I'm leaving on a voyage of exploration." To the quizzical eyebrows, Columbus rushed to explain. "I'll be searching for more gold deposits south of Española and beyond."

"But what about the Santo Tomás mine?" Fray Buil asked.

"Santo Tomás will not produce large quantities for España. What we have found is miniscule. But I have high hopes that with the Indians' help we can rest assured of the output."

By the incredulous reflections in their eyes, Columbus saw that the men weren't convinced, except for his brother, Diego, who obeyed and worshipped him.

Diego spoke to the men present. "My brother, the admiral, knows what he's talking about. Just trust him. He has been chosen by the Lord to enrich España."

Columbus was pleased with his brother's comment. Diego's invocation of the Lord had conveyed the authority for the men to trust their leader.

Columbus gave him a grateful smile. He congratulated himself that under his supervision Diego would make a fine priest for the church. "I promise you that the gold will flow by the end of this year."

"And what about Isabela and building the fort?" asked de Caravajal.

"All of you present here will form a council to supervise the men and the building in the colony. I trust that during my absence you'll maintain order among the men and the Indians."

"Which men will direct the council?" de Carvajal asked.

"My brother, Don Diego Columbus, will be in charge as president." A satisfied smile appeared on Diego Columbus's face. "Pedro Fernandez Coronel and Fray Buil will report to him as regents. And you, Alonso Sánchez de Carvajal, with Juan de Luján, will be their officers."

The men nodded, accepting their duties without protest, which gave Columbus great satisfaction. He turned to the other men standing at attention.

"Now, for the expedition. Francisco Niño, you will pilot the *Niña*. My good friend Juan de la Cosa, with whom I've weathered many dangerous storms—" His men sighed with relief at the reference. Braving the deadly Atlantic squall on their return to Palos the previous year was no small feat. De la Cosa nodded as he smiled at Columbus, who concluded, "You'll sail on the *Niña* as my first mate."

Columbus continued. "Alonso Medel, I want you as her master. Pedro de Terreros, you'll be my boatswain as before. We'll take sixteen seamen and gromets on the *Niña*."

Alonso Pérez Roldán jumped in. "What about the *San Juan* and the *Cardera*, Admiral?"

"I was just getting to those. Alonso, you will master the *San Juan* with sixteen men, and you, Cristóbal Pérez, will lead the *Cardera* with fifteen."

The men seemed pleased. Columbus felt relieved now to explore the islands beyond Española. He turned to the Benedictine monk. "Fray Buil, we need your blessing for the voyage."

The ecclesiastical man of God promptly complied. He made the sign of the cross while the men kneeled in the small space and petitioned the Lord for safe sailing. *"Habeto pacem et reperio vestri somnia. Ire cum Domino."*

The men were still in their prayers, when a voice cried out, "Almirante! Almirante!"

Columbus raised his head to see a man from the colony in Santo Tomás running toward him, panting and out of breath.

"What is it?" Columbus asked, his voice quivering.

"The cacique Caonabó . . . is arming his men to attack Fort Santo Tomás!" He bent down, placing his hands on his thighs to catch his breath. "Margarite sent me to bring relief soldiers!"

Columbus gasped as his muscles tightened under the shock. He turned to Ojeda. "Take one hundred men, horses, and arms and make haste to Santo Tomás!"

"Aye, aye, Admiral!"

"Send back Margarite and remain there as governor."

Ojeda broke out in a large smile with the promotion. "I'll serve with honor, Admiral."

After Ojeda left to prepare for the reinforcement trip inland, Columbus sighed at the tasks and responsibilities he had to shoulder: maintaining peace between his garrulous men as well as ensuring their safety under his command. No one alive knew the hardships involved in commanding unruly men in a strange land with dangerous Indians, and most of all the struggle to maintain harmony between Spain and this new world. At least Ojeda was a man after his own heart with great capabilities, swift to carry out orders. Throughout the night, Columbus saw to the rescue party's preparations and predawn departure. When the last men marched west into the woods under Ojeda's guidance, his heart ached for their survival. *I know Ojeda will come through.*

Dawn broke slowly with a faint line at the horizon, then illuminated tall palms capping the tip of the Cordillera Septentrional Mountains. Columbus waited for the full sun to illuminate the entire sea. The salty air filled his nostrils and lungs and mind, and he looked forward with unabated anticipation to the marvels he would discover. The excited feeling was similar to discovering the love of a new mistress.

The crew had prepared themselves all through the night, getting but a few hours of sleep. They were energized though, eager to sail and escape the humidity and construction work. A sailor was a sailor no matter what, and no amount of reward could force him to become a mason. The smiles on their faces expressed their yearning to set sail.

Columbus, too, felt at ease only when the floorboards moved beneath his feet. Being on terra firma made him itch for the swaying of sea waves and the open expanses he lived for. Now new islands beckoned him with gold yet to be discovered. His mind was at ease now that he had left all the preparations and instructions with the council on land. When he returned, he expected to find the colony built with houses and a brand new church.

63

A Glint of freedom

ALI STOOD BY THE MAINMAST early in the morning, letting the wind caress his face and cheeks. Beneath his feet the sea moved like a gigantic body propelling the pirate ship forward to a new destination. Where? He didn't know. They headed south along the African coast and had passed several settlements dotted with forts and whitewashed houses. Forts appeared aligned at intervals along the coast, presenting a strong image to any ship considering attack on the gold mines. Somehow he had the strange feeling he'd been here before: the same coast, same towns, and same forts. They were now approaching a fort in the distance that brought a shock of recognition. He took another good look at the harbor and stood frozen on deck. He was back at La Mina!

No! Not again! It was indeed a nightmare—one with no waking. He turned from the railing and slid down to the plank floor, venting his grief and anger by clenching his teeth and fists. No sound passed his lips. His despair was bottomless. When finally facing the horrible truth, he tried convincing himself that at least he wasn't slaving in hot pits, blown with dust and baked by blazing sun, but his grim despair didn't let go. *I must escape or I'll go mad!*

As he contemplated escape, he noticed a Portuguese caravel docked in the harbor. He recognized the flag on the mast, displaying the eleven yellow castles with five white blue-dotted shields. In some respects his memory was now firmly anchored—he recalled the smallest details of maritime travel and high-flying colors. If he could communicate with the Portuguese ship, they might grant him asylum. He considered his shabby state and overgrown beard. With his appearance, no one would provide protection—especially to a man called Ali. He needed a new identity!

While scrubbing the deck, his mind ran over many names he'd heard over the last two years: Afonso, Diego, Pedro . . . None suited him. What about León, Fernando, or Juan? No. None sounded Portuguese. Perhaps José after his younger brother? He had sorely missed him over the last two years. So José it would be. Now he needed a family name. After much consideration, he came up with Tavares Sílva. *José Tavares Sílva.* It was a solid name.

Plans to evade Mustapha and the cook's watch over him ran through his head. The deep night would help in giving him an escape window. He then organized, mentally, what he needed to survive. The last few days that he'd gone to the kitchen's corner by the forecastle to pick food for his master, he found himself among a cornucopia of baked bread, cooked lamb, and various fruits and nuts. All were laying there for the taking.

When the cook's back was turned, he grabbed a couple of flat breads and some nuts and hid them in his pocket. He'd also grabbed a skin filled with water and dropped it near one of the boats on his way to the cabin. When no one was looking, he hid the food and the skin in the boat, covered by a canvas. By the end of the day, after shuttling four trays filled with food to the chief's cabin, he had stashed away enough food to last him a few days.

The opportunity to flee came that same night, when the caravel lay to off La Mina's harbor. Night had fallen, and only two lanterns shed diffused light on the stern and one on the bow. The rest of the ship lay in darkness. The pirates had imbibed rum and beer with their supper, except for Aruj and two men on watch. Aruj had retired to his cabin and was sound asleep, the cook lay snoring on deck, and Mustapha was on watch at the stern. A young apprentice pirate huddled in the crow's nest, but Ali knew for certain the lad would soon fall asleep.

With slow crawling movements, Ali reached one of the boats stacked on deck and slid the cover off. At the bottom lay the stashed food and water. He peeked at Mustapha's undefined outline lit by the lantern as he paced the starboard deck on his midnight round. His boots pounded against wooden beams on deck as he did his watch. Ali's eyes followed Mustapha's movement back and forth to pinpoint when to begin his escape—which would be when the second-in-command sat down momentarily.

Silently, Ali unrolled the rigging and ropes holding the boat, and fed the ropes through the pulleys. But then the rusty chain let out a loud creak, and Ali froze. Mustapha turned his head toward the sound and quickly approached the port side, trying to peer through the moonless night. He stood listening for a number of minutes while Ali held his breath and ground his teeth. Mustapha turned from port, moving starboard, then aft to the stern. In the crow's nest above, the young pirate didn't stir at the sight of Mustapha's sudden prowl on deck. Ali knew the youth must be asleep.

Ali sat still for a moment. Then he fed out the ropes, lowering the boat along the hull in small increments. With all his strength, he worked on one side at a time, and when he heard the boat hit the water he stopped to listen. He peered into the darkness for Mustapha, but no movement came. *He must've dozed off.*

Ali rejoiced as he climbed over the gunwale to slide down the line attached to the boat. The transom's hard surface met his foot, and he felt for the bottom planking. Moving fast, he released the lines holding the boat and began to row away from the ship. When the starboard and port lanterns began to fade, Ali increased his rowing speed.

The faint lights from shore grew brighter and larger as Ali vigorously rowed. Then a series of bells sounded in the night. Either his absence from the pirate ship or the missing boat had been discovered. He looked frantically to shore, when he noticed the Portuguese ship still in the harbor. He approached the vessel, rowing with fury until he came close to its hull. Silently he paddled around the ship, and when sure no one had noticed him, threw a grappling hook attached to a rope up to the gunwale.

His first attempt failed. He tried a few more times until finally one of the three hooks caught the wood gunwale. He then pushed the boat adrift before climbing the hanging rope. Scrambling over the gunwale, he looked frantically for a place to hide. Stacked boats near the railings beckoned to him. He pulled a corner of the sturdy cover off a boat and slipped under, then breathed out a sigh of relief. In the distance, he heard the bell still ringing on the pirate ship. After minutes went by, the bell stopped ringing. Ali suddenly heard a commotion around him.

"Isso é um pedido de socorro?" a voice asked in Portuguese.

"Calm yourself, first mate. There were no flares. It can't be serious," another voice replied.

"Aye, aye, Captain."

"Go back to sleep now," the captain's voice said.

Calm returned to the night, and Ali began to doze off. He startled when his head went down to his chest. *I mustn't fall asleep!* By dawn he'd think of a way out of his dilemma. That was his last thought before he fell asleep with exhaustion.

64

Changes

*J*SABELLA SAT ON THE PORCH, admiring how the spring brought back its full array of budding flowers, newly germinated vine seedlings, and fresh air breezing above nature in bloom. She had welcomed this change in season, and with it new growth in Salvadore. He had acquired a large vocabulary of many sentences in both Spanish and Portuguese. Juanita had also taught him Caló, the language of Romani gypsies. Isabella had watched Juanita teaching Salvadore the fandango pirouette dance descended from many groups including Moors, Jews, Andalusians, and Indian gypsies. She thought with wonder of the many peoples' cultures merging together then distilling down to her little son, who was becoming part of a greater humanity.

But her little son was bereft of a father. Was she selfish to refuse him a protector, a man he could look up to? Miguel was his real father, and no other could ever take his place. Yet, what then of her own adoptive father, Don Arturo? He remained the father she loved, while her real father had abandoned her.

Ana's words came back to her. Even though Avram wasn't Salvadore's true father, could he replace Miguel? She suddenly felt unsettled, as if she had given up on Miguel altogether.

The grounds around the house were quiet and peaceful, bringing back a soothing feeling from deep inside her. She looked east toward the vineyards and saw Avram at a distance, walking rapidly toward the house. When he saw her on the porch, he slowed. Perhaps, she thought, he was reticent to approach her. God knew how many times she had rejected him. She had been unusually harsh on him.

"Isabella, I didn't expect you to be waiting here," Avram said as he stepped up the stairs to the porch.

"I . . . wasn't . . . waiting for anyone."

"Then can I help you with anything?"

"No. Thank you, Avram." She then quickly asked, "Is anything wrong with the vineyards?"

"Well . . . not exactly."

"Then why are you here in the middle of the day?"

"I wanted to check with you, to see if I should begin rehiring seasonal workers."

"Of course. You know what needs to be done. I leave you in charge."

Avram's face reflected surprise. "Thank you, Isabella. Just wanted to make sure it was all right with you."

"It is." Isabella smiled at him, which brought another surprised look to his eyes.

"Well then, I'll see to it." Avram turned on his heel and walked away back to the vineyards.

When Avram disappeared over the hill, she laughed with abandon, as if a weight had suddenly lifted off her shoulders. She went into the house smiling and ran into Ana carrying linens.

Looking curiously at her, Ana stayed mute for a moment. She then said, "It's good to see you smile, Isabella. Any reason for it?"

Isabella stopped smiling and replied, "No reason at all. I just left Avram, who asked me when to begin hiring."

"And . . . ?"

"I told him to go ahead. I'm going to check on Salvadore." Isabella quickly left Ana, who had a satisfied smile on her face.

65

Exploration

BY NOON ON THE TWENTY-FOURTH of April the *Niña,* the *San Juan,* and the *Cardera* were ready to sail from Isabela. The sea spread before them in cerulean blue against white frothy waves, and they headed west for Monte Cristi, where Columbus planned to lay to for a few days. From there they would sail to La Navidad.

The following morning, they reached a protected cove at Samaná Bay in Monte Cristi, west of Isabela.

Columbus gazed from the quarterdeck at an idyllic scene from paradise. He could never grow tired of nature's beauty offered in vivid colors and pleasing surroundings. The clear cyan waters in the bay flirted with white sands and deep-green palm trees that came near the edge. Flocks of pink flamingos waded in the waters, their plumage contrasting with the emerald-shaded forest above them. The moisture in the air raised the sweet perfumed scent of the mariposa flower. Agaves grew wild, and the sea grape's rounded leaves, bearing clusters of purple and whitish berries, offered nature's bounty. In this contemplation of nature, Columbus decided to pay a call on his old friend the cacique Guacanagari.

"Lower the boats!" Columbus ordered on the sixty-ton *Niña.*

"Aye, aye, Admiral," said the *Niña's* master, Alonso Medel, who quickly carried the order to Francisco Niño, the pilot.

Before disembarking, Columbus issued further orders to his boatswain, Pedro de Terreros. "We'll take six able seamen with us, and the rest of the crew should continue their tasks on ship. Make sure to watch that the gromets don't dawdle!"

Each ship lowered their boat, and the parties rowed ashore under the able direction of Juan de la Cosa. The canoes landed on the pristine beach, and the sailors stepped onshore, their boots picking up wet sand made of myriad colorful silica grains. After a ten-minute march they arrived at the village to find it empty. Guacanagari and the natives had fled, likely in fear at the sight of three caravels they hadn't seen before.

"Admiral, we can't stay here. We have much ground to cover," de la Cosa advised.

"You're right, de la Cosa. Let us proceed to the island of Juana."

"Then we ought to leave right away."

With the *San Juan* and *Cardera* following, the *Niña* sailed away from La Navidad. Six leagues west lay a small island that looked like a round turtle that Columbus called La Tortuga. The waters along the shore were choppy due to rip currents and large breaking waves caused by high onshore winds. The rip current pulled strongly at the ships through a trench between sandbars. Attempting to land onshore would be madness. The ghost of the *Santa Maria*'s wreck came back to Columbus's memory.

"We'll lay to by the island," he told de la Cosa. "Keep the sails set during the night."

After Compline prayers that night, unsettling thoughts troubled Columbus. The search for gold was uppermost on his mind. The safety of his men in Santo Tomás was another thought that beset him. What if the cacique Caonabó came with thousands of strong Indians with bows and arrows and tried to set fire to the newly built fort? What if his men died one by one? An image of his men lying dead by a burned-out fort was more than he could stomach. *No*. His men would conquer the cannibalistic Caribs with the Lord's help.

Last, but not least, thoughts of his living daughter came back to him. He yearned to see her, and yet could not bring himself to allow himself such an indulgence. It could only lead to disaster. His true identity, once revealed, could wipe out all he had gained. He must at all costs keep her identity a secret.

The following morning the winds coming from northwest, with a current rising from the west, made it impossible to cross the Windward Passage between Española and Juana. The three ships returned to Española to wait out another night.

On Tuesday April 29, the ships finally crossed the Windward Passage to Juana, fifteen leagues west-northwest of Española, landing on Punta Maisí. A large cross was unloaded from the *Niña* and mounted on a promontory on the cape.

"I take possession of this cape in the name of our sovereigns in España," Columbus declared. The party kneeled and crossed themselves, their faces full of devotion.

He gathered his officers and pilots. Francisco Niño, master of the *Niña*; Alonso Pérez Roldán from the *San Juan*; and the *Cardera* master, Cristóbal Pérez; along with their seamen sat down to a council.

Columbus addressed them. "I value your opinion greatly. What would be the best course to explore this mainland?"

"Admiral," de la Cosa, the mapmaker and mariner, said, "We already explored the northern coast of Juana on our first voyage. I say we go south."

Cristóbal Pérez affirmed de la Cosa's suggestion. "I agree, Admiral. Anything good can only happen going south."

Columbus mulled Cristóbal Pérez's last words as ambiguous, but he showed him courtesy by nodding his head in agreement. "Then south it'll be. *Vámonos!*"

66

A New Identity

ALI AWOKE INSIDE THE ROWBOAT to the ship's swaying movement and loud voices on deck. Huddled in his hideout, he held his movement in check. His stomach began to growl, and he cursed himself. In his haste, he had forgotten the food and water provisions in the pirate boat. While he mulled how to evade discovery, the boat cover was suddenly pulled back, and two sailors stared at him with surprise.

"Captain! Captain!" one of the sailors hailed in Portuguese. "We found a stowaway beggar!"

The other sailor took one look at him and said, "You're a dead man!"

The captain approached and observed Ali with curiosity. "You know the penalty for traveling penniless. Do you?"

"Please, Captain. Please hear me out," Ali begged him. "I'm not a beggar." He looked down at his shabby trousers and shirt still wet and mucked by the escape and thought he was done for. He raised his head to the captain and said, "I can explain everything. Please give me a chance."

"All right. I give you one minute. Speak!"

"You see, Captain, I was captured two years ago by slave traders and sold into slavery."

"What is your name then?" the captain asked.

"I'm A—" He gulped and took a swallow. "I'm called José Sílva. That is, José Tavares da Sílva."

The captain raised his eyebrows. He turned to his mates and yelled, "Tie him to the mast!"

"But why, Captain? Why?" Ali begged.

"Because I know a liar when I see one."

"But I told you the truth!"

The captain crossed his arms. "All right then, why did you hesitate?"

"I can explain everything." Ali's voice was strong.

"Bring him to my cabin!" said the captain.

With the captain leading, the two sailors grabbed him by the arms, shoved him forward to the upper deck and into the cabin, then waited aside for the interrogation to begin.

The captain sat in a chair and quizzed Ali. "Now tell me the truth. Who are you?"

"I swear to you that I'm a Portuguese man caught by pirates and sold to the slave market."

"What is your real name?" the captain insisted.

Ali hesitated, hoping to be believed, then took the plunge. He related all that he knew for certain: the pirates who saved his life by pulling him out of the water but then dumped him in the slave mines, the escape from La Mina, recapture by slave owners, and then capture again after the second escape by pirate Aruj.

At the mention of Aruj, Ali saw a new interest in the captain's eyes. Ali fell quiet, hoping against hope that he had convinced the man.

"All right. I believe you," said the captain, at which Ali gave a long sigh. "But if you sold me a bill of goods, you'll be sorry for the day you set foot on my ship."

Ali reassured the captain by speaking in perfect Portuguese. *"Não se preocupe, Capitão. Eu lhe disse a verdade.* You can call me José."

"We'll head back to Portugal after delivering our goods," the captain said. "I'm Captain Da Costa, you'll —"

Ali suddenly felt faint. He wobbled, trying to support himself on the table near him while raising a hand to quell the captain's concern. "It's nothing, Captain. Nothing. I must be hungry that's all."

"You had me worried there for a minute." Da Costa turned to his two sailors. "Feed this man, then put him to work. Now go!"

Ali thanked Da Costa with a nod as he followed the sailors out. His head burst with swirling thoughts and conflicting feelings. Who was he really? Why did the name Da Costa make him flinch with such a strong gut feeling? Was his memory coming back in bits and pieces? Had he heard this name before?

While he followed the two men, he noticed the sailors stopping their work to look at him. All he wanted now was some food and drink to quench his thirst. A sudden peace descended on him. He felt certain that his true identity would present itself soon.

67

Punishment

AS HE WOKE UP, OJEDA smelled the sweet perfumed scent of flowers blowing in the groves near Santo Tomás. He heard the camp wake up to another smell wafting to his nostrils— breakfast cooking on spits over fire.

"Trae más agua!" A voice called for water over the din of three hundred men busying to begin their day while another commanded that the fires be minded: *"¡No dejes que el fuego se apague!"*

His men had caught and killed a crocodile then grilled it on a wooden platform resting on sticks, the Indians called barbacoa. Swaying palm trees, long-necked blue herons with great wingspans circling low, and the sounds of nearby waterfalls displayed nature's best splendor.

The men's rations of tack biscuits had run out, and they were forced to eat the Indian diet of cassava bread and tuberous roots. The grilled meat was welcomed on this day in which the men would exert their energies cutting wood and hammering planks to build the fort. A wall composed of mud and wood encircling a small area designated to become a future town was already in place, missing only a gate. Inside the fort, crude huts had been built and were awaiting their palm frond roofs. The party Ojeda sent to the coast for more supplies would add manpower upon their return. All went according to plan. Furthermore, the predicted attack from the cacique Caonabó hadn't materialized, and peace reigned over the Cibao region.

Ojeda rubbed his hands in delight at the progress made in the colony. By tomorrow, the Indians would be recruited to begin mining.

The cook pulled him out of his contented musing by serving him breakfast. He took a bite of the freshly cooked crocodile meat, savoring its chicken-like flavor and dense texture.

Two of his men imitated cackling chickens to show fowls twisting over fire. "*¡Ooo! ¡Ooo! ¡Me estoy quemando!*"

Just then a cry came in the distance from a Spaniard racing toward the fort with two companions. "Captain! Captain Ojeda!"

Alarmed, Ojeda threw the rest of his meat into the fire and ran to meet him. "What's wrong? You were supposed to head to Isabela!"

The man spoke haltingly, short of breath. "The Indians transporting us across the river stole our belongings and ran to the groves near Pontón!"

Ojeda grabbed four armed men and hiked to the groves. They searched for an hour, and after failing to find them decided to call on the cacique from Pontón's village. The march took them a good part of the day, and when they arrived sweating profusely at the village of Pontón, they found it deserted.

Ojeda was furious. He had used up precious hours on a futile chase, and the Indians would pay dearly for his lost time. He said with rage, "We'll destroy all their belongings!"

His men stayed silent but followed obediently. Ojeda went directly to the cacique hut and slashed everything in sight. He cut the hammock ropes and broke the makeshift tables and stools into pieces, while his men threw the few clothes that belonged to the chief out of the hut. When they were done with the cacique's hut, they went on a rampage through the other huts, throwing out all the possessions the Indians had. The grounds became littered with native cotton clothing, furniture, ropes, and crude tools.

Just then, the cacique walked haltingly toward the ransacked village with his arms up, swaying back and forth while saying over and over, "*Òmàko kaje ròmun' kynkano.*" To Ojeda it meant surrender. He put down his sword and waited for the cacique to approach.

"You have thieves among you. Bring me those men!" Ojeda yelled as he pointed to the trees.

The cacique apparently understood his words. He turned and waved his hand toward the trees.

"Macana! Macana!" he yelled to his men. *"Mòkaron sampura morykaton!"* At those words, Indians began to emerge from the trees, pushing three men in front of them. The three Indians held the Spaniards' clothes in their arms. The men were brought to the cacique, where they threw themselves at his feet. They offered him the stolen clothes.

Ojeda retrieved the clothing comprising a couple of old vests, worn-out hats, and red capes.

"These men must be punished!" Ojeda yelled at the cacique.

Grabbing and dragging one of the Indian thieves, he raised his sword and cut one of the Indian's ears off. Blood spurted down his cheeks and naked torso. The man covered his mutilated face with his hand and ran screaming into the forest. With the help of his men, Ojeda tied the cacique and two of his relatives with ropes cut from the huts. The remaining two thieves were also tied up.

Ojeda told the robbed Spaniards, "Take these men back to Isabela for a beheading when the admiral returns!"

The men hesitated for a moment, then left the village, heading north to Isabela with their prisoners.

"Let's go back to our work now!" said Ojeda.

68

Counting Days

JOÃO WORKED ALONGSIDE THE MEN in Isabela, pushing and placing logs along the length of the fort. The work proceeded slowly, the men stopping now and then to rest and chat among themselves. For his part, João kept working steadily, not wanting to garner attention—or ire—from the council. Columbus's brother, Diego, council president, walked the grounds from time to time, checking on the work's progression. As for the other officers in charge, Fray Buil occupied his time baptizing the Indians, but Alonso de Carvajal, Captain Coronel, and Juan de Luján made rare appearances at the working field. For all intents and purposes, the men in Isabela's colony were left to their own devices.

The same conditions existed at the gristmills being constructed near the river a few leagues upstream from the fort. All the material to build the mill was being collected by the Indians. The Spaniards kept them felling trees, cutting, sawing boards, and constructing the paddled waterwheel. The wheat planted by Columbus's men when they had first landed was about to be harvested. The water sluice and millstones were ready for the wheat to be separated from the chaff and ground into flour. But the work progressed slowly. João thought they might starve until the relief ships arrived from Spain with food supplies. At any rate, he had a cache of food—grain from open sacks, tack biscuits that hadn't been invaded by bugs or moisture, and a complete barrel of molasses he had hidden near a palm tree one night while all were asleep.

The sun went down, Compline hour came upon them, and the men quit their work to pray. João joined them in prayers, and quiet descended upon the colony. When they were done with the night meal, he was joined by one of the men he had helped stow away.

"When will you make your move?" León asked him in a low voice.

João took his time answering. When he began, a long sigh escaped his throat. "We still have a long way, Léon. We're not quite ready yet."

"When will you be ready?"

There was no point in answering when he didn't have the answer. "You and the others must be patient. In the meantime, I want you all to befriend the natives and learn everything you can. We will need them someday." He fell quiet, then said, "At least you're out of reach from evil hands. There's an ill wind now in Europe."

"What do you mean?"

"There are rumors that the Inquisition is coming back."

"Back where?"

João hesitated again, wondering whether to tell León or not. "You mustn't worry. It won't happen overnight."

León's voice came out trembling. "Is it coming to Portugal?"

"Yes."

León exhaled his grief. *"¡El Dio mio!"* He then said with a moan, "My wife and three children are living in Sintra."

"As I said," João tried to reassure León, "It may be a couple of years. By then I intend to gather all Jews and Conversos and ship them to the New World."

"A miracle is what we need."

"Yes, a miracle would help," João said as if in prayer. This time he didn't cross himself, but he uttered, *"Be'ezrat Hashem."*

69

South from Juana

IN ORDER TO DISCOVER WHETHER Juana was a continent or an island, Columbus had his three caravels sail southwest from towering Punta Negra. He had seen part of this coast the previous year but had never ventured farther beyond that point. He was disappointed to find that the tall mountains in the background didn't provide enough moisture to create lush tropical groves and vegetation as were found in the northern peaks. When they disembarked on shore, they found that the coast was arid, lacking palm trees, and had but a few rivers. Instead of luxuriant forests he found instead cacti and blue agave plants that held moisture in their spiky and fleshy leaves. When they sailed to the southern tip, they found a large deep harbor in the shape of a sickle. Columbus named it Puerto Grande.

Columbus took a small party of ten men and went to look for a village but found only three empty huts. On the beach, they found two iguanas cooking on spits with a large dog watching the fire. The fearsome mastiff didn't stir or bark and remained unperturbed by the men's presence.

One of his men cracked a joke: "That's a dumb dog!" They all laughed, including Columbus, who needed a diversion from his concentrated focus.

"Let's go back to the ships and get some grub!" Columbus said with one of his rare smiles.

The bay, populated with large fish, provided a satiating dinner for all his men. After vesper prayers, Columbus watched from deck the darkened sea that was partially illuminated by a hazy moon. His thoughts went to the voyage ahead and the safety of his men. He felt eager to start colonizing the forts being built on Isabela and Santo Tomás. Once their hold on Española was firm, Spain would earn its place in history. These lands would become Christianized for the Lord's glory.

The following morning, they sailed west up the coast to the last cape, where Columbus decided it was the farthest point he would sail to before heading south. He named the cape Cabo de Cruz. From that point on, the sea was covered in weeds—another reminder of their first voyage.

All at once, many Indians suddenly came in their canoes to see the men from heaven. Columbus and his men were offered freshly baked cassava bread, grilled fish, and fresh water. The Indians were paid with hawk's bells, small mirrors that surprised them with their images, and colored glass beads. The Indians' happy faces bore large smiles at those gifts.

On Saturday, May 3, the *Niña*, *San Juan*, and *Cardera* reached thirty-three leagues south-southeast from the southernmost coast of Juana, arriving at a small island Columbus called Jamaica. He recalled from his first voyage that the Indians had called the island Babeque or Jameque, and said the island was rich with gold.

As before, the islanders paddled canoes to greet them with offerings of water and food. Columbus ordered his men to distribute the trinkets they'd brought with them. None of the natives carried or wore any gold ornaments, which brought disappointment to his heart.

"Let's go ashore!" Columbus ordered.

Of all the islands he and his men had visited so far, this was the most beautiful. The Spaniards were treated to an enchanting world. Palm trees came to water's edge, fanning the beach with shade; birds sauntered between fronds, chattering and tweeting; turtles were aplenty, nesting in the sand; and the white-crested surf filled the air with a hypnotizing rhythm. Intoxicating flowers showered their senses with sensual fragrance. Bougainvillea abounded near hibiscus, and water lilies made white carpets on the surface of inland ponds. The men were so taken that they stopped their actions to smell the flowers.

"Let's go back to the ships," Columbus said. The party then returned to their ships and sailed to another harbor.

"Admiral!" de la Cosa alerted Columbus. "The Indians are armed!"

Columbus saw many Indians paddling their canoes toward the ships, armed with bows and arrows. "Don't harm them!" he ordered Juan de la Cosa. "I don't want to start hostility with the Indians. Let's sail away!"

They sailed to yet another harbor, which Columbus called El Puerto Bueno. Again Indians canoed to the ships, shooting arrows at the sailors. Sheets of finely chiseled reed arrows raining down made them duck below the railings. Arrows fell everywhere, and one struck the cook, Maestre Diego, in the leg.

"Dr. Chanca, take care of Diego!" Columbus yelled, then turned to his crossbowmen. "Give them hell!"

A rebounding volley of metal-tipped arrows filled the skies, wounding many Indians. They retreated to the line of trees and shot their arrows, now fewer, from there.

"Stop the arrows!" Columbus ordered.

During this lull, the Indians retrieved their wounded men lying on the beach, and then they all disappeared into the forest.

"We taught them a lesson," the men from the ships yelled in unison.

Right after the brief confrontation between the Spaniards and the Indians, many more canoes showed up with peaceful, friendly natives wanting to trade with them, and valueless trinkets exchanged hands. Columbus decided to moor in the harbor to repair a leak on the *Niña*. While they caulked and repaired the hull damage, a young Indian came to the ship. The youth then kneeled down and made the sign of the cross.

Surprised, Columbus said to de la Cosa, "Ask him what he wants,"

The Indian translator spoke to de la Cosa, his face filled with surprise. De la Cosa turned to Columbus. "Admiral, this young boy wants to go with you to Castile. He wants to be baptized!"

Columbus approached the youth and with a paternal voice said, "We welcome you to our faith."

"Translate those words to him," he said to de la Cosa.

Many canoes suddenly appeared with the boy's relatives, tearfully begging him to return to his village, but the boy hid from them and remained on the *Niña*.

Columbus reached out to the youth, patting him on the head with wonder. "I want him to be treated with kindness."

De la Cosa nodded.

By Friday May 9, the ships sailed along the shore, but the weather turned sour with strong gales. Progress was slow, and they lay close to shore. On Tuesday May 13, with the sea calm, Columbus decided to return to Juana. The ships sailed for six hundred leagues along the southern coast to round a small cape, and he reluctantly and sadly had to admit that Juana was truly an island and not the mainland of Cipangu.

70

Dilemma

FOR MORE THAN A YEAR, Isabella had waited for a miracle that would bring answers to many burning questions. Her dual identity of growing up Catholic yet born of a Jewish mother had opened a door into a world full of desires, fears, and dilemmas. The question of Miguel's whereabouts—of whether he was still alive or dead—hadn't been answered. Nor did it seem it ever would be. She had to accept the awful truth that she had lost him forever. Now she needed to turn to her young son and protect him.

With new political developments unfolding every month in Sintra, she was forced to confront the reality of their situation. Should she leave Portugal or risk being stripped of home, wealth, and security? But what better place could she call home? Spain was closed to her unless she returned to the old Christian faith. She had already paid the price of losing the only father she ever had.

On a more positive note, her situation with Avram improved each day. She spoke to him with ease and no avoidance on her part. He approached her with an apparent wish to serve and attend to her needs. He had doubled his efforts with the hired help, making sure they were taken care of in their cabins and seeing to their well-being. Isabella considered him part of her small family and her cousin by marriage to Miguel.

"Daydreaming again, Bella?" Ana's amused voice pulled her out of her thoughts.

"I was just thinking about Salvadore," Isabella said quickly. She became absorbed with the challah dough she was kneading.

Ana took a cup of flour and poured it into a bowl with salt water and mixed it vigorously with the wooden spoon. "What about Salvadore?" she asked.

Isabella didn't reply and fell into silence.

Ana raised her eyes from stirring the dough. She added more flour and asked, "Well? What about the boy?"

"I'm worried about him growing up in these troubling times."

"I understand your concern. We have to come to grip with our situation."

Isabella stopped her work, then flung a small piece of dough on the table. "I know what the authorities have for us—more of the same prejudiced hate!"

Ana listened to Isabella's outburst, folding the firming dough. "You know that if you go back to Spain, you'll always be hounded as a Jew or Converso. For Avram and me, we have no choice but to accept our fate and leave. We both decided not to convert. You have a choice. Go back and be a new Christian."

Isabella jerked her head back in surprise. "How can you suggest such a thing!" Her voice rose. "I can never go back again. I made my choice when I married Miguel and returned to my ancestors' religion. I will never go back to a religion that endorses torture and death."

Ana smiled at her. "I never expected any less of you." Then she said with a grave voice, "You must therefore decide when to leave Portugal."

"We will all leave this land I had called home. The question is, where will we go?"

"Some Jews at the market confided that many already left for El Levante and Turquía."

"I'm sure we can find safe passage to Turquía," said Isabella. "We have a ship. We can sail anywhere we please."

"*Mi querida* Bella, Not all countries will welcome us."

"I don't know," Isabella said hesitantly. "I'll ask Avram for his advice."

71

Mirage

ALI, NOW CALLED HIS BY chosen name, José Tavares Sílva, had become integrated into the Portuguese ship. The vessel he sailed on was christened *Esperança*, giving him cause to hope for his own freedom. But a nagging thought troubled him enough to distract him from his chores: What was his true name? If the captain's name Da Costa made him flinch, might his name be Da Costa as well?

"José! Get back to work!" The voice of his master, Martinho, startled him.

"Aye, aye, master," he said, plunging back into his tasks.

"José?"

He looked up from coiling ropes. "Yes, master?"

"When I called your name before, you didn't reply."

Ali could see into Martinho's squinting and narrowed eyes. "I was daydreaming. That's all."

"You never speak of your family or your town? Why?"

His body suddenly became hot, and his heart began to race. "I . . . don't talk much because I'm an orphan."

"But someone raised you, didn't they?"

This time Martinho's voice became insistent, demanding an answer. He needed to silence his master's suspicions. He had to think of something quick.

"I had no parents at all. The orphanage gave me to a couple that worked me to the bone. They were mean and starved me." He glanced at Martinho and saw a shade of pity in his eyes, or perhaps Ali saw only what he expected to.

"But then your name, Da Sílva—was that your true name?"

"No, it was the name of the people who took me in."

Appeased now, Martinho turned around and walked away when captain Da Costa hailed Ali to his cabin.

As he climbed the few steps to the upper deck, Ali's pernicious worries began again. *What could he want from me? Were my lies discovered?*

"Come in, come in, José." The captain stood ceremoniously at the door, inviting him into the cabin.

Ali tried to quell the turmoil inside of him by removing and twirling his cap.

"Sit down, José. I want to ask you a few questions."

Ali sat hesitantly, still twirling his cap.

"I want to ask you," the captain began, "how big was the pirate ship you were on? How many men sailed on her? And how many cannons did they have?"

"Captain, I served the pirate captain and cared for his meals and personal dress. I wasn't authorized to dwell on deck for very long. The hold, the stern, and belowdecks were forbidden to me."

"Surely you must have seen the covered cannons and could count them with your eyes?"

"I'm not sure, but there must've been at least six cannons. Two at port and four at starboard."

The captain's face lit up with satisfaction, but he didn't seem convinced that Ali had been kept out of certain areas. "From what you've told me, they kept you as servant." He looked to see if Ali agreed, which he did. "Why didn't they sell you at the nearest port?"

"I'm just as baffled as you are, Captain. The pirates traded slaves from port to port. Yet I was spared. Perhaps as a Portuguese white man they hoped to get more for me?" Ali kept silent about his discovery in the pirate's cabin—the documents and charts with trading information.

"It's all very puzzling," the captain said.

Ali kept quiet.

"All right. You may return to your chores."

"Captain? When does the *Esperança* expect to return to Portugal?"

"I can't give an answer right now. We're picking up slaves at several more ports along the coast. I'd say in four months."

Ali squashed the moan that almost escaped him. His mind now raced with the burning thought that he had to get to Portugal in a hurry. Why, he couldn't grasp. He had the foreboding thought that calamity might strike if he didn't return to Portugal soon.

72

Return to Juana

THE SAILS BLEW GENTLY ON the *San Juan* and *La Cardera*, and on Columbus's flagship, the *Niña*, as he stood on deck, stymied by a fruitless search. They had covered many leagues between Juana to Jamaica and discovered that Juana was a true island and not the mainland as he had obstinately insisted to his men. He felt bitterly disappointed that gold had eluded them on Jamaica. The Indian translator talked to the natives, who confirmed that gold didn't exist on Jamaica. With the little gold he had found so far, Spain would curtail future voyages, and perhaps his reward and pay.

The ships sailed around a jutting cape he called Cape Santa Cruz, with the loveliest shorelines and abounding with green trees, teal waters, and many bright red long-legged and long-necked cranes nesting near shallow water. They also found many turtles laying their eggs on the beach, and crows similar to those in Spain flew high above their heads. Many small birds enchanted them with their tweeting, heightening the sense that they had found paradise. Columbus was so taken by the sight he called all the islands El Jardín de la Reina, befitting the queen's gardens in Granada's palace.

"Ask the Indian translator how many of those islands are as beautiful as this cape."

De la Cosa turned to the Taíno Indian, and by sign gestures he made an arc with his arm. *"¿Dónde están las islas más hermosas?"*

At this the Taíno translator shook his head.

De la Cosa repeated the question, and the Indian replied, *"Cairi Caico."*

"He says, Admiral, that many beautiful small islands exist far away."

"Then let us sail further west-southwest!" Columbus ordered.

As the ships sailed that day, they counted at least seventy-five more islands between Juana and Jamaica in the Caribbean Sea. The sea had turned choppy, and mist rose on the water, limiting visibility. Columbus feared grazing dangerous shoals with unseen rocky protrusions below the surface that might crack the keels or dash holes in the hulls. Adding to the men's fears, thunder and lightning swept upon them from the east.

Columbus yelled the order, "We must strike all sails!"

After much work heaving and furling sails, the men expected a deluge to fall from the sky, but by evening the squall had diminished to light rain and weak winds.

On the following day, they came upon a large island Columbus called Santa Marta. A party of men landed on shore and found the village abandoned and the Indians gone. The huts were empty except for a few dogs lying peacefully on the hard-beaten floors.

"Let's get back to the ships," Columbus said.

The ships continued sailing northeast among numerous islands populated by red cranes and many diverse birds, including parrots of bright-red, yellow, and royal-blue plumage. As they approached the coast of Juana, sea turtles covered the waters. The sailors caught several of them to be roasted for the night meal. The ships sailed on through passages becoming narrower as they negotiated a sea covered with abundant weeds. Several times his men became frightened when the keels scraped unseen shoals.

The Indian translator told Columbus that the sea was full of many—innumerable—islands, forming an archipelago off Juana. Most were heavily wooded, while some were mere flat sandy beaches devoid of mountains and trees. By evening the men had counted one hundred and fifty islands.

Between the islands, the sea held dangerous shoals and reefs, and the ships had to maneuver carefully through narrow channels.

While navigating one channel they encountered three Indians fishing near the shore. Columbus hailed them to canoe to the ship and board. They calmly approached the *Niña* and came on board. Columbus gave them some trinkets, and the Indians reciprocated with nets and fishhooks made of bones.

"Admiral, we're running low on water," de la Cosa said.

"We'll stop at the nearest island south of Juana."

The three ships continued their exploration along the western coast until they came to an island fifty kilometers south of Juana. The small island measured about thirty leagues in circumference, and the men rowed ashore to search for wood and fresh water. Upon landing on the black sand beach, Columbus named the island San Juan Evangelista. The island was covered in pine trees, and hundreds of parrots abounded everywhere, creating a cacophony of high-pitched sounds unfamiliar to the men's ears.

They sailed further northwest, passing many smaller islands, when the sea turned deep green, with pockets of pure white at intervals.

"We may be coming upon shoals," de la Cosa advised Columbus.

"Keep on sailing for five more leagues," Columbus said.

They continued until the sea became the color of milk. The sounding plummet went down and measured two fathoms deep by the knots, with no sediment in the concave bell. Columbus was puzzled, as were his men, until after another four leagues the sea turned deep black. Now he could read fear in his men's eyes. But the ships continued without incident until they reached the far reaches of Juana's southwestern coast.

The ships sailed on, and Columbus felt the weight of navigation taking a toll on his health. His bones ached, and he lacked restful sleep. Furthermore, provisions were dwindling on all three ships. He thought at that moment that if he'd had ample food provisions, he might have gone back to Spain. The colonies were well manned by Ojeda, Margarite, and the six hundred men distributed among Isabela and Fort Santo Tomás. They would see to it that all ran smoothly. He had trust in his men to build the towns and search for gold. But no sooner had these tempting thoughts occurred to him that he castigated himself. His presence and leadership were needed on Española, judging by his men's greediness for women and gold. Further hostilities between the Spaniards and the Indians were ill advised and to be avoided at all costs. It was now the end of July, and he had best return.

He gave the order: "Make sail back to Jamaica. From there we'll sail for Española."

He then sat down to write a few lines in his short journal.

June 30: My men have been fed on rotten biscuits with little wine to nourish them. I humbly hope that Their Majesties will speed supplies to the New World. Even though we've had a smooth voyage, we must return to Isabela. Dr. Chanca has been keeping a complete journal with descriptions of the islands we named in the name of Christendom and the realm. Their Highnesses now possess many vast lands that will bring gold, commerce, and souls—.

A large thud shook Columbus and catapulted all his papers and the journal off the table. He barely caught himself as his seat wavered. He ran on deck to see to the commotion, and the sight that greeted him made him tremble with shock. The *Niña* had run aground and suffered considerable damage but was still navigable. With great effort and his trust in the Lord, the ship was pulled off by the prow, and dragged by *La Cardera* and *San Juan* to deeper waters. Trembling at the thought of how close they had come to being marooned without provisions, Columbus and all the men kneeled and thanked God for their salvation.

By July 31, the small fleet approached again the east coast of Jamaica, and the scented fragrance of flowers brought back memories of their first arrival on the idyllic island. The temptation to remain in Jamaica was irresistible, and Columbus thought they needed a much-desired rest. This rest stretched till August 15, when he finally gave the order to sail. From the eastern point he called El Cabo del Farol, they directed their bows toward Española.

73

A Mother's Concerns

QUEEN ISABELLA SAT WITH A burdened heart in the hall of justice, ministering to the disputes and petty grievances of her subjects. Why must men make hardships for themselves by being contrary and argumentative? If the inhabitants would go about their daily lives without incidents and fighting among each other, heaven would descend upon earth. Instead, she had to put out fires around her to appease her Spanish subjects. To add to her burden, Ferdinand hadn't returned from his Naples campaign, leaving her to shoulder the burden and govern on her own.

She let out a moan that didn't escape her spiritual advisor, Cardinal Francisco Jiménez de Cisneros.

"What ails you, my child?" Cardinal Cisneros asked. He kissed his rosary, and Isabella followed his lead by kissing hers with reverence.

"Thank you, Cardinal. Your presence near me gives me comfort."

"You know that I'll always support you in any clerical endeavors."

"Yes, and I do thank you for that too." She stopped, sighed, and then said, "As you well know, my children are my first concern after the well-being of my subjects."

"I do know the forbearance you show your subjects. Your children are lucky to have you as their mother."

"It is my children that inflict the greatest grief." She fell quiet. "My son Juan is still too young to marry, but will eventually form an alliance with Margaret of Austria."

"Then what concerns you, my queen?"

Her confessor Cisneros's smooth voice gave her comfort. She ventured to say, "As you know, it's my eldest daughter that concerns me at present."

Cardinal Cisneros gestured for her to continue.

"Isabella, Princess of Asturias, has been waiting to hear from Manuel I of Portugal."

"But that should bring you much joy."

"A wedding is by nature a joyous event, but months have passed since we've heard any news. My daughter is tired of wearing the widow's cloak."

"Is the prince not ready for his vows?" Cisneros asked.

"That isn't the reason for this silence. You see, we've stipulated the condition to the forthcoming king of Portugal that his country will have to be Christianized before my daughter joins him."

"Isn't King John II still in power?"

"He's still protecting the Jews in Portugal."

"Aha," Cisneros uttered. "Now I see the dilemma. Portugal has a sizeable population of Jews in its midst."

"Especially since those Jews are the same ones my husband and I exiled two years ago."

Cisneros nodded in silence.

"I can't in good conscience let my daughter marry into a kingdom filled with heretics. So you see, Cardinal, I have much to complain about."

"My queen, you have been a paragon of faithfulness to the church. I admire you for your zeal to the Catholic dogma."

Queen Isabella was about to dismiss the cardinal's praise of her, when he continued. "I'll support you in any effort to rid your daughter's path of heretics."

Queen Isabella smiled with relief to have a friend in the cardinal. "I thank you, dear cardinal, and so will my husband when he learns of your support."

Cardinal Cisneros waved his hand.

"You have supported my family and my realm with your piety. You have been my confidant as well, since my dear friend Fernando Núñez Coronel left us to be with his maker." Queen Isabella's eyes held sadness.

Cardinal Cisneros crossed himself; Isabella did the same. "I know he was a great comfort to you and the realm in his wisdom. His name will be remembered for many generations to come. I'll remember him in my prayers."

Isabella nodded approval at the cardinal's statement. Then she returned to matters of state. "I will conduct the business of the hour now."

Cardinal Cisneros kissed her ring, then left the empty hall for the antechamber, which was populated with many subjects and claimants bringing their complaints and lawsuits.

"Let the first claimant enter," Queen Isabella said.

74

Harvest

THE HARVEST SEASON BEGAN WITH farmhands begging for work. Avram supervised the hiring and placement of seasonal workers in various parts of the vineyards and groves and made sure they had daily food provisions. Isabella had delegated all farming responsibilities to him, and he saw very little of her during his workday.

Juanita brought Avram and the workers breakfast from the house: black bread, scallions, boiled eggs, and cheese with lots of hibiscus drink. The second meal of beans and rice with codfish cakes was served to the men in the evening near their cabins. The workers were well fed and supplied with plenty of work and a pay of four cruzados per month. Many times Avram had to refuse hiring excess workers who had heard of the estate's good pay and working conditions.

As he supervised the workers and rows in the vineyard, his thoughts went to Isabella. She seemed to have made peace with the fact that Miguel would never be found. Avram fought conflicting feelings about his cousin's death, hoping that perhaps Isabella would look upon him as a suitor. At first she had put a distance between them by ignoring him, not communicating, and refusing to share in the events of their lives with him. Worst of all, forcing a kiss on her had alienated her. But now, his luck had turned.

Isabella's stance toward him had mollified, her voice softened when she spoke to him, and he'd caught her taking furtive glances at him.

"Avram! Avram!" Isabella's voice startled him as if she had materialized from his thoughts. He looked up to see her carrying the breakfast basket, fighting its weight. He ran to meet her and grabbed the food supplies from her hands.

"This is too heavy, Isabella. I expected Juanita to show up. But I'm glad to see you."

She lowered her head, avoiding looking at him. He hoped for a moment that her heart beat fast in synchronicity with his own.

"Juanita was unavailable, and Ana is too tired to carry it. So I came instead."

He observed her face, but couldn't read any hint of affection in her eyes. She was as mysterious as a sphinx.

She then asked in a level voice, "How is the harvest going?"

"Let me show you," Avram said.

They walked into the vineyard, between rows of heavy grapes ready to be picked. Isabella stopped to taste one of the black muscats and delighted in its taste. "I think these are ready for jam. Ana will be pleased."

"This loose, sandy soil helps the taste. In eighteen months these grapes will rival the Colares or Porto region."

Isabella seemed pleased with his statement. "Thanks to you, Avram, we have a good crop."

"Isabella?"

"Yes, Avram?"

"Have you given any thought to leaving?"

"Yes. I have."

"And?"

"We were ordered to report to the authorities in Lisbon. They've given us one year to complete our departure. I intend to use every bit of it, then leave on the last day."

"But where will you go?"

Isabella hesitated at first. She then said, "I spoke to Ana about this. She suggested Venezia or Naples. But I prefer going to Turquía." She took one look at him and quickly added, "Of course, you'll travel with us."

Avram could barely keep his joy and happiness from showing.

75

Perilous Outcome

THE *ESPERANÇA* CARAVEL CALLED AT more ports along the northern shore of Serra Leão, trading in slaves brought from the interior and held in barracoons until loaded on board. When the ship landed at port, a brisk exchange took place, wherein silver coins were paid for older slaves and gold coins went to the trader who had young slaves in their prime.

At one such port, Ali stood on deck watching Captain Da Costa supervising the exchange taking place on the dock. Since Ali was a former slave, the port was forbidden to him.

"Make sure to stay off the gangplank, José," Martinho, his master, reminded him. "I'll administer the flogging myself if you dare set foot in port or run away!"

Blood rose to his face. "But, master, I'm no longer a slave. Besides, why would I want to leave ship?" Ali faced him. "This ship is taking me back home."

A scowl appeared on Martinho's face, which surprised Ali. He scratched his neck. *Why are they watching me? Don't they believe me to be a Portuguese man just like them?*

"José!" Martinho yelled at him. "Get to work! See that each slave is securely chained below deck."

Ali followed the rows of African slaves as they descended into the hold. They were thin and malnourished, their ribs poking through soiled linen shirts. Their eyes held a glazed look. Beneath their expressions, he sensed fear resided in their eyes—the same fear he himself had felt each time he was chained.

"Move along, move," he urged as each one descended the rope ladder into the bowels of the cavernous hold. One of the last slaves to descend was a young lad with penetrating eyes that he focused on Ali. In them Ali thought he saw a muted message: *save me*! This look deepened Ali's conflicted feelings of pity toward him. There wasn't much he could do to save this boy.

"Sit, sit!" he told the young slave, then turned and ran up the ladder.

"Did you check their chains?" Martinho's voice stopped him mid-climb as his head appeared above the hold.

Ali made an about-turn. "I'll double check them!" he yelled as he descended back into the hold. *That was a close call!* If Martinho had discovered he hadn't secured their shackles, he'd be marked for flogging. As he went around pulling on each chain, the lad's eyes followed him. When done, Ali scrambled up the rungs and took a long breath of fresh air on deck before closing the heavy hatch.

76

Return to Española

THE VOYAGE WAS ROUGH, WITH many gales coming down from the Windward Passage, during which Columbus lost sight of the other two ships. Somehow with the *Niña* being a faster ship than the other two, he had distanced himself from his party. On August 20, ten leagues from Cabo del Farol, Columbus set his eyes on Española. He spotted its western end, a cape he named Cabo San Miguel. Immediately, he sent men ashore to climb a mountain to look for the two ships in the distance. No fires or sightings of the ships were signaled back to the *Niña*. On August 23, a cacique came on board, addressing Columbus as admiral. Much to the admiral's surprise, this cacique knew a few words of Spanish. Columbus was now sure they were on Española.

Two days later, they still awaited the lost ships. Before leaving the cape, his men spotted seals sleeping on the beach and killed six of them, as well as many pigeons nesting nearby, and turned them over to the cook. Four days later, to Columbus's great relief, the lost ships were sighted.

All three ships now headed west from the southern coast of Española to a small island twelve leagues away that Columbus called Beata. The island seemed small with jagged rocks, mangrove swamps, and forests, and was inhabited by Taínos, so they sailed back to the coast of Española.

From the ship they sighted plains on the heavily populated southern coast of Española, and an elongated lake that could be seen at a great distance. Many canoes rowed toward the ships and communicated that Christians from Isabela were in their village. Columbus greatly rejoiced at the news.

The ships sailed further along the southern coast, then dispatched a boat with ten men to alert the settlements of Santo Tomás and Isabela that they had returned safely from their voyage. Before the men even landed, they were attacked by Indians shooting arrows. From his vantage point on the ship, Columbus saw the natives waving ropes in their hands, signaling that Columbus's men would be tied up. Columbus sent more men and boats ashore, which forced the Indians to drop their bows and arrows and come speak to the Spaniards. Bread and water were brought from the natives. His men accepted the food supplies, and they sailed on.

Suddenly his men sighted a large fish as big as a whale swimming near shore. The fish had a hard back like the shell of a turtle, with a sizable head.

They encountered flocks of many varieties of birds flying and gathering on the island, alerting Columbus that a storm was brewing.

The ships sought refuge on September 15 on an island lying off the eastern coast of Española. The Indian on board called it Adamaney in his tongue.

The storm unleashed its fury upon them. When it calmed, the moon came out and was then eclipsed, which brought great distress to his men.

"We're done for! How can we navigate in darkness?" his men moaned.

"Stop your whining!" Columbus bellowed. "You're as bad as scared women, the lot of you!"

The men fell silent. At the moon's reappearance, they began to laugh at their lack of courage.

Columbus took measurements and discovered a distance of five hours and twenty-four minutes on the quadrant between their position and Cadiz in Spain. By September 24, the ships sailed east to another island Columbus called Isla Mona. They had now been away from Isabela for several months, and chronic fatigue induced Columbus to speed to the colony with haste. He was also weary of jotting down all the points of exploration and relegated the complete task to Dr. Chanca and João.

The demands of navigation; a poor diet; and his old, tired bones made Columbus gravely ill. A high fever took hold of him, and Dr. Chanca and de la Cosa urged the crews to speed to Isabela. On the journey, Columbus lay sweating profusely and suffered a loss of memory and sight. On September 29, the ships dropped their anchors offshore Isabela, and Dr. Chanca and the Indian with the herbal remedies cared for the admiral.

77

The Decision to Leave

A FLURRY OF ACTIVITY HAD taken hold of Isabella as she moved about the house, giving orders to Juanita and Raquela and slamming doors in her flight to the fields. Then she returned without any sort of purpose to justify her hectic pace. She felt Ana's eyes following her while she crossed the kitchen to the alcove where her desk was. Without much ado, she went through her books, adding columns of numbers, then closed the books as fast as she had opened them. Then she looked around for something else to do. From the corner of her eye, she saw Ana approach her desk and tried to ignore her.

"Isabella?" Ana waited patiently to be acknowledged.

Isabella replied without lifting her eyes. "Yes?"

"What's going on? You're moving so fast I can barely follow you with my eyes."

"I know you've been watching me," Isabella said. She looked at Ana and waited for her to comment.

But Ana stayed mute, shaking her head.

"What is it, Ana? Have I done something to shock or insult you?"

Ana said, "It isn't that. You're behaving oddly. Has something happen between you and Avram?"

Isabella saw a worried look on Ana's face. "It isn't anything like that. As a matter of fact, I've gone out of my way to be polite to him. All is well between us."

Ana let out a sigh. "That's good. I was worried about it."

"Look, Ana." Isabella met her eyes. "I'm treating Avram with respect and friendliness. And in no way differently than I treat everyone else in this household."

"But Avram *is* different. Isn't he?" Ana replied with insistent eyes, trying to penetrate her thoughts.

"Yes. He is." Then, for no reason whatsoever, the turmoil that Isabella was trying hard to push down erupted. She broke down crying with an intensity that surprised her. Tears streamed freely down her face, and she couldn't stop them.

"Now, now," Ana said in a soothing tone. "I know what's troubling you. It's Miguel, isn't it?" She came close to Isabella and held her in her strong arms. "Perhaps Avram is right. Pursuing this 'White Ali' lead of Sekou's was a false trail from the mind of an old man. It will lead you nowhere."

At the sound of those words, Isabella's anguish and pain surfaced again, and cries of deep grief engulfed her body until she shook with sharp emotion she couldn't control. "I'll ne . . . ver . . . see him again. Never." She wiped at the torrent of tears streaming from her eyes with the back of her hand.

Ana let go of Isabella, pulled a cloth from her pocket, and wiped her tears as a mother would her child. "You know that Miguel's memory will always be with you. He wouldn't want you to be sad and unhappy. He'd want you to live your life, as well as make your son happy. A sad mother makes a sad child." Ana looked into Isabella's face for any sign of acceptance. "Make peace with your soul, my child."

Isabella calmed down somewhat, and her thoughts slowly regained clearer and sharper focus. She grabbed the cloth from Ana's hand and wiped her face again, blew her nose, and tucked the cloth in her pocket. She forced a fleeting smile. "I'll have it washed, then get it back to you."

Ana smiled at her.

"Ana," Isabella said with gravity, "we must put our plans into action."

"What plans are you talking about?"

Ana, too, seemed to push away the realization that soon they would have to leave. It was up to Isabella to make the final decision and tear everyone in this household away from their cherished home.

"Yes. We have to prepare to leave." Ana bent her head with resignation, then nodded.

It was now Isabella's turn to comfort her. "We still have a number of months to put everything in order, but we can begin now." She put her hand on Ana's shoulder and said, "We will find a new haven and settle down in a better land."

Ana had tears in her eyes.

78

A Prison without Bars

ALI WALKED THE DECKS OF the *Esperança* with a feverish pace. He had been on the ship for several months and felt like a lion pacing his cage. The slave cargo had been delivered at the next port, a new contingent had been loaded again into the hold, and Captain Da Costa once again bargained prices with slave traders. Ali couldn't fathom why a Portuguese captain lowered himself to profit from slave trading from port to port. So far they had covered many points along the shores of West Africa, where forts and holding pens dotted the cliffs and landscape. He had, naively, believed the captain's promise that once the run ended, they would return to Portugal. But each time they delivered a shipment, the vessel set sail for another delivery along the coast.

"José!"

Ali jumped at the sound of his fake name.

"What did I tell you about wasting time?" Martinho's voice sounded ferocious.

"I'm sorry, master. I'm going as fast as I can."

"You weren't working at all, but dreaming again!"

"I wasn't aware," Ali said, which was true in part. He did dream most of the time now—about escaping.

"Go back down into the hold and bring the barrels up like I told you!" Martinho was still fuming.

Ali hurried to the hold to retrieve those barrels. Deep in the dark cavernous storage, he squinted at the supplies against the wall and found what he was looking for: wine barrels propped in a row, one on top of another. He dislodged one of them and rolled it down. It was heavy, filled with the red liquid to quench his captain's thirst. *Why would he need so much wine?*

Holding on to the heavy barrel, he supported its weight and slid it gently so that it wouldn't crash on the hold's floorboards. His muscles taut, he succeeded in setting it down and began to roll it toward the opening of the hold.

"Send down the net!" he yelled to Martinho waiting above.

The net was lowered, and he pushed the oak barrel into the waiting rope. He repeated the procedure twice. When secured, he pulled on the netting. "Go ahead!" He followed the barrels with his eyes, then grabbing the rope ladder, lifted himself out of the hold.

He let a sigh of relief for the job accomplished.

"Now bring one barrel to Captain Da Costa." Martinho's voice was calm and smooth.

Ali rolled the barrel along the deck while the crew watched him with smiles on their faces.

"Come on, lazy bones!" a crewman shouted at him.

"Lazy yourself!" Ali murmured between his teeth. He lifted the barrel up one deck to the captain's quarter. Out of breath, he knocked on the door.

"Come in!" Da Costa said.

"Where do you want it, Captain?"

"Just put it against the wall, or that corner." Da Costa pointed toward the stern window.

Ali went to prop the barrel next to the window, when he noticed a ship sailing astern. A black flag flew high on the mast with crossed bones and a skull.

He turned to the captain and yelled, "Pirates, Captain!"

Da Costa didn't flinch. "Well, our guests are here." A long laugh followed. The captain grinned with a satisfied demeanor.

More slave trading, Ali thought, then stepped out on deck. His eyes glued on the pirate ship, he recognized the caravel. Aruj the pirate! What the devil?

He waited no longer. Making a dash for the hold, he opened the heavy hatch, jumped on the first rung of the rope ladder then closed the hatch above his head. He descended into the hold, and weary eyes shining in the semidarkness raised to him in surprise. The shackled slaves all stared at him. Ali sneaked behind the rows of crates and bales against the walls and found a small corner between two stacks of cargo. There he waited, his head a jumble of mixed thoughts. If the pirates discovered him, he wouldn't just be flogged; he'd be beheaded or quartered.

After an interminable time, during which Ali hoped his absence wouldn't be discovered, he breathed a sigh of relief. Once again, he yearned for that elusive freedom that slipped away from him year after year.

He heard a commotion above, with loud voices and scurrying feet on deck. The pattering sounds increased, and the overhead hatch slid open with a squeal. The voices now came nearer, and several lanterns gleamed above the slaves sitting in the center. Sailors checked the faces and shackled bodies. Ali crouched into a fetal position, making himself smaller and inconspicuous.

Lantern lights suddenly flooded his eyes.

"I found him!" Ali recognized Martinho's gloating voice. The master had an ugly flash in his eyes and a victorious smile on his lips. "He's hiding like a woman!" Martinho punched and hit him on the head with the flat side of his *kilij* scimitar.

The blows stunned Ali for a short moment. He then cried in agony, "Why? Why are you treating me like an animal?"

"Because you're an animal and a disgusting slave," Martinho yelled at him.

"Why do you hate me?" Ali shot back.

Martinho was about to strike him again, when the sailor behind him cautioned, "Go easy, master. Aruj doesn't want his merchandise damaged."

Martinho relented. "Take him on deck."

His hands tied, Ali was dragged up the ladder, then through the decks to Captain Da Costa's cabin. When pushed through the door, his heart sank. Aruj was seated on one of the chairs facing Da Costa. Aruj took one look at him and said with a contented smile, "There's my white Ali. My escaped slave."

Da Costa came close and punched Ali's nose. Ali cringed with pain.

"You lied to me! You're no Portuguese."

"But I am!" Ali shot back in anger. "I lived in Portugal for one year!" He stood stunned for a minute. *Where did this information come from?*

Da Costa turned to Aruj. "He's all yours."

Aruj signaled to one of his pirates, and a money purse changed hands. Da Costa bowed with contentment but didn't check inside the purse.

"Bring him!" Aruj ordered.

Cuffed, Ali was dragged from the *Esperança* caravel to the pirate ship's deck.

Aruj said to one of his men, "Don't hit him or flog him yet. I'll deal with him later."

Thrown into the pirate's hold, Ali sat chained amid the cargo in a stupefied and forlorn state. In his gut, wrenching pain tore at him as if the master had already impaled him. He might as well make it easier and finish the job for the pirates by jumping ship and drowning at the first opportunity.

Memories tore a hole into his mind and flooded him. He would never again see the beautiful woman calling him. Calling him? But of course! She had called him Miguel. Miguel was his true name!

And hers was Isabella.

79

Back to Base

COLUMBUS WAS CARRIED ON A plank board as his men disembarked from the *Niña*. His forehead burned and he stirred, moaning with fever. In his foggy awareness he felt a deep sense of defeat. True, he had conquered more islands for the Crown and added more exploits to his fame, but gold in large quantity remained elusive. If gold in great deposits wasn't found soon on Española, he might as well die now from his fever rather than face the monarchs back in Spain. He had but a few months to motivate and energize his men to put the Indians to work in amassing substantial gold. Only then could he return to Spain with the honors due him.

"Put him down gently, gently, I say!" Ojeda's voice came to Columbus's ears. With effort, he lifted himself on his elbows to take in a view of where he was.

"Whoa! Easy, Admiral. Everyone here is caring for you. Please lie down and leave everything to me."

Columbus stared at Ojeda fussing around him and lambasted him. "Stop treating me like a woman. I must get up!"

"Please, please, Admiral. You must get better first," Ojeda begged him.

"Yes, Admiral. You must allow us to treat you. You have a nasty fever that needs to be looked after." This was Dr. Chanca trying to steady him.

He watched the physician prepare a diluted powder in water for him that he slipped between his lips. Some of the liquid dribbled on Columbus's chin, reigniting his impatience.

"Enough!" he said. He wiped his chin and said to Ojeda, "Call the council to my tent."

Ojeda hesitated for a moment, but Dr. Chanca nodded for him to carry out the order.

Within minutes, Columbus's brother, Don Diego, and the men he placed in charge—Pedro Fernández Coronel, Fray Buil, Alonso Sánchez de Carvajal, and Juan de Luján—appeared by his bedside. Columbus sat up in bed with Dr. Chanca's help, then pushed the doctor's hands away from arranging the blanket around him.

Columbus faced his makeshift assembly and demanded, "I want a detailed account of everything that happened while I was gone."

They all looked at each other, deciding who was to begin. Then Diego spoke, "I bring good tidings to you, Cristoforo. Our brother Bartholomew is here on the island."

Columbus felt joy in his heart. He opened his mouth to say something but no sounds came out, his surprise overwhelming him. He then regained his power of speech. "I'm overjoyed! I haven't seen him in years. Where is he?"

"He was sent inland to see the mines for himself, but will return shortly," said Diego.

Disappointed to have missed Bartholomew, Columbus asked the question burning on his lips. "Give me an account of the Santo Tomás mines in the Cibao."

Ojeda had a serious look on his face when he spoke. "Admiral, we've made much progress building the mines and hiring the Indians to work. The gold is still in its initial stage in mining. We hope to finish the mill first, then begin the gold operations soon."

"You mean there's nothing to show for it yet?" Columbus asked.

"I didn't say that," Ojeda said. He glanced at the council, each one nodding, including Diego. "What I'm saying is gold hasn't been produced in bulk yet."

"What do you mean, Ojeda?"

"We're having a little trouble with the Indians. They're not used to working productively. They don't show up for work, they slack off on the job—talking and laughing—and they don't understand teamwork."

Columbus mulled over Ojeda's words, then said, "What you're saying is that they're lazy. Have you bribed them with trinkets?"

"Yes, we did, Admiral. They received these free when we first came upon them. They even took some of our personal belongings, thinking they were free. We had to beat them to retrieve those items."

A silence fell over the small space where they congregated. Columbus looked at each one of his men, then asked, "There is something else, isn't there?"

Ojeda spoke first. "We had trouble with the cacique, Caonabó. You remember, Admiral, that Cacique Guacanagarí accused Caonabó of the destruction of the fort at La Navidad?"

De Luján added, "Yes, Admiral. He also attempted the assault on Fort Santo Tomás just before you left for Juana."

"Of course I remember. I sent you with Margarite and one hundred men, horses, and arms to fight him!"

"We arrived just in time to fight and repel them," Ojeda affirmed. "We did catch Caonabó's relative, another cacique, with two other men accused of stealing."

"Well done, men!" Columbus was certainly pleased with Ojeda's leadership of Fort Santo Tomás. "Where are these men now?"

"They're awaiting execution, Admiral. We thought it best for you to administer justice," Ojeda said. "I suggest beheading."

Pallor showed on Fray Buil's face. He raised his hand to stop the discussion. "Admiral. Will this be necessary?"

Columbus pondered Fray Buil's question and the punishment awaiting the cacique chief and his thieves. He then shook his head. "I will let this matter wait for now. I'm feeling better with Dr. Chanca's care and badly need a rest. Awaken me if Bartholomew arrives this afternoon."

As soon as the men vacated his hut, Columbus fell into a deep and restful sleep, the Indian potion having a positive effect on his fever.

80

Decisions and Acceptance

A FEVERISH PACE LED BY Ana overtook the whole household. She moved about, instructing Juanita and Raquela to inventory the contents of all cupboards in the house. Next, she listed all their wine bottles and jam pots in the cellar and gave that inventory to Isabella. Isabella took a cursory look at the items and felt a curtain had fallen before her eyes. She was faced with the reality that their lives in Portugal were coming to an end. Another life would begin, but where? A messenger had been sent to the Jewish communities in Istanbul with no reply so far. A request for asylum reached Abravanel's home in Naples, but he couldn't be located since he was on a voyage to Sicily.

"That's that!" Ana voiced her displeasure. "Our lives are weighing in the balance, and we can't find asylum anywhere!"

"But, Ana," Isabella intervened. "We can't rely on Isaac Abravanel for our livelihood any longer, nor on anyone else, for that matter. Besides, according to the letter we received, he is only temporarily unavailable. The Abravanel family fled to Sicily with the king of Naples because the king of France has just invaded Naples."

"That's what I would expect from my cousin. Always gallivanting here and there helping royalty. What about us, his brothers and sisters?"

Isabella was surprised to hear Ana's displeasure. "Ana, you know that's unfair. Need I remind you how he already helped us, as well as many others? We were slaves, and he gave us shelter and fortune."

Ana lowered her head in silence. Isabella recognized that Ana must have felt mixed emotions just as she did. The feeling of abandonment, difficulty of another exile, and not knowing where they might end up created confusion. Those were powerful feelings feeding the fear of the unknown.

By now Isabella had accepted that, as a Jewess, she would have to prepare herself to flee at a moment's notice. Her life so far had been turned upside down, going from nobility to becoming a fugitive and a slave. But luckily her misfortunes had been turned around when Abravanel saved them from slavery. She owed her benefactor her life and her little son's life. By now she had made her peace that Miguel might never be found, and for the sake of her son, she must live her life, wherever it might take her.

Avram dropped in from the fields to check on the household. Isabella had come to accept and appreciate that he took the time to see to their well-being. He seemed surprised to find the four women going through the entire house.

"Are we getting new furnishings?" he jested.

"No," Isabella replied. "I wanted to take stock of all unnecessary items we can't take along."

A shadow fell across Avram's face. He too had pushed away the thought of their departure. "I understand," he said. "But why now? We still have many months."

"Yes, we do," Isabella replied. "However, this way, if we must flee suddenly, we'll leave nothing important behind."

"Isabella, I must speak with you alone," Avram said.

From the corner of her eye Isabella saw Ana and Raquela exchange glances. Isabella fought mixed feelings. *I hope it isn't what I suspect.* "Of course, Avram. Let's go outside."

Avram followed her to the front porch, and they sat on the wooden bench. Isabella busied herself arranging and rearranging her skirt's folds. She swatted a couple of flies badgering her, tucked a strand of hair behind her ear then turned to Avram. "Yes?"

Avram coughed, moved about on his seat, and with a redness spreading across his face, said haltingly, "You know, Isabella, that we will undergo a rough voyage by the beginning of next year. That's why I thought, with all the women under one man's protection—"

Isabella raised her hand to stop him, but he continued. "All the people coming along with us—Salvadore, Ana, Juanita, Raquela and her children—must be protected."

"Yes, I know that," Isabella said with minor impatience. She wanted this awkward moment to end, while Avram was winding round and round.

"What I mean to say is, if you would care to honor me by becoming my wife, I can better protect you and your son as well as the other women."

At that moment, Isabella visualized Miguel's arms around her waist, so close she could hear his heart beating and feel his lips melting upon hers. She pushed the thought away.

"Isabella?"

She stayed silent a few moments longer. The looming thought facing her was the protection of her son and his well-being. Yet what about her own happiness? And what about Miguel? Should she give up on him too? Fate was cruel and unforgiving, but her duty to her son was foremost. She took a deep breath and turned to Avram. "I will try to be a good wife to you, Avram," was all she said as she lowered her head.

Avram put a hand on her chin to lift her face toward him. Then he grabbed her hands and kissed them. "You've made me a happy man."

"I'll go back inside now to continue our inventory," Isabella said without looking back, leaving Avram with a pleased smile on his face.

When she came back to the sitting room, all eyes were on her.

"Well?" Ana asked.

"Well, what?" Isabella didn't look back at her.

"Did he propose?" Ana pressed.

After a silence, Isabella nodded her head.

"Mazal tov!" Ana screamed with joy. Raquela and Juanita congratulated her by hugging her tightly and repeatedly.

She tried to escape the effusions of joy, her heart dead, unfeeling, and unresponsive. "Please, please, girls, you're suffocating me."

"All right everyone. We've got work to do!" Ana ordered.

The three women went back to their work, separating glassware from clay dishes and folding linens. They organized everything for Isabella to decide what to take and what to leave behind.

Standing near the women, Isabella stared at the work in front of her while inside she felt torn asunder between her duty to her son and her loyalty to Miguel's memory. She could taste bitterness on her palate and unspeakable dread. The dread that Miguel would never hold her again in his arms, that she would never smell and feel his being, what made him special to her, or know happiness as she'd known it for such a brief time when love enveloped both of them in a tight embrace.

She lowered her head in agony and squashed a painful cry in her throat as she tried to become used to the idea that she would marry soon. Once she took that step, it would be too late to regret her decision.

81

A Last Attempt

SHACKLED IN THE HOLD, ALI talked himself little by little into believing he was Miguel. He was driven with one thought in mind: escape. How or where, he hadn't worked out yet. All he knew was if it killed him in the process, so be it. He couldn't live another moment on this ship or without finding Isabella. As his memories began to unknot and weave slowly into his present, he felt a momentous event was about to take place in his life. What was it? He had no clue.

A thought pierced his brain—he recalled that a bounty was on his head. He had seen the truth in that document he found on Aruj's table. The words appeared in his memory as if he had read them yesterday: "Find the slave Miguel for the sum of four thousand dirhams . . ." Who had placed the reward? The owner of La Mina? Someone else? If so, whom?

Miguel silently plotted ways of escaping. Throughout the day, over and over, he hatched ways to slip away from the hold. What if he used that brief moment when the meals were brought down, his hands were untied, and the guard's back turned? Couldn't he use that precise minute to hide? But a head count took place immediately after the meal and he'd be found out. He sat in the darkened hold at his wit's end.

Whenever he felt he had to relieve himself, he flung the excess chain against the wall of the hold where he sat, making a racket for all to hear. The slaves in the hold yelled at him to stop banging his chains, stating retribution would come swiftly. Sitting in their own excrement, the slaves didn't dare ask to be let out, resigned to their miserable fate. The hold's odor made him ill, and he longed to breathe fresh air.

"Stop that infernal sound, all of you!" A head appeared at the top of the opened hatch, and cold water was splashed on all sitting below.

High-pitched screams rose to the top of the hold, gaining volume, with Miguel adding his voice to theirs. "Go ahead, men! Shout at the top of your lungs!" He encouraged the chained men. "Shout: 'We want to be freed! We want to be freed!'"

He didn't know if the chained men understood his Portuguese cry, but they replied with a low chant of their own that grew in intensity. *"Tunataka kuwa huru! Tunataka kuwa huru! Tunataka kuwa huru! Tunataka kuwa huru! Tunataka kuwa huru! Tunataka kuwa huru!"*

The slaves dragged the chains linking them to one another on the plank floor, magnifying the terrible sounds rising to the deck above them.

The hatch opened again, and Miguel heard Aruj's familiar voice above his head, yelling at the sailors. "Can't you keep these dogs quiet? Tell them they'll be flogged if they don't shut up!"

"Come on men, yell louder!" Miguel exhorted them, and the chained men obliged.

"Bring the instigator up first!" Miguel heard Aruj call.

Several pirates climbed down and homed in on Miguel's corner. They unchained him and dragged him along the floor. His bare feet picked up splinters from the coarse flooring, and his toes began to bleed. The pirates dragged him up the rungs of the rope ladder and brought him on deck. They threw him down with force, and some of the pirates began to beat on him.

"Stop! Stop!" Aruj yelled at his men. "Bring him to my cabin before he's flogged!"

More dragging and shoving followed. Miguel's thoughts were muddled, but he felt victorious. If they were going to kill him, perhaps now he'd be completely free from the yoke of slavery.

When Aruj faced him in the cabin, he signaled for his men to let go of his twisted arms. Miguel stood all bloodied, facing Aruj. Aruj eyed his men, nodding them out of the cabin. The pirates hesitated, fearing for their chief, and Aruj opened the cabin door for them to leave.

Aruj walked around Miguel, then stopped to face him. "I've been patient with you. I even spared you from flogging, to see if you'd reform and stay put. Haven't I treated you with care? Eh?"

Miguel stifled the cry inside his throat and fell upon Aruj with his fists. "You call that care?" The scream escaped his lips in a fury of anger and burning thoughts of revenge. "You held me against my will, even though I told you that I'm a Portuguese man!"

Aruj fended off Miguel's blows by grabbing his hands and holding them in a vise grip. He then let go and broke up in laughter. Eventually his roaring laughter ended with a snort. He sat down panting, leaving Miguel smoldering and grinding his teeth.

Miguel came close to Aruj and confronted him. "Someone put a bounty on my head. I want to know who did. I saw the document. I'm a Portuguese man, and now I have proof!"

"What kind of proof can you give me?" Aruj laughed again, on a more sarcastic note this time. "You're called Ali, and as Ali you're an Arab."

Miguel pushed back his soiled sleeve and came closer to Aruj, who shuffled back in his chair.

"Look, look, I'm whiter than you are."

The calm look hadn't left Aruj's face. "That is no proof. Perhaps your Arab mother whored with a white man somewhere. That's why your skin is lighter."

It was too much for Miguel to bear. He drew in slow and steady breaths. His poor mother suffered torture and death to protect him and his brother José. He shuddered. José! His brother! It was all coming back to him!

He said with a suppressed calm. "My name is Miguel Costa, I'm a Portuguese man. My wife's name is Isabella."

A shadow passed over Aruj's face that he didn't conceal. He said quietly, "We'll have proof of this when the next ship crosses our path."

Miguel was confused. What did he mean by that? Why the next ship?

"In the meantime, you'll stay in my cabin." Before Miguel made a show of victory he added, "But chained, mind you. You're valuable in gold pieces. If you try to escape, I'd rather kill you and put an end to this."

Miguel nodded. He had won a first round. Convincing Aruj was no small feat, but could he trust Aruj? The next few days would tell whether he was rescued or sold again.

82

A Happy Reunion

"ADMIRAL! ADMIRAL!"

The voices woke Columbus from a deep sleep. His fever had abated during the day, but each night it had risen again. He had lain on his mattress in the cabin for three weeks with no sign of improvement. He had lost much weight and appeared like a ghost of himself, swimming in the loose sleeping gown. Dr. Chanca came on board several times daily to administer his potions, accompanied by his Indian helper. The bark powder mixed with water was forced through his lips twice a day, though he spat out most of the vile-tasting remedy.

"You won't get better, Admiral, unless you take your medicine." Dr. Chanca sounded exasperated.

"You must listen to the physician," his brother Diego warned.

"Admiral! Your brother Bartholomew has returned!" Ojeda came into his cabin shouting.

"All right, Ojeda. All right. Call him immediately to my cabin." Columbus gestured for Dr. Chanca and Diego to help him up.

Diego was smiling as he told Columbus, "Our brother has much to tell you."

With Dr. Chanca and Diego helping lift him, Columbus sat upright on his bed with much pain. His hands and joints were swollen out of proportion.

He stood on the floor of the cabin, his face flushed from the effort, feeling somewhat dizzy.

"It's all right, Admiral. It'll pass. You've been lying down for days," Dr. Chanca reassured him. "I'll be close by, belowdecks, if you need me." He then left Columbus's cabin to give him privacy.

The door flew open, and Bartholomew stood on the threshold, a large smile across his face and his arms wide open. "Cristoforo! My dear brother!"

Columbus moved unsteadily on his weak legs and enveloped his brother tightly. As he held Bartholomew, who was much shorter, he felt as if he were hugging a child.

Diego stood aside, hands hidden in his long-sleeved black priestly robe, smiling timidly at the brothers' reunion. When Bartholomew came to greet him in a tight embrace, Diego's face broke into a large smile.

"My little brother." Bartholomew slapped his back with pride. "You'll make us proud in the priesthood."

Diego flushed under the praise while trying to hide his embarrassment.

"I'm overjoyed to see you, Bartholomew," Columbus said, feeling stronger with the family reunion. "How long has it been since we parted? Years?"

"Feels like it." Bartholomew laughed with glee. "Too many years, if you ask me. It seems like yesterday when we were drawing maps in Lisbon's Customs House." He slapped Columbus on the shoulder. "I want to know everything that's happened to you: the voyage, the monarch's reception—" Bartholomew stopped abruptly. "I have news from the queen about your children," he said, smiling.

"What news?" asked Columbus.

"You must know by now that both Diego and Fernando are under the queen's wing. They're being groomed as pages for Queen Isabella's heir and son, the Infante Juan, Prince of Asturias. She also made me a *caballero*. I'm now called *Don* Bartholomew." A proud smile spread across Bartholomew's face.

Columbus grasped Bartholomew's hands and shook them. "I'm truly blessed to have a distinguished brother like you. I'm also overjoyed and blessed that my sons were well received at court." He then became serious and asked his brother, "Tell me, Bartholomew, of the trek inland."

"You mean in the Cibao region?"

Columbus nodded again. "Have you found much progress? Are the fort and mine completed? Are the Taínos falling in line with the work?"

"Whoa, whoa!" Bartholomew said with a smile. "One thing at a time." He then became serious. "First, let me tell you that I sailed back with the three caravels with the provisions and medical supplies you requested from Antonio de Torres and the queen. And I'd like to give news from home."

Columbus raised eyebrows. "You mean Spain?"

"No, I mean your ancestral home, Genoa, you fool," he said to Columbus without derision or intended insult to his big brother.

"How's everyone? Father, my little sister Bianchinetta?" Columbus asked.

"Bianchinetta is well. She has a son."

Diego kissed the cross on his rosary.

"And father?" asked Columbus.

Bartholomew kept quiet. He then said, "Our father isn't well, Cristoforo."

"What's wrong with him?"

"He's been ill for a long time."

Columbus lowered his head, slight guilt seeping through him. "You know very well that if our father had been successful in the wool trade, we'd be there alongside him to help."

"Yes, perhaps," Bartholomew acknowledged. "But then you wouldn't have discovered the New World, or earned the riches that will be yours, or had your sons so well taken care of." He shook his head. "You were meant for greatness, big brother—oh, and before I forget." Bartholomew pulled from his doublet under his mantle a folded and sealed missive that he passed into Columbus's hand.

Columbus recognized his father's seal pressed by the beloved ring he'd played with as a child. He raised inquisitive eyes to Bartholomew. He was about to break the seal, when dizziness overtook him. He had just enough time to stuff the note into his garment before his knees began to give out. He tried to sit down, his legs wobbling, but the chair was beyond his reach. Bartholomew and Diego ran to his aid and gently brought him to his bed, then saw to it that their brother lay comfortably.

Diego ran out to call Dr. Chanca from the lower deck. The physician came inside in a huff. "He's still weak, and shouldn't exert himself."

Bartholomew nodded and spoke to Columbus in a low voice. "You rest now, brother. Tomorrow, I know you'll be stronger." He signaled for his brother, Diego, to join him outside

⁓⌇⌾⌇⁓

When Dr. Chanca caught up the brothers outside the cabin, Bartholomew asked the doctor, "What's wrong with my brother?"

Dr. Chanca first shook his head, then said, "The admiral has accomplished a lengthy voyage to Juana, Jamaica, and many other islands in between. It's a lack of sleep, you know, and proper diet."

"But he seems in pain," Bartholomew insisted.

"I'm afraid he has a condition called *la gota*. It comes and goes. An inflammation of his joints." Dr. Chanca looked down at Bartholomew through his spectacles to see if he understood.

Bartholomew shook his head and asked, "But he will recover, won't he?"

"Absolutely. With much rest and a varied, healthy diet, he'll be fit in no time at all."

Bartholomew let out a sigh of relief. "That is good, because we have other fish to fry." In response to Dr. Chanca's inquisitive eyes, he hastened to add, "There's much trouble with the Indians in Cibao. Ojeda will fill you in. It's all got to do with the cacique chief imprisoned with two of his men. His people want him back."

Dr. Chanca shook his head. "May the Virgin protect us in this time of trouble."

Bartholomew and his brother both crossed themselves and said a silent prayer.

83

The Treaty of Tordesillas

ALL ATTENDEES IN THE CONSISTORY of the Sacred College of Cardinals were seated anxiously to hear Pope Alexander Borja give his sermon and news to the thirty-four priests. Strife between the members of the college had existed since the fourth century, when the priests then were mere clerics assisting the Pope. With cardinal titles, however, these clerics became a consulting body of legates and delegates with all befitting honors.

At present, rumors were spreading among the cardinals that Pope Alexander had admonished his camerlengo for lapses in his duties. The words circulated between the priests as they waited nervously in their seats.

"Cardinal Carafa and Cardinal Sforza are missing from the chamber. I wonder what it means," Cardinal de Carvajal, bishop of Cartagena, whispered to Cardinal Alessandro Farnese.

Farnese scoffed. "Perhaps, his protégé son, Cardinal Cesare Borja, has caused trouble for his father."

"You two have been deadly enemies, haven't you?" asked de Carvajal.

Before Farnese could reply, Camerlengo Carafa entered to announce Pope Alexander's entrance.

All the cardinals stood as Pope Alexander VI, Rodrigo Lanzol Borja, followed by Cardinal Sforza entered the chamber and sat down. The chairs squeaked on the parquet floor as the cardinals sat back down.

"Pope Alexander VI will conduct the meeting of the cardinals," Camerlengo Carafa announced.

"All right, all right, Camerlengo." Pope Alexander made a sweeping movement of his hand. He hated these rituals and introductions by the camerlengo, claiming they wasted his time. "What is the order of this meeting?" he asked.

"Your Eminence, we're here to discuss the next election of cardinals."

Pope Alexander waved his hand again to stop the camerlengo. "Please, Camerlengo, read this document before we proceed." Pope Alexander handed him a tightly wrapped cylindrical leather parchment.

Cardinal Carafa untied the red ribbon on the document and unrolled it. "It proclaims here . . ." He hesitated, tilting his head and the document to decipher the cursive writing. "That on 5 September, 1494, in Lisboa's archives in Portugal, said document entitled Treaty of Tordesillas is ratified and signed by all parties . . ."

A murmur followed this first paragraph of the lengthy treaty. The cardinals shifted in their chairs, the tassels swinging on the wide brims of their red galeros, knowing that a good hour would be spent listening to this important but tedious document.

" . . . that the lands lying to the east of 370 leagues from the Cape Verde islands would belong to Portugal, and the lands called Cipangu and Antillia, west of the meridian of 370 leagues, and signed by the crowns of Castile and Aragon on 7 June, 1494, in the city of Valladolid, and by Portugal 5 September, 1494 . . ."

The reading went on for another thirty minutes, then it ended with many sighs of relief from the camerlengo and the rest of the cardinals. The impatience in the hall was palpable. A reading of the newly elected cardinals was the genuinely anticipated order of business for the meeting. The cardinals and those to be promoted waited breathlessly as the camerlengo unfurled a new parchment.

"On the year of our Lord, 20 September, 1494, we proclaim Luigi d'Aragona as cardinal of Santa Maria in Cosmedin . . . and on the year of our Lord . . . we proclaim . . ."

Another hour passed while the cardinals whispered their pleasure or displeasure to find that their ally or archenemy had scored another victory. Cardinal Carafa threw a murderous look at Cardinal Sforza. The seated cardinals caught the bitter glance, and they began to whisper again.

84

The Elusive Dream

SAILING INTO AND OUT OF the many ports along the African coast became a blurred world for Miguel, who saw his greatest wish for escape become ephemeral. The entire crew had been alerted to guard against his escape, and their eyes followed his every move. The chores loaded on him were increased to keep him occupied without an idle moment. When he protested—with no ill repercussion threatened other than a beating—Aruj dismissed him. "In good time you'll be released to your new master."

This comment befuddled and confused him. *What new master*? He'd had so many that he'd forgotten the number. The only thought still whirling in his mind that brought him solace was the image of Isabella. Was she still living on the estate south of Sintra? Or had she left Ana's protective world? Thoughts and memories were revealed more and more to him each day, bringing him joy as well as sorrow. Had he lost her forever? And what about Avram? He had had feelings for Isabella since their departure from Cordova. And what had happened to José later, once under Obrigon's kind care?

"Oh!" Miguel lamented, holding his aching head between his hands. He had promised his mother that he'd care for his brother. This promise had been broken. The guilt and sorrow pervaded every pore of his body and brain. But he hadn't been defeated yet! *I'll survive to get my revenge!*

"Hey, Ali!" Mustapha's voice startled him. "Dreaming again? You'll polish the decks again for slacking off!"

Miguel turned his head toward him. "My name is Miguel, not Ali anymore." He clenched his hands on the line he was coiling and felt fury down to his bones.

Mustapha said slowly, "You call yourself whatever you want. To us you'll be Ali, a lowly slave." Mustapha smirked.

At that moment, Miguel wished he had a knife or sword to carve out that sarcastic look on Mustapha's face. Instead, he turned back to his work and let Mustapha's penetrating eyes follow his movements. *I'll get my revenge one day*!

85

Dark Clouds Above

WITH GREAT PATIENCE FROM DR. Chanca, Columbus regained his health again. He stepped out of his cabin one morning on the *Mariagalante*'s upper deck to take a whiff of fresh air, then slowly migrated down to the lower decks. As the men worked, he looked over their shoulders, to make sure they weren't dawdling—especially the young recruits who had a tendency to stop their work and banter around.

"Make sure the lines are coiled properly!" he told one of the young boys.

"Yes, Admiral," the boy replied obediently.

Columbus returned to the main deck and saw a man precariously balancing on the ratlines as an acrobat would on a rope extended between two poles. *This man is endangering his life.* His eyes still enflamed, he couldn't see clearly who it was.

"Watch out, you up there on the mast! I won't have bumbling idiots on my ship!"

"It's all right, Admiral. I'm Antonio de Torres! Remember me? The master of the *Mariagalante*," the sailor yelled down from the mast.

Columbus rubbed his eyes and looked up again. He could barely make out de Torres due to the lingering inflammation in his eyes.

Bartholomew, who was present on deck, came upon him and intervened. "You must let them do their job, Christoforo." He put his hand on Columbus's shoulder.

"I feel caged. I must disembark and see to the running of the island." Columbus burned with frustration at his immobility.

"Take your time and regain your health first," Bartholomew urged.

"I won't wait any longer." He turned and called for Pedro de Terreros, his personal steward. "Get my clothes ready. I'm going ashore!"

Bartholomew looked helpless to stop him. "Perhaps we should consult with Dr. Chanca?"

"No. He tends to me as if I were an old man."

By then Pedro had come with a long overcoat even though the weather was balmy. The trees swayed under a gentle breeze, and the sky was painted cerulean blue.

Columbus breathed a long sigh as Pedro helped him into the brownish-red overcoat. "I feel good and fit. Launch the boat!"

Within minutes Columbus found himself with two men rowing the boat and Bartholomew at his side.

"What news of Ojeda and Ginés de Gorbalán?" he asked Bartholomew.

His brother remained silent and waved a hand in front of him. "You'll have plenty of time to hear news."

"No. I want to hear it now!"

Bartholomew startled under the command. "Well, the Indians are giving us some trouble, brother. But here we are onshore."

Columbus felt fit enough to jump onto the sandy beach, and he marched to the fort with Bartholomew tagging behind. His men scraping barnacles from the bottom of two caravels lifted their heads at the sight of their commander-in-chief walking by. *"¡Buenos días, Almirante!"* the men shouted. Columbus saluted them with a smile on his face.

He said to Bartholomew. "Call Diego, Ojeda if he's here, and Ginéz de Gorbalán. Make sure to find Alonso Sanchez de Carvajal, Captain Coronel, and Juan de Luxan from the council and send them to me. Then I want to see the cacique Guacanagari immediately!"

Bartholomew left to find the men, and Columbus smiled as he regained his lost authority. *My men must know that I rule them.*

As the men began to arrive, one at a time, Columbus stayed silent. When all were present, he began to pace up and down the entrance to the small garrison built with bricks.

"I know I've been too ill to guide you. But now we must begin the work we were meant to carry out in these lands. Our most important cause is the welfare and baptism of Indians. The gold is secondary. I promised our queen that the work of the Lord would go on." He turned to Diego sitting quietly and asked, "How many men, women, and children have you baptized since I left for Juana?"

Diego remained silent. He shifted on the block of stone that served as his seat and raised his face to his older brother. "We have tried very hard to baptize them, but they fought us tooth and nail."

"Why do you think they refused the true faith?" Columbus asked, trying to restrain his voice from rising.

Sánchez de Carvajal said, "They complain all the time that we're working them too hard. That we're stealing all their food and keeping them hungry, and—"

Columbus stopped him. Anger rose to his throat, but again he controlled it. "Diego, I made you the council head of the colony, and nothing has happened while I was gone. Not an ounce of gold, or new baptized souls, or a finished mill." He turned to Ojeda and Gorbalán and faced the two standing men. "What's the story on Cacique Caonabó?"

Ojeda spoke, "He is still hiding, but—"

Gorbalán interrupted Ojeda. "His men were stealing from us. Ojeda punished some of them, but the cacique's relative is awaiting execution along with the two thieves."

"Execution?" Columbus roared, unable to control his anger now. "Who authorized an execution? Answer me?"

Both Ojeda and de Gorbalán lowered their reddened faces with confusion.

"And where is Margarite in this whole mess?" Columbus addressed them all.

The men remained silent, and Diego finally spoke. "Brother—Admiral," he said, correcting himself. "I gave Margarite special instructions not to harm the Indians but to continue exploring as you commanded him. And Fray Buil was harsh with the natives. I warned him to be gentle with them, but he disobeyed me."

"And what was Margarite's answer?"

Diego remained silent with an embarrassed look on his face. He arranged and rearranged the cuffs on his bell sleeves, then raised his head. "He took the three caravels, Admiral, and returned to Spain with Fray Buil and other renegades."

Columbus shuffled back to the chair behind him and sat down in shock. While he had been exploring the islands of Juana and Jamaica, a mutiny had taken place in Isabela! He couldn't trust these men or his own frail brother, Diego. *It is my own fault for designating him president of the council.*

"Is all this true?" he asked Bartholomew, who he thought to be levelheaded and accurate.

"It's true, Brother. I woke up one day to see the caravels missing. Thank the Lord, though, we had unloaded the food and supplies we had brought with us."

"There's another thing, Admiral," de Gorbalán said. "Some of Margarite's men were left behind, and they're roaming the island and extorting gold and precious ornaments from the Indians."

This was more than Columbus could stomach. Mutiny, theft, and complete disregard for his instructions had taken place during his search for gold. He couldn't rely on his men, nor could he punish them in front of the Indians. As admiral and chief, he would lose all authority, and the Indians wouldn't follow orders then and would become totally unruly.

"We must capture all the culprits. I want these mutineers shackled in chains and brought back to Isabela. When we catch Caonabó and his thieves, we'll send them back to Spain to be tried and executed. We'll take care of any Indian that disobeys work orders by punishing them. The same goes for the lazy Indians who don't want to work. We have much to do, men. Go and begin!"

86

Another Voyage

"WHEN CAN WE GET MARRIED, Isabella?" The question left Avram's lips almost reluctantly. He turned to face Isabella almost shyly. He feared a change of heart on her part that would leave him crushed, but still relied on her promise to marry him.

Isabella, walking alongside Avram, hurried to circumvent weeds in the vineyard's path. She then stood overlooking the vineyards from the small hill and let out an impatient sigh. He sensed she was thinking along the same vein as he; the crops planted in the springs were now ripe and ready to be picked. If they waited any longer, the new crop would overripen.

He waited for her reply, then asked again, "You do want to marry me, don't you?"

She raised her head and looked directly at him. "But of course I do. I promised, didn't I?"

Avram let a sigh of relief pass his lips.

"You do know, however," Isabella said suddenly, "that if we don't reap this season's crops, we may be in for a sorry return. With all the expenses planned for the voyage next year, we must be prudent not to overspend."

Avram was befuddled. "Why should this stop us from getting married? The workers have been hired, the merchants have placed their orders, and

Ana said we'll move the merchandise by spring of next year. I don't understand why the delay."

Isabella listened to him quietly and took her time in answering. "Because—" She stopped and said in one breath, "I plan to make one more voyage to Morocco."

"Another voyage?" Avram was completely taken by surprise.

"Yes.

"But why?"

"We can do better selling the wine to the North African market—faster and more profitable than here in Portugal."

Avram was confused. "But the voyage would be costly, when you can sell right here."

"I've made up my mind, Avram. And I want you to stay and oversee the estate and the harvest while I'm gone. I will take Sekou with me, since he knows those waters."

He struggled to change her mind. "Sekou is an old man. He knows little of sailing these seas. You will be endangering your life and his." He felt his voice being strangled by mounting desperation.

Isabella shook her head. "I cannot change my plans. The only thing I need from you is to look after Salvadore. He looks to you as a father, you know?"

The mention of being a father to Salvadore took Avram by surprise, but it pleased him. Isabella had enough trust in him to watch over her boy, soon to become his own son. But it did not explain this sudden voyage on her own.

"There's one thing I'd like you to do for me," Isabella said.

"What's that?" He began to feel frustrated, overlooked, trampled upon.

"Keep Ana in the dark about my plans to sail till the last minute."

A rash of emotions suddenly overwhelmed him. She was rejecting his help and protection by leaving him behind. He should be at ther side, in the future role he'd be playing as husband, father to Salvadore, and in charge of her affairs on the estate. He only wanted to help and feel needed and be a part of this family—to recover a semblance to the family he had lost by the death of his parents and brothers.

Why was she remaining aloof, almost as separate from him? If they were to be joined in matrimony, all their plans, voyages, and future undertakings should be done together, as husband and wife. Why was she resisting him and postponing their wedding?

He felt great frustration as his voice could not be heard, and his needs and desires were swept aside. However, he feared that if pushed too hard she might change her mind and not marry him. Could he afford to lose her? It would tear his heart out. He had come to love her when he first set sight on her the day she arrived with Miguel and his brother, José, from Granada. No, he loved her too dearly, enough to swallow his manly pride.

His chest caving in and his neck bent, he said, "I will keep your plans a secret from Ana."

87

Plans for Escape

THE LONG WEEKS AND MONTHS passed at an excruciating crawl for Miguel, who breathlessly waited for his chance to escape. A few times he had evaded the suspicious eyes following his every move, but those moments were far and few in between. He craved to be alone. All his chores took place on deck: bringing trays to Aruj in his cabin, climbing the mainmast to look for other caravels, and helping the cook prepare meals. If only he could find an hour of peace and quiet to calm his perpetual anxiety, he might be able to come up with a plan for slipping through.

As he pondered routes of escape, Aruj appeared on the upper deck near his cabin. He stood above his men working on deck, standing with his legs planted wide on the planks, his gleaming swords at his belt, caressing his red beard. *"Beni dinle!* Hear me out!"

Intrigued, the half-naked pirates, wearing their trousers rolled to the calves, dropped their tools, ropes, and chisels and gathered on the main deck below Aruj. They eyed their mates standing nearby with question marks in their eyes.

"I called you all here to announce that we'll be looking out for a special ship."

The men turned to each other again while nodding their heads.

"This ship holds much treasure, and we can't let it slip between our fingers. The first one who spots it will be rewarded double!"

"Aye, aye, Aruj. But how are we to recognize the caravel?" asked one of the pirates.

"Yeah. And what kind of treasure does it carry?" asked another.

Aruj lifted his hands to stop any more questions. "A loaded Portuguese caravel, with many cannons, supplies, and goods. Why, just the caravel itself is worth its weight in gold!"

The men standing below laughed raucously. They slapped each other's backs, grabbing their neighbor and jumping up and down.

"Glorious victory to us, *Baba Oruç* Aruj! Victory belongs to us, Baba Oruç!" The sailors slipped swords out of their belts and brandished them in the blue sky above as if heaven itself were under attack.

The pirates shouted over and over until Aruj quieted them down. "Remember to be on the lookout. If this glorious catch is successful, we will sail home to Midilli!"

"Hurrah, hurrah!"

Miguel couldn't understand the fervor with which the pirates shouted their joy. Perhaps booty was all that mattered, while to him freedom was the ultimate reward. *But when will it come?*

That night the pirates celebrated by drinking anise-flavored *raki*. They danced the rich, rhythmic movements of the *Halay* in a line. Sailors played a melodic tune on the *kaval*—a shepherd's wood pipe—and the *sipsi* woodwind. The air that filled the musicians' cheeks transformed to song while the men's bare feet slapped the wooden deck, which creaked under their hops and jumps.

As Miguel watched the cheering men and dancing figures in the lantern light, he thought perhaps that if the men got dead drunk, they wouldn't notice his disappearance. At the next drunken performance he would make his escape.

88

Preparations for a Wedding

QUEEN ISABELLA SAW THAT HER eldest daughter was well prepared for the long voyage to Lisbon. Already, the widowed princess of Asturias was exchanging her black gown for a deep blue silk dress with an orange sash around her waist. Her maid brought the princess her pearl necklace of gold filigree and slipped it around her neck. Gold bangle bracelets completed the outfit. The queen looked at her daughter, and pride filled her heart. Wed to Manuel, heir to John II, the princess would someday become queen of Aragon, Castile, and Portugal. This would fulfill Isabella and Ferdinand's dream of uniting the two kingdoms under one Iberian flag. She sighed at the thought.

"Mi reina," the princess moaned, "Manuel isn't king yet. Our marriage will not take place unless his uncle John dies." She blinked back tears about to appear in her eyes.

"Hush, daughter." Queen Isabella put a finger to her lips. "It's bad luck to speak of death when you're promised to be married."

"But, Mother—"

The queen interrupted the princess with reproach in her eyes.

"But, *mi reina.*" The princess corrected herself. Her daughter knew the strict rule that Isabella be called queen by all her subjects, including her own children. "What am I to do while Manuel waits to be king?"

"You will have your duties as a lady-in-waiting to Queen Eleanor of Viseu."

The princess lowered her head in submission. The queen expected her children to obey her in all matters and to trust her judgment.

A tap on the door brought in Lady Beatriz de Bobadilla with a missive for the queen. Queen Isabella tore the seal and quickly read the few lines:

Pope Alexander VI, Rodrigo Lanzol de Borja, sends his blessings to the Catholic Queen Isabella of the house of Trastamara and Catholic King Ferdinand I of the house of Barcelona, and the good news that the kingdom of Portugal has accepted the Treaty of Tordesillas.

The Queen looked up with joy from the note to her daughter. "We've been blessed with good news. It is a good omen for your marriage to Manuel and his good luck. You are indeed marrying a fortunate man."

1495

89

A Hard Road

TIME PASSED ON ESPAÑOLA UNTIL the months blurred and the days all blended into one long uninterrupted struggle. Columbus felt that the rewards for conquering many islands and the road to heaven were reached through an excruciatingly hard climb. Each time he thought progress had been made with the Indians, a disruptive event came along to undo his work. Margarite, the military nobleman, had ruined any chance he had to cooperate with the natives. A bad feeling now existed between the colonists and the cacique chiefs on the island. Guacanagari was the only chief who remained his loyal friend. But the road was hard to winning back the natives' confidence.

Columbus sat outside the door of his small room in the almost-completed fort, still recuperating from his illness, and admiring the incomparable view in front of him. The fort in Isabela was constructed on a small hill overlooking the sea. From his vantage point, he could look on his three ships swaying in the unprotected harbor beyond Isabela. The skies were free of clouds, and the last bit of the summer season still lingered. The perfume of flowers permeated the air mixed with smells of the Indians grilling iguana barbacoa for the evening. In the distance, he saw fires ignited by natives to burn the dense foliage and prepare the soil with rich potassium ashes. The following weeks would usher in the planting season.

His thoughts returned to his worries, when something nagged at him. He recalled, precisely, that when he was recuperating from his illness, Bartholomew had given him a letter from their father, Domenico. He now wanted desperately to read the letter, but it had disappeared. His last memory of that letter was of him stuffing it into the pocket of his long sleeping gown. He searched the few clothes he possessed and his voluminous papers, but nothing turned up. When he asked his steward Pedro de Terreros to conduct a thorough search, the letter remained lost. Columbus was crushed.

"Admiral?" De la Cosa approached.

Columbus raised his head from the mass of papers he'd been perusing on a makeshift table. "What is it, Juan?"

De la Cosa's voice was charged with excitement. "Admiral, I bring you a report on the Arawak villagers."

"You mean the Taínos?"

"Well, Admiral"—De la Cosa hesitated before explaining respectfully—"the Taínos and Lucayans are both Arawak Indians."

Columbus smiled at his long-time friend and fellow mariner. "How did you learn all this?"

"I spend time with the natives, Admiral, trying to learn all about them."

Columbus sighed. "I wish that the men I left in charge had done the same."

De la Cosa ventured to ask, "You mean concerning the trouble we've had with some of the chiefs?"

"Not only the chiefs but their subjects too. Entire villages are refusing to work," Columbus said, shaking his head. "What kind of report were you talking about?"

De la Cosa's face broke into a large smile. "The villagers produce, twice a year, strong crops of cassava roots, mahiz, sweet tubers the Indians call *boniata* that grow underground, mani cacahuete, and beans . . ."

Columbus tried to pay attention to de la Cosa's long recitation of crops, but his attention waned due to his other woes.

De la Cosa became animated as he explained the natives' slash-and-burn method. " . . . and the amazing part is, they grow them in checkerboard fashion, not in rows. They use *coas* sticks to—"

"De la Cosa, all this is extremely interesting, and will open up new markets in Europe, but I need the latest report on the gold mining in Santo Tomás."

"For that I'll call Ojeda, who just returned this afternoon."

De la Cosa left him, and Columbus went back to his gloomy thoughts. If gold in large quantities was not found soon, would the Spanish monarchs recall or replace him? Who knew the lies and slander Margarite and Fray Buil were telling at court? A shiver ran through him. He'd be the laughingstock of the entire court, especially his enemies and detractors.

He spotted Ojeda climbing the short hill to the fort. He walked to where Columbus sat. "You wanted to see me, Admiral?"

Columbus peered at Ojeda between his spaced fingers he'd raised to block the sun. "Tell me the latest numbers in gold production."

"Well, it's like this, Admiral." Ojeda started slowly. "We have gathered a small amount of gold powder that was given to the adelantado, your brother Bartholomew, for safekeeping."

"What do you mean by 'small amount'?" Columbus felt his anxiety rise again.

"About this much." Ojeda gestured with both hands to describe a small box.

"That's all?" Columbus could hardly conceal his disappointment.

Ojeda lowered his head at the poor showing.

"All right, Ojeda. We need to motivate the Indians, but they also have to obey our orders."

"How can they, Admiral? They're afraid of the renegade soldiers abandoned by Margarite after he returned to Spain who still roam the island and the Vega Real. They're stealing food from the Indians, and raping and kidnapping their women for their own pleasure."

If Columbus hadn't suffered from inflammation in his joints he would've barged out, found the culprits himself, and put them to the sword. But he was as good as nailed to his chair, relying on his brothers to manage the colony. It was up to him to lead and force everyone on the island to buckle down to his orders and find more gold.

Abruptly, he had an idea. "I want you to gather all the young men ages fourteen and older on the island and force them to pay a tribute of gold dust equal to a filled hawk's bell. In exchange, each man will receive a brass token to wear about his neck. The ones not wearing this visible proof of their compliance will be severely punished."

Ojeda hesitated at first to acknowledge the order. "But, Admiral, the Indians in Maguana have been told not to cooperate with the Spaniards. The cacique Guatiguaná leading the Caribs in the province of Xaragua is massing them against us. They're prepared to fight us over the imprisonment of Caonabó's relative and the other two men."

"Those men are thieves. They'll get their punishment as soon as we deal with Guatiguaná!" Columbus stopped, out of breath, trying to control the anger rising in his chest. "We will fight back. Prepare a strong party of two hundred armed men, horses, and hounds to fight Guatiguaná. We'll show them who is running this island. If they fight back, they'll be enslaved and shipped to Spain!"

"All right, Admiral," Ojeda replied, ready to fight.

90

Alarming News

"HAVE YOU HEARD?" RAQUELA BARGED into the kitchen and slapped an empty basket on the floor.

Both Ana and Isabella, working at preparing dinner, raised their heads from their tasks. "Heard what?" replied Ana without stopping peeling her carrots.

Isabella looked at Raquela's sweaty face. Even though the weather was cooler at the end of October, running in from the fields took effort for Raquela.

"The king is dead! John II is dead!" Raquela screamed.

Both Isabella and Ana stopped their work and looked at each other.

"*¡Por la vida de Dios!* We might as well be dead too!" Ana covered her mouth in dread.

"What does it mean?" Isabella asked her. She tried to conceal her alarm.

"What it means," Ana began, "is that we've lost a monarch who welcomed us, kept us, and protected us. The new monarch will abide by Spain's wishes and change Portugal to a Catholic country through and through."

Isabella said in a halting voice, "We will have . . . to leave sooner. I'll finalize the voyage with Avram."

Raquela, who had remained silent, began to cry. "What will happen to us?" She sobbed and wiped tears from her eyes.

Isabella came around the table to hug Raquela. "We *will* take care of you and the children." Isabella comforted her. "Who will play with Salvadore if you leave us, eh?"

Raquela smiled through renewed tears.

Isabella gently asked, "Have I said something to make you cry again?"

Raquela shook her head and stopped crying. "They're tears of joy. You have been like a sister to me, and Ana a mother."

Ana acknowledged Raquela's comment by smiling and nodding her head.

"All right then. Let us continue our work," Isabella said calmly. She continued sorting the provisions and making a list of supplies they'd need on their grand voyage. She felt confident that everyone in her charge would be cared for and fed as before. As a wealthy widow, she had the means to keep and feed at least one hundred people for several years.

But she felt a shadow descend upon her. A feeling of dread enveloped her, and she wanted to crawl into bed and give way to the scream mounting in her throat. With great effort, she restrained the cry.

91

A New Monarch

THE ASSEMBLY IN THE GREAT hall in Lisbon's palace was hushed, awaiting their new monarch's entrance. A cluster of officers, palace courtiers, dukes, and counts stood by, whispering to each other with concern. Now that John II of Portugal was dead, a whole new regime was to follow. From the highest noble to the lowliest servant, they were at risk of joblessness overnight. The nobles had the most to lose, living in castles donated by the dead king along with the funds to maintain their costly lifestyles. A few men among them, though, had the foresight to ensure they kept their estates, ranks, and lives of idleness with a few well-placed bribes.

The guests mingled, dressed in their finery of elaborate gowns, feathered hats, and swords gleaming on men's waists. The scent of expensive perfume and sandalwood filled the air. Isabella, Princess of Asturias, stood smiling among them in a rose-colored brocade gown sporting fur-lined turned-back sleeves over a blue silk kirtle, tied with a soft sash at her waist. Bystanders in the audience knew of the princess's anticipated wedding to the new king. Heads were nodded to her, acknowledging her rise to queen consort of Portugal. A gold necklace encircled her neck with a pendant over her gown.

"Manuel I, king of Portugal and the Algarves and of the House of Aviz."

Every one in the gilded hall bowed as King Manuel I walked with carefully measured steps, while his attendants carried a heavy red brocade train that descended from his shoulders. The king looked in the direction of Princess Isabella and smiled with his eyes. She returned the smile as she saw that he wasn't as old as he appeared in the cameo painting presented to her in Cordova. As a matter of fact, she found him quite handsome. His high eyebrows capped intelligent blue eyes, and he bore a proud, Roman aquiline nose and medium-length soft beard.

The king sat on his elevated throne, and his attendant tapped the parquet floor with his staff.

The assembly waited breathlessly to hear their fortunes—or, in some cases, misfortunes. Manuel I remained silent a moment or two, gazing upon the crowd.

"My dear subjects and sons and daughters of the proud realm of Portugal," he began. "I am your humble servant and will uphold your laws in this cherished country."

Everyone in the audience hall let out sighs of relief that rose to a low hum.

"We are but a few years away from a new century and a new dawn to descend upon our beloved kingdom. I proclaim as your king to do my utmost to advance our people in the coming sixteenth century!"

As King Manuel's voice rose, the assembly rebounded in cheers. "Long live our king! Long live Manuel I!"

King Manuel smiled at his audience, then continued. "You may well know of my inquisitive nature. I intend to expand and move the boundaries in exploration of the New World. We've been blessed by the Treaty of Tordesillas—the papal bull ratified by Pope Alexander Borja. All lands east of a meridian of three hundred and seventy leagues from Cape Verde belong to Portugal."

"Long live Portugal!" the audience shouted.

"Furthermore, I vow that our kingdom will be unified under one religion, the Roman Catholic faith."

The cheers rose again to the ceiling painted with religious motifs, cherubs, and sacred figures in heaven with a beauty that rivaled any of the churches in the realm.

King Manuel now looked to the audience and said solemnly, "Now for a new announcement. Let me introduce to you my future bride, heiress to the kingdom of Castile and Aragon—Isabella, Princess of Asturias." King Manuel stood up, descended the three steps from the throne and waited for the princess to join him.

The audience cheered and applauded the princess, who walked to her future husband and gave him her hand. King Manuel then led the princess of Asturias out of the hall and to a balcony overlooking a plaza packed with waiting citizens.

The king approached the balcony's balustrade, still holding the princess's hand.

Great cheers burst from the crowd. "Long live King Manuel! Long live the king!"

King Manuel then presented the princess, bowing his head to the people below the balcony. "This is your next queen consort."

The cheers rose in crescendo as Princess Isabella smiled to thousands of faces raised to her—rows of men, women, and children waving colorful flags. She blew kisses to them, and the cheering renewed.

Her mission was clear. *I will be their Catholic queen of unified Castile, Aragon, and Portugal under one faith.*

92

Battle

KNEELING IN HIS TORN TROUSERS, Miguel scrubbed the wooden planks on the upper deck, the skin of his knees resting on the rough wood while his hands slid the pumice stone back and forth. Every day he scrubbed all three decks; main, upper, and above the stern, until the stripped wood gripped the soles of heavy boots walking to and fro without slipping. While his back strained under the effort and the skin of his hands became red and scaly, the pirates sat playing cards on deck.

Miguel would throw murderous glances at these lazy no-good men enjoying themselves. He kept promising himself that one day he'd be free of the tyrannical yoke that had kept him prisoner these last three years. When thoughts of Isabella permeated his mind, he fought back tears. *All I need is pirates making fun of me.* He suddenly scrubbed the floor harder and faster.

Near him on the upper deck, two pirates sat shuffling their cards in their greasy palms while periodically throwing coins on a mound between them.

"By Allah! Abdul Aziz, you're cheating!" one man said in a raised voice.

"I did not! Look who's talking, Fahri. You cheated Ergin yesterday. He told me so!" Burly Abdul Aziz shot back.

"Why you good-for-nothing—!" Fahri reached to grab Abdul Aziz, but the latter anticipated his move and scampered across deck to take refuge by the stern.

"I'll get you for this!" Fahri shouted as he ran across deck, his sword brandished.

"Silence!" Mustapha's voice sliced through the air, his cutlass gleaming in the cool sunlight bathing the pirate ship.

At that moment, Aruj stepped onto the upper deck, throwing glances about him. "What's the meaning of this noise?"

Miguel had stopped his scrubbing, following the scene while chuckling to himself. *I wonder who'll be whipped tonight.*

By now Mustapha had dragged the culprits by their ears to the center of the main deck, while the remaining pirates, pulled away from scanning the ocean, gathered around.

"Why all the ruckus?" Aruj asked again, his angry voice projecting to the lower deck.

"I'll have them whipped, Effendi," Mustapha strongly affirmed.

Aruj said, "All right. Tie them to the mainmast!"

"Ship ahoy! Ship ahoy!" The bearded pirate in the crow's nest shouted while jumping up and down in the small lookout.

At once all heads turned west, to where the pirate was pointing.

Aruj squinted as he peered at the horizon of the vast Atlantic Ocean to detect the speed of the approaching caravel. He rushed down to the main deck without a glance at Miguel standing fixed in his spot.

"It's a Portuguese merchant ship!" the pirate above them screamed.

The call to action set the pirates in a frenzy as they armed themselves, climbed the ratline rungs, and prepared the cannons for firing.

"Keep the cannons filled and ready to fire!" Mustapha and Aruj ordered simultaneously.

Miguel, meanwhile, had become lost in the shuffle on board. They had forgotten about him, and the pirates' eyes were now focused on the unsuspecting ship getting closer and closer. He had to think fast, but stealing another boat in daylight was out of the question. *What to do?*

He suddenly thought of an idea. All he had to do was slip unnoticed to the hold until the battle began, though he might be cornered without an exit. If the Portuguese were the victors, the hold would be searched thoroughly. He sat frozen and undecided, still unable to formulate an escape route. Meanwhile, the Portuguese ship had sounded the alarm, their decks becoming as busy as those of their enemy's. Miguel could see squinting, tense looks on the pirates' faces as they lightly ran fingers down their blades.

A six-pound cannon shot burst from the Portuguese ship. Then silence reigned as the warning shot fell into the water. The enemy ship waited for a response from the pirate ship that didn't come, then a call to battle sounded from both ships carrying clearly across the remaining league.

"Get ready to board!" The pirates' voices carried across the waters.

The next cannon shots ignited in the air with sulfur and fire. Then the pirates fired a series of shots at the Portuguese ship, which answered immediately with a volley of their own. Both ships sustained light damage to their hulls in this first round. The Portuguese ship lost its mizzenmast, which crashed and collapsed into the water but was still attached to the ship by cordage. Sulfur stung Miguel's eyes and nose with a musty and acrid smell, and white smoke began to blur the Portuguese vessel. The pirates, hanging on masts and ratlines with one leg propped against the rails on the port side, eyed the Portuguese sailors positioned starboard. A sudden thud shook both ships as they collided. The pirates threw their boarding axes and grappling hooks across the small divide while holding small parrying daggers between their teeth and the short curved blade of the cutlass sword in hand.

Standing frozen with apprehension on the upper deck, Miguel saw the Portuguese sailors braced for their opponents with hanger swords, grasping the shell guards, blades gleaming in the sun. They prepared to board the enemy first. They fired their espingardas at the pirates braced on ratlines who were pinned and cornered like birds caught in a net. The first cries of the wounded were heard, and the Portuguese threw down their gangplanks, but the pirates had already boarded by jumping across from their ships and were the first to engage the Portuguese sailors.

A mêlée ensued on both ships, swords causing maximum damage as organs were slashed, hands chopped, or eyes pierced in a pitched hand-to-hand battle. The cry of wounded men and the call to kill filled the air. Miguel watched the battle move closer to the upper railing. The pumice stone, still in his hand, fell out onto the boards. Fearing for his life, he dashed starboard, climbed the rails, and dove into the sea.

The water splashed cold around him as he descended below the surface. He turned around and propelled to the surface. On the pirate's starboard side, an eerie calm existed as opposed the port side, where the battle raged. Silently, he swam to the bow, then peeked above at the combatants still brandishing their swords. Dead bodies of pirates and two dead Portuguese floated on the water between ships. Miguel dove under the dead men, then swam underwater around the stern of the Portuguese ship to her port side. All was calm, as the main battle was concentrated on starboard. He then retreated to the rudder, hoping no one would turn the tiller and catch him between the blade and the hull.

There he waited for a long time in the water, hidden from view. He heard more cries and skirmishes between the combatants. Peeking around the side, he saw pirates dragging Portuguese men to the pirate ship. Other pirates carried chests and crates on their shoulders. He feared the pirates had won the upper hand in the battle.

The water surged, and a swell raised him up and down. The pirate ship was breaking away. Within minutes the brigands were sailing away.

It was time to make his move. He grasped ropes attached to the fallen mizzenmast and hung on for dear life. The Portuguese were bound to cut the mast to lighten the load—that is, if anyone was still alive.

A few minutes passed before he heard voices above him.

"See to the wounded! Take them to the surgeon!"

There were living men after all, he thought with relief. He emerged dripping wet from the water, and crawled up the partially submerged mast to its base still tangled against the ship's hull. He climbed over the gunwale and found himself on a bloodied deck with bodies strewn all over.

A sailor shouted at him: "You there! Help me carry this man to the infirmary!"

Miguel complied, and they both lifted the wounded man, who was moaning and whispering monosyllables. "Where's . . . my wife? My . . . son?"

Poor man, Miguel thought. The man lost all sense of time. Perhaps he was nearing his death. They lowered the wounded man below deck, where a makeshift medical station was created amid the rows of cannons. The floor was soaked in blood, and sailors were covering it with straw. The physician cared for the wounded and at times administered last rites.

Miguel found himself alive and unharmed among the wounded, the dying, and the dead. Perhaps God in his wisdom and grace had watched over him and seen to his salvation. He suddenly felt that his suffering had ended and that his life would continue as intended.

"Seize this man!"

Miguel found himself suddenly encircled by sailors.

93

New Recruits

ISABELLA STARED AT THE ESTATE growing smaller as the carriage distanced itself. Then the trees hid the figures of Ana holding her son, and Avram in the background.

A gnawing sense of guilt assailed her as if she had abandoned all of them. It had been magnified by Ana's teary parting words: "I fear. I fear you may not come back."

"Hush," Isabella had replied. "I'll be back, and then we'll leave for a safe haven. You'll see."

But Ana cried harder, her sobs interrupted only by Salvadore's small hand caressing her face. Her distress was alleviated by the gesture, and she had kissed his little fingers.

Isabella sighed.

Sekou, sitting across from her bench, patted her hand in comfort. "*Senhora Patróna*, we back soon."

Isabella tried to smile, but a grimace pasted her lips together. Sekou's words didn't soothe her conflicted feelings. She could only justify her actions by trying to find Miguel one last time. It was for the good of her son to find his father, was it not?

"Thank you, Sekou, for your words. We will be back soon." She then fell silent.

The carriage arrived at the junction at the outskirts of Sintra where the road to the port began. She sat up and tapped the roof of the carriage. The vehicle stopped, and her driver came to the window.

"What is it, *Patróna*?"

"I want you to take a detour. Head for Castelo dos Mouros."

Her driver nodded, then climbed up to the driver's seat and took the fork in the road toward the castle. It was a mere kilometer, and soon they arrived at the foot of the ruined castle, where a few men and women worked a small patch of land. Isabella could see plants and vegetables growing in rows.

One of the men raised his head at the arrival of the carriage, leaned on his hoe, and lifted his hat as she approached. *"O que podemos fazer por você, senhora?"*

"It's what I want to do for you," she replied, and without waiting for another question from the man, she turned to Sekou in the carriage and signaled for him to follow her up to the castle.

They climbed the narrow stone steps of the north-facing wall of the Moorish castle. Children playing out front stopped to stare at her and Sekou. Behind, the people working their gardens also watched. Through the ruins of a portal that at one time had been grand, Isabella entered a stone courtyard and was surrounded by inhabitants who led her to a roofless chapel. Everyone in the chapel watched with curiosity.

Isabella looked at canvas tents protecting the people from harsh weather and sun. The thin men, women, and children were dressed shabbily, and Isabella found fear in their rapidly blinking eyes. The silence was thick with suspicion. Some of them scratched their necks or shuffled their feet, while others stood with their lips pressed into a grimace. The men moved to wrap their arms around their wives' shoulders while the mothers hugged their children.

Isabella spoke to erase the looks of alarm, agitation, and open distress. "The kingdom of Portugal will exile us from this second home we found after Spain. But you have a way to escape this existence."

One of the elderly men, with a long white beard, came close. "Where is this hope you speak of? It's only a dream. We've been chased many, many times in history. What is different now?"

Isabella nodded to agree with him. "I have the means to transport all of you to the kingdom of Turquía. The pasha opened his doors to the Spanish Jews three years ago. Now he'll welcome us again."

Some of the people nodded, while others raised objections. The questions flew from their lips.

"How can you be certain he won't close the doors to us?"

"What if the Portuguese close their gates and don't let us leave?"

Isabella couldn't help smiling at the last comment. "I know Portugal will want you to leave. First they will force you to convert—just like they did in España."

Again, murmurs filled the large chapel space.

A voice suddenly broke through the muttering. A young man shouted, "I know who you are. You're the senhora at the winery estate. The one who employs us each fall at harvest."

A murmur rumbled through the crowd. Isabella acknowledged the comment with a nod.

She continued her passionate speech. "I have the means and the ship to take you away. You'll be safe crossing the Mediterranean Sea on my ship, the *Liberação*."

"What about pirates roaming those seas?"

"The *Liberação* is equipped with many cannons and skilled sailors to protect you." She stopped pleading and waited to see that they understood her, but no one came forward. "We will leave in a few months' time. The ones who want to join me on this voyage must come to the harbor when we leave."

"And when will that would be?" a young woman clutching her two young sons asked with a steady voice.

"I will let you know when the time comes." Isabella turned to leave, when several men and women encircled her.

"We're looking for our sons who left many months ago for the New World. Have you heard any word from them?"

Isabella was puzzled by the question and at a loss to help them. "How did they travel, and who recruited them?"

"He was a seasoned mariner, and our sons were hired on the ships that left in 1493."

"But who employed them?"

A silence fell. No one ventured to answer her, until one of the men spoke. "The mariner was called João."

"João Treves!" Isabella shouted. "He's my uncle."

"Yes. That was the name he gave us. He took away our sons—Isaac, and our youngest, Emanuel."

"Our son Moisés was also recruited."

"Elías is my son, and his friend Enrique was also hired," said a small woman, her eyebrows drawn together.

One woman came close to Isabella and whispered, "My husband, León, left on this voyage too."

The names came at her from all sides. Pained gazes, clasped hands, and wrinkled brows showed Isabella the depth of their concern.

Isabella was overwhelmed by the sheer number of names. "The man is my uncle," she said. "You can be sure they'll be protected from harm. He has years of sailing experience."

"But how can we leave here? If we go with you, they won't find us when they come back."

Their cry was heard loud and clear. These families were caught in a dilemma: to leave or stay.

Isabella couldn't give them an answer. "I will let you know the minute I hear anything from my uncle. But the rest of you—do get ready to leave on this voyage." She turned and, followed by Sekou, headed for her carriage and the port of Lisbon.

94

A Last Battle

A GLORIOUS MORNING DAWNED WITH flights of harried birds flying above their camp on Española, the breeze gently swaying the caravels in Isabela's harbor, and the men attired for battle.

The Spaniards were prepared to fight the four principal caciques and their kingdoms: Caonabó from Maguana, Higuanama from Higuey, Behechio from Jaragua, and Guarionex from the Vega Real. These chiefs ruled thousands of villages and had gathered one hundred thousand men to war against the Christian colonists. Riding alongside Columbus was Cacique Guacanagari from the Marien region, who had played no part in killing the men at La Navidad. Guacanagarí had stressed to Columbus from the start that these other caciques were his enemies.

The horses moved restlessly, as if they sensed whispers of death in the air while waiting for their riders to mount. The grounds were crowded with men outfitting themselves with cuirasses and arms and their helpers bringing them water and food to sustain them on the campaign.

Columbus applied gentle pressure to his horse's flank and trotted to the head of the columns of soldiers.

"We're headed to the Cibao region to punish the men who killed our comrades." He steadied himself on his swaying horse and continued. "They pilfered the fort at La Navidad and enticed other Indians to commit crimes against Her Majesty's men!"

"Vamos a matar a todos!" his men shouted in agreement.

"We're marching against these evil Indians to teach them to never disobey us or fight us!"

"Son carne muerta! Con la victoria!" the men shouted.

"Then follow me, soldiers!" Columbus roared.

The columns of men moved out, as the rest of the colony cheered them on.

Columbus spoke to his brother Bartholomew, the adelantado, riding to his right, and Alonso de Ojeda on his left. "We will surprise them by hitting them on several fronts."

Ojeda was swift to question Columbus. "With much respect, Admiral— how do you intend to do that? They're spread out over many kilometers. We can't cover that much ground with only two hundred of us."

"Yes, I'm aware of that. Don't forget our twenty horses and hounds ready to tear into them."

Ojeda came back again. "But, Admiral, how can we fight them all? We'll be surrounded in no time."

"I intend to split our men down the middle, and direct the attack from two fronts. The Indians will be surprised by our two frontal attacks. We'll then send in the cavalry and hounds to finish them."

For a short moment, Ojeda remained silent, pondering with his head lowered. Then he looked up and gave Columbus a large smile. "By St. George, Admiral, it sounds like a winning strategy!"

After a seven-day march to Cibao, the men sorely needed rest. They pitched camp by sunset at the base of the Cordillera Mountains, which they would be climbing the following morning. Columbus gave the order not to light fires, fearing giving away the camp's location to the enemy. The men drank and ate a cold meal of tubers and a sweet orange mush that the Indians called *boniata*, provided by Guacanagari's people.

Early the following morning, as the mist began to rise on the mountain near the Puerto de los Hidalgos pass, Columbus's men prepared to descend into the great valley of Vega Real. The white mist covered the men and animals, aiding in their plans to surprise the native enemies. The march downward was laborious, with stones rolling under the hooves of their horses, which bucked with fear and unseated a few of the unskilled riders. A continued hush, ordered by Columbus, kept each man silent and caressing his horse's flank to keep it quiet. They slowly descended until they hit the valley floor after a grueling two hours, during which men fell off their horses, with many suffering scrapes or minor broken bones.

"Call Dr. Chanca from the rear." Columbus alerted one of his aides. When the physician appeared, Columbus said, "Five of my men are wounded. Treat them right away. I'll need them for the fight."

Dr. Chanca looked befuddled by the order. "But, Admiral, if they're wounded, what good will they be?"

"Never mind their worth. I need every man to fight a hundred thousand natives!"

"Right away, Admiral," Dr. Chanca answered.

Columbus called Bartholomew and Ojeda. "This is where we'll split up," he said to Bartholomew. "You take one half the men, and you, Ojeda, the other. Post them in the jungle at fifty-meter intervals. This way the Indians will think there are many more of us. Make sure everyone is well hidden behind the trees. On my orders, we'll attack simultaneously."

"What about the mounted men, Admiral?"

"The men on horses will follow the foot soldiers. Make sure each rider has a hound with him."

Both men nodded, then left Columbus to relay his orders.

They waited until noon, well-hidden behind trees and in bushes, when the blaring of trumpets rose from their ranks. The men on foot lunged forward, each supplied with a sword and an axe. The mounted men followed the foot soldiers at a medium gallop, careful not overrun the soldiers charging on the front line. Behind the horses were soldiers with arquebus firearms. The villages were reached within minutes, where the Indians were absorbed in preparing a noon meal, unaware of the danger.

The sight of men charging toward them with shining arms reflecting the sun and the horses following them brought a great fright to the Indians who believed that man and beast were one and the same. The hounds running alongside the horses' flanks lunged and planted their sharp canine teeth into the Indians' naked legs, tearing their skin and muscle to the bone. Guacanagari, marching with Columbus's men, had supplied one hundred of his men armed with crossbows and arrows. They finished off the wounded men running to the forest behind the huts. The sound of arquebusses firing what seemed to be flashes of fire into the thousands of terrified Indians brought the armed resistance to a stop. Many of the tens of thousands armed Indians did not materialize as feared. They melted away into the thick forests.

Within an hour, the Spaniards had conquered the Caribs and rebel Taínos. The terrified Indians surrendered and begged on their knees to be forgiven. Columbus searched for Caonabó among the Indians, but he had fled into the surrounding forests with his wives and children.

"Run after them!" Columbus ordered ten of his riders, led by Ojeda. The horses disappeared into the forest, trailing dust as their hooves hit the sandy ground.

Columbus waited half an hour in the village now overrun with his men, pacing restlessly back and forth. The many captured Caribs sat on their haunches, their eyes darting from the moving admiral to the line of trees.

A flurry of people, both mounted soldiers and bound Indians, suddenly sallied forth from the forest. Women and children followed behind the captives, crying and moaning in their native language. Caonabó was manacled with his legs in irons.

"Good work, Ojeda!" Columbus roared with satisfaction. "Where did you find him?"

"We caught him crossing at the mouth of a river!" Ojeda shouted. "Before he could climb Cibao's southern mountain."

"Bring them to me!" Columbus ordered. Ojeda dragged the shackled Caonabó and forced him to kneel in front of Columbus.

Columbus turned to de la Cosa. "Find out if he had our men killed at La Navidad."

De la Cosa communicated through signs and a few Taino words he'd learned from the Indians. "Spaniard men you killed?"

With animal fear in his eyes, Caonabó remained silent. His face glistened in the late afternoon sun.

De la Cosa asked him again, but to no avail. Caonabó was determined not to speak. His lips sealed tight, he wiped sweat from his forehead on his arm. His chains and necklace made of shells and small bones jangled at his movement.

Columbus's impatience and anger mounted as de la Cosa failed to make progress with Caonabó. Guacanagari came forward. The cacique raised his hand and questioned Caonabó.

"Cacicazgo maguana Cacique Caribe Caonabó canima mynu lu baina pyrywa?"

Upon hearing Guacanagari's speech, Caonabó spat on the ground, nodded several times, then turned his head away. A mocking smile played across his lips.

Guacanagari turned to Columbus and nodded. "Cacique kill men from heaven."

Columbus bowed his head to thank Guacanagarí. He ordered Ojeda, "Take that miserable Carib back to Isabela to be shipped to Their Majesties to do with as they please."

95

The Last Voyage

ISABELLA WENT OVER MAPS AND documents with a fine-tooth comb. Both she and Avram had already gone up and down the coast of Africa, from Morocco to the Portuguese Gold Coast and south to the Pepper Coast, the furthest point the *Liberação* sailed.

Isabella now wanted to go beyond that shore. There hadn't been any sign of Miguel since his escape from La Mina, so where could he have gone? A sense of panic and a choked feeling grasped her no matter where she channeled her search. The pirate ship under Aruj's command should have found him by now. Clearly, Aruj had led her on these last two years. What else could she surmise? If nothing turned up on this voyage, she'd have to disassociate herself from those brigands.

Ana was right. They were thieves and profiteers. What else could one expect from pirates? She'd been warned, but disregarded Ana's caution. She suddenly laughed at her own stupidity. No matter. It was now up to her to find Miguel before it was too late. This urgency brought back to her commitment to the men and women at El Mouro castle and the voyage out of Portugal.

She called Lourenço da Sintra, her second-in-command, to her cabin. "These are the coordinates for this voyage. See that they're recorded in your log book."

"Yes, Captain." Lourenço glanced at the coordinates, then tried to follow them on the map lying on the table.

"Well, Lourenço?" Isabella stood before him with a smile on her lips, dressed in black trousers and a white blouse buttoned up to the neck that was covered by a vest, with her black hair tucked under a cap.

Lourenço looked up from the chart, biting his lip and with a worried gaze in his eyes. "We're going way beyond ports we've covered so far."

"And why should that bother you?" She crossed her arms, waiting for a logical reply.

"Because once we are beyond the Gold Coast, we face many dangers."

"What types of dangers?"

"With all due respect, Captain, these waters are controlled by many factions and many pirates. There's no telling—we could be attacked from all sides."

"It's a chance I'm willing to take. Now go and carry out my orders."

Lourenço paused for a moment that wasn't lost on Isabella. *He must obey me*, she thought as he left the cabin and closed the door behind him.

Isabella stepped out on the quarterdeck and abandoned herself to the breeze buffeting her. Far off the portside, the African continent revealed itself as a flat line dotted here and there by forts surrounded by small towns of square whitewashed buildings and kilometers of sand dunes without vegetation on the perimeter. She leaned against the rails to admire the sea hugging the ship, the bow cutting white-crested waves, and the immensity of water reaching to the horizon. The sky was still clear—the minimal rainy season hadn't begun for these lands.

If everything went according to plan, she would find Miguel. But no matter what the outcome, she would head back home without regret, knowing she had explored every path in her quest.

She turned from the rails and saw Sekou sitting on the floorboards. She waved a hand at him, and he smiled back. She saw change in the old man daily as the progression of age slowed him down and felt a sense of duty toward him. After all, it was his reported sighting of "White Ali" that had prompted this last voyage. If Sekou was right, and Ali was not the imaginative ramblings of an old man, she would find Miguel.

She approached Sekou and sat on the deck beside him.

"If you want to go back to your village, we can take you now."

Sekou raised his head, and a gentle look was in his eyes. "I see my village all day."

"I don't understand, Sekou. Do you mean you think of it every day?"

Sekou nodded. "I no return to my village. I stay with you. You good to me."

Isabella hugged the old man. "I want you to stay with us. You are my only thread to 'White Ali,' who was my husband."

Sekou smiled at her. "White Ali my friend and—"

A cry rang out above their heads.

"Ship to starboard! Ship to starboard!" the sailor called out from the crow's nest.

Isabella peered from the right-hand railing at the ocean, and a speck on the horizon seemed to be headed their way. She ran down to the main deck and began to ring the bell near the stern. The pealing attracted all the sailors around the mast, as well as Lourenço and Joham Alvaro, the pilot. All eyes turned to the ship growing larger by the minute.

Isabella called out to the men. "Prepare the cannons. Now!"

A mad shuffle rumbled on deck and below as every sailor ran to ready the cannons with fireballs.

"You'll fire on my orders. But not before!" Isabella warned them.

As the men on board waited breathlessly for the anticipated battle coming their way, the caravel came closer. The sailor in the crow's nest yelled, "It's a Portuguese flag!"

The men below and on the upper deck cheered, but Isabella yelled at her sailors, "Wait for my order!"

Soon the ship came a few yards to the starboard side of the *Liberação*, and Isabella breathed a sigh of relief. She recognized the new rectangular flag, bearing seven yellow castles on a red background with five blue shields in the center and Portugal's crown on top. This was King Manuel's new flag—the new king who would chase them out of Portugal. Isabella swallowed her grudge down hard and gave the order to fire the customary salvo of recognition: a cannonball into the water.

The Portuguese ship bearing the name *Esperança* replied in kind.

Soon the short, round captain, followed by his wiry second-in-command, boarded her ship, and the captain bowed to her from his waist down.

"We're pleased, Captain, to cross paths with one of our countrymen's ships. Captain Álvaro at your command. This is my second-in-command, Martinho."

Isabella was pleased to be recognized as the captain. "Captain of the *Liberação* at your command, and here is my second officer, Lourenço da Sintra."

The captain gazed at Isabella for a moment and said, "It is my honor to meet one of the youngest captains I've ever seen."

Isabella smiled. "My father died not long ago, and I had to take over." Isabella saw Lourenço's face redden as he restrained himself from blurting out the truth. *Oh well*, thought Isabella. A white lie never hurt anyone.

She turned to Lourenço. "Tell the cook, Hanrrique, to bring a bottle of our best wine. Please follow me to my cabin, Captain."

Once in the cabin, Isabella made room for Captain Álvaro by removing the documents she had strewn about her table and chairs.

Captain Álvaro observed her with curiosity under his eyelids that partly covered small beady eyes. Isabella felt his eyes on her, and she hoped he hadn't suspected the truth about her.

"You seem to be taking a long voyage, Captain . . ." He waited to hear her name.

"Oh, I beg your pardon. It's Captain Treves."

"Treves, eh. Then you're Portuguese?"

"Yes, it was my mother's name." *What a pesky man!*

Captain Álvaro repeated, "You're so young, Captain," he strained the word *young* in a diminutive fashion. "Where are you headed?"

At that moment, Lourenço arrived with Hanrrique, carrying the wine on a tray. Isabella waited for the cook to serve them. Once the glasses were filled, Captain Álvaro drained his immediately. Martinho did the same. The cook quickly filled their glasses again. Both Isabella and Lourenço drank a small amount and she put her glass down.

"To answer your question, Captain. We're looking for a young slave that escaped our ship."

"That is most interesting. What did he look like, and what was his name?"

Isabella hesitated at first, feeling Lourenço's eyes weighing heavily on her. "He was young, went by the name of 'White Ali.'"

Captain Álvaro, who was drinking his second glass, choked, then coughed several times. Martinho nearby rolled suspicious eyes to Captain Álvaro's glass and put his hand on his sword's pommel. When the captain stopped coughing, Martinho relaxed his grip on the sword.

Isabella waited anxiously for the captain to catch his breath.

Captain Álvaro then said haltingly, "I know that man. He was on our ship!"

Isabella and Lourenço sat upright on their chairs, their ears perked up.

Isabella's voice trembled. "You mean you had him in your hands?"

"Yes, we did. We turned him over to Aruj, a fearsome pirate."

Isabella slumped against the back of her chair. "But why?"

"Because the pirates attacked us and asked for him."

"Where has the pirate ship sailed to?"

"We don't know. Those are not questions we ask of them. But if it's any consolation to you, Aruj operates from the Bosphorus Strait, where he controls the slave trade in the Black Sea and the Sea of Marmara near Turquía." Captain Álvaro looked curiously at Isabella. "If you want to find your slave that's where you should search. Be prepared though to pay a high price."

A heavy silence fell in the cabin. Isabella spoke first, "We're very grateful for the information you provided, Captain Álvaro. We will provide you with five bottles of wine to take with you." Isabella felt that one second more in the captain's presence and she would tear his face with her nails.

The captain bowed. "My sincere apology for losing that slave. You know you cannot retrieve any man, slave or freeman, once the pirate Aruj gets a hold of him."

Isabella nodded.

"Thank you for your hospitality, Captain Treves—and the wine!" He bowed and left the cabin with the silent Martinho in tow.

They left as fast as they had boarded. Isabella sighed with relief to see the ship distance itself from theirs. Left alone, she descended to the throes of despair. All her effort, searching, and months of hoping to find Miguel had been in vain. Now she must face the realization that Miguel was lost to her and to Salvadore, his son.

She sat alone in her cabin, her eyes dry with her throat gripped in a vise. She wasn't going to cry. Suddenly she raised her head and thought in a flash—if the pirate Aruj operated in the Levant by Turquía, where she had planned to find a new home, that's where she'd continue her search. She got up and went to call Lourenço.

"Let's head back to Lisbon."

96

Slavery

PEACEFUL DAYS FOLLOWED THE TAMING of the rebellious Caribs and natives after their subjugation by Columbus's small army in the Cibao region. Now any Spaniard could safely walk through the forest without being robbed or attacked by bands of armed Caribs. Caonabó sat in chains in his locked hut with two Spanish guards watching over him day and night. He tried to escape several times, shaking the bars of his bamboo-and-palm-frond hut trying to topple it, but to no avail. He also blasted at his guards with a flurry of Taíno words they didn't understand. Then he fasted for seven days. When one of his wives came to see him, she brought him food and tearfully pleaded for him to eat. Caonabó ended his fast and fell into a depression afterward, not yelling, talking, or trying to escape.

Columbus, meanwhile, glad for the peace afforded them, tried to get back to the running of the colony. The task ahead of him was a monumental undertaking. He was no closer to mining large quantities of gold, instead reduced to collecting small amounts of gold dust panned in the rivers of the Cibao region. The fort in Santo Tomás had been finished a number of months. The mill to grind gold from ore extracted from the nearest mountain sat idle, and their food supplies were dwindling again. They were reduced to a diet of fruit and tubers cultivated by the Indians. Fish was plenty, but his men craved meat and pork. The barrels of wine and beer were drained to the last dregs. The wheat planted the previous season had germinated, and white flour would be plentiful in a month or two, but that wouldn't supply nourishing food. Dr. Chanca warned Columbus that if food and medicaments weren't supplied soon, the men were liable to fall sick again.

The admiral sat in his cabin, desperately trying to find a source of income to offset the scarcity of gold and to pay for supplies. Finally he thought of a way out. For a long time he had toyed with the idea of slave trading. The Caribs on Española could supply the slave market in Seville. All they had to do was round up Carib natives by the hundreds and send them on the next voyage. After all, since the Caribs were mortal enemies of the Taíno, this slave trade would be legitimate. He called Antonio de Torres to his cabin.

"I want you to select four caravels and take as many as fifteen hundred Caribs from various islands to be sold as slaves in Seville. My brother Diego and Michele de Cuneo will accompany you."

To de Torres's stupefied look, Columbus added, "You can appropriate the *fustas*, the Caribs' large canoes, to catch them and bring them by force to Isabela's harbor."

"But, Admiral, it will take weeks to gather them. And besides—" He stopped for a moment, unsure of delivering the next words, then said resolutely, "If I recall in the last letter from Their Highnesses, they were against that idea." He looked down, afraid of the reaction his words would cause.

"Are you questioning my loyalty to the monarchs?" Columbus's voice rose with indignation.

De Torres shook his head. "No . . . no, Admiral. What I meant to say—"

"You meant to say that these Caribs deserve our compassion. What compassion have they given the Taínos, eh? They've been oppressing them for years, stealing their wives and their children, castrating the young boys, and even eating some of them!"

De Torres stood shocked by Columbus's fury and outrage. "I was only inquiring, Admiral. I wasn't questioning your command."

"That's good, de Torres." Columbus breathed a sigh of relief. "We go back many years, you and I, in good time and bad times. What I need now is your loyalty and obedience."

"You have them, Admiral."

"Good. Go and carry out my orders, then." Columbus turned to his table to continue his work.

A spectacular sun rose on the horizon line and painted massive clouds above in a reddish pallete. Much of Isabela's colony was awash in furious activity. Three weeks had passed since Columbus gave the order to capture Caribs, and fifteen hundred awaited their fate as they sat on the sandy beach chained to one another. The Spaniard guards stood over them with espingardas, ready to fire at any move from the wretched men and women. The Indians' grim faces took on a reddish tint from the orange sun now above their heads, and a low moaning came from their throats as they anticipated their deaths. Caonabó sat among the Caribs, silent and resigned to his fate. His wives stood by crying their hearts out, and pleading for the admiral and de Torres to free him. Columbus supervised the operation but remained silent, an internal battle taking place between his head and his heart.

"Begin loading the caravels!" de Torres ordered the guards.

Diego Columbus, garbed in his monk's robe, made the sign of the cross as the slaves boarded one by one. Michele de Cuneo, the noble explorer, stood by with his right hand on his sheathed sword, ready to use it at any sign of rebellion.

De Torres glanced at Columbus several times to watch for a change of mind, but the admiral didn't stir.

The line of captured Indians moved slowly, and the shackled women started weeping in earnest. They fell on their knees, their children bundled on their backs, impeding the march to the waiting caravel.

"Wait!" Columbus shouted.

De Torres looked to him, ready to embrace any change of orders when Columbus approached him.

"I want you to choose four hundred of the best males and females for embarkation."

De Torres nodded.

"The remaining Indians can be divided among the Christians to do with as they please."

"There are more Indians than there are Spaniards, Admiral. What do we do with the rest of them?"

"You can release them," Columbus said.

"I will, Admiral."

Columbus saw de Torres smile before nodding then proceeding to divide the mass of Indians into three groups. He signaled for one group to be allowed to leave. Their chains were removed, and they fled the beach. In their haste to escape, mothers ran into the forest, leaving their children behind. When the freed adults emptied the beach, many young children and infants were left crying on the sand.

Columbus looked at the abandoned children and said to de Torres, "These children can be given to the Taíno, who will care for them."

"Admiral, these are Carib children. I don't know if the Taíno will take them in."

"We will force them to care for them," Columbus said. He then turned to de Torres and stressed, "Make sure to keep an eye on Caonabó. He's liable to jump in the water and escape."

"But, Admiral, just the chains—"

"If he escapes, you'll have to answer for him."

De Torres nodded.

Columbus then went to embrace Diego. A lump lodged in his throat at parting from his little brother. "Take care of yourself, and give Their Majesties my undying loyalty."

Diego nodded, tears forming in his eyes. "I will, Brother."

"And make sure," Columbus stressed, "to dispel any rumors or slander Fray Buil and Margarite spread about me at court!"

Diego nodded again. "Send my good-byes to our brother Bartholomew in the Cibao region. I will miss him."

"I will, Diego."

By noon that day, the caravels sailed from Isabela with de Torres waving his good-byes from deck. As the ships became small dots, then disappeared from view, Columbus made the sign of the cross praying that the voyage might pass without danger.

97

The Race Home

TWO SAILORS DRAGGED MIGUEL WHILE he resisted, trying to throw them off. One mariner clamped a hand on his mouth, preventing him from shouting, while the other held both his arms behind his back. Miguel continued to twist and to wrench his body back and forth to throw the men off balance. All three crashed to the bloodied, stained deck in front of the cabin. In the blink of an eye, he could see blood from the battle still moist as it soiled the floorboards. No amount of washing could ever erase where a man had died.

Freed from the sailors' hands, Miguel clambered to his feet and shouted at the downed sailors. "I'm a free man, just like you!"

He took in the bedlam on the decks below. Sailors shouted, running to and fro across decks. Ten men pulled and heaved, trying to lift half of the foremast from the water—an impossible task. Wounded men lay on deck, moaning and crying in pain, while the physician threw his hands in the air at the enormous task before him. Smoke rose from the hull above water where hot cannon balls had found their targets.

A stocky bearded man, giving orders to the sailors scrambling up from the planks, glanced at Miguel. "What's this man doing here?"

"Captain, we caught this stowaway from the pirate ship!" Said one of the sailors.

The captain turned to Miguel and yelled, "Who are you?"

Oh no. Here we go again. Miguel bowed to the captain. "Captain, I'm a sailor too. I was kept captive by the same pirates who attacked your ship."

The captain expressed bewilderment at first, then peered closely at Miguel. "You do look Spanish or Portuguese. How did you fall into pirates' hands?"

"Captain, this would take hours. But I assure you, I have honorable intentions to tell you the whole truth."

"All right. Now that you're here, go and help the physician with the wounded."

For the next two hours, Miguel lent a hand to the wounded, applying cloth to their bleeding wounds and making sure they were protected from the sun, while trying to comfort them as best he could. When done, he climbed the upper deck to the captain's cabin. He found the captain changing his bloodied clothes.

"Come in," said the captain.

Miguel, still in his bloodstained clothes, waited for the captain, who was rummaging through his table cluttered with torn and crumpled documents and trying to put his papers in order. He lifted a torn map, one half hanging ragged with the other half strewn on the floor among important archives, records, and credentials. He suddenly swiped everything off the table with a raging burst of impatience. "Look at what these evil men did! They stole all my bills of lading, important documents—even the deed to the ship!" The captain collapsed on a chair and wiped his brow.

Miguel could see the man's eyes watering.

"If I may be so bold as to suggest something?" Miguel said.

The captain turned his eyes on him, as if just remembering Miguel's presence. "What can you do that I haven't thought of?"

"I will sift through your papers and find the missing pages and logs."

"Why, are you a mariner too?"

"I was the captain of my ship three years ago, before I fell into pirates' hands."

The captain took a good look at him and asked, "What was your ship?"

"I sailed the *Liberação*, a two-gun caravel from Lisbon, to various cities in North Africa."

"Then you're a compatriot, like me." The captain smiled, forgetting for a moment his woes, lost documents, and fallen men.

"Yes, Captain. I'm at your service." Miguel bowed, and the captain replied in kind.

"I'm Captain Luis Borges Santos."

Miguel bowed again. "I'm Miguel Costa."

"Well, Captain Miguel Costa, you're welcome to help in any way you can." Before Miguel could reply, he added, "And after supper you can tell me everything that's happened to you. Now if you'll excuse me, I have men to bury at sea."

Captain Santos left the cabin, leaving Miguel in charge of the papers. Miguel thought how quickly he had won the captain's complete confidence. If pirates had stolen the most important documents, what was left to organize or repair? He pulled back his bulky wet ballooning sleeves and began to sort the mounds of documents on the floor.

98

A Date Is Set

IT HAD BEEN SEVERAL WEEKS since Isabella came back empty-handed again, but her resolve to find Miguel after they left Portugal for Turquía still burned in her heart. The sooner they left, the faster she could resume her search.

It was a disorderly time on the estate. Hired men brought in cartloads of empty bottles to be filled with the wine that had fermented in oak barrels over the last few months. Isabella, Avram, and Ana sampled the red wines but found they were not ready for market.

"I can taste the oak, but the alcohol content is still low," said Ana.

"I agree," Avram commented after drinking a cup.

"No matter," Isabella said. "We have a long voyage ahead. The wine will be ready when we arrive in Turquía."

Avram glanced at her with a wanting look that Isabella found slightly discomforting. She lowered her gaze to the wine bottles on the table. He had asked her the same question several times over the summer—to set a date for their wedding. But she found many excuses to avoid doing so. Now that they were leaving Portugal, she felt burdened by his expectations.

"I'm ready to reward our workers. Would you please gather them, Avram?"

Avram stood still for a moment, then acquiesced with a nod. Within a short time, a group of workers lined up in front of the house. Isabella, followed by Ana, stepped in front of the weary-looking men. Their worried faces reflected sadness. *They sense the end of their livelihood*, thought Isabella with a heavy heart.

"I want to thank you for all your hard work—" Isabella stopped for a moment. "Over all the years you've worked for us." She looked into the men's faces, who were squinting without smiles. *These poor men*, she thought again. "Your hard work made much profit for the estate." Their eyes rose to her lips. "That's why we want to reward you." She turned to Ana, who carried a bucket full of small purses. "Each one will get a year's wages and two bottles of our wine."

Smiles lit the men's faces as they glanced at each other, and a murmur rumbled down the rows.

Ana distributed the coin purses, and Avram gave each their ration of wine. Now the men's voices were louder and happier. Isabella was glad for the little she could do for them. This would settle them until they found other means of employment.

"Thank you, mistress, for your kindness," one worker said.

"Yes, we thank you from the bottom of our hearts," said another. They all agreed by shouting together, "We won't forget you!"

Fighting back tears, Isabella nodded and smiled. "Good-bye, men. May the Lord keep you."

"And may the Virgin keep you safe on your voyage," the workers replied in one voice.

Isabella lifted the hem of her long dress and turned to enter the house. Ana and Avram followed with the empty bucket. Isabella turned back to see the men remaining silent and motionless in the yard. They began to disperse a few at a time, reluctant to leave a place where their work had been valued.

99

A Last Attempt

FINALLY, ON A SHIP SAILING toward Portugal, Miguel began to feel a taste of freedom and a renewed connection to Isabella. When he thought he might see her in a few months, his hands trembled in anticipation. Yet, he had been given no set date for the ship's arrival at Lisbon. Whenever he asked Captain Santos—who was still lamenting the loss of his men and seething over his stolen cargo—he merely replied "soon." He had told the captain his ordeal of the last three years and believed the man's frank assurance to return him home to Lisbon.

Miguel had become indispensable to Captain Santos by setting course along the African coast, checking and rechecking coordinates on his maps, jotting down measurements and leagues, and helping with the maintenance on deck. The captain knew how to maximize Miguel's workload, using every minute of the day and some of the night. When Miguel finished his shift, all he had were two hours' rest, then he began the next work assignment. At one point Miguel wondered whether he would have been better off remaining shackled on the pirate ship instead of being tied here to a rigorous work schedule. Freedom was dear and costly.

Meanwhile, Miguel learned interesting information about the caravel and its cargo. The ship didn't carry slaves in its hold, like the previous caravels he'd been trapped on. When he asked casually of the contents, sailors told him they contained iron implements that the pirates couldn't carry away on their raids. The shipment had originated in Guinea and held heavy crates that were nailed shut. He tried to guess their contents, but couldn't chance pulling the nails to take a peek inside. After a while he thought he'd better mind his own business and not risk his safety or his goal, which was to hold Isabella in his arms again.

"Ship ahoy on starboard!" the sailor shouted from the crow's nest.

Captain Santos, Miguel, and the crew ran starboard. A caravel sailed the waves toward them with great speed. No flag was hoisted on its mast.

Captain Santos alerted his men. "Keep a close watch on that caravel!"

The caravel kept getting closer, when the sailor in the crow's nest yelled, "They're hoisting their flag!"

Miguel could see the flag unfurling on the mast, when a cry went forth, "It's one of ours! One of ours!"

At the sight, the men on deck cheered.

Miguel gave a sigh of relief. In these treacherous waters, any friendly sight brought welcomed news. It was curious why their mast had been bereft of a banner. Perhaps the ship was sailing home? His excitement rose as the leagues between the two ships shortened.

The seventy-ton ship made a close approach and fired a two-gun salute into the waters. Miguel noticed that a Portuguese flag flew that was different from their own. Theirs bore a crown mounted on a coat of arms with eleven castles. It flew side by side with a black flag. *Must've lost good men at sea*, he surmised. It was clear that Santos had also noticed the anomaly, but remained silent.

"Hurrah! Hurrah!" the men cheered as the other ship replied with a similar salute and the bell by the stern rang, calling on all hands.

Within the next thirty minutes, the two ships floated side by side as Captain Santos welcomed his counterpart. Miguel was struck that the ship bore no name on its hull.

This captain was a tall man of approximately forty-five years of age, with a black goatee and distinguished look. He wore the rank of admiral on his uniform. Miguel recognized the insignia of the marine royal house. Next to him stood a young boy.

"Welcome aboard the *Tres Magos,* Captain." Santos bowed.

His counterpart bowed too. "I'm Captain Francisco de Almeida. We're returning from Galle on an exploration voyage in the Indian Ocean. This is my son, Lourenço de Almeida. Just turned fourteen."

Standing nearby, Miguel felt a tremor. He pressed his right hand to his heart. A son. He had a son. Where was *his* son? The memory exploded and seeped through his brain as he remembered Isabella awaiting the birth of their child. A son? He began to feel weak on his legs, and his head felt giddy.

Captain Santos glanced curiously at him. "You're as white as a sheet, Miguel," he whispered.

Miguel regained his composure and whispered back, "I'm fine, Captain."

Captain Santos returned his attention to his visitor. "Congratulations, young man." Captain Santos bowed to the boy. "How exciting your voyage sounds, Captain! I wish I could've accompanied your ship to the Indian Ocean. Please follow us to my cabin."

When they were all assembled in Captain Santos's cabin, and after wine was served, Captain Francisco de Almeida spoke. "We were searching for the cinnamon spice found in Galle."

"And did you find it?" Captain Santos asked.

"That is a secret for now, but I can tell you we will have it in Portuguese hands as soon as the small country is in ours."

"My congratulations, Captain Almeida. Indeed a proud discovery for Portugal. As for spices from the New World, we still wait for the benefit of Spanish Admiral Cristóvão Colombo's discoveries to trickle into Portugal."

Captain Almeida nodded.

Miguel, meanwhile, stood silent near Captain Santos, watching the young boy paying attention to his father. *My own son may be two or three years old by now.*

"You must have noticed, Captain Almeida, the shambled state of the *Tres Magos,*" Captain Santos began. "We were forced into battle by a pirate ship led by Aruj, a vile heathen. We lost five men, and the pirates stole goods and supplies."

Captain Almeida shook his head with a saddened face. "I grieve for you, good captain. This is the scourge of the seas now. I hope we can stop these cutthroats and criminals someday."

Captain Santos's lips were shut tight in recollection.

"I'm sorry to add to your sorrows," said Captain Almeida, "but, Captain Santos, I must bring your attention to your outdated flag. King John II passed away on October 25, this blessed year." Captain Almeida stopped to cross himself, followed by everyone in the small cabin. "The new flag now belongs to our new king, Manuel I from the House of Aviz."

Captain Santos was visibly startled by the news. A pained look covered his face. "I mourn our King John. He did much for Portuguese exploration. A monarch who had a vision of the future."

Captain Almeida nodded.

Captain Santos glanced at Miguel, then addressed Almeida. "My good captain, you're headed home to Lisbon, I presume?"

Captain Almeida nodded. "After a short detour, we're sailing straight to Lisbon."

"Could I impose on your hospitality and have Miguel Costa sail home with you? This man has seen many horrors in the last three years, and he's anxious to return home to his family."

"It would be my pleasure to have him join our ship."

Miguel Costa fell suddenly mute. Then he burst, unable to contain his joy, "Captain Almeida, I'll never forget your kindness. Thank you, Captain Santos. Thank you!"

Captain Almeida smiled at him. He turned to Captain Santos. "We'll see many changes now with a new king. His marriage to Queen Isabella's daughter is now official. To honor this alliance, all foreigners and heretics must leave Portugal within the next year or convert. Much change is indeed upon us."

A tug at his heartstrings sent a shiver through Miguel, and a dampening spirit quelled his bursting joy. Again, all Jews would be stripped of their homes. He lowered his head in a foreboding mood.

"All right, young man—we now head home!" Captain Almeida said to Miguel as he got up and took leave of his host

Miguel, meanwhile, felt invisible chains tugging at him. He shrugged off the feeling and elated in the thought of shortly seeing Isabella and his son.

100

A Perilous Journey

ANTONIO DE TORRES CHECKED AND rechecked his coordinates as he sailed, pushed along by the winds.

Columbus had instructed him to sail with the westerly trade winds blowing from west to east, to carry the caravels straight to European lands and to Spain. But de Torres decided to sail along the island arc of the Lesser Antilles and on his own to pursue a southerly route where the winds were weaker. A few island discoveries on his part might boost his own name and add to the admiral's prestige.

The caravels sailed along the arc that Columbus had explored on his second voyage, and de Torres felt satisfied he was following a familiar course. The men on the ships were all seasoned mariners, and Michele de Cuneo at his side displayed his gallantry and added a touch of nobility to the expedition. Diego Columbus provided nourishment to their souls as he conducted Mass on board: Lauds in the early morning hours, Matins following Lauds, Vespers at sunset, and Compline night prayers with punctuality.

As the sun shed its last rays, it illuminated a broad part of the sky and bathed it in an eerie orange hue. The few clouds above their heads took on reddish tints with a few tropical showers scattering water into the ocean like the stream from a sculpted fountain.

"*Deus, in adiutorium meum intende. Domine . . .*" chanted Diego as the men sang after him. Bent to their knees on deck, they repeated the sacred words. The sailors on the other ships conducted their services as well, and prayed for a safe voyage. After prayers, each of the men retired to his spot on deck and began to play cards.

The hours passed, then after Compline the men on deck wrapped themselves in their blankets and went to sleep.

"The hour is nine in the evening by the *ampolleta*!" the gromet cried as he roamed the decks.

Below deck, muffled moaning and cries rose from the hold where the Carib slaves were chained. They had no nightly meal, after having earlier eaten a serving of a concoction of beans and bread with rationed water.

The only ones still awake were de Torres and the boy in the crow's nest. De Torres paced the deck, stopping now and then to peer through the darkness surrounding the caravel. The other three ships were lights dotting the darkness half a league away. De Torres hated having to curtail the Indians' rations, but with what they'd been allocated for the voyage, there was hardly enough to sustain his men for the entire crossing. While stopping at a few islands on the way might procure more food supplies, he felt reluctant to spend too much time island hopping. So far he had spent two weeks searching for undiscovered lands, but the admiral had already perused this part of the Antilles. He shivered on the cold deck and pulled his shirt collar close to his neck.

"Oh well, better hit the bunk," he said aloud.

Two weeks followed the first two since leaving Española, and the men were becoming antsy. They began to show signs of boredom, and complained of the cold seeping into paradise. A poor combination—strong winds and a pervading sense of wasted time.

"Antonio?" Michele de Cuneo spoke with familiarity. The two men had become close friends, especially since they were quartered in the same cabin. "What do you say we sail for Spain?"

De Torres didn't answer at first, fixated on a spot along the horizon.

"If we don't leave now, we may starve on the crossing," de Cuneo said, his voice taking on a reproachful tone.

"Michele is right." Diego seconded the noble cavalier. "With all due respect, de Torres, my brother has already covered these parts of the Caribee. We must head home."

Diego seemed to have gained strength in the absence of his older brother, the admiral. "If we don't, we will lose the cargo."

De Torres turned from contemplating the many islands ahead and the large island of Boriquén. "It's time. Raise all sails!" The order went through to the other ships via the bucket extended on the pulley.

⁌✑⁊

The ships sailed 145 leagues northward, and as soon as the strong wind of the westerlies caught the four caravels, they were on their way. The sea was gentle with white foam on small crested waves. Schools of gold fish swam around them, and the sailors used this lull to catch the fish caught in green weeds against the hull. Now their diet was being sustained from the sea. Some of this manna found its way to the Indians sitting in the suffocating hold. Diego, who had taken pity on them, sneaked additional rations of bread and water to them.

Two more weeks passed in the bliss of fishing, working, praying, and playing cards on the ships. Now the men were ready to arrive, and their anxiety rose two notches above their usual state of mind. Small fights broke out now and then, but de Torres restored calm with threats of lashings.

"Come on, men. We're almost home. Your patience will be rewarded," he shouted from the quarterdeck.

"Antonio." Diego came to him.

"What is it?"

"You must come down the hold."

"Why?"

"We may have a problem on our hands."

De Torres looked into Diego's eyes, and what he saw didn't please him. There was sadness and grief in them.

"Lead on, Diego." He followed Diego into the hold.

The darkness hit him first, then a cold wave enveloped his body, and a pungent and acrid smell hit his nostrils. De Torres brought his hand to his nose to keep the offending smell from penetrating his lungs. As soon as his eyes adjusted to the darkness, he saw forms lying on the plank floor. Some slept and others sat or reclined against the hold wall.

"Why are these men and women so still?" he asked Diego from under the hand covering his mouth and nose.

"Because they're dead, Antonio."

De Torres startled as if someone had gut-punched him. "What do you mean, *dead*?"

"Just like I said," Diego retorted, his voice angry.

"But how could they have died so quickly?"

"Because these men and women are not used to these conditions! They're used to sunshine and fresh air! Here in the hold, they're suffocating!"

De Torres fell silent. He'd have to answer for these deaths and would be blamed for the loss of precious cargo. The admiral would be furious. No less would be the monarchs, who advocated being gentle with the natives. He knew the whole idea of shuttling slaves had been a bad idea. He had counseled Columbus to forgo the idea of shipping slaves to the Old World, but Columbus resisted him. Now he felt cornered. How was he to explain this turn of events?

"There's another thing you should know," Diego said firmly.

De Torres felt dread. "What thing?"

"Caonabó is also dead."

Shocked, de Torres fell speechless.

"Do you realize what this means?" Diego asked the question with a seriousness that overwhelmed de Torres. The king of the Caribs was dead, and the repercussions from Spain would touch everyone connected with his charge. *He should've seen to their care himself.* He hit his forehead in anger.

De Torres lowered his head in agony. "Call all the men on deck, and let's bury them at sea."

The next hours were hellish for all the men on board his ship as they brought bodies from the hold. The same ordeal was played out on the other ships when more Indian deaths became apparent. About two hundred bodies from all ships were slowly dumped into the cold water of the Atlantic, slipping off the decks one by one. The remaining Indian survivors were not on deck to see their brothers and sisters being buried at sea. Diego officiated at the funeral, saying a short prayer for their souls.

"May these souls reside with the Almighty, and may they find paradise in their innocence."

De Torres then gave the order to feed the Indians extra rations and bring them on deck for fresh air, a few at a time. Afterward, Antonio de Torres became moody and silent. Michele de Cuneo tried to cheer him without success.

"I see land!" cried the man in the crow's nest.

The sailors ran to starboard, and a faint line appeared on the horizon. The men cheered and jumped up and down in their joy. A high rocky promontory appeared before them.

"I see Cape Spartel on the shores of Morocco!" one of his men shouted.

"Yes, we're entering the Straits of Gibraltar!"

"We're finally home!"

De Torres felt relieved. At least he had preserved all his men's lives. It was sad and regrettable that two hundred natives had met their deaths, but no one knew what to expect from these Indians, who simply couldn't survive as well as Europeans or African slaves.

Now, though, he would have to face the consequences of his superior's faulty judgment.

101

Winds of Change

FOR THE FOUR MONTHS FOLLOWING Antonio de Torres's departure with the caravels full of Carib slaves, Columbus had been having nightmares. One night, in painful detail, he dreamt that the slaves he shipped home were returning to Española carrying arrows and spears spiked with poisonous acid from cassava residue. He genuinely felt the pain as an arrow pierced his shoulder. In a panic, he tried to pull the arrow out, but it had become fixed in his bone. Sweat dripped from his brow. As he wiped it, he realized he had been dreaming. His left shoulder still ached, and his arm was partly numb. He realized his old ailment had come back. He rubbed his shoulder to stimulate blood flow to his arm, and the pain subsided.

He got up from the bunk and saw through his enflamed eyes that it was high morning. He ran to his trousers and shirt draped over the chair and stepped out of his loose sleeping gown. Cold water splashed from a pitcher refreshed his sore eyes and face. Leaving the cabin, he squinted his bloodshot eyes to see clearly. His cabin boy, Pedro de Acevedo, was still slumbering on deck, wrapped in his blanket.

Columbus shook him violently. "Wake up, Pedro! Why didn't you wake me?"

The lad, who had grown to the age of fifteen, vehemently protested his innocence. Pedro rubbed his eyes still full of sleep and began to tremble. "Admiral, I was given strict orders not to wake you!" He stood quickly.

"And who gave you that order? Eh!" Columbus softened his voice. "You know that I must oversee the colony's daily affairs. Otherwise everyone will run amok on this island."

"Dr. Chanca gave the order." Pedro stood ashen.

"All right, Pedro. I'm no longer angry with you. Go and find Diego to bring my breakfast."

Columbus smiled as he saw Pedro running down the steps. *He's a good lad.*

Diego de Salcedo showed up shortly with a tray of food.

Columbus dug into the freshly caught grilled fish and tore off a big chunk of cassava bread. *Thank the Lord—the natives know how to bake calabash without its poison*!

"Diego, call de la Cosa and the priests to the *Mariagalante* within the hour."

An hour later the men showed up. Columbus waited for them on the main deck.

"I called you here because it's high time we converted the natives."

A smile appeared on Fray Ramón Pane's face, of the Franciscan Order. The three Jeronymite monks nodded with approval.

"How do you intend to get them baptized? Fray Buil tried and failed," Fray Pane said.

"Fray Buil was a weak man. That's why he fled and ran away from his sacred duty," Columbus said with annoyance. Anything that reminded him of Fray Buil and Margarite set him in a wretched mood. He pictured the cowards at court spreading lies and falsehoods about him. He took a deep breath.

"Beginning tomorrow, I'd like to have a Mass in the morning and another at night. And in between have the Indians baptized until the whole of Española is Christian."

Fray Pane nodded dutifully.

"That's much better." Columbus sighed with relief. "Now, de la Cosa, have you heard word from Ojeda at Santo Tomás?"

"Yes, Admiral. He has followed your order. The Indians are now carrying the copper coin around their necks when they fulfill their obligation. The gold dust is supplied every three months in the calabash shell to the contador. The cacique Manicaotex has to do the same every two months. That's worth one hundred and fifty castellanos, Admiral."

"What about the other natives who live far from the rivers?" Columbus asked.

"These Indians are providing tributes of spun cotton instead of gold. We should be able to send the next shipment home in a few months, as your brother Bartholomew, the adelantado, ordered."

"That's good news. I knew I could depend on my adelantado. Thank you, everyone, for doing your duty to España! Dismissed."

After his council left, Columbus mulled over the affairs of the island. There were six hundred and fifty Spanish souls on Española, including some women and children who had arrived from Spain to join their husbands. His brother Bartholomew had organized the gold dust tributes and had required strict obedience from the natives. Columbus felt satisfied with the report.

But where was the real progress? The one sure thing that he had anticipated would happen after a year or two? By now the crops should have been providing enough food and starch to nourish the colonists. Wheat, barley, and other crops were meager, even though the soil was black with nutrients. It was manpower they lacked. The colony needed more working hands. Except for a few dozen men working hard in the fields, none of the rest of the nobles or military men wanted to soil their hands in the earth. Columbus sighed under the pressure of his burden. Something must be done.

A sudden wind rose and whipped his face. The trees swayed violently, and sand began to cloud his vision. Both the natives and the Spanish began to run for cover. Dark clouds gathered above their heads where the sun had shone a moment ago.

"De la Cosa!" Columbus yelled as he ran to the stern. He didn't see Juan but yelled, "Make sure the anchors are properly secured in the harbor. See to the tiller!"

He then ran back to the few men on deck and prodded them with some instructions. "Lower the sails! Check the rigging!"

By now the winds blowing from the southeast grew to hurricane proportions. With great cracking sounds, trees were uprooted and fell to earth. The native huts offered no resistance to the power of a violent and capricious wind. Some huts were lifted entirely and torn apart by that powerful force, tumbling round and round until they disappeared from sight. The families who had cowered in their huts a moment ago huddled together, embracing each other for protection. Their cries became drowned by the loud cacophonous roar. All hell had broken loose.

From the main deck, pitching dangerously, Columbus saw the beach and shore disappear under the blasting sandstorm. Holding on to the railings and guided by a line tied for safety, he laboriously tried to return to his cabin, but no such luck was afforded him. With a loud bang and a horrendous crack the three caravels lying at anchor in the unprotected harbor capsized onto their portsides! Columbus's heart cracked with the ships. The *Cardera*, *San Juan,* and *Gallega* broke up, sending masts still attached to rigging into the water; hurling planks on shore; and covering the sea with beams, barrels, and crates.

Without those ships they were done for—isolated from the Old World. The *Niña* and the *Mariagalante* were the only ships remaining upright and proud, though the *Mariagalante* was badly damaged.

Columbus tried laboriously to pull himself up the quarterdeck, but the violent pitching below his feet threw him back each time he tried. A board hit him on the head as he pushed against the wind. On the last try he felt arms around his shoulders.

"I've got you, Admiral. Hold on to my waist!"

Columbus tried to counter the wind by twisting his head, but the blasted sand penetrated his mouth, nostrils, and eyes, preventing him from seeing who held him. He closed his eyes, feeling the sand grinding under his eyelids.

Another push up the last steps and both crouched figures scrambled for the cabin. The unhinged door banged back and forth under the force of the wind. Strong arms pushed Columbus into his cabin as the wind swirled around the structure. One last shove, and they both fell inside. The door was slammed hard, then shut tight. Now only the wind whistled as it seeped through cracks in the door.

"Here, Admiral—lie down here."

Columbus opened his inflamed eyes and saw João's figure moving like a ghost. "João?" he called out.

"Yes, Admiral. It's me, João. Don't try to move. You have a nasty bump on your head."

Columbus brought his shaking hand to his head and felt a sticky wetness that wasn't seawater or rainwater. He looked at his fingers and was surprised to see blood.

"Where are the men on the ship? Pedro? De la Cosa? The others?"

"We won't know until the wind ceases, Admiral."

Columbus nodded, in a trance. All power had gone from his mind and limbs. He felt frozen.

"We'll sit out the storm in your cabin," said João as the wind punctuated his remark by growing in sound and fury. The floorboards under their feet groaned and squeaked as if about to be torn asunder. As the room swayed and pitched, the men waited out the storm together.

102

Hope Raised and Dashed

MIGUEL TOILED MANY HOURS ON deck: helping to hoist the sails, checking passing ships from the crow's nest, taking night watch duties, and shuttling meals to the captain's cabin. When he had free time, he dreamt of Isabella and his son. *A son, or perhaps a daughter*, he thought with pride. He felt an urgency to reach Portugal's shores. *The old king is dead, and the new king is mad.* Mad because he was ridding himself of all Jews in Portugal. Mad because he listened to Queen Isabella's wish for a Catholic Portugal. It was the basis for the marriage between her daughter, the Princess of Asturias, and King Manuel of Portugal. The phrase "a Catholic land" rang in his ears.

He kept asking Captain Francisco de Almeida when the ship would arrive in Portugal.

"All in good time," the captain answered with a smile.

"But approximately, when do you expect we'll sight land?"

"Young man." The captain's face turned serious. "If I had the answer to that, I'd be decorated with the highest mark. I promise you—you'll be the first to disembark once we touch Lisbon. You can expect two months at the most."

"Thank you, Captain," Miguel said with a quiet sigh and dropped shoulders.

Two months! A lot could happen by then. He relived all over again the mad rush to port in Seville with Guerida on their tail. The search the Beneluz family had been subjected to on board and Isabella's temporary disappearance were more bad memories. Although now that they weren't fugitives, Isabella and her son would likely be leaving the estate—to go where? A cold sweat covered his brow, and an uncontrollable fear pervaded down to his bones. She would leave without him. He would lose them both!

He descended to the depths of despair. There must be something he could do to speed up the ship!

He lived in a constant state of agitation, fear, restlessness, and lack of sleep. He couldn't hold down much food—his anxiety getting the better of him and spoiling the taste in his mouth. He began to taste bitterness in his mouth and bitterness in his mind. Within a week, he had lost a substantial amount of weight and turned moody.

The other sailors on ship eyed him quizzically as they carried out their duties. On one particular morning, he was carrying the captain's tray and let it slip from his hands as he tripped on the steps to his cabin. Two sailors rushed to his side and helped him get on his feet.

"You better get another tray," one recommended.

Miguel nodded, and after clearing the food splattered on the plank's floor, he shuffled to the cook's corner. Midway there, he collapsed and lost consciousness.

❦

"What do you think, Doctor?" Captain de Almeida asked.

The physician shook his head. "He's undernourished—all skin and bones."

"But I don't understand," de Almeida said. "Why would that be? No one is starving on my ship."

"Captain, it's true *you* don't understand. This boy is dying from love. All he has talked about for the last months is his sweetheart back home."

Captain de Almeida's mouth slacked in disbelief. "But why withhold nourishment?" He cleared his throat. "He was most anxious to return home to his wife and son. I should think he'd keep fit to see them. It is most curious. As if he were afraid he won't find them?"

"I'll keep an eye on the young man," the physician said. "I'm worried about his fever. Make sure he drinks plenty of water."

Captain de Almeida nodded.

The physician wiped the sweat off Miguel's burning forehead. Then, supporting his head, he poured water between his opened lips. Some of the liquid found its way down his throat, while the rest spilled on his sweaty shirt.

Miguel gagged, then coughed. "Wait . . . Isabella. Wait . . . for . . . me."

The physician and the captain locked glances and nodded in agreement.

103

Leaving the Hearth

UPON HER RETURN, ISABELLA HELD Salvadore in a tight embrace against her chest. She had missed him with a ravenous hunger for the love that fed her lonely life. Bitterness and disappointment from her last voyage weighed heavily upon her. She had known that the odds of finding Miguel were practically none but hadn't wholly believed it until the end. Hope against hope, she had trusted her intuition and convinced herself that by some miracle he would come to her like a dream that materialized out of her love for him, but that belief had evaporated into thin air. Tears rolled down her cheeks, and Salvadore looked at her with innocent surprise.

"*No llores,* Mama." His little hand cupped her chin as if to say he was there for her.

"I'm not crying, my love. I'm happy to see you."

Contented by her answer, Salvadore nodded, his red curls shaking about his young face.

Ana rose from her chair and gently took Salvadore from Isabella's arms. "I'll take him to the kitchen. Why don't you join us later?"

Grateful, Isabella nodded silently and watched Ana leave the room with Salvadore. In a way, she was glad Ana had interfered, and as soon as the door closed she vented her grief and despair. She let go of her tears and shook under great pain. She cried to her heart's content.

"Good-bye, my love. Good-bye," she whispered between sobs. She wept bitterly for a long time. When her pain became lighter, she wiped her wet eyes and face with her long sleeves. Rummaging in the pocket of her dress, she pulled out a cloth and blew her nose. She waited a while longer to compose herself, then hurried to the kitchen.

Wrapping her woolen shawl tightly around her shoulders, she couldn't help thinking that the days had cooled considerably since winter had descended upon Portugal. The rains fell periodically, and at those times birds, wild rabbits, and weasels—that Salvadore loved to run after—hid in the oak forest nearby. When the skies cleared, a few black-headed gulls would venture inland and compete with eagles and peregrine falcons in the hunt for small creatures. But foremost, a heavy silence hung over the estate, adding to Isabella's sense of loss.

She entered the kitchen and found everyone warming themselves by a fire in the big hearth. The only ones absent were Avram and Sekou, who had gone to the vineyards. All the workers had been dismissed, and any vestiges of grapes growing on the vines would be abandoned to hungry birds.

Ana observed her with keen eyes, scrutinizing her appearance and puffy eyes.

Salvadore left Ana's warm lap and ran to Isabella's arms. She lifted and twirled him around the kitchen. Raquela's children, Sarina and Aron, rose with excitement, but they were now too big to be lifted.

"We want to hold hands with Salvadore," Sarina called out.

Isabella motioned them to join hands in a circle, and they did so with great enthusiasm. To Raquela and Ana's delight, they sang and danced a *jota* until they collapsed out of breath on the floor, giggling and screaming their joy.

As soon as they all calmed down, Isabella asked that Juanita join them.

"She was cleaning the upper floor," Raquela said. "I'll go find her."

Just then Avram and Sekou entered the kitchen. Avram had an inquiring look in his eyes at seeing them all assembled.

"Have I missed something?" he asked.

Isabella turned to him and said, "I have an announcement to make."

A surprised look lit his face. Isabella could swear he had blushed slightly. She disregarded the thought as Juanita entered.

"Please sit down, Juanita. You're part of this family too."

Juanita lifted Aron from his chair and helped him on her lap.

"I've made a decision. We'll be sailing to Istanbul in Turquía. Remember when Pasha Bayezit II welcomed us to his country three years ago?"

"That's right!" Ana said. "I remember the pasha sent his ships from Istanbul to gather Jews and bring them to his kingdom."

Questions flew, and Isabella smiled at the excitement mixed with a certain amount of fear. Sekou sat on the floor, as was his custom, but his crooked smile showed how much interest he had in the news.

"But that was three years ago," Ana said. "How do we know if they'll still invite us with open arms?"

Isabella nodded. "He will. I know this fact from the Jews in El Mouro Castle who receive family letters from Istanbul. I tell you—we'll be welcomed."

"When are we leaving?" Raquela asked.

"What about our personal belongings?" asked Juanita.

"We'll leave within the next six months. And yes, Juanita, you can take your belongings with you."

"And how do you propose we'll travel?" Ana asked, still leery.

"Why, on the *Liberação*, of course!" Isabella said with the pride of a captain.

Avram remained silent with his customary patience, leaving the women to ask all their questions first.

"But we still have time," Ana interjected. "They gave us an entire year to sell our lands and homes. Why rush?"

"If we leave earlier, we'll catch the first buyers for our property. Rather than wait till the last moment."

"And have you found a buyer yet?" asked Raquela.

Isabella didn't reply right away. Instead, she said, "I want to leave Portugal after the winter. By then I'll have a buyer."

She cleared her throat as if gathering courage to announce the next news. She looked in Avram's direction and saw his hopeful eyes set on her.

"Right after we leave the harbor, Avram and I will marry on the *Liberação*."

Avram came to her side and held her in his arms.

"Mazal tov!" Both Ana and Raquela screamed with joy.

Isabella tried hard to show her joy and not disappoint them with her lack of exuberance.

"Speak! Speak!" All looked to Avram.

"I'm a very happy man. I will do everything in my power to make Isabella and Salvadore happy."

They all applauded until Isabella put an end to the applause. "We have much to do. So let's organize ourselves within the next weeks."

A loud knock on the kitchen door startled them. They all turned to the door and saw an official standing in his velvet doublet and stockings, an expensive sword at his side, and a helper at his flank.

"Is this the Costa household?" the official asked.

A hush fell over the kitchen.

"And who wants us?" Avram asked.

"We're sent by the Crown. We need to know your adherence to our religion, or if you're of another faith?"

The question raised shivers in Isabella. She was sure the others felt it too. She raised her head and enunciated clearly. "No one here is of the Catholic faith. And yes, we will vacate our home and lands to sail from Portugal." She saw Juanita smile at her approvingly.

The official stood taken aback by her statement. He regained his composure. "In that case, you will have till summer of next year to leave Portugal. Any land or structure remaining will revert to the Crown."

You bet it will, thought Isabella in a flash. It was all happening just as before in Spain. The Portuguese crown benefited from all wealth belonging to Jews who couldn't sell what they owned. In the end, they'd be offered a pittance for their homes, land, mills, vineyards, and shops. But Isabella would make sure it wouldn't happen that way.

The official scribbled on a parchment with a quill pen dipped in the ink bottle held by his helper. He approached the large kitchen table and sprinkled white powder on the fresh ink. He rolled the document and presented it to Isabella.

"Bom dia." The official left the kitchen, followed by his attendant, and silence fell again on the small crowd.

"We've known this would happen for several years now," Isabella said, reassuring everyone. "But we won't let them overcome us. Right?"

"Yes!" the adults all answered in a united shout.

104

Rebuilding

THE DEVASTATION FROM THE HURRICANE was total. The new fort at Isabela had been demolished, along with the mill. Columbus had lost three ships, and the Indian population moved inland with whatever they could salvage. All that remained were ruins, a few bricks that had been the first town built in the New World. The demolished settlement had lost a number of colonists as well— four men, three women, and five children. The ones remaining alive thanked the Lord for that miracle. Fray Ramón Pane, Fray Juan de Borgoña, and the three Jeronymite monks conducted a Mass, and a funeral lament sung by the congregants rose to the cloudless skies.

"We grieve and lament the children, women, and men lost to us," Fray Ramón Pane eulogized. "These souls came with the best intentions to this new land to build new homes . . . may the Virgin protect their souls." He made the sign of the cross, and the six hundred and thirty colonists on Isabela did likewise.

Columbus felt deep sadness as he stared at his hands locked in prayer. An aching chest and blurry eyes still plagued him. He had had a streak of bad luck in the last year, when success in establishing settlements and commerce eluded him. And some of his own men—Fray Buil and Margarite, who he thought were close colleagues—had rebelled against him and now spread rumors. He felt confident, though, that Antonio de Torres and his brother Diego would represent him at court and vouch for his pure intentions and strict leadership. Everything he had done was intended to benefit the Crown, leave a legacy for his sons, and help Spain become a stronger power in Europe.

The voice of Fray Pane came to his ears as though from a distance. "Let us pray together." Another prayer ensued, and then the service was over. The twelve bodies were buried, the mounds sealed with rocks, and a cross placed to mark the graves.

Columbus rose from the ground with difficulty and walked in front of the crowd to Fray Pane's side. The Franciscan priest shook Columbus's hand and stood aside.

"My most beloved colonists and friars," Columbus began. "I stand before you today as a humble servant of the Crown and of Their Majesties, *los reyes Católicos.*" He stopped to gauge the audience and saw faces burdened with grief and lingering traces of fear. They'd had a fearsome reminder that they were mere mortals in the hands of elements beyond their power.

Columbus continued. "We will rebuild. We'll rebuild our town, harbor, mill, and the heart that makes it a Spanish colony to be reckoned with!"

The colonists listened with new interest, their faces turned to him. In that instant, he felt a presence hovering above him that gave him strength. His mission was to be an emissary and a force of change. To create a new world, where the Catholic faith would embody this change.

"The first work we'll undertake in the name of the Lord is the crafting of a new vessel. We can use the salvaged parts and timber from the wrecked ships and build a new one. The first ship to be built in the New World!"

By now the colonists felt uplifted. "Hurrah for the admiral! Hurrah for our leader!"

Columbus smiled with pleasure. He put out his hand to stop the cheering. "Now my friends, let us begin the holy work of the Lord!"

The colonists scattered to carry out Columbus's orders. The men returned to the harbor for the rebuilding of the ship. The women picked up the care and feeding of six hundred and thirty-nine bellies, helping the cooks and using food supplies that they scavenged from the damaged ships.

Columbus called on his council, which included Juan de la Cosa; Ponce de León; Dr. Diego Alvarez Chanca; and Diego Marquez, the royal inspector.

"I asked you here to tell you that we'll begin building three other forts: a fortress to be called Esperanza near the River Yaqui, and Magdalena Fortress across Puerto de los Hidalgos in the Royal Vega by the river Jalaqua, and Santa Catalina town near Estancia Yaqui."

"Will you build only one ship?" asked de la Cosa.

"That's all the timber we have. Cobbled together we can erect a strong ship like the *Niña*, captained by de la Cosa."

De la Cosa smiled, pleased by the mention. "Do you have a name for the new ship, Admiral?"

Columbus thought for a brief moment. "It will befit this new ship—the first built in the New World—to be called *Santa Cruz*."

"Admiral, I have another name for the *Santa Cruz*. Let's call her the *India*!"

"Officially it will be *Santa Cruz*, but the men can nickname her the *India*." Columbus and all assembled received the new name with approval. He turned to the friars, who seemed somewhat at a loss in the bureaucratic planning of works. "As for you men of God, we depend on your skills to force the conversions of the natives."

The friars nodded in agreement and relief that they had a role in the building of the faith among the heathens.

"All right, men. We have a lot of work in front of us."

After the men left him, Columbus sat for a long time, contemplating the task ahead of him. He anticipated his men would be energized and overjoyed by their mission, the sheer amount of work, and at constructing the towns. He wasn't too hopeful though, knowing how the Spanish noblemen had acted all along, preferring to let the sailors do all the work and not lending their horses to carry burdens. But he had to believe that his leadership, and that of his brother Bartholomew, would supply the discipline to get these tasks accomplished.

Another concern tugged at him. He felt a great urgency to return to Spain, to see if Torres had carried his orders and extinguished the lies Buil and Margarite had no doubt disseminated at court. He longed to tell everyone in his own words the truth about the treachery of rebels, the islanders' resistance to obeying him, and the nobles' refusal to work. As soon as the first town was built, he would return home.

105

Preparations for a Grand Voyage

THE CARRIAGE TAKING ISABELLA AND Avram to the Castelo dos Mouros made haste on the winding road, climbing the Sintra Mountains. The rectangular towers shortly appeared before their eyes, and as the fog lifted to reveal the castle's stony structure, it strengthened Isabella's resolve. She wrapped the long overcoat tightly around her body, as the temperature for November felt icy.

"Please, Isabella, won't you listen to reason?" Avram begged of her.

"I can't abandon these people. I gave them my word," Isabella said. "Besides, they'll be a great help throughout the voyage. You know—helping with chores, the sails, the rigging."

"But think of the expense. Having to feed them. Seeing to their safety?"

"I told you, Avram, and I'll say it again. I won't let them die on other ships or at the hands of pirates."

"Yes, I know about pirates. I lost my whole family to them!"

Isabella felt pity for Avram. His mother's and brothers' death, then the disappearance of his father, all left him with indelible and painful memories. We go through life juggling suffering and relief, and pain and joy. Hadn't she had her share of affliction and anguish? The loss of her adoptive mother, Estrella, would always have a place of guilt in her memories. The abandonment of her adoptive father, yet another. There was also the loss of the man that took her heart with him. She tried to chase away memories of Miguel and his gentle, loving nature. Although, she was left with a son who brought sunshine and love into her life. She now possessed a mother's love, which could never be extinguished.

"Isabella?"

Avram's voice startled her. "Yes, Avram?"

"Well?"

"We've arrived." Isabella descended from the carriage, followed by a reluctant Avram.

Right away, the children playing on the stony bridge ran to her with smiles and laughter. Isabella was surprised by the welcome reception. Children had a great capacity to retain pleasant memories, she thought. Two of the children held her hand and gently dragged her toward the entrance. The parents came to greet her and, accompanied by a small crowd, they all entered the castle's dilapidated reception hall. Many more men and women came out of their pitched tents as they heard the commotion spreading in the castle hall.

Isabella smiled at everyone and let go of the children's hands.

An elderly man with white hair approached her and Avram. "Welcome to our humble home."

Isabella nodded with a smile. "Thank you," she whispered.

"I'm Ben Baruch. I was gone the last time you came," he told Isabella. "I'm sort of the rabbi and spiritual leader."

Isabella gently bowed her head. "I'm pleased to meet you. I want to know how many of you live here."

"Together, with men, women, and children, they are sixty-five of us. That's thirty children and the rest adults."

Isabella quickly calculated that by adding her household, they'd be at seventy-five souls. As a carrack ship with a wide berth, the *Liberação* could accommodate at least ninety.

"We're planning the voyage to Istanbul by the beginning of next year. I'll take all of you here at the castle. We'll let you know when we expect to leave and what to bring with you."

A silence followed her announcement. Now that freedom beckoned them, a natural fear set in. They were probably torn between leaving for a better future with unforeseen dangers and remaining in the safe and familiar environment until they were forced to leave, Isabella thought.

Ben Baruch spoke. "The clothes off our back are all we possess. We'll travel light."

Everyone laughed with comic relief. "We're leaving behind our jewels and fine linens!" someone in the crowd jested, followed by a renewed wave of laughter.

Isabella noticed that Avram had remained mute the whole time, without any expression on his face. *I wonder if seeing these poor people has given him a change of heart.*

"Good-bye then," Isabella said. "We'll return for you in a few months."

106

Recovery

THE ILLNESS MIGUEL HAD FALLEN into was slow in its departure. He could only recall burning in a fever that brought shivers and chilled his bones. One of Captain Almeida's servants applied a wet towel to his forehead every hour to help cool his fever. The captain's face hovered over him. "How is he?"

"Still no good," the physician replied.

"Keep him watered and feed him more soup."

"All right, Captain."

Miguel heard the words and replies as if in a trance. As if they talked of someone else lying in the same bed.

He kept repeating, "Isabella, Isabella, don't leave. Don't leave me." The floor under his bed swaying and pitching told him that they were still at sea.

Words came back to him: "Hold on, young man. Hold on. Isabella will wait." The words were disembodied, and he tried to lift himself, but everything was a blur of elongated figures hovering in the cabin.

The fever ravaged his starved body. His hands went to his chest, and he felt his ribs protruding, the skin thin.

The physician's voice came to his ears. "You must eat!"

"I will Doctor." Miguel promised.

The physician brushed his hand against Miguel's forehead, then cupped it more firmly, trying to feel his temperature. "I say, your fever is cooling." He laughed. "The captain will be mighty happy."

"Thank you, Doctor," Miguel said. "I'm beginning to feel much better."

"All right, young man."

At the moment, Miguel actually felt very old. He felt years had passed, as if ten years had been squeezed into the space of a few weeks.

"How long have I been ill?"

The physician didn't reply at first. With his brows knitted, he then said quietly, "Two months."

"Two months! I must get up. I must leave the ship."

"You can't get up, because you're weak. And you can't leave the ship."

"Why can't I leave the ship?" he shot back.

"Because we're in the middle of the ocean. Unless you want to swim home—and the waters are extremely cold."

Miguel tried to rise, but the physician's hands pushed his shoulders down. "You mustn't exert yourself, or the fever will come back!"

Suddenly, a flood of tears overcame him. Miguel wept and wept for a long time until there were no more tears.

"Why do you weep?" the physician asked.

Miguel then told him about Isabella, about his son, his years as a slave, and his fear of not finding her. He talked and talked until he felt spent, but made sure to leave out the details about the decree hanging over his head. And with his recounting came great relief.

"My poor man. It must've been a horrendous experience. But you're getting better now, and soon you'll be reunited with your wife and son."

"Thank you, Doctor, for your help."

"It was my duty and pleasure to help you recover," the physician said. "Now try to get some sleep." With those words he left the cabin.

Left alone, Miguel felt great calm descending upon him. In no time he fell into a recuperative sleep.

꧁꧂

"We must do something to help this young man, Captain," the doctor said.

Captain Almeida's features were somber, his brows creased in thought. "Our hands are tied. We're on a secret mission, one that I can't divulge right now."

"I understand, Captain. You do your job, and I'll do mine. I just can't help wanting to reunite this fellow with his beloved family."

"As do I. But these orders came down from the king himself. No one must know our destination, not even my own son, who keeps asking for his mother."

"All right, Captain. But if this man isn't returned to his family, I'm afraid he'll fall into a desperate and depressive condition. One from which he may never recover."

The captain and the physician both fell quiet, each to their own thoughts.

107

New Towns

THE ISLAND OF ESPAÑOLA WAS alive with activity. The new ship, the *India*, was being built; houses of timber were raised; the natives had returned after the frightful hurricane; and life on the island became peaceful for the Spaniards. The system of collecting gold dust from each Indian from the age of fourteen on became law in the colonies. Anyone malingering or refusing to work and collect the gold was punished severely. Columbus approved, after much soul-searching, the cruel method of amassing gold for Spain as the only way possible. He faced the bitter truth that the Indians had gathered the gold he had previously seen in ornaments and masks after years of labor. The gold paid as tribute was gleaned by panning it from sand and gravel in streams and rivers, and by clearing the land and strip-mining to find more substantial deposits. Finding nuggets were rare occurrences. Yet, Columbus was desperate for a big find, one that would justify all his years of wanting and waiting for the legacy he sought.

One day, Bernal de Pisa, the contador, came to him in his newly built one-room house.

"Admiral, the Indians are complaining that the work is too hard." He stopped before finishing his next sentence. "The tribute is hardly filling our coffers."

Columbus stopped writing in his journal and looked up at de Pisa. "You told me last month that our tribute to Spain was meeting its quota."

"I did, Admiral, but we had great hardships after the hurricane. Building the new towns has taken a toll on the treasury."

"What do you mean?"

"We have to pay the men—the contractors who came back with de Torres on the last voyage and the soldiers keeping the peace. Some of these men are supporting their families."

Columbus fell quiet. "You're right. I'd forgotten that the work performed was not on a volunteer basis." He sighed.

De Pisa stood quite silent. He seemed somewhat indignant that Columbus suggested the work was voluntary.

"Thank you, de Pisa, for reminding me of my obligations to the men. I also have an obligation to the Crown for subsidizing the supplies sent from home."

"Perhaps we can try the other islands for tribute?" de Pisa suggested.

"I'll have to think about that. We're already spread thin as it is. Thank you, my good man," Columbus said to end the conversation.

De Pisa bowed with his head, then left him.

From the window, Columbus watched de Pisa walk away and spotted João approaching. Since João had practically saved him from being swept off the *Mariagalante* during the hurricane, he felt a debt to this man who had been a thorn at his side. Although he hadn't forgotten being blackmailed, he tried hard to greet João with friendliness when he entered the room.

"What can I do for you, João?"

"Admiral, I'm just inquiring when you'll be making your return to Spain."

The question took Columbus by surprise—not that he hadn't thought about it the last few months. As a matter of fact, it was imperative for him to return home as soon as possible.

"I don't have an answer for you."

"I understand, Admiral, that the Crown wants to establish a monthly shuttle to the colonies."

"And where did you hear of that?" Columbus asked, surprised by the leak.

"Why, from de Torres before he sailed."

Columbus was unable to comment. "It hasn't yet been finalized yet by the Crown."

"Admiral, I must return to España. I miss my niece and my grandnephew—your grandson."

Columbus sat frozen at the statement.

"I should think you'd want to see your daughter and her son," João stressed.

Columbus felt guilt mixed with annoyance. He had always been a good father to his two sons, always seeing to their wealth. This new duty was beyond his capability as a father.

"You don't have to remind me, João. I know my obligations."

João drove the last nail home. "So do I. You must return and meet your daughter and grandson. I'll be traveling with you on the next ship leaving Española. Thank you, Admiral." João turned on his heels and left him in seething angst. Sooner or later, Columbus would have to meet his newly found daughter and grandson. Perhaps it was high time to return home.

A sudden noise startled him. He ran out to see his men assembled by the shore and four caravels entering port. He ran as fast as he could, his arthritic limbs still not fully limber, and arrived out of breath among his men.

The caravels flew flags bearing the crown of Spain. Sailors were finishing coiling the rigging, and a smiling Antonio de Torres waved from deck. Near him, stood a man in black garb with a serious look upon his face. *A new explorer or official*, thought Columbus. *Good. I'll put him to work too.*

The first to disembark was his brother Diego. Columbus embraced him, happy to see him. He took him aside and asked him, "What news do you bring me from home, little brother?"

"I'm so glad to see you, Christoforo. It's been four long months."

"So what have you heard?"

"The only rumor I heard from court and courtiers was that the gold promised hasn't amounted to much so far. Other than that, Margarite and Fray Buil were absent."

Columbus reflected on what Diego had told him. "Thank you, Brother. I'm going to receive de Torres and this new visitor."

De Torres, in the meantime, had disembarked with the new visitor following behind.

"Admiral!" de Torres called with joy. "It's good to see you!"

"And you," Columbus said as he embraced de Torres.

De Torres turned to the visitor. "I'd like to present to you, Admiral, Juan de Aguado, from the queen's household."

De Aguado bowed his head. "I'm privileged to meet you, Admiral." He handed a letter with Spain's royal seal to Columbus.

Columbus broke the seal right away, anxious for good news.

To Cristóbal Colón, Admiral of the Ocean Seas.

King Ferdinand II, and I, Queen Isabella of Trastamara, introduce Juan Aguado, our chamberlain who speaks on our behalf. Please accord him any help to aid him in his work. We are giving an order to reduce the royal payroll to five hundred colonists. You are commanded, furthermore, to apportion food rations to everyone, including men punished for misdeeds. The chamberlain is bringing food supplies and experts in metallurgy to aid in the extraction of gold and silver. In matters of sending chained men to Spain, we want you to desist from any further shipment of slaves.

Signed Queen Isabella I   Signed King Ferdinand II

The letter was brief, without the customary pleasantries Columbus was accustomed to. The letter's address made no mention of his title as Viceroy of the Indies. Columbus lifted his eyes and saw an air of smug satisfaction in the chamberlain's eyes.

"Of course we will help you in any way we can, Chamberlain," Columbus said. *What would happen to his brother Bartholomew, the adelantado?* Was he to resign his position as governor of the island, which both monarchs had awarded him previously? This was all troubling.

Juan Aguado bowed to Columbus and turned to a slew of scribes following him.

"Take notes from every colonist and native. I want this work done within a month!" Aguado ordered them.

As soon as Aguado left them, de Torres turned to Columbus. "Admiral, I have bad news regarding the last voyage."

"What more bad news can you bring I haven't heard already?"

"I did my best to keep it a secret from the sovereigns, and asked my men to seal their lips. But news does travel fast." De Torres shook his head with a contrite look on his face.

"What is it?" Columbus raised his voice with impatience and dread.

"We lost two hundred natives at sea."

"What do you mean? How could you have lost them?"

"Well, Admiral," de Torres began. "First, the food supplies dwindled and I had to cut rations, on the other ships as well. . . . and . . ."

"And . . . ?" Columbus urged him on with impatience.

"They died one by one, from the cold, hunger, and lack of fresh air."

Perhaps that was the worst news Columbus could have heard at that point. It stunned him. Notwithstanding his low opinion of the Caribs—as cannibals and enemies of the gentle Tainos—they were souls, after all. And his action to enslave them had contributed to their deaths.

A voice inside his head suddenly rose with the words, "*We have to be good to animals and people. . . .*" These words were tied to a vague, fleeting memory that visited now and then when he had to make moral decisions. He chased the thought away and turned to de Torres.

"See that the men under your supervision are dealt with kindness and justice."

De Torres showed surprise in his eyes. "As you order, Admiral."

108

A Secret Operation

MIGUEL HAD RECOVERED COMPLETELY FROM his illness, but his state of mind had descended into despair. He'd been told that the ship was making a short voyage to Tangier for an important assignment. He tried to obtain more information about the reason for the detour, and why arrival in Portugal had been pushed further out, but no answer came forth. Everyone around him seemed either uninformed or not willing to impart a shred of news. Fed up and nearing the end of his patience, he confronted Captain Almeida in his cabin.

"Captain, I don't want to be presumptuous, but I must ask you a question."

The captain raised an eyebrow. "What is it, young man?"

"I'm most grateful to you for giving me free passage on your ship. However, I believed that we were going directly to Lisbon."

"You were correct."

"Then why are we headed to Morocco?"

The captain examined him, got up from his chair, and paced the cabin. "You see, you haven't been long a sailor or captain. There are things that go beyond the duties of a captain at sea."

"Like what?" Miguel asked.

The captain showed surprise at the question. Nevertheless, he had great patience. "A captain's duties aren't only to lead voyages and expeditions but to also provide for the safety and well-being of his men and his country as well."

Miguel would go as far as possible with his questioning, until the captain put a stop to it. "How does an extended voyage to Morocco affect the safety of Portugal's citizens?"

The captain sat and looked him straight in the eyes. "You see, Portugal seized power in Tangier in 1471 when we fought the Moors. We've been in Morocco since, and Portugal does not want to lose this post. Especially since Ceuta has fallen to Spain."

"But how does this impinge on going to Portugal?"

"Look, young man. I've told you more than I should. It is a secret mission. The best I can tell you is we'll leave Morocco in March of next year at the latest."

Miguel lowered his head in resignation. The captain had confided information likely reserved to his rank. Pursuing the conversation further might jeopardize Miguel's return to Portugal. He bowed to Captain Almeida.

"Thank you, Captain. You have been most gracious."

He left the cabin with the doomed feeling that he had lost Isabella.

1496

109

The Return Home

THE FORTRESSES AND TOWNS OF Magdalena, Santa Catalina, and Esperanza were nearly completed. Columbus had Ojeda and Bartholomew supervise all the work from the rebuilt Fort Santo Tomás and divided the colonists among all the towns. Several children were born in the New World in the interim, marking and highlighting the Crown of Spain's rights and possessions of Española forever to be held in perpetuity. The caravel *India* floated proudly in Isabela's harbor, swaying side by side with good old trusty *Niña* and the rest of their ships, while the *Mariagalante* still underwent repairs. Much progress was made in planting crops, and food was in adequate supply, brought by Aguado in the name of the queen. It was time for Columbus to return to Spain.

Bartholomew would accompany the departing ship as far as the next harbor on the northern coast of Española to search for a new capital site. Columbus had divided and delegated the main jobs among his most trusting men: his brother Bartholomew overseeing the colonies under Juan Aguado; de Torres as his right-hand man for odd jobs; his other brother, Diego, to help Fray Ramón Pane with the natives' conversion; and Ojeda with the strip-mining and collection of gold dust. So far, no other gold nuggets had been found, and Columbus had badly wanted to show Aguado, the chamberlain of the queen's household, Española's potential. This, the chamberlain ignored, and he went about gathering information from colonists who were sick, tired, and aching to return home. The expression "as God may return me to Castile" was often heard from the colonists' mouths.

By now Columbus was at his wit's end. His own health had deteriorated even more; the slightest trip inland inflamed his joints. Furthermore, his eyes—which had healed before—began to puff and tear at the slightest wind. He began to hum in his head the litany to return to Castile.

One morning, he called de Torres and de la Cosa to his headquarter cabin now on the *India*.

"Within a week, I want you to supply the *Niña* and the *India* to return to Cadiz." Both men's eyes bulged at the sudden news. "There's nothing to worry about. We'll leave the island in capable hands. Now that we've rid ourselves of renegades and discontents, there's not much to fear."

As promised, Columbus's officers fulfilled his orders. Both caravels, the *Niña*, and the *India*, were stocked with supplies, plants, thirty natives, and two hundred and twenty-five men eager to return home. The *Niña*'s master was Alonso Medel, and the *India* would be captained by Bartholomé Colín, who was to steer the brand-new tiller.

"Admiral, we're bursting at the seams," said de la Cosa.

"I know, de la Cosa. But these men don't want to stay on the island. I can't force them," Columbus replied. "Now that we're ready, let's hoist the sails!"

"Raise the sails!" De la Cosa's voice thundered from the quarterdeck of the *Niña*.

The sailors ran to their posts and onto ratlines and yardarms, and knots were untied, unraveling the square-rigged sails. The freed canvases flapped in the gentle breeze, regaining their full dignified curves.

"Raise the anchors now!" the order followed. The heavy anchor emerged from the waters and dripped salt water on the freshly scrubbed deck.

The same orders were carried out on the *India*'s decks, in order to prep and initiate her for the long voyage. She glided majestically out of the harbor, following the *Niña*.

"Hurrah! Hurrah!" Shouts carried from shore from all the men, women, and children who stayed behind and had gathered to see the launching of both caravels. The men on deck reciprocated and roared back with their own shouts of joy.

Columbus watched and supervised the launch with a rare smile on his lips. He stood on deck with Bartholomew and Diego, waving to the crowds on shore, hoping they would miss him a bit. No matter. He looked forward to seeing the Spanish shores of Cadiz and his sons at court in Cordova. His whole being was geared for this blessed event of returning to familiar shores—though part of him dreaded getting bad news there.

With a wind blowing from the east, the caravels glided on the surface of cerulean waters, heading for home.

A few days later, the caravels arrived at Columbus's first objective: a safe harbor where he planned to erect the capital of Española. Columbus, Diego and Bartholomew took a reconnaissance trip inland and came upon a valley by the east bank of the Ozama River.

Bartholomew said, "Brother, I believe this is the spot where I will build the capital."

Columbus evaluated the level terrain at the mouth of the Caribbean Sea, its sheltered harbor among forests, and the tall mountain in the background, and sanctioned the spot as heaven on earth. Pleased, he said solemnly, "We will call this first capital Santo Domingo after our father."

"Amen," Bartholomew said, agreeing with his brother.

"Now, my dear Bartholomew and my dear little Diego, it's time for me to depart." The three brothers embraced for a long time. "You will be cautious on your return by land."

Columbus rejoined the caravels and watched as his brother, surrounded by several of his men and Indians, waved good-bye.

The caravels close-hauled along the northern shore of Española for twelve days until March 22, when the last cape, Engaño, disappeared from view. They then sailed a passage between Española and Boriquén, passing small islands along the way and harnessing the wind by tacking from starboard to port.

As the *Niña* passed Boriquén Island, with the *India* following close behind, Columbus noticed João deeply absorbed in taking measurements by the binnacle box. This was an unusual level of interest on João's part, since he wasn't on duty that morning.

"João! Get up here!"

Startled, João turned toward him. "Right away, Admiral."

When João reached him, he stood erect in front of him without any artifice.

"What were you doing by the binnacle box?"

"Just taking coordinates as you'd agreed to, Admiral."

"I already have de la Cosa doing the same thing. I want you to cease your dead reckoning. Dismissed!"

"Aye, aye, Admiral." João left him for other chores.

On Saturday, April 9, the caravels stopped at Mariagalante Island.

By Sunday, April 10, with provisions running low, Columbus decided to stop at Guadalupe Island and drop anchor. The men on board grumbled, for it was their day of rest.

"Send down armed boats!" Columbus ordered.

A party of twenty men landed ashore, when suddenly they were showered with hundreds of arrows shot by a horde of women natives. The Indians aimed their bows and shot wave after wave of arrows. Several sailors went down with superficial wounds. Columbus signaled the men on ship to reply with lombard shots. The women dispersed and hid behind the tree line.

"Send down two native men!" Columbus signaled again.

Two Taínos swam ashore from one of the caravels and told the women they only wanted to barter for provisions.

The women were curiously adorned, with their knees and arms bandaged in white cotton. They replied, *"Lu Cairi."*

The translator said to Columbus, "They small island people."

"And?" Columbus asked.

"Eporyi makuto, mahiz, casabi. Men in island give." The Carib pointed north on the island.

Columbus knew by now that *mahiz* was corn flour for bread, and he also recognized the word for cassava.

The men boarded the ships again, the wounded turned over to the physician on board, and they made sail for the northern part of the island. When they arrived, the men were waiting in ambush for them with bows and arrows. The arrows flew again from shore. But upon seeing the armed boats and having lombard shots fired at them, the natives fled.

Columbus gave the order to search the square huts nearby. The Spaniards found a treasure of cassava dough, and they immediately baked the bread on barbacoa griddles over fires. The looting and plundering of huts continued until nothing was left of value. Colorful parrots were stolen in great numbers, along with what looked like wax and honey, and woven cotton cloths.

Columbus thought the island must be peopled by women, with the men visiting only to lie and mate with them. It brought to mind Herodotus's story of the Islands of Females in the far regions of Asia, the same as the island of Matinino populated by Amazonian women. A rare smile appeared on his face.

"We will stay for a week on this island," Columbus said. "To bake as much bread as we can. Gather plenty of firewood for the hold, and fill the water barrels to capacity. We'll catch fish along the way."

"Aye, aye, Admiral." De la Cosa went to carry out his order.

On April 20, the caravels, filled to the gills with provisions, weighed anchor and headed for Spain. They had lost a month stopping at islands, and they sailed to catch the easterly winds. But in the horse latitudes, between thirty and thirty-five degrees north, the winds were light and progress was slow. The decks were overcrowded, and men slept in shifts.

On May 20, food rations on both ships were cut in half. A cup of water and five ounces of bread were handed out per day. By June 8, the men rebelled and confronted Columbus.

"Admiral, the men are hungry and thirsty!" one sailor blurted out.

"I say we repay the Caribs with their own customs. We'll eat them!" said another.

"That'll make you sick!" one of the friars cried with repulsion, covering his face.

"In that case," the man who suggested eating them proposed, "let's throw them overboard."

"Hold on, men!" Columbus raised an angry voice. "These men are humans, and we are not cannibals."

When calm was restored and the ships returned to the business at hand, a surprising announcement came from the crow's nest.

"Land! I see land!"

"Blessed be the Lord," a grateful Columbus said. "Take in the sails. We're too close in at the Azores." Again, Columbus harbored concerns of running aground in the manner of the *Santa Maria*.

The coast of Portugal appeared in all its glory, thanks to Columbus's skill of dead reckoning and navigation by the heavenly bodies. By June 11, the caravels rounded Cape St. Vincent and entered the Bay of Cadiz. The only driving thought now on Columbus's mind was to race to court and stop all gossip and falsehoods spread by Fray Buil and Margarite.

110

Leaving the Land

THE DATE OF DEPARTURE WAS getting nearer, and despite Isabella's promise to leave earlier than the Portuguese decree, she stalled for time. The food supplies weren't sufficient, the refugees at El Mouro Castle were not organized, the sale of the estate was still pending, and something deep inside her told her to pace herself, to slow down and make sure all loose ends were tied up. Ana was pleased with the delay, but Avram had turned morose, remarking that his marriage to Isabella would be postponed indefinitely.

"If you wait any longer, Isabella," Avram pleaded with her, "we'll be stuck in Lisbon with all the other caravels. Not unlike Seville a few years ago."

The mention of Seville brought into focus those hopeful yet horrible times. With the memories, the image of Miguel at her side plunged her back into those wrenching days. She had no reason to delay any longer; she'd given her promise to Avram. She'd promised those families a safe passage on the *Liberação* to a new land, and most of all, she would see to her son's safety. The sooner they left, the safer they'd be.

"I know what I'm doing, Avram. I want to prepare for all contingencies. Perhaps purchase more food supplies at the port and check again that all regulations for sailing are in order."

"We've checked and rechecked them. There's nothing more to oversee." Avram's voice raised in exasperation.

"I know, Avram. I'm sorry I'm putting you through this. It's better to be sure than to look back with hindsight where we failed."

Avram was about to reply, when Ana, out of breath, ran into the sitting room.

"Isabella, Avram—we have a visitor!" Her face sparkled with joy. She stood aside to let in a seasoned man in his prime with white hair and a ruddy complexion.

To Isabella he appeared to be a mariner, with a face tanned by the sun at sea, and a muscular, fit body. Yet, he also seemed familiar. Where had she'd seen him before?

"Don't you recognize me, Isabella?" The low, hoarse voice startled her.

She scrutinized his face, when a flash of recognition dawned on her. "João! No! It isn't possible."

"It is possible," João stressed. "We're finally reunited!" He opened his arms to receive Isabella to his chest.

Isabella stood in shock, shying away from embracing him.

"That's how I'm welcomed?" João laughed.

She ran into his open arms and hugged him, then suddenly broke out in tears.

"Whoa, whoa! I hope these are tears of joy."

Isabella stopped her crying immediately. She alternated between cries of joy and bursts of exasperation. "Why have you not contacted me before? Where have you been?"

João said, still smiling, "Please, Isabella, one question at a time."

"Give him time, Isabella." Avram spoke with a soothing voice.

She presented Avram. "This is my fiancé, Avram."

João hesitated as he stretched a hand to him with a serious look. "Congratulations. I didn't know."

Avram nodded, then fell silent.

"To answer your questions, Isabella, I was away on a long voyage. You've heard, I'm sure, of what we've discovered on the other side of the world?"

Isabella nodded and Ana interjected, "We only know that our lives have been changed forever."

"Are you speaking of events coming to bear in Portugal?"

All three affirmed João's assumption.

"We're forced to leave again for new shores. Why can't they let us be?" Ana's voice broke.

João fell quiet. He then said, "Remember, Ana, when I proposed to find a new land for Jews, Conversos, and others who were persecuted?

Ana nodded. "It was a dream long ago. Now we have to leave yet again."

"I have the answer for the problem of repeated exile."

Eyebrows went up quizzically.

"Before I go into it, I need to speak to Isabella alone," João added.

Ana looked at Avram, and they both headed for the door. "You'll find us in the kitchen by the hearth," said Ana.

After they left, João sat and motioned for Isabella to do the same.

"I came here," he began, "for a specific purpose. To lead you to your birth father."

Isabella sat confounded. She hadn't thought about that father for a long time. As if he hadn't existed until João mentioned him. "You found him?" she asked with a strangled voice.

"I have. But first I want to fill you in on your mother. My sister."

Isabella fell quiet, but her heart beat rapidly in her rib cage. She put her hand on her chest to calm it.

João began by telling her about his sister Sarita, her dalliance with Isabella's father—a sailor who never returned after leaving for sea—and the birth of a daughter unknown to this father. "So you see, Isabella, your father never knew that your mother became pregnant with you. You can't fault him for not knowing that you were born."

"But why didn't he come back?" Her question was a cry to understand circumstances beyond her control.

"Because he fell for the lure of the sea, and for the glory that he sought." He stopped, then said with a conciliatory voice, "No matter. Forgiveness is the only possible thing in this life. Without it, hate will obliterate love."

Isabella lowered her head deep in thought. She then raised it and asked him, "Where is my father now?"

"He's in Seville, after a long voyage from the New World."

"Seville?" Isabella echoed. "Seville. I can also visit with my adoptive father there."

"As you wish. I must warn you, though, he's aged considerably."

"I must see him. At least to try to convince him to join us on our voyage to Istanbul."

João didn't answer her comment. He nodded.

"I will give Avram instructions to prepare the *Liberação* for sailing," Isabella said.

111

The Race to Lisbon

THE DAYS WERE FILLED WITH CHORES for Miguel, but the nights were full of nightmares. He imagined all sorts of calamities that might befall Isabella and their son. He dreamt one night that the arm of the Inquisition had reached into the safe haven where his wife and son dwelled. He feared for their lives and his inability to protect them from harm.

By now, his complete memory had returned, and with it the pain of the loss of his mother in the inquisitorial jail. He also feared for his young brother, José. He must be at least fourteen now. He had promised his mother to protect and look after his brother. Yet, he hadn't been able to prevent his own fall into slavery. Why did they have to suffer? Why was their religion marked for persecution? Why was any religion, for that matter? For a millennium and centuries upon centuries, one religion would persecute another, then there would be a backlash of cruelty in a revengeful cycle. So much for religion, he thought, disgusted by its ugly record. Yet, it wasn't religion per se but more the individuals who preached false beliefs from pulpits, marring the beauty of faith.

"Hey, Miguel!"

The voice startled Miguel from his deep thoughts. "Yes, what is it?" He raised his head to see Bento, the master, looking down on him. From

Miguel's seated position on deck, leaning against the mainmast, he must have looked like a loafer.

"Are your chores done?" Bento had a kind look in his eyes, accentuated by a smile.

"I have, Master Bento."

"Then the captain wants to see you."

"Right away, master." With a stab of anxiety, Miguel headed for the captain's cabin. *Perhaps we're finally leaving this African coast*, he hoped.

When he entered the cabin, Captain Almeida greeted him silently.

Now Miguel's heart sank with a greater premonition of bad news.

"We're docking in Tangier. You can take a few hours' leave to go ashore."

"But, Captain, when are we sailing to Lisbon?"

"As soon as our business in North Africa is done."

"Can you at least tell me how much longer?"

The captain fell silent. "Another week at the most. That's all I can reveal."

"Thank you, Captain. Thank you for the shore leave. May I get an advance on the wages I earned?"

The captain took two *ceitil* copper coins out of his pocket and set them on his desk. He then dismissed Miguel.

Miguel grabbed the coins, nodded his thank-you, and ran out of the cabin. In a great hurry he went down the gangplank and heard Bento's voice behind him, "Where you going?"

Miguel didn't answer and kept running through the docks to the market square. From his recollection, Matigoro's house wasn't far from the marketplace, and he reached it within a half-hour run. At the front gate, he shook the metal bars when a bell couldn't be found. No one answered his call.

"Matigoro? Matigoro?" He called again and again. An older man came out of a nearby house on the narrow, cobbled street and listened to Miguel's frantic calls.

"The man who owned this house no longer lives here," he said.

"Where is he?" Miguel yelled.

"First, calm down," he suggested in a soothing voice. "He left last year, never to return. His house now stands empty."

Miguel stood distressed by the news. To what destination had Matigoro traveled? He thanked the neighbor, then left for the docks.

He arrived at the docks and scanned the crowds of merchants and vendors doing brisk business. Memories flooded him of the ordeal when he and Isabella had been sold as slaves. It had been their luck that Matigoro had been there to save them. These last few years, luck and misfortune cancelled each other out in a streak of catastrophe and salvation. Three years of his life had been snuffed out under his feet. In a fit of angry despair, he yelled at the top of his lungs, "Bastards! Thieves! Snakes!"

The crowds around him stopped their haggling and purchasing to look in his direction. Afraid, now that the attention was turned on him, he circulated among the crowd with his head low and made his way back to the ship.

Bento smiled at him. "How was your afternoon, mate?"

Without replying, Miguel fixed his eyes on the deck planks and attacked the rigging, rolling and unrolling the lines. Within minutes, the rage that had overtaken him subsided, and he continued the soothing work and let it penetrate his mind.

112

Pilgrimage

THE CARRIAGE THAT TOOK ISABELLA, her son, and João to Seville skirted small towns and hamlets. João chose to travel the secluded roads at night to cover the four hundred kilometers in the space of ten hours, stopping only to take nourishment at three inns and to exchange their horses. Salvadore slept through the hours, stirring now and then to ask for water.

Ana had objected strongly to Isabella taking Salvadore with her. She predicted terrible things that might happen to them: arrest, attack, accidents on the road, and many other calamities. "This isn't a voyage for a young boy. You may be endangering him!"

Isabella tried to calm her down. "Don't worry. We'll take good care of him." She understood Ana's anxiety. Ana had grown close to Salvadore, as if she were his natural grandmother.

"Upon our return form Seville we will meet as planned on the *Liberação* Isabella reassured Ana.

She then added, "don't forget to deliver the deed and keys to the house to the tavern owner in Sintra as I instructed you."

Ana had nodded with a gloom on her face.

Isabella's attention returned to the present in the carriage bouncing over the uneven road. As the two strong Arabian horses galloped at a fast pace, they passed Lisbon then Setubal, avoiding unnecessary stops. It was hot and humid for a July night, and Isabella wiped Salvadore's wet forehead, but the child kept on sleeping. When Faro appeared, they felt the salty air and knew they were traveling near the lagoons and the sea at the frontier with Spain. At the border their papers were examined at length while Isabella worried they would be found out. They were then waved on and she breathed a sigh of relief. At last, when they skirted Huelva and the town of Dos Hermanas, their destination neared.

Isabella envisioned the small town of Dos Hermanas where her life had unraveled. She sifted through her memories of Maria's chicken farm where it had all begun: her kidnapping; imprisonment in the Alhambra; escape to Córdoba with Miguel and his brother, José; and the exodus to Seville, where her new life began with Miguel.

It had burned indelible memories in her mind that could never be erased. She had to keep those memories alive. Trying to forget them would mean cutting Miguel from her mind and life as if he had never existed. New memories would be added after she married Avram, but Miguel's would be front and center in her life.

She turned her attention to the road as the kilometers to their destination grew fewer. Her anticipation and excitement at seeing her adoptive father grew to intense proportions.

A worry planted by Ana nagged at her. "How safe will it be to enter Seville?" she asked João.

"We'll be arriving in the early morning hours. Neither the merchants nor the neighbors will be awake."

Isabella sighed with relief, but Ana's worries kept nudging her.

The carriage entered the sleeping city, rolled through the narrow streets then entered the familiar neighborhood where Isabella grew up. After a bend in an alley, João eased the horses, stopping gently in front of the house. Isabella's hand brushed her throat with nervousness.

"Come on, Isabella," João urged her. "You go in first, and I'll carry Salvadore."

She descended the carriage steps, opened the front metal gates, crossed the courtyard, and knocked on the front door. She didn't want to wake the entire household by ringing the bell at this early hour. She waited a few moments while João joined her with Salvadore still asleep.

The small peep window in the door opened, and a white-haired woman peered out. Her eyes widened, and she covered her mouth in shock and surprise. The door creaked on its hinges, and Isabella fell into dada Hannah's arms—her nanny. Though she was still as corpulent as ever, she had aged, and only her eyes revealed a youthful disposition untouched by her advanced years.

"¿*Qué milagro es este*? My little girl. What miracle is this?" Hannah repeated. Instant tears rolled down her cheeks.

Isabella hugged her and kissed several times on both cheeks.

When they finished embracing, Isabella turned to João and said, "My uncle, and my son, Salvadore."

"I remember him," Dada Hannah said, pointing at João without smiling, but her eyes fell on the boy. She grabbed the sleeping Salvadore from João's arms and pressed him against her wide chest. "He's a beautiful boy. So handsome."

Dada Hannah turned and led Isabella and João through the tiled hallway and into the sitting room.

Isabella found the room the same as if she had left it yesterday. The chairs had acquired a patina these last few years, but the room was clean and freshly aired out.

Dada Hannah gently deposited Salvadore on a leather-cushioned wooden bench and quickly said, "I'll be right back."

Within ten minutes, Don Obrigon's bent figure, walking haltingly and followed by dada Hannah, came into the room, and he and Isabella collapsed into each other's arms. The tears from father and daughter mingled as they sobbed, happy to see one another. When they calmed down, Don Obrigon bowed his white head to João, recognizing him from his visit the previous year.

"And who's this beautiful boy?" Isabella's father asked with soft eyes falling on the slumbering child.

"This is your grandson, Salvadore. Miguel's and my son."

Her father pulled a wooden chair close to the bench and watched the boy sleeping soundly. "Can I wake him?" he asked timidly.

"Of course," said Isabella. She sat Salvadore on her lap and quietly kissed him on the cheeks.

Salvadore opened his eyes and surveyed the people around him with surprise. He smiled at Isabella and jumped off her lap. He stopped at Don Obrigon's chair and, turning around, asked, "Who's this, Mama?"

"This is your *abuelo*."

Salvadore opened his arms and went to hug his new grandfather. At that, everyone in the room laughed with glee at the boy's gesture.

"He has a good heart," Don Obrigon said with a hoarse voice as he hugged his grandson. He raised his eyes to Isabella and said, "I heard what happened to his father."

Isabella stared into space, unable to comment. Then she turned to her father. "Father, we want you to come with us."

"Go with you? Where?"

"We're no longer welcome in Portugal. We leave right away for Turquía. Please come with us. Please," she begged him.

João added his encouragement. "You can be near Isabella and your grandson and see them everyday."

Don Obrigon remained mute for a long time. He got up and paced the room. He coughed suddenly, cleared his voice, and looked at the faces staring at him. "There's nothing more I'd want to do." He stretched out his arms. "But you see, I'm not well. My physician would surely forbid a long voyage because of my health."

A rush of thoughts and emotions swirled in Isabella's head: nurse her father, postpone the voyage and her marriage to Avram.

"I know what you're going to say." Don Obrigon stopped her before she could speak. "You know you won't be safe here."

"He's right, Isabella," João stressed.

Isabella turned a mournful face to her father. "How can you ask me to leave you?"

"It's for the best." She saw her father's resolve about to break down, but she believed the voyage might be fatal for him. "As soon as we're established in the new land, I'll come visit you."

Don Obrigon gave her a gentle smile, grateful that she didn't insist on him joining them.

João suddenly stood. "We must hurry," he announced.

Isabella went to her father and wrapped his small frame in her arms. Tears came to her eyes and rolled down her cheeks. Don Obrigon coughed and held her in a tight embrace. He kissed her wet face and held her for a long time.

Salvadore came to his mother and grandfather still holding each other and wrapped his small arms around them.

Don Obrigon eased himself from Isabella's grasp and bent down with great difficulty to Salvadore's level. "You will take care of your mama, won't you?"

Salvadore nodded as he flexed his arm to show his budding bicep. "I strong. Take care of Mama."

The whole room exploded with relieved laughter.

Dada Hannah hugged Isabella to her immense frame. "I will take good care of your father."

Isabella nodded with a smile.

They made their way out the door and into the carriage. With a heavy heart, Isabella watched her father and dada Hannah wave as the carriage hugged the corner of the street. Both were dear to her, and they'd forever remain a treasured part of her life, but it hurt to realize this might be the last time she'd see them.

113

The Reckoning

THE FIRE BURNED IN THE great hearth, warming Columbus's arthritic bones. He sat garbed in a black Franciscan monastic gown of coarse brown fabric. He had preferred this comfortable and simple attire since his days at the Monastery of La Rábida. The friary robe reminded him of humility whenever his thoughts rose to his lofty ambitions. His host, Andrés Bernáldez, a churchman and chaplain to the archbishop of Seville, provided a comfortable stay for the weary but famous traveler in his home in Seville.

While awaiting an invitation from the Catholic monarchs to join them in Valladolid, Columbus enjoyed whiling away the days talking to his host, checking his papers, and making progress on a treatise he'd been working on for a number of years. In it, he opined that the time had come to conquer Jerusalem. All his energy was to be channeled for that holy mission. Meanwhile, a third voyage to the New World was uppermost on his mind.

"Admiral?" The voice of Bernáldez awoke him from his reverie.

"What can I do for my most gracious host?" Columbus asked the curate.

"I've been reading your journals from the second voyage, and I'm amazed how this Indian chief befriended you."

"If you're speaking of Guanahani, he was my most loyal cacique." Columbus closed his eyes, remembering the image of a weak yet wise chief.

"He gave me the most support in our battle with the Caribs and against the traitor chiefs who aligned themselves with Caonabó."

"Yes, but don't you think this Caonabó thought he was defending his land against outsiders?"

Columbus didn't reply at first. Then he said, "It was bound to happen that his island would become a Christian land. So his was a lost cause."

Bernáldez didn't comment. Columbus saw that he disagreed with him. But it was fate and the superiority of the Spaniards that had given them this victory over heathens.

"There's another thing that baffles me," Bernáldez said.

"What is that?"

"According to Fermín Zedo, the Sevillian goldsmith, no virgin gold could be found in Española." Bernáldez spoke with amusement in his eyes. "But the nuggets you brought back that I've held in my hands, and the beaten gold, tell me otherwise."

"As you can see, my detractors are many, my friend. That's why I'm distressed that Their Highnesses haven't summoned me yet to court."

Bernáldez tried to reassure him. "They will. I'm sure they—"

A tap at the door interrupted him. An old servant entered. "There are visitors in the front parlor to speak with Admiral Columbus."

Columbus was surprised. Who could have known he was staying with the chaplain?

"Let them in," Bernáldez said.

A few moments later, with unbelieving eyes, Columbus saw João standing before him with a boy and a young woman who gave him a start. He knew right away who the visitors were, yet it astounded him that they had sought him out. He sat with his mouth agape.

Bernáldez stood and said, "Well, I'll leave you to them." Before Columbus could speak, his host left the room and closed the door behind him.

"Admiral, I promised to bring them to you," João said. "This is your daughter, Isabella, and Salvadore, your grandson."

Columbus sat frozen and speechless.

Isabella stood away from the door, yet still far from the mature man who sat without stirring or uttering a word. A rush of feelings and thoughts swirled in her brain. Here was the man who had given her life. The father she never knew. The one who abandoned her mother, Sarita. Salvadore's hand pulled on hers.

"Who's the man, Mama?"

Isabella regained her power of speech. "Salvadore, this is your grandfather."

Salvadore shook his red curly hair. "No, no!" he cried with stubbornness. "This is not Abuelo!"

João turned to Isabella with a grave look. "Isabella, this is Cristovão Colón. Columbus, as he is called. Your real father."

Isabella remained motionless. She didn't know whether to believe this was her true father or a complete stranger facing her. She stared at Columbus—at his white hair interspersed with a few reddish curly strands at the temples, his piercing blue eyes.

Salvadore suddenly let go of her hand and ran to this new grandfather. The boy leaned against Columbus's chair and raised a smiling face to him.

Columbus bent to the boy and lifted him to his lap. "I am your grandfather," he said in voice devoid of emotion. Salvadore reached for Columbus's curls and twirled them around his fingers. Columbus hugged his grandchild, then turned his eyes to Isabella.

"You appear just as your mother did at her age." Columbus fixated on Isabella's features.

Isabella regained her voice, which came out slightly raspy. "I never knew my mother. Perhaps you can tell me about her?"

Columbus made a sign for her to approach. She came close, and he reached and caressed her face. She kneeled before his chair and sat on the cold tile floor.

"She was a beautiful woman, and you look very much like her. She laughed at life, and . . ." Columbus unleashed a torrent of words as he spoke of those times when they were happiest and in love.

Isabella couldn't help asking the question that burned her lips. "Why didn't you come back?" The question was a cry that burst from deep within her soul.

Columbus bent his head, looked at Salvadore, and hugged him again, slow to reply. "I had a mission in life. The Lord had summoned me to do his work. He shone the light that guided me to his goal." Isabella heard him talk of his sacred mission, the hurdles he suffered, all the ridicule he endured for years, and now of finally being vindicated by history and his sheer determination.

For a long time Isabella had dreamt of meeting her father, and now, as she sat by him, she felt disappointment and a bitter taste in her mouth. All he talked of was his dreams, his mission, and his trials. Here was the fantasy father she had yearned to meet. Yet it seemed that he would remain a fantasy. No more and no less.

Columbus then spoke with a truer and clearer voice. "I know that I could have been a better father to you. But you see, those were difficult times. We earned a pittance for our work, and worked as beasts of labor. I had to make a difference for myself and for my parents." He stopped, then opened his mouth to say something, then closed it without uttering a sound.

Isabella, somehow, sensed he held back words he didn't want to utter.

"Isabella?"

She turned to João's voice.

"We have a long road ahead of us."

She tore herself from the moment and went to lift Salvadore. "We must leave now."

Columbus's face went slack and pale. He stood and put his arms around Isabella.

She hugged him back, and he said, "I will keep this treasured time close to my heart and remember it always."

She tried to understand his words, but João signaled it was time to leave.

"Good-bye," was all Isabella could say before parting from the elusive father who entered her life then quickly stepped out of it.

With haste they all left the house, saying a quick thank-you to the host. Columbus did not follow them outdoors.

Isabella felt numb throughout the return to port in Lisbon. She felt devoid of feelings, regrets, or anger. Her mind had emptied. The only father she regretted leaving was her adoptive father, Arturo Obrigon—the father who had raised her and saw to her joys and disappointments with tenderness and caring. Now she needed father figures no longer. She'd be both a mother and a father to Salvadore.

She shook herself from her deep thoughts and turned to João. "Let me take the reins and you can rest."

"No." João said in a firm voice as he whipped the horses.

As the kilometers were bridged, Isabella noticed that João looked over his shoulder at the road behind them. "Why are you constantly looking back?"

João didn't answer and whipped the horses to a faster gallop.

João's actions stirred the worry she'd harbored before. Were they in danger? Fear grabbed Isabella. She hugged a sleeping Salvadore to her chest and covered him with a woolen blanket. As the night descended, a chill penetrated the carriage, and she wrapped herself tightly in her shawl. When they approached the city of Faro and kept riding fast, she turned to João, "Aren't we stopping at least for a meal?"

"No!" João replied sharply without any explanations.

Isabella fell quiet and didn't disturb him after that. How could they evade danger if she couldn't see it? The road disappearing behind their carriage was dark with many bends. If another carriage had been chasing theirs, no sounds, horses, or men threatened to overtake them.

She squeezed Salvadore's small frame in her arms. Then they passed the road sign marking the border with Portugal. From that point on, João slowed the horses but kept pushing on. At last, Lisbon came into view, and with it she saw João relax his hold on the reins.

"It seemed as though we were fleeing from danger," she said to João.

"We were," João said. "There were five riders in the distance who followed us on the road past Faro."

Isabella gave a start. "Why didn't you tell me?"

"It wouldn't have mattered. I could tell they were Spanish soldiers by the flag they carried. I wouldn't be surprised if they served in the Inquisition army."

Isabella shivered at the thought of having escaped and having endangered her son.

"The sooner we leave this accursed land, the better we'll be."

"Amen to that," João said.

The carriage carried them to Lisbon, where all awaited them on the *Liberação*. They arrived late in the night, and the glowing lanterns on deck pinpointed the way to the caravel.

Isabella said, "Tomorrow we set sail for Turquía."

114

A Momentous Discovery

AFTER HIS VISITORS LEFT HIM, Columbus sat for a long time thinking it had all been a dream. A dream he'd wake from, the memory fleeting away. But as hard as he tried to erase thoughts of the visit, they hung tenaciously. He had met the daughter he had repudiated and his grandson, and he couldn't deny that they were linked to him. Isabella's and Salvadore's looks screamed at him: *How could you deny your flesh and blood?* Indeed, how could he? Not only had he demonstrated reluctance to embrace them with warmth and affection, he also made no new connections with them. He had set a barrier between himself and his daughter and grandson, knowing that he could never establish a bond. For doing so would open up a Pandora's box. Most of all, the fact that his lineage branched into the Judaic faith would create complications for him. He had seen what the Inquisition had done to Marranos and Conversos. Due to that, he had buried deeply his origins. He had to reject his association with that daughter and grandson.

"Daydreaming again, Columbus?" His host came into the room. "Who were your visitors?" Bernáldez asked with unrestrained curiosity.

Columbus took a few moments to reply. "It was one of my sea mates with his relatives. They came to inquire about my health."

"That was most charitable." Bernáldez examined his face. "My friend, are you feeling all right?"

Columbus looked at his host with questioning eyes.

"You do look pale. Perhaps that visit was unnecessary."

"I'm quite fine. Really." He steadied his voice to reassure Bernáldez.

"I'll leave you then, until supper tonight."

"Thank you," Columbus replied.

After his host left him, Columbus felt restless, and he paced the room lit by the fire in the hearth. He moved sluggishly to a large table that held all his papers and proceeded to examine them. He felt compelled to plunge into the charts and maps before him. Now was as good a time as ever to prepare for the third voyage. He would propose it to court, to go further beyond the chain of islands in the Antilles.

He looked for Paolo Toscanelli's map, the one document that never left his side. He had cherished the map since he was a young man. That same map had fired his imagination when he sat with his brother Bartholomew, dreaming of great conquests of the seas and of finding Cathay and Cipangu. He recalled the letter sent with the map, telling of great marble-columned cities filled with gold and silver, gems and spices. He knew for certain that one day he would find all those treasures. That further south of his explorations lay a great continent.

Under a pile of documents he found the folded map, and as he lifted it, something fell out of its fold. His eyes fell on the sealed letter Bartholomew had given him that he had misplaced! This was the lost letter from his father, Domenico. His heart leapt with joy. With trembling hands he tore the seal and began reading it.

Cao Figgio Cristoforo,

By the time you read this letter, I won't be in this world. There is so much I wanted to say to you, but perhaps a better time would be when we meet in heaven. I was always proud to have had you as my son. I haven't been successful in my life with the wool weaving; otherwise, you and your brothers would've remained home next to your mother and me. But, as we say in Genoa: "Your children are like the wind. They come, then they leave."

You know that I've been honest to tell you the truth about your origins. I was frank to tell you when your mother and I adopted you the fact that you're a Converso. And now it is high time to tell you the whole story of your birth.

You were brought to us as a young boy by an old man called Abilio. He confided in us that you were born of a Jewish mother from Tomar by the name of Isabel Gonçalves Zarco. She died young and told the old man of your high birth. You see, my dear boy, João Gonçalves Zarco, who was your grandfather and a great Portuguese navigator, was in the service of Prince Henry. It was at the court in Portugal that your mother Isabel met Fernando, Duke of Beja. You were born from that union. Your mother then fell out of grace with her father and fled to Sintra. Your birth mother named you Salvador, and we selected for you the name Cristoforo because, like the Savior, you would help your fellow men.

So you see, dear son, you were born of nobility, but you could never prove it to the father who abandoned you. Your mother and I always loved you as our own son, and you returned the love and respect to us by your gentle nature. Be happy, my son.

Your loving father, Domenico Colombo

Columbus sat stunned. His whole life he had chased the elusive dream of nobility and titles. Yet it had been his heritage all along, without his knowledge, hovering above his head. Why had his birth father not recognized him as his son? Why had he abandoned his birth mother? He sat empty without stirring, devoid of emotions in his mind and heart. Numb.

As the shock began to wear off, he noticed the uncanny similarity with which life's offenses kept repeating themselves. In a way, the same pattern had occurred through him and his daughter, Isabella. He stood and went to the recessed window to look upon the Guadalquivir River flowing past his host's home. He wanted to stop the carriage carrying Isabella and his grandson. To tell them he was sorry for sending them away, that they were a noble part of the Portuguese land and history. But they were gone.

I had good reasons to sever my ties to Isabella, he told himself. A vital reason for cutting the bonds rather than fostering a familial thread.

Yes, he had recognized his son by his mistress Beatriz, and Beatriz did not jeopardize his career. His own birth father had abandoned him. And somehow, fate had reciprocated to punish him for having abandoned his daughter. In order to keep the titles and benefits bestowed upon him by the Crown, he had to keep his true origins a secret—a secret that his adoptive father, Domenico Colombo, had carried to the grave.

Columbus walked to the vast hearth and dropped the letter into the fire.

115

The Third Exodus

ISABELLA STOOD ON DECK, GAZING for the last time on Castle São Jorge dominating Lisbon on the hill. A harbor bustling with shouts; milling travelers congregating on the docks; and captains giving orders to load cargo, animals, and people desperate to board caravels brought to mind the last time she sailed from Spain. Those were memories she would rather forget. Miguel had stood then by her side. Now he was gone, and she felt deeply his empty presence. She sighed with a heavy heart.

The *Liberação* was moored at a distance in the harbor, swaying gently with its sails folded, buoyed by small waves entering the short stretch of the Tagus River. The men on deck helped unravel the sails from the yardarms and tie the loosened rigging into coils and knots. By ten in the morning, the order went through to depart, and the travelers huddled on the *Liberação*'s deck watched, mesmerized, the anchor being lifted from the cold water. The shank emerged first, then the trident shape of the flukes on the end of the arms followed as it was lifted and tied securely to the cat hook off the railing.

"Sails ahoy!"

"Anchor up!"

"Rigging and lines tied!"

The calls were made as João helped check and recheck that all was ready for departure. The *Liberação* stood proud, her sails blowing in the gentle breeze, when Isabella noticed a boat rowing toward them with great speed. A man stood in the prow, signaling the *Liberação* with his hands and encouraging the four men rowing fast and furious. The boat grew in size as it approached, and the uniformed man who was motioning shouted at the top of his voice, "Stop and disembark!"

Isabella looked at Avram. "What is it?" Avram looked as befuddled and clueless as she felt.

João, standing nearby, yelled to the refugees serving as new sailors on the ship, "Drop anchor!" The anchor rolled back into the dark waters of the harbor, while Isabella prepared to face the official climbing the rope ladder thrown over the gunwale.

The officer was stout with a medium-length beard. He carried himself with an aura of pride in his demeanor, mindful of his important duty.

Ana, who stood next to Isabella, turned pale. "I hope we won't be delayed all day."

"Don't worry," Isabella replied. "I'm sure it's a minor thing we've overlooked."

Ana took Salvadore's small hand and led him starboard, where Raquela and the other passengers were gathered.

Meanwhile, the officer bowed to Avram, assuming he was the captain. Avram glanced at Isabella, and she encouraged him with her eyes.

"I'm the customs' inspector, and leaving port is forbidden."

Isabella protested. "Why, Inspector? We provided all necessary and signed papers."

"That's quite true," the inspector answered. "But according to the number of passengers on board, you must pay an additional tax per head."

Everyone surrounding the inspector fell quiet. Avram spoke for Isabella, "How much is the tax?"

The man checked his papers and counted a few lines. "You must pay an additional four hundred reais."

Isabella, Avram, and João stood shocked. Then Isabella said, "Pay him, Avram."

"But—"

"Pay him!" Isabella demanded.

"You must come back on land," the official said. "There are papers to sign and stamp."

João said. "I'll wait here for you, Isabella, and mind the ship," He reassured her.

"All right." Isabella called out to Ana," Please take care of Salvadore while we're gone."

One of the *Liberação*'s rowboats was lowered for Isabella and Avram as he rowed behind the inspector's boat.

They reached the docks within ten minutes, fighting a slight current. Avram tied the boat to the dock and with Isabella headed to the large whitewashed barracks where maritime transactions were conducted. Through a series of corridors with attending rooms, the inspector led them to a small room with a table and chairs.

"Sit down." He signaled with an outstretched hand.

Isabella sat, her legs feeling somewhat weak. She suddenly feared that it was happening all over again: the mass exodus four years ago, the chase by Inspector Guerida, the shipboard search, her hidden cache in the ship's wooden sidings, and all that followed. They would bleed them dry. She then remembered she was a rich merchant and captain of her ship. She quickly slipped a money purse into Avram's hand. He nodded and laid the money purse on the table.

Isabella said, "Here's enough to pay the taxes and some for your troubles."

The inspector looked at Isabella with indignation. He hesitated for a moment, then pocketed the purse. "All right. You may sign these papers while I go to the head inspector to get your ship released." He left them to gaze at the documents placed on the table.

They affixed their signatures at the bottom and waited for the inspector to return.

Isabella, feeling a bit faint, got up and turned to Avram. "This room is stuffy. I'll be waiting for you outside." Avram looked surprised as she left him.

The air tasted crisp and salty helped clear her head. She walked slowly along the docks through the throng of rushing travelers, her footfalls heavy yet silent. The time went by as she waited for Avram to show on the docks, and she wondered why he hadn't left customs. Perhaps the snag hadn't been cleared up? She kept walking the length of the docks with anxiety, watching the channel where the Tagus River merged into the Atlantic. It had been a good life living off the land in Portugal. It had made them rich with experiences beyond gold and silver—seeing the flight of the falcon, breathing the freshness of the forest, holding a grape between her lips and tasting its sweetness, and experiencing motherhood in all its pain and joy. She would miss Sintra, where her mother had lived at one time and the memories tied to her history. Now the future beckoned to her and her son— to continue living the rich life offered to her.

She reached the end of the docks, when she saw an unkempt beggar with a long beard standing with his eyes fixed on the *Liberação*. She felt pity for the poor man. He probably wanted to leave to find a better life but couldn't afford the voyage. She hesitated for an instant, then turned to head for the maritime office. Avram must be done and waiting for her. With a quickened pace, she strode toward the customs building.

"Isabella! Isabella!" The cry tore into the depth of her being. It was a familiar voice laden with pain, love, and hope. She turned and saw the same beggar walking haltingly and hesitantly toward her. He then screamed her name again and again, and began to run toward her.

"Isabella! Isabella! Isabella!"

When the beggar came close, she scrutinized him. The first things that hit her were the deep-blue eyes, and the long matted black hair framing a dark, tanned young face. Her heart stopped.

No! It wasn't possible! *Yet, maybe it is—maybe it is Miguel!*

Her mind swirled with contradictory thoughts. The man stood transfixed like a statue in front of her. He raised his arm to touch her face. She held her breath, yearning for it to be true, when she saw his eyes searching hers.

She gave a piercing cry. "Miguel! Is it you?"

Miguel opened his arms, and she fell into them. They both fell to their knees and searched for breath as their lips met. All their hunger for each other's love was fulfilled at that moment. Isabella couldn't control her laughter and crying as she kissed him over and over.

"I thought I'd never find you," she said, hugging him, then kissing him again and again.

"Isabella, my Isabella," Miguel said softly, while caressing her teary face. "The thought of you is what kept me alive. To return to you." He bent his head backward and, looking up at the sky, laughed with abandon, offering his happiness to heaven. Looking into her eyes, he said, "It isn't a dream! You're real." His face was lit with delight.

Isabella laughed with glee. "Of course it's me. I can't believe it's you holding me! Where have you been? What happened to you? How did you survive?" The questions flew out of her mouth between short breaths of amazement. She touched his head, his face, and his lips to make sure he was real.

"All in good time. First, tell me—do we have a son?" Miguel said as he shook her.

Isabella laughed with joy. "Yes, my love. His name is Salvadore." She turned to the harbor and pointed at the *Liberação* swaying on the water.

Miguel reached with his hand in the air to touch the ship. "My son is there on the ship. I can feel him."

She reached with her hand and caressed his cheeks, then kissed him again on the lips. He answered her tender kiss by returning all his love and by kissing her face, her neck then her mouth in a sealed kiss that took her breath away.

Isabella pulled away first, then laughed again with abandon. "My husband. My love. You don't know how much I've missed you." Tears of joy now mixed with tears of pain ran down her face as she recalled her longing for Miguel. It was the pain of yearning for him, for his touch, his love and his caring. At that moment she knew that life was blended with great moments of happiness and times of sorrows. That one cannot bear sorrow without joy to erase the pain.

Avram waited a long time for their papers to be processed and stamped. When the inspector finally returned, he had a satisfied look on his face.

"It's all in order. You may now leave port with your wife."

Avram was about to correct the inspector, then thought that since their betrothal would happen soon enough, he'd let the remark pass. "Thank you, Inspector." He gratefully bowed, then left the building.

Outside, the clear air and a strong winter sun greeted and blinded him for a moment. He looked at the *Liberação* and was reassured to see it bobbing on the waves. *Let's sail away to my hard-earned happiness*, he thought, his head full of pleasant thoughts of what awaited him. He then searched for Isabella but couldn't find her. He walked the length of the docks, when he saw in the distance a couple embracing on their knees, then standing up. One of them was Isabella! Isabella kissing and embracing a beggar!

He dropped the documents in his hand. His heart broke with pain at the unbearable recognition. He knew instantly that the man was Miguel, who had come back to life to take Isabella away from him. No, it couldn't be! Not his love! Not Isabella!

Avram put his fists to his head and fell to his knees, weeping his despair and sudden loss between clenched teeth. She was no longer his Isabella the moment Miguel materialized. Had she ever been his? Had she ever loved him?

Painfully, he admitted to himself that he had never fully possessed her love. She had given him many reasons for delaying their wedding and remained distant from his affections—her thoughts kilometers away from him. What a fool he'd been. He now felt unjustly robbed. Robbed of the life he could've had with her. He had lost her.

He squelched a cry of pain deep inside his throat. He had not only lost his entire family, but Isabella as well. He was now alone in the world.

The pain of this realization churned his insides and made him feel faint. There was only one thing he could do now: disappear from her life as if she'd never existed.

He turned brusquely around and walked away from the port, the documents lying on the pavement.

Isabella remembered that everyone was on the *Liberação* awaiting her and Avram. Avram! My God, she had forgotten about him. How would she break the news to him? He'd be destroyed! She wavered between conflicting thoughts—between complete happiness and anguish, muttering to herself.

"What is it, Isabella?" Miguel asked, seeing her agitation.

"I can't explain right now, Miguel. But we have to find Avram."

"Why? Isn't he on the ship?"

"No. We were waiting to clear papers for the voyage, and I must go find him."

Miguel nodded and followed her along the docks as they made their way through the throngs of people. When they arrived at the customs office, no one had seen him.

"I gave him his signed documents. You're free to go," the inspector said.

Isabella rushed out of the building and grabbed her face in guilt and regret. Avram must've seen them! He must've seen the miraculous reunion when she and Miguel embraced and kissed with great happiness. What to do now?

She then spotted some documents lying on the dock. When she picked them up, she recognized the signatures. Their customs papers! She shuddered. *He saw us*!

"Let's return to the ship." she said with a faltering voice.

"I can't," Miguel said.

Isabella saw a shadow had passed Miguel's eyes. "Why?" she said in a strangled voice.

A grimace rose on Miguel's lips. He opened and closed his mouth without sound. When he spoke, the words came out with struggle and a pained look on his face. "I must find my brother, José."

Isabella was speechless. She wanted to help Miguel's find his brother. On the other hand, she knew the search would be useless. It was too late to pull him out of the monastery in Palos de la Frontera. He must have been indoctrinated by now into the priesthood, and no amount of begging or bribery, or even kidnapping him, would bring him out. José was lost to their faith.

"Miguel." Isabella spoke gently to him. "Let's board the *Liberação*, and I'll explain what happened to your brother." She took Miguel by the arm and pulled him toward the edge of the docks. "Please come with me."

Miguel took one look at her and reluctantly followed her with despair on his face.

He must've sensed that his brother is beyond reach or dead, Isabella thought with great sadness. Her eyes turned to the docks and found the boat moored where it had been left, and within minutes they both boarded the *Liberação*.

The shock and amazement at seeing Miguel left everyone who knew him stunned beyond belief.

Ana couldn't help touching his head, face, and hands to see if he was real. So did Sekou, who laughed a great deal to see his old mate. João embraced his nephew. But when Raquela brought forth Salvadore, Miguel kneeled before the child and held him at arm's length to take in every part of him: his face, his eyes, the red curls on his head, and the scent and feel of his small body bouncing with the freshness of new life. Miguel couldn't remove his eyes from his son.

"Aren't you going to kiss him?" Isabella asked, laughing.

Everyone around them laughed with joy.

Miguel held Salvadore in his arms for a long time, then kissed him with reverence. He had a son!

"Where's Avram?" Ana asked suddenly.

Isabella startled to remember the painful task awaiting her. "I don't think he's coming back," she said in a mournful voice.

Ana demonstrated her immediate understanding with the glance she gave Isabella and Miguel.

"All right! We have a voyage to begin. All hands on deck!" João gave the order.

Isabella went to him and said quietly, "We can't leave yet. We have to wait for Avram to return."

João rubbed his brow. "Do you truly believe the man will come back?"

"But how can we leave him here? What will happen to him?" Isabella cried with guilt pangs.

"Now listen to me. He knew his place, and it wasn't at your side. He'll survive the blow."

Isabella bent her head as she realized she had her own small family to be concerned with. She nodded with a heavy heart and went to find Miguel holding Salvadore.

The anchor was weighed again from the sandy bottom, all sails readied for the voyage, and when the *Liberação* glided out of the harbor, many shouts rose from the decks. They were cries of relief and cries of hope. The refugees from El Mouro's castle huddled together, their faces gazing at the horizon.

João stood in front of everyone assembled on deck.

"I have an announcement to make!"

All faces turned to him, hanging on his words. Miguel wrapped Isabella's shoulders with one arm and held his son with the other. He searched Isabella's eyes for a clue, but she shrugged her shoulders.

João said. "I have sailed the Mediterranean and the Atlantic for over twenty years. I have sailed to the New World and seen amazing lands and sights."

Everyone around him waited with anticipation for what he was getting at.

Ben Baruch called out, unable to contain his impatience, "Yeah, yeah. Come on, man, tell us your mind."

João smiled with glee as if he were nursing the suspense for his announcement. "There's a shore that will be a safe haven for us. A distant island called Boriquén. A land where we can begin to live with freedom— each man, woman, and child."

Miguel hugged Isabella and smiled at his little son. She returned his smile and thought, *We will be as free as the birds of the skies and the fish in the ocean. Free to live our lives.*

The End

Epigraph

EXILE WAS VISITED UPON THE children of Abraham in repeated epochs. Each time, it strengthened their ties to the land and renewed hope in themselves and the power to survive. And through many generations they begat many children, and many remembered that they were once slaves and were now free.

1492 – 200,000 Jews are expelled from Spain
1497 – 20,000 Jews are expelled from Portugal
1497 – 300,000 Moors are expelled from Portugal.
1609 – 150–200,000 Moors are expelled from Spain

The Characters

The Spanish Court

    Queen Isabella de Trastamara—queen of Castile and León

    King Ferdinand of Aragon—king of Aragon, Castile, and Sicily

    Isabella—princess of Asturias and Aragon, eldest child, widow of Afonso, prince of Portugal

    John—prince of Asturias, and heir to Castile and Aragon

    Joanna—princess of Asturias and Castile, second daughter

    Maria—princess of Asturias, third daughter

    Catalina—princess of Aragon, fourth daughter

    Señor León de Castañeda—painting instructor to John, Prince of Asturias

    Beatriz de Bobadilla—Leonor's sister and Queen Isabella's lady-in-waiting

    Leonor de Bobadilla—sister to Beatriz de Bobadilla

    Pedro Gonzalez de Mendoza—grand cardinal of Spain

The Portugese Court

    King Jonh II Reign—1481 to 1495

    King Manuel I—To marry Isabella Princess of Asturias

Christopher Columbus's Family

    Christopher Columbus—"Admiral of the Indies and of the Oceans," Cristóbal Colón (in Spanish), Cristoforo Colombo (in Italian), and Cristóvão Colombo (in Portuguese)

    Domenico Columbus—Columbus's adoptive father

    Susanna (of Fontanarossa) Columbus—Columbus's adoptive mother and wife of Domenico

    Bartholomew Columbus—Columbus's second brother

    Bianchinetta Columbus—Columbus's sister

    Giacomo (Diego) Columbus—Columbus's youngest brother

    Giovanni Pellegrino Columbus—Columbus's brother (deceased)

    Filipa Moniz Perestrello—Columbus's dead wife

    Diego Colón Moniz—Columbus's first son

    Beatriz Enriques de Arana—Columbus's mistress

Fernando (nickname for Ferdinand) Colón—Columbus's second son

Ferdinand of Portugal, Duke of Viseu and Beja—Columbus's birth father

Isabel Gonçalves Zarco—Columbus's mother

João Gonçalves Zarco—Columbus's grandfather, navigator under patronage of Portugal's Prince Henry

Sintra

Isabella Obrigon Costa

Salvadore—Isabella's son

Ana Sarauel—midwife

Avram Beneluz—Isabella's cousin

Raquela—living in household

Sarina—Raquela's daughter

Aron—Raquela's son

Juanita—living in household

José Costa—brother to Miguel Costa, snatched by the Convent of La Rábida near Seville for the priesthood

Isaac Abravanel—Ana Sarauel's cousin, living in Sicily

Benvenide Matigoro—purchaser of Jewish slaves in Tangier, Morocco

Mariners and Colonists

Christopher Columbus—Admiral of the Indies and of the Oceans

Bartholomew Columbus—Christopher Columbus's brother, governor of Española

Diego Columbus—younger brother to Christopher Columbus, primed for bishopric, member of council

João Treves—Mariner on Columbus's ship and uncle to Isabella Obrigon Costa

Juan Aguado—chamberlain from the queen's household

Fray Bernal Buil—Benedictine monk

Fray Juan de Borgoña—Order of St. Francis monk

Alonso Sánchez de Carvajal—mayor of Baeza, Spain

Dr. Diego Alvarez Chanca—Seville physician, second voyage chronicler

Fernando Núñez Coronel— member of council

Pedro Fernández Coronel—alguacil or mayor of the Indias

Juan de la Cosa—chart mariner aboard the *Niña*

Michele de Cuneo—Columbus's childhood friend from Savona

Maestre Diego—cook and boatswain (contramaestre)

Dieguillo—young translator

Archbishop de Fonseca—royal chaplain sent by the Spanish monarchs

Gil García—alcalde mayor (principal judge)

Ginés de Gorbalán—soldier and mariner

Juan Ponce de León—young noble adventurer

Juan de Luján—member of council

Juan Manrrique—former foreman, remained in Cadiz

Melchior Maldonado—envoy to the Holy See, sent by sovereigns Queen Isabella and King Ferdinand

Mosén Pedro Margarite—commander of fort in Española and servant to the royal household, soldier and profiteer

Diego Marquez—inspector (*veedor*)

Jeronymite monks—three monks native of Burgundy and Picardy

Alonso de Ojeda—soldier and mariner

Fray Ramón Pane—Franciscan Order priest

Francisco de Peñalosa— queen's personal servant, uncle to Bartolomé de las Casas

Bernal de Pisa—gold keeper (contador)

Pedro de Terreros—admiral's personal steward

Antonio de Torres—master and owner of *La Capitana* (*Mariagalante*)

João Treves—Mariner on Columbus's ship and uncle to Isabella Obrigon

Diego Tristán—gentleman volunteer

Fermín Zedo—Sevillian goldsmith

Beltrán and Gaspar—servants of Their Highnesses

La Mina Mines

Ali—slave suffering from memory loss

Sekou—slave and friend of Ali

The Ships

Columbus's Fleet on the Second Voyage

Santa Maria (Mariagalante also nicknamed the *Capitana)*—carrack
(merchant) ship, 200 tons, flagship for Admiral Christopher Columbus
Antonio de Torres—master

La Gallega—carrack (merchant) ship

Niña (Santa Clara)—Square-rigged caravel,
Juan Niño, owner
Juan de la Cosa—Captain, chart maker and seaman
Francisco Niño—pilot
Alonso Medel—master
Pedro de Terreros—boatswain and ex-steward on first voyage
Diego Tristán—boatswain and public notary

Pinta—caravel, identical to the first Pinta ship

San Juan—caravel
Alonso Pérez Roldán—master and pilot

Cardera—Caravel
Cristóbal Pérez Niño of Palos—master

Colina—caravel

Fraila—caravel

Gallarda—caravel

Guitierre—caravel

Bonial—caravel

Rodgria—caravel

Triana—caravel

Vieja—caravel

Prieta—caravel

Gorda—caravel

Quintera—caravel

Santa Cruz—caravel. Also called the *India*. First ship to be built in the
New World

Stowaways on the *Mariagalante*

Elías—stowaway youth

Isaac—stowaway youth

Emanuel—stowaway youth

Moisés—stowaway youth

Enrique—stowaway youth

Léon—stowaway, along other adults from El Mouro Castle on other ships

The *Liberação*

Isabella Obrigon Costa—captain

Miguel Costa—former captain and presumed dead

Avram Beneluz—first-in-command

Lourenço da Sintra—second-in-command

Joham Alvaro—pilot

Hanrrique—cook

Fernando—sailor

Benvenide Matigoro (Ansar)—Moroccan slave master

Al-Aziz—ship Ali was aboard after being captured

La Esperança —Portuguese: "hope"

Captain Álvaro Da Costa

José Tavares da Sílva—AKA Ali

Martinho—master

Captain Treves—AKA Isabella

El Mouro—Juan de Luna, captain of ship where Isabella and Miguel were stowaways

Tres Magos —Portuguese ship, battles with Aruj and the pirates

Luis Borges Santos—captain

Portuguese—unnamed spy ship
  Francisco de Almeida—captain
  Lourenço de Almeida—Captain de Almeida's son
  Bento—master

Pirate Ship and Slave Owners
  Aruj the pirate—Ali's slave chief
  Mustapha—Ali's first in command on pirate ship
  Effendi Yusuf Zaim's— Ali's slave master
  Abdul Aziz—pirate
  Fahri—pirate
  Ergin—pirate

Islands' Present Names

Babeque—Jamaica
Boriquén—Puerto Rico
Cipangu—Japan
Española—Dominican Republic
Hayti—Haiti
Juana—Cuba

Language Translations

Arabic

Ahlan wa sahlan!	You are most welcome!
Al-Aziz	The Mighty. Allah's Name: Al-'Aziz in the Quran.
Anta! Ibta!	You! Move!
As-salamu alaykum	Peace be upon you
Dãmit Hayãtak	May you live forever
Hal beemkani mosa'adatuk?	Can I help you?
Lah?	No?
Qef!	Stop!
Maa ismuk? (or *Sho Ismak?*)	What's your name?
Saariq! Intadhir duuruk!	Wait for your turn!
Shoukran.	Thank you
Ta'ala ma'ee!	Come with me!
Tawa-qaf!	I don't know anything!

Swahili

Tunataka kuwa huru!	We want to be freed!

Portuguese

Portuguese	English
Que aconteceu?	What happened?
Pergunte a ele o que ele quer	Ask him what he wants
Não se preocupe, Capitão	Do not worry, Captain
Eu lhe disse a verdade	I told you the truth
Senhora Patróna	Lady boss
O que podemos fazer por você, senhora?	What can we do for you, ma'am?
Isso é um pedido de Socorro	This is a cry for help
Você encontrou o que?	You found what?
A que devo o prazer da sua companhia?	To what do I owe the pleasure of your company?

Galician

Galician	English
Bre, Salvadore, bre os ollos que ten	Hey, Salvadore, hey what eyes you have

Spanish

Spanish	English
Bre, Salvadore, bre ojos tienes tu	Hey, Salvadore, hey what eyes you have
Mientras tanto, ve con la protección de Dios	Meanwhile, go with God's protection

Caribbe and Taino

*(This is an approximation of the language in Columbus's time)

Aajàta. moro po	You want to
Aji, ciba cohoba cinchona	Hot with fever bring cinchona
Atantymoko	Sit down there
Bohio	House
Carib lu lucairi Pinagua	Carib tribe and island people took their canoes with sail.
Casabi, chicha, yucca, mahiz	Cassava, corn for (beer) yucca, corn.
Cacique Taíno Guacanagari caneyes	The Cacique Guacanagari is in his square house
Lu y guey	Your people are well
Cairi Caico.	Many small islands exist far away
Cacicazgo maguana cacique Caribe Caonabó canima mynu lu baina pyrywa?	Chiefdom Maguana cacique Caribe Caonabó kill Spaniard people blood with bow and arrow?
Eporyi makuto, Mahiz, Casabi	Men, deep baskets, supply corn and cassava flour for bread.
Kynoro	Scarlet macaw
Macana! Macana!	War clubs!
mòkaron sampura morykaton!	They beat the drums!
Mynu! Mynu!	Blood! Blood!

Taíno caçábi	Taíno cassava bread
Pyjai. *Pyjai*	Shaman
Yayagua, Anana.	Pineapple
Òmàko kaje ràmun' kynkano	Stop it! I tell you!

* Taíno expressions are compounded from *Talking Taíno* by William F. Keegan and Lisabeth A. Carlson, and for *The Carib Language* by Henk Courtz.

Men left at La Navidad — first Voyage.
All Deceased

Cristóbal del Alamo—mariner
Francisco de Aranda—mariner
Diego de Araña—master-at-arms of fleet, captain at La Navidad, cousin
    to Columbus's mistress: Beatriz the Araña
Gabriél Baraona—mariner
Juan del Barco—mariner
Domingo de Bermeo—cooper
Pedro Cabacho—mariner
Diego de Capilla—mariner
Castillo—silversmith
Juan de Cueva—mariner
Rodrigo de Escobedo— secretary of fleet, lieutenant at La Navidad
Francisco Fernández—mariner
Gonzalo Fernández—mariner (from Segovia)
Pedro de Foronda—mariner
Diego García—mariner
Francisco de Godoy—mariner
Jorge González—mariner
Pedro Gutiérrez—representative from the royal household, Lieutenant

Francisco de Henao—mariner
Guillermo Ires—(William Harris or William Penrise, from Ireland)
Antonio de Jaén—mariner
Francisco Jiménez—mariner
Martín de Lograsan—mariner
Tristán de San Jorge—mariner
Diego de Mambles—mariner
Sebastián de Mayorga—mariner
Diego de Mendoza—mariner
Alonso Vélez de Mendoza—mariner
Juan de Mendoza—mariner
Diego de Montalban—mariner
Juan Morcillo—mariner
Alvar Pérez Osorio—mariner
Juan Patiño—mariner
Hernando de Porcuna—mariner
Pedro de Talavera—mariner
Bernandino de Tapia—mariner
Diego de Tordoya—mariner
Diego de Torpa—mariner
Luís de Torres—interpreter of Arabic, Spanish, and Hebrew
Juan de Urniga—mariner
Francisco de Vergara—mariner
Juan de Villar—mariner

Reproduction of Paolo dal Pozzo Toscanelli's Map, 1474.

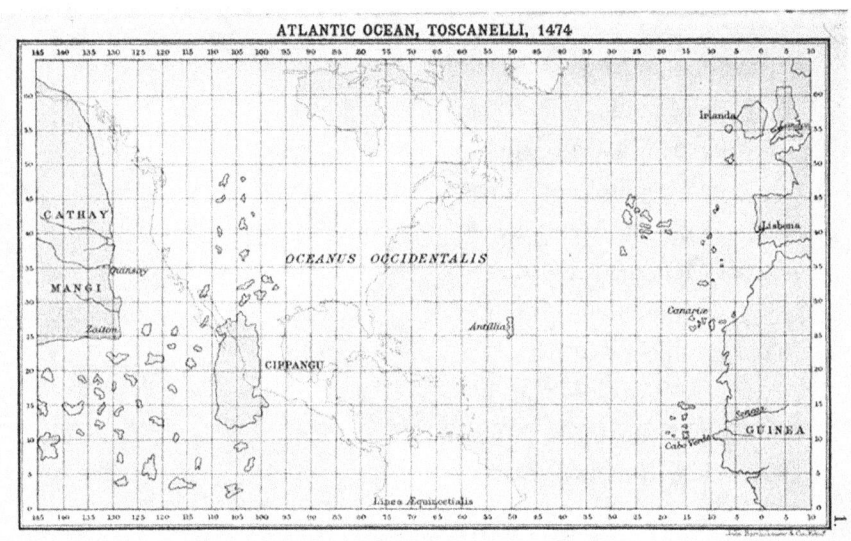

From Lawrence J. Burpee, An Historical Atlas of Canada, (Toronto: Thomas Nelson and Son Limited, 1927) 4. Map by John Bartholomew and Son, Ltd., Edinburgh Geographical Institute.

A map of the West Indies, in Christopher Columbus's handwriting

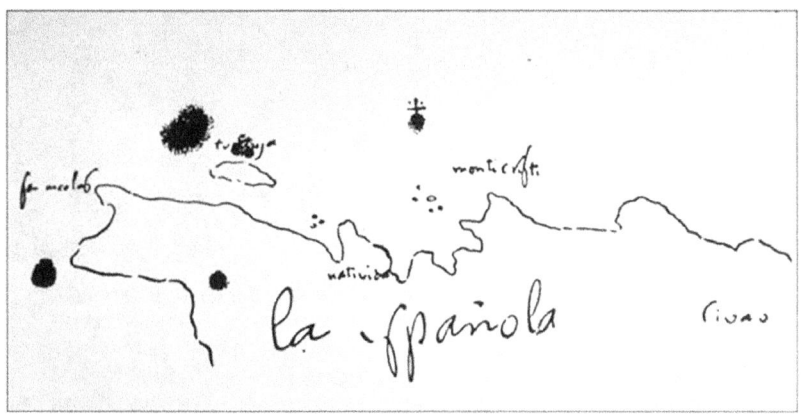

West Indies, Christopher Columbus, 1492-93

Source: http://www.henry-davis.com/MAPS/Ren/Ren1/302.html

Source: http://www.henry-davis.com/MAPS/Ren/Ren1/302.html